Becoming Tonus 0

A Baby Boomer Tale About Growing Up

Nick Toth

outskirts
press

Outskirts Press, Inc.
http://www.outskirtspress.com

ISBN: 978-1-9772-5711-6

Outskirts Press and the "OP" logo are trademarks belonging to Outskirts Press, Inc.

PRINTED IN THE UNITED STATES OF AMERICA

This is dedicated to Nick and Phyllis Toth who provided the most loving homelife that any child could possibly hope for.

Special thanks to my wife, Judy, who always has my back.

With gratitude to, John Filan, Dave Hackenberg, retired, Toledo Blade and Tim Rogers, retired, Cleveland Plain Dealer. And to my brothers and sisters, children and grandchildren, nieces and nephews, who are always there to support, encourage and help one another.

This is dedicated to Nick and Phyllis Toth who provided the most loving homelife that any child could possibly hope for.

Special thanks to my wife, Judy, who always has my back.

With gratitude to, John Filan, Dave Hackenberg, retired, Toledo Blade and Tim Rogers, retired, Cleveland Plain Dealer. And to my brothers and sisters, children and grandchildren, nieces and nephews, who are always there to support, encourage and help one another.

DO YOU REMEMBER THE 1950s?

- TELEVISION SIGNING OFF AT MIDNIGHT
- WALT DISNEY'S DAVY CROCKET
- SALK POLIO ORAL VACCINE
- HULA HOOPS
- I LOVE LUCY
- ALLEN FREED COINED THE TERM ROCK-N-ROLL
- ELVIS PRESLEY ON THE ED SULLIVAN SHOW
- BIRTH OF McDonald's
- THE BIG BOPPER
- ROTARY PHONES AND PARTY LINES
- STEVE ALLEN AND THE TONIGHT SHOW
- SPUTNIK
- FIDEL CASTRO
- ALASKA AND HAWAII ADMITTED AS FORTY-NINTH AND FIFTIETH STATES
- MARBLES
- TEN-CENT BOTTLES OF COKE
- MILK DELIVERED TO YOUR DOORSTEP
- YOYO'S
- NEWSPAPER COMICS: DICK TRACY, NANCY, AND SLUGGO, FEARLESS FOSDICK
- HIGBEE'S VISITS WITH SANTA CLAUS
- CLEVELAND INDIANS AND 1954 WORLD SERIES
- BASEBALL CARDS
- TYPEWRITERS
- SOCK HOPS
- DIME STORES
- GIGANTIC SNOWSUITS
- JELLO DISHES WITH FRUIT INSIDE
- ROLLER RINKS
- PITCHING BASEBALL CARDS
- THE MICKEY MOUSE CLUB AND MOUSEKETEERS
- CIVIL DEFENSE DRILL – DUCK AND COVER
- POODLE SKIRTS AND BOBBY SOCKS
- DINERS AND JUKEBOXES

PART 1

THE BEGINNING

It began in the summer of 1947. Joseph Jr. was born. His father, having returned a WWII veteran after fighting in the Pacific, married his high-school sweetheart, beginning their life-long love affair. His dad, lovingly known as Big Joe, brought home with him a bad back and a Purple Heart. A bad back that lasted the rest of his life and the Purple Heart that sat in his drawer. Mom was dad's high school sweetheart, and like so many other baby boomer women had waited patiently for him to come home. They married almost immediately. The age of the Baby Boomers was just beginning and would impact all their lives. Together they would raise six children, and as the Roller Derby television commentators of the 1960s would say: *THE JAM WAS ON*

Joseph would be called Joey, 17 years later, Tonus 0 (Tonus *OH*) was born.

While Joey and his family lived with Grandma K., mom and dad saved up money, and like many boomer families, they moved from the near-westside of Cleveland to the suburbs. Joey's parents chose Parma, a small growing community of approximately 25,000. By the time he was an adult, Parma would be a city of over 100,000. It seems that all Baby Boomers had the same idea.

The family was Catholic. Mom had converted dad before they were married. Dad was so glad to be out of the Philippine jungles, and the terrors within those jungles, that mom could have talked him into being a Buddhist monk and he would have said yes. Joe and Phyllis were devout Catholics. Their six children would attend Catholic school for all twelve years.

In 1950 they welcomed a second child into the family, Grace. Joey was now a big brother and he loved it. He watched over Grace constantly, taking care of her, listening to her whine and cry, and would try to entertain her. He was her big brother and he protected her. The family continued to grow, and in 1952 another sibling was born, a son named Douglas. Mom and dad were not wasting any time.

LEARN TO RUN

Two weeks before Joey would start kindergarten, his dad came home with a surprise, a shiny, two-wheeled bicycle that he had won in a raffle. Joey had never seen anything so huge! He wasn't a very big kid and could barely get on the bike let alone ride it, but his devoted dad worked with him constantly. After days filled with falls, bumps, and bruises, a pleased and proud dad announced to Joey and his mom that he was able to ride the bike. He would be allowed to ride it down to the end of the block, turn it around, and ride home. Absolutely no further and absolutely nobody else could ride it. When the family moved to Essen Avenue in 1950 there were about fifteen homes on the street. Five years later there were almost sixty. And by the time he was eleven years old, there would be close to one hundred.

On a rainy Sunday a week before kindergarten, Joey was anxiously waiting for the rain to stop so he could take his bike out for a ride. When it finally did, off he went. Halfway down the block, he noticed an older boy, a much bigger older boy, on a much smaller bike following him. Before long, he caught up and started riding in circles around him. The boy asked, "Are you the new kid that lives on the corner? "Yes" replied Joey. "My name is Patrick what is yours?" "Joey," he said. Patrick said laughingly "Joey, sounds like Dick." Joey looked at him puzzled but did not respond. Then he asked, "Are you a pussy?" Joey replied, "we have no pets." Patrick laughed again as they reached the end of the block and Joey had to get off his bike to turn it around.

Joey was about five feet three inches, weighing no more than fifty pounds. Patrick was at least five foot six inches and a good one-twenty. Joey was thinking that Patrick was the ugliest creature he had ever seen. Years later while Joey was watching *A CHRISTMAS STORY* with his children, he saw the bully Farkas and he thought, holy shit that is Patrick.

As he got off his bike, Patrick was getting off his. He walked up behind Joey and asked, "Can I ride it?" to which Joey replied, "My dad said no one else is allowed to ride it." "Oh" as he put his arm around Joey, put him in a headlock, threw him to the ground, and jumped on top of him. Joey could barely breathe let alone talk. Patrick said, "your dad is not here now, is he?" He got up, got on Joey's bike, and rode away. Joey sat on the ground with tears in his eyes and wondered what to do. Patrick returned in about ten minutes, got off the bike, stood for a second, and again asked Joey "are you a pussy?" This time Joey had no response, Patrick laughed and got on his bike and as he pedaled away, he said to Joey "see ya pussy." Joey quickly got on his bike and pedaled home. He parked it in his garage, just like his dad had shown him. He walked towards his house while Patrick was still pedaling around in the street. As Joey got to the side door, he opened it but decided not to go inside. Instead, he walked around to the front of his house and saw Patrick still on his bike about forty yards away. He yelled out "HEY PATRICK". Patrick turned his bike around and started to pedal toward him. As he got closer Joey yelled out to him "Patrick you look like a freckled face baboon" and ran like hell to his side door. Patrick was pedaling hard now and as Joey got in the side door, he shut it and locked it, caught his breath, and walked into the kitchen. Mom greeted him by asking how his ride was. He answered, "fine mom, I also practiced my sprinting a little." "Oh good," said mom as Joey looked out the window at a beet-red Patrick who was giving him the finger. Joey had no idea what the finger meant but he knew it couldn't be good.

That night as Joey lay in bed, staring at the ceiling he thought; it's good that I am fast, but I must learn how to fight.

MONSTERS IN PLACES THAT YOU WOULD NEVER THINK

The big day arrived. The first day of school. Joey and all of his five siblings would attend grades K through eight at Saint Charles elementary school which was just two blocks away from their home on Essen Avenue.

Baby Boomers were everywhere, and Saint Charles was packed. Classes were held in auditoriums, cafeterias, coat-rooms, and portable trailers. Kindergarten, as well as grades one and two, were split sessions. One in the morning and one in the afternoon. There were almost fifty kids in each class and each session.

Teachers had their hands full. They were paid very little, and the lay teachers rarely stayed longer than two years. The nuns on the other hand were lifers. They used their teaching experience to develop hand-to-hand combat skills as well as learning C.I.A. interrogation techniques. Joey and his friends would develop counter techniques over time, but in the first week of school, he was still a Rookie.

The first week of kindergarten was uneventful. The kids sat at tables, not desks. There were anywhere from six to eight at a table. The teacher was a tall muscular lady named Miss Boris. She ruled her class with an iron hand as well as a yardstick. The students would soon find out just how iron her hand was.

The first couple of days Joey walked to school with his mom or dad. By the third day, mom realized that Joey could walk with a boy and his mom who lived down the street. Martin and his mom walked every day even though his right leg was in a full cast. Martin had the dreaded disease called polio. On their daily trip, Joey became aware of two things. One, it was extremely difficult for Martin to walk in his brace, and two, the course they took went right by Patrick's house. Joey was extremely vigilant.

They sat at the same table with about six other boys. By week two the enamor of going to school had worn off. Sitting at a table full of boys also enhanced the opportunity to goof off. Goofing around in school became in vogue. Joey was good at it and in time he became very good at it, like almost every day.

Miss Boris's version of martial law was breaking down about week three. Anyone paying close attention would have been able to recognize the signs of an upcoming nervous breakdown. Unfortunately, no one was. One day with about 30 minutes left in class, Miss Boris rang the little bell she kept on her desk, with the idea being the class should be quiet. On this day, the idea wasn't working so she rang it again. Again, it did not work so she started to bang her yardstick on the desk while yelling "QUIET DOWN CLASS." This had the desired effect, except at Joey's table, they were simply having too much fun. Martin had put on a fake nose and glasses which caused the whole table to double up with laughter.

Unfortunately for the boys, their backs were turned to Miss Boris who was staring at them with the look in her eye that all the kids had come to fear. The class suddenly became dead still as Joey and his buddies continued to have a good time. Miss Boris started toward their table as the rest of the class watched thinking *this is going to be good*. Joey was the first to realize the abnormal quiet that had enveloped the class and he looked up to see a rapidly advancing Miss Boris. He said "whoa boys" and Martin and the other boys turned to look. Unfortunately, Martin had not taken his fake nose and glasses off. However, he was not a bit phased. You see Martin felt protected by his brace and polio. Martin was wrong. As Miss Boris approached the table Joey had the same knot in his stomach that he had when Patrick threw him to the ground. Much to his horror Martin suddenly realized he was still wearing the fake nose and glasses. As he was removing them Miss Boris threw a right haymaker of a punch that hit him square in the nose, a punch that would have made Muhammed Ali proud. Blood from his nose was immediately pouring out on the table. Miss Boris grabbed Martin by the shirt and pulled him to about eight inches from her face and screamed "I RANG THE BELL". She turned to Linda, who was the teacher's pet #1, and told her to get some tissue. Miss Boris then turned calmly around and walked back to her desk.

By dismissal, Martin's nose had stopped bleeding, and, on the way out of school he said to Joey "not a word of this to my mom." They walked home in silence. Martin would eventually be cured of polio. By eighth grade, he was on the same basketball team as Joey. By 1957 there was a Polio vaccine. For three days that summer millions of Americans would stand in line all over the country to receive three sugar cubes of the Salk vaccine which in a short time would completely wipe out polio. What a different place America has become.

Later that night as Joey lay in bed staring at the ceiling he thought: HOLY MOLY there are monsters in places that you would never expect.

WHAT'S UNDER THERE?

I t was Halloween. The kiddies were all dressed and ready to have a swell old time. There were princesses, hoboes, and witches, there were lions and tigers and bears (*OH MY*). Joey was a leopard, mask, and all. His younger brothers would be wearing the same costume for the next fifteen years. The afternoon started with alphabet lessons, to which absolutely no one was paying attention. Miss Boris was doing her best to control the class as well as herself, although she was not in costume, she was the scariest person in the room.

Finally, with an hour left in the class, Miss Boris announced that it was time for the party. The kids could do whatever in their seats, and orderly lines would be formed to go up and get snacks. More sugar was exactly what they needed. Joey's table immediately started playing tabletop football with a folded paper being used as the football. Three different games were going on at their table and they were barely aware of what was going on around them. Miss Boris called out table nine (the table behind Joey's) to come up for their treats. At table nine was the teacher's pet #3, Louise Beeker. The boys were barely aware of the table being called as they were locked into their games. Joey hardly felt the swoosh of *Louise the Chinese* princess skirt as she walked by.

The boys called Louise Beeker '*Louise the Chinese,*' not because she was Chinese but because it was the only thing they could think of that rhymed with Louise. What else could you expect from 5-year-old boys (by the way most of the boys had never even seen an Asian person and had no idea where and what China was. To them it just sounded right.)

Louise's princess skirt had at least five petticoats under it with at least one lock on each. Joey and his buddies were paying no attention to the trek for snacks as they were immersed in tabletop football.

Suddenly the class quieted down, without even being yelled at. Martin, who had become an expert at recognizing the shaping process of Miss Boris's normal face into her Frankenstein's face said "BOYS we are going to have a problem." Miss Boris was turning into full Frankenstein mode as she was talking to Louise while she was staring at their table. Martin started shaking. His memory of his bloody nose was etched in his mind. The more Louise talked the more twisted Miss Boris's face became. As Louise started to point at their tables total silence descended on the class. Terror descended on Joey's table.

Miss Boris screamed, "JOSEPH COME UP HERE." Even though Joey was the only Joseph in the class he looked around hoping to see someone else stand up....nobody did. As he rose from his seat and started toward the front of the room his buddies all started humming a funeral dirge. As he got to about five yards from Miss Boris's desk she started screaming "WHY DID YOU DO THAT?" Joey was scared. He was more scared than when he had called Patrick a freckled-face baboon. Here, there was nowhere to run and hide. Joey had no idea what Miss Boris was talking about. However, he did remember Martin getting punched right in the nose and he vowed that Miss Boris was not going to be able to do that to him. He would keep his head down even as he spoke to her. As he got to the front of the room, he noticed that Louise was sobbing. Miss Boris screamed again "WHY DID YOU DO THAT?" to which Joey answered, "DO WHAT?" "You know what" Miss Boris screamed again as she went into a complete frenzy. She then yelled, in front of the entire class "YOU LOOKED UNDER LOUISE'S DRESS." His buddies snickered, Louise sobbed louder, and the little girls pulled their legs together and held their dresses down.

Joey was very puzzled. He was thinking why would I do that? He looked at Louise and as he backed out of Miss Boris's punching range he said "NO I DID NOT" to which Louise responded with loud sobbing and Miss Boris screaming at Joey to get out in the hall. As they went outside Miss Boris said to the class, "the door will be open, and I do not want to hear a sound." There was not. Joey, Louise, and Miss Boris all stood in the Hallway. He was keeping a good distance away from Miss Boris's right hook. Miss Boris looked at Louise and asked again, "what did he do?" Between sniffles, Louise answered he picked up my dress and tried to look underneath it. Actually, it would have taken twelve locksmiths and two sticks of dynamite to get under that dress. They both were staring at Joey like he had three eyes as he responded, "NO I DID NOT." Miss Boris stuck her head in the class and said "JoAnn," who was teacher's pet #6, "please come out here." JoAnn, please go down to the office and ask Sister Jane to come here. We have a problem."

Sister Jane was the principal of the whole school and if Joey was not scared earlier, he was downright petrified now. Sister Jane looked at Miss Boris and then at Louise and then at Joey and asked, "what is going on here?" Miss Boris said, "Tell Sister what happened Louise, who promptly responded Joey looked under my dress." Normally Joey would have responded with some type of remark due to the fact Louise called him Joey, but common sense told him to keep his head down and his mouth shut. Sister Jane was staring at Joey like he had three eyes and asked him "Did you look under her dress?" To which Joey answered, "NO I DID NOT." Sister Jane asked again "WHY DID YOU DO THAT?" to which Joey said, "I didn't." Things were now getting intense. Sister Jane said, "I am going to ask you once and only once more WHY DID YOU DO THAT?" Joey again said, "I DIDN'T!" "That's it, I am calling your dad." Miss Boris echoed "I will call Louise's Dad." Joey was thinking the joke is over. "I am doomed." He was also ut which Dad would get there first. Either way, he was acked, so he just waited.

Big Joe got there first, and Miss Boris promptly informed him what his oldest son had done. Big Joe immediately looked at his son and said, "WHY DID YOU DO THAT?" to which Joey answered "I DIDN'T" which promptly set off another forty minutes of interrogation in which they all just kept asking the same question. Joey answered the same way every time. He was wondering though how three adults could not be a bit more creative in their questioning. Like using waterboarding or sticking fingers in light sockets. Things like that.

Finally, the bell rang. Girls filed out first staring at Joey while they continued to hold their skirts down. However, a girl named Shirley smiled and winked at him. The boys came out next giggling behind their hands and making the shame, shame sign. As the students were leaving Sister Jane told Big Joe to take him home and he can return on Monday. Louise's dad was leaving with Louise and was giving Joey the evilest of evil eyes. Big Joe glared back at him as if daring him to say something. He did not.

The ride home was in complete silence. When they got home Joey was told to sit down, mom and dad were going to talk in private. Joey's little sister Grace was staring at Joey while she was holding her skirt down. Mom and dad could be heard talking in the other room and when they came out mom was crying. Through her tears, she asked Joey "WHY DID YOU DO THAT?" to which Joey sighed.... "I didn't." The grilling went on through dinner and finally at 7:30 dad said to Joey, "GO TO BED." Joey's parents remained downstairs long into the night discussing if their five-year-old son was a pervert.

That night as Joey lay in bed staring at the ceiling he thought, they all grilled me for hours, Louise was hysterical, Miss Boris was completely off her trolley, and Sister Jane was close to throwing me out of school. Joey thought to himself 'I do not know what girls are keeping under their skirts to cause such a ruckus, BUT SOMEDAY I AM GOING TO FIND OUT' and as he fell asleep the last thought he had was of Shirley winking at him.

WINNING, HITTING, AND FICKLE FANS

In the 1950s professional boxing was in vogue. Television brought the Friday Night fights right into your living room. Joey's parents were big fans. Friday night fights were a ritual for Big Joe and his wife. As Joey got older, he was allowed to watch with them. However, at five years old he was in bed at 7:30. He would listen to his parents talk about the fights the next day.

It was January and school was moving along. Joey was finding it quite boring. Flashcards for words as well as flashcards for adding and subtracting were fast becoming old news. One day Big Joe came home and said to his wife "I want to talk to you about something. Joey, go play with your sister." (Which was the same as saying "Joey you are going to Purgatory.") As Joey left the room Big Joe said, "what do you think of entering Joey in the Golden Gloves?" (The Golden Gloves was an amateur boxing tournament that took place throughout Cleveland. Hundreds of kids from age thirteen and up would enter the tournament. Both newspapers, the Plain Dealer and the Press would cover the event as if it were the WORLD SERIES.) Mom wondered aloud, is he old enough? Big Joe responded quickly. "They are having an opening exhibition bout between two five-years-old to kick off the tourney. It will be the first match, and both local newspapers will cover it. Three full rounds and Joey Maxim will be the ref." (Maxim had been the local Cleveland boy who had become the Light Heavyweight champion of the world.

He was mom's favorite fighter and recently retired). "What do you think?" Mom thought for about 15 seconds and said "I think you fell off the ladder at the Fire House and fell on your head. We need to get you some help. Patrick has beaten him up both times they fought; I would prefer that my oldest son be given the chance to grow up somewhat healthy. He has no idea how to fight." Dad quickly responded, "Patrick is way bigger than Joey, it is unfair to judge him by those fights and I will have Abe train him." (Abe was a childhood friend of dad's who was cut from the same mold as Big Joe and his other childhood buddies were. He was a WWII veteran like most of dad's friends and he had also boxed in the Army. His older brother was on his way to becoming one of the most prominent criminal defense lawyers in Cleveland.) "It would be a great experience for Joey, dad said, and we can start training him in two days." Mom reluctantly said, "O.K. but you need to make sure that he will be matched with someone his size." Big Joe said "NO PROBLEM." We will begin training on Monday. Mom said, "let's go see what Joey says." They went to ask Joey who had been listening to the entire conversation from the living room. Dad asked, "do you want to box in the Golden Gloves?" "Like on TV?" Joey asked. Dad said, "yes, just like that." "Will Patrick be who I am boxing?" Mom quickly responded, "No you will be matched with someone your size." As she said this, she glared at Big Joe who promptly repeated mom's promise. Joey quickly responded, "yes, I want to do it."

When Monday came Joey was ready to go. While other five-year-old kids were watching Howdy Doody, Clarabelle, and Mr. Bluster after school, Joey began his training. Dad had bought a speed bag for the basement and a body bag for the garage. Abe showed up four days a week and the training sessions began. They had about three weeks to prepare. Abe taught him well. Jab, jab, right cross, keep moving to your right, away from his power hand, keep your chin down, don't throw roundhouse punches, keep your punches straight and crisp. Four days a week he drilled these fundamentals into Joey's head. Joey was learning. The time passed quickly and soon it was the night before the tourney began.

As Joey slept his parents sat in the kitchen talking with Abe and his wife Gretchen. They had no children of their own, so Joey was very special to them. They talked together for a while and then finally mom looked at Abe and said "well what do you think? "Abe quickly responded, "I think he is going to flatten him." They all laughed hard. Big Joe told mom and Gretchen that nobody could train Joey as well as Abe had and while looking at Abe, he said "you have done a great job." A lengthy silence followed. Finally, mom commented, "you trained him well BUT you never hit him. Joey has NEVER taken a punch square in the face." Mom then asked the magic question "Who is he fighting?" Big Joe looked at Abe and Abe avoided his eyes. Mom thought UH–OH. Dad finally answered, "he is fighting Ronnie Nagy." Mom loudly asked, "you mean Yoshi Nagy's kid?" (Yoshi was another west-side kid who grew up with dad and who also fought in WWII) Abe said, "yes that is the kid." Mom loudly said, "that kid is at least twenty pounds heavier than Joey." Dad chimed in, "everybody is twenty pounds heavier than Joey and he is not nearly as big as Patrick."

The silence that followed was broken up by mom as she looked square into Abe's eyes and said, "what do you really think?" Abe looked right into her eyes and said "Phyllis, JOEY WILL FLATTEN HIM." Mom said, "that's nice, but I want to hold the white towel that I will throw in the ring if Joey is getting creamed." Abe and Big Joe agreed, and with that, they all said goodbye and goodnight.

FIGHT NIGHT

The big night was here. The gym was packed. Both boys wore fighter robes. They both had their hands taped as if they were regular boxers. They both came out of a tunnel of people and headed to the ring. The ring was surrounded by floor seats that were all filled, and more people were standing in the aisles. There was a balcony that hung over and around the ring that was filled to the brim. Both fighters took off their robes before heading to the pre-fight conference with the referee. It was then that for the first time in his life Joey heard jeers. People started yelling "you are going to get killed kid, tell your parents to feed you, get the ambulance ready, I have a sandwich here if you need to eat something." They yelled to the ref; "Joey you need to stop this now. That kid is going to get killed." You see Ronnie Nagy was at least twenty-five pounds heavier than Joey and was a stocky five-year-old. Joey looked like a poster boy for hungry children. Both boys were called to the center of the ring for a pre-fight meeting with the ref. The jeers continued. The ref spoke about the rules and then sent the boys back to their corner to wait for the bell.

The bell rang and the crowd was screaming. As they moved toward each other Abe was yelling jab, jab, right cross, but even though Joey was listening he was also watching Ronnie come out. Joey saw that Ronnie's left hand was hanging below his waist.

Joey knew that was not the way he was taught. As Abe was yelling jab him, jab him, Joey quit listening and led with a right hook that landed firmly on Ronnie's chin and he went down. There was a stunned silence for about two seconds as Joey found the neutral corner that Abe had taught him to go to when he knocked Ronnie down. As he stood in the corner, he saw his mom who had gotten to her feet and was cheering loudly for her oldest son. She was waving the white towel above her head. Suddenly it dawned on the crowd the skinny kid had just flattened his opponent. The screaming was deafening. The ref too was stunned. He never expected he would have to count a five-year-old out. He hesitated a good five seconds and then began the count. Ronnie got up and was ready to go. The ref took him to his corner and checked with his dad and they both said he was ok. The fight would go on. The fans had completely changed their allegiance They were now fans of the skinny kid. The next two rounds were clearly one-sided. Joey used jab, jab right cross as he pedaled and moved around the ring. He was proving to be unhittable, and the fans were going nuts, Abe's training had paid off. The final bell rang after round three. The ref took both the boys to the middle of the ring and raised both their hands to signify a draw. The crowd immediately started to boo and yell and scream. There is no way that skinny kid did not win that fight. The ring announcer went quickly to the middle of the ring and with the microphone, in his hand, he explained to the crowd that this was an exhibition bout between five-year-olds and there were no winners. Almost immediately Abe went to the center of the ring and raised Joey's hand and the place went berserk. As they walked through the crowd to return to the locker room Abe and Big Joe had huge grins. The fans were still cheering for the skinny kid. Waiting at the door were his mom and Gretchen. Both were crying tears of joy. Joey got hugs from both, got dressed and they all went to dinner.

That night as Joey lay in bed staring at the ceiling, he thought about things that he would ALWAYS remember. How the fans had made fun of him and when they saw he was winning they were on his side. He would never forget that. He also thought WINNING IS GOOD...you just cannot beat the feeling of winning, and jab, jab, right cross is good, BUT IF I AM EVER IN A FIGHT, I WILL ALWAYS BE THE FIRST HITTER (and he always was).

THE INTERMEDIATE YEARS

Life lessons show up when and where they show up. Joey experienced four unforgettable life lessons when he was five years old. He was now eight going on nine years of age. Mom and dad had their fourth child. A baby girl who they named Tina. Joey now had three siblings and there were still two more to come. He went through the first, second, third, and fourth grades. He was blessed with four excellent teachers, three nuns, and one lay teacher. They were all sane and they genuinely liked kids. (He would not realize until later in life that all teachers were not sane and lots of them did NOT LIKE KIDS.) His memories of those years were always pleasant. Life lessons are not at all limited to school. The summertime and sports would provide many different types of learning opportunities.

Between the ages of 6, 7, and 8, baseball, much to Mom's delight became Joey's sport. Also, there was the addition of a dog into the family. As if mom and dad did not have enough on their plate. Enter a boxer puppy who was immediately named Muscles. Muscles would become a protector and friend to all the children for the rest of his life.

A GREAT PLACE TO PLAY

Dad brought home a glove, a ball, and a bat. On his off days from the firehouse, he would always have time to play ball with his oldest son. Each day of summer was spent with Joey being out in the yard, playing baseball either with dad or the many kids who were now starting to show up in the family backyard. There was Roger and Ducky and Bobby, actually there were two Bobbys, Freddy, Billy, Wayne, and Slugger. Patrick started to hang out and play ball. They were all different ages with Joey usually being the youngest. New kids would appear out of nowhere and ask to play. They were never turned away.

During the summer of his eighth year, there were enough kids to play organized games. There just wasn't a convenient place to play. They tried playing in the backyard, but Mom quickly tired of hearing the hard baseballs hit the house, especially while baby Tina was napping. Whiffle balls and bats had not become popular yet. One Sunday the family was returning from church in their '53 Ford Victoria. As they traveled down Essen Avenue, and they were passing the Parma Show, Joey looked out the window and had a thought. He wanted to ask his mom and dad if they could expand the neighborhood area he could play in. Mom and dad had strictly forbidden him from going up Essen Avenue towards the Parma Show. It was too close to Ridge Road which was the main thoroughfare through Parma. When they got home and were sitting down to have lunch,

Joey took his shot and asked. Both parents immediately asked why. He explained that the Parma Show parking lot was empty on week-day mornings and afternoons and would be a wonderful place to play baseball. It had yellow poles that could be homerun fences and a huge wall in left field that would be just like the Green Monster in Boston. Both mom and dad talked a bit and while still forbidding Joey to travel to Ridge Road they both agreed he could go to the Show parking lot during the day. For the next seven years, the Show parking lot became the number one baseball field in Joey's life as well as for the many different kids who would play there. Years later as he was watching the movie Sandlot with his children, the sum-mer memories of baseball flooded back to him. Naturally, he would share many of those adventures with his kids, at least the ones he could share.

THE RESCUE

The next day would be the beginning of playing baseball in the Parma Show parking lot. It would become a summertime way of life for the boys in the neighborhood. Even though Joey wasn't looking for them, life lessons would be found everywhere.

The boys would play through the morning, stop for lunch, and come back and play more. Between ten and twenty boys would show up every day. Occasionally people in the neighborhood would stop and watch them play. Often there would be cheers for some of the better plays that the kids would make. The boys loved it. One of the regulars who would stop by, and watch was known as Tony S. He was 18 years old and drove the coolest white Oldsmobile convertible. He had hung around this corner during his teen years, and he currently worked for his dad in a neighborhood shoe store on Ridge Road. He also traveled with several different older girls who all had one thing in common. They were all GREAT LOOKING. Tony S happened to know Joey through Joey's dad. Big Joe would bring the family shoes to the shoe store and often he was with his dad when he did. Tony would always talk about how much he liked watching the kids play ball. He would also go to the Snow Road firehouse during Big Joe's shift to get some mechanical help with his convertible. The firemen would find their way outside to talk and look at his car. Also, as was mentioned, Tony S always traveled with knock-out women and the firemen didn't seem to mind talking to the girls. Occasionally little Joey was there also. He and Tony would talk, and Tony would give him some baseball pointers. When the girls would say "Tony who is your cute little friend?" Joey would blush and constantly the question would be in his mind, I wonder what's under there? Someday I may ask Tony.

Late in the summer of 1956 as the boys were playing ball in the Show parking lot a group of older boys, much older, showed up. Their leader, Pat, said, "Hey can we play?" Roger who was the oldest of Joey's friends said, "sure we will stop, and we can pick new teams so the sides will be even," to which Pat said, "No, we will play you guys, we stay as a team". Roger looked at Joey who shrugged his shoulders and the game was on.

The newcomers slaughtered the much younger kids and while they did, they made fun of them. They called them names and made fun of how they looked as well as how they played. Finally, Pat said, "we are out of here" and as he was saying it one of his guys took the ball and threw it on the theater roof. They walked away laughing. As they walked away Joey yelled, "DON'T COME BACK." The boys laughed and gave him the finger. (By now he knew exactly what that meant) The boys were silent for a while and then Roger said, "we have other balls let's play" and they did.

The next morning, they were playing ball again as the older boys showed up. Joey immediately said, "forget it, you are not playing." Pat asked, "are you sure you don't want us?" While he was asking one of his pals named Rhino came over to Joey and asked "What's your name kid?" to which he responded, "Joey." Rhino said, "Joey sounds like Dick." Joey rolled his eyes and answered, "yes, I have heard that before." Rhino replied, "Dick, no hard feelings" and he took out a chocolate candy bar and gave him a piece of the candy. Joey thought it was a Nestles bar and said "thanks." The older kids were now roaring with laughter. Rhino said to Joey "you better hurry home real quick Dick." Roger walked over to Joey and whispered; "I think they gave you Ex-Lax" to which Joey asked rather loudly, "what is Ex-Lax?" The older boys were roaring now. Roger said loudly, "it makes you shit you better head home...NOW." Joey immediately got on his bike and pedaled home as fast as he could. The rest of the boys had lost interest in playing and took off. The older boys still laughing yelled, "WE WILL BE BACK TOMORROW."

Joey's mom told him this is no big deal just do not go far from the bathroom. Grace asked her mom, "what is wrong with my brother?" Mom said, "he ate the wrong thing, but he is ok." Dad came home for his lunch hour and asked him how he was doing. "Ok," he said, but he noticed a different look in his dad's eyes.

The next morning, he had breakfast and started off to play ball. Mom said, "Hey where are you going?" "To play ball mom." His mother said to wait, and she stood and looked at her son for a while. Finally, she said, "be careful Joey, go ahead and have fun." Joey met Roger and they walked together as other boys met them. Nobody asked any questions. There were fewer boys than normal, and the others knew why. They picked up sides and warily started to play. Around 10:30 the older boys showed up again. Joey and his friends instinctively gathered together. Pat laughed saying "you pussy's aren't thinking of fighting us, are you?" (Joey now knew what being a pussy meant). Pat looked at Rhino and said, "what do you guys think," as they started to walk towards Joey, Roger, and the rest of their friends. Joey was holding a bat and he didn't let it go. As the older boys got closer out of nowhere coming around the corner peeling its tires was a white convertible. It was Tony S and three of his friends. Tony slammed on his breaks and he and his three friends jumped out of the car. They all carried clubs. Tony put his club down and said, "I do not need a club for these punks." He punched Pat right square in the face, then took him to the ground, punched him twice more then jumped up looking for whoever was next. Meanwhile, his huge friend Marco went right to Rhino and gave him similar treatment. The other four bullies didn't move as Tony's other two buddies came toward them with clubs ready. They quickly responded, "we had no part in this" and surrendered. They saved themselves an ass whipping. Tony turned back around and grabbed Pat by his shirt. He told Pat, "Apologize to these guys now." to which Pat quickly said, "I am sorry." Tony grabbed him again and said "you ever fuck with these guys again we will use the clubs. If you don't know who I am ask around." Pat responded in a very low voice "I know who you are, and I am very sorry." Meanwhile, Marco called to Joey while Rhino lay on the ground. "Come over here." Joey walked over, and Marco said, "you want to kick him or punch him go ahead." Joey thought for a couple of seconds and said, "No thank you Marco" and he looked at Rhino and said, "someday I will be older and bigger, I will never forget you." Tony yelled, "get the fuck out of here, and do not let me see you anywhere near here again." The boys got up and left. Tony and his guys were getting in their car. As Joey went to them, he signaled to his friends to follow him. Each of them thanked Tony and his three buddies. When they were done Tony got out of the car and took Joey aside. "Let me give you some advice Joey. I watched you fight in the golden gloves," Joey interrupted "you were there?" "Of course, I was there that's all your old man could talk about when I first met him. Anyway, I watched you handle a much bigger kid. You were trained and so you won. That will not be the case all the time. Stay away from guys like this, they were way bigger than you guys. Also keep hitting the ball, widen your stance, and most importantly do not grow up to be like me. I will see you around." He got in his car, and they left. The boys went back to playing ball.

That night Joey lay in bed thinking for a long time. How did Tony know? He thought about the look in his father's eyes at lunchtime. It finally dawned on him; Tony knew because dad knew. Dad sent him. Joey did not know if there were more life lessons in store for him but if there were not, he knew he had just learned THE MOST IMPORTANT LIFE LESSON OF THEM ALL. ALWAYS NO MATTER WHAT TAKE CARE OF YOUR FAMILY it is great to have friends, but it is, REALLY, GREAT to have parents who love and care about you. Also, never take candy from strangers.

DAD LAYS THE GROUNDWORK

Late in August of that same summer, a new group of boys showed up. They were fully equipped as if they had come to play. Their leader, Jeff, asked Roger if he and his buddies wanted to play a game. They said they lived just across Snow Road by the firehouse and that they were a Little League team that just wanted to play a practice game. Douglas, one of the younger boys who was an everyday player at the lot asked "Little League? Do you guys have uniforms and everything?" Jeff replied, "we have shirts and caps that are paid for by the pizza place across Ridge Road." Roger was looking at Joey and Joey was looking at the other guys that were regular everyday players. They all remembered what happened the last time when the older kids had shown up and asked the same question. All of them were staring at Joey who shrugged his shoulders and said, "let's play." So, they did. They played the game and had great fun. Both teams played well. When the game was over Jeff asked if was ok for them to come back tomorrow to which Roger and Joey simultaneously agreed, no problem. The boys would spend the last three weeks of summer playing the Pizza Shop Little Leaguers. There were no umps, no parents, and no arguments or fights. They just had fun playing ball.

At 5:00 each night the family would gather promptly for dinner. A tradition that would last until Joey was married and moved. There was mom and dad, Joey, Grace, Douglas, and baby Tina.

Family dinner was one heck of a good time for years to come. After the blessing, Joey immediately told dad and the rest of the family about playing against a Little League team at the Show parking lot. Dad thought for a while and then started to ask questions. He asked Joey "How good were they? How did your team play and how did you play?" Joey replied good and good and ok in that order. "Dad we more than held our own." Dad asked if they were going to play tomorrow to which Joey replied "of course."

The next day during Big Joe's lunch break he walked across Snow Road to watch his oldest son play ball. The boys all saw him standing and watching the game and almost all of them said hello. Joey was shocked that the Little Leaguers knew him. They all lived so close to the firehouse that they stopped in often, especially when Big Joe was working. Dad stayed for about thirty minutes, and he was genuinely impressed by how well both teams played. He said goodbye to the kids and walked back to the firehouse with a little gleam in his eye. The next night at family dinner, after prayer, it was Big Joe who spoke first. He looked at both his sons and said first to Douglas "how would you like to be a bat boy on a little league team?" Douglas said, "What's a bat boy?" mom and dad laughed hard. Dad looked at Joey and asked, "how would you like to play Little League baseball next year?" Joey shrugged his shoulders and said, "Can we start now?" Mom and dad looked at each other and again laughed very hard.

THE LOU GEHRIG'S

The school year came and went, and it was summer again. Which meant baseball and that meant Little League. Dad's friend, Bernie, was going to sponsor a Little League team as well as help Big Joe coach. He brought some players with him from his neighborhood including a "lights out pitcher" and his son who was a very good centerfielder. Much to Joey's surprise, Big Joe had approached some of the Little Leaguers that he saw play in the Parma Show parking lot against Joey and his friends last summer. Most of those kids lived right around the firehouse where Big Joe worked, and they often would come to the station, and dad would bring them inside and let them slide down the fire pole. The biggest surprise was Patrick. You see most of the boys from the Snow Road area were in the same grade as Patrick. When they told dad that Patrick could hit, it was easy for Big Joe to say ok when Patrick came to the house asking if he could play on the team. It was the summer before Joey would enter fifth grade. Not only was Little League baseball about to start but Joey would also be eligible to play football and basketball for his school. He couldn't wait to play all three. Also, by the time fifth grade would be over Joey would learn about every four-letter word that young boys were not supposed to say. But that is a story for another day. Summer started and it was baseball, baseball, and more baseball. The team would be called the Lou Gehrig's. Big Joe would hold practice every day he did not go to work at the firehouse. Usually, three days a week but sometimes four. Whenever there was no practice Joey would holler for his old friends who were all too old to be on the team and they would go to the Parma Show lot and play pickup games just as they had for the previous three summers and just as they would for at least four more summers to come. Big Joe ran organized and disciplined practices. Joey was surprised. Practices were not nearly as much fun as the games at the Parma Show lot. But there were so many new things that he was being taught. How to turn the double play, relays, and cut-offs as well as how to hit a fastball on the outside half of the plate and many other fundamentals. He would often hear the kids talking about Big Joe. How tough he was but how funny he was also, and on top of that what a good coach he was. In the second week in June, it finally was game time. 7:00 clock at the diamonds behind the newly built Parma Town mall just outside Byer's Field football stadium. The Lou Gehrigs were ready to go.

Joey played second base and batted eighth. The Lou Gehrigs were far superior to the Rocky Colovito's who they played that day. The fact is that they were far superior to every team in their league. They were undefeated in league play and the city playoffs started the week after the Fourth of July. Meanwhile, everything was not perfect. Patrick was back in Joey's life. Making matters worse Patrick had an afternoon paper route and his papers were dropped off on the corner right in front of Joey's house. (Cleveland had two daily newspapers at that time. The morning paper was called The Plain Dealer and the afternoon paper was called the Cleveland Press.) Joey's battles with Patrick began again and Joey would always lose. Usually, they would happen in Joey's front or backyard and they never happened when Big Joe was home. Joey could not figure out how a baboon like Patrick could know that until he realized Patrick in his slow head had figured out that if there was no baseball practice then Big Joe was at work. On those days Patrick would always pick a fight and Joey would always end up on the bottom of his 160-pound body. They must have battled twenty times that summer, and Joey lost nineteen of them. One day Joey's mom noticed

Patrick on top of Joey and pushing his head into the ground. She ran to the door and yelled at Patrick to get off. He slowly did and he said, "We are only playing." Mom said, "it sure doesn't look like it." The next day and the next day and the next day the exact same things would happen. Finally on the fourth day in a row mom saw them fighting again. This time she walked outside, but this time she had Muscles with her. In the last few years, Muscles had turned into a full-fledged Boxer dog, with clipped ears and a developed chest. He had fallen in love with Joey as well as his brothers and sisters and became their fierce protector. Muscles was growling at Patrick as mom yelled "GET OFF HIM...NOW, OR I WILL LET HIM LOOSE". Muscles was starting to strain on his leash as a terrified Patrick got to his feet saying, "please don't let him loose, please." He was almost crying with fear. Mom responded saying "GET OUT OF OUR YARD AND STAY OUT. IF I SEE YOU FIGHTING WITH MY SON AGAIN, I WILL TURN THIS PUPPY LOOSE ON YOU." As he walked away Patrick looked at Joey and said very quietly "that ain't no fucking puppy." Joey went in to have lunch with his mother and said "thanks mom." They both thought that the bullying would now stop. They both were wrong.

That night Joey lay in bed staring at the ceiling. He was thinking of his dog Muscles. You see Joey liked the dog, but he had to clean up after him. The dog pooped like a horse and Joey constantly complained about having to clean it up. But tonight, Muscles was king in his mind. He vowed he would never complain again, AND he didn't until two days later when he had to clean up again. Before he fell asleep, he thought about his mom. He thought back to his Golden Gloves fight and mom standing up and cheering for him and now how she saved him this afternoon. He thought, mom is definitely not soft, it's great to have a mom like that. She had even taught Muscles that family was everything and Muscles was now a full-fledged member of the family.

HOLY MOLY

The Little League playoffs were beginning. There were four divisions of Little League baseball in Joey's age bracket. The playoffs for the Parma City Championship began the Wednesday after the 4th of July. Four teams would play a single-elimination tournament. One and out. No second chances. The Lou Gehrigs would play the Mickey Mantle's at Byers Field. The Mantle's had a great pitcher, and they too were undefeated. The Gehrigs had the same record as well as a great pitcher. Joey couldn't wait.

Parents from both teams were there as well as many of their friends and relatives. Abe was there with his lovely wife. As they walked up to the diamond mom hugged them both and said to Abe "well, what do you think?" Abe looked at mom and answered, "Joey is going to flatten them." They all laughed hard. Little did they realize how right Abe would be once again.

Joey's grandma, his mom's mom, was at the game too. For Joey, she had always been a sweet old lady who loved him dearly. This past season he learned differently. She went to all the games. She yelled constantly at umpires, opposing managers, and even the other ten-year-old players. Joey would hear her during games and think HOLY MOLY grandma is gonzo. He was right! The game began and after six full innings of a seven-inning game, the Gehrigs had not scored. Patrick had struck out three straight times and Joey had struck out twice. They only had three total hits and no runs. The good news was the Mantles had not scored either. It was now the top of the seventh with the Gehrigs coming to bat. All the parents were standing and cheering for their kids. Grandma was clearly the loudest. Joey was up third that inning. The first two batters had their best contact of the night and hit the ball on the button, but they were right at someone. Joey was up with two outs. Abe yelled out "Joey, jab, jab, right cross." Joey smiled. The first pitch to Joey was a ball. Then he fouled off the second pitch and the third was a called strike. The Mantle's pitcher made his only mistake of the night. He took a little off his fastball and Joey tagged it. It was a line drive to right field about ten feet from the foul line. The right fielder couldn't get to it. As Joey hit first base, he saw the ball go by the right fielder, as he rounded second base, he looked at Bernie the third base coach. Bernie was yelling "come on Joey" and as Joey got closer, he was waving him home. As Joey headed home, he saw Jeff, the Gehrig's third baseman yelling "SLIDE, SLIDE." Joey slid and knew he was safe as he hit the ground. The catcher was on top of him, and Joey pushed him off to go celebrate. As he started to get up the ump yelled "OUT, OUT, YOUR OUT." Joey turned to the ump yelling "WHAT??" Gehrig's parents were yelling as Big Joe was hustling down the first-base line, and players were screaming. Joey SNAPPED. He went after the umpire. He tried to punch him, but the umpire was way too tall to hit so Joey tried to tackle him and of course, that did not work either. Joey was crying with rage as he felt himself being picked up off the ground. He tried to kick whoever was picking him up and then he realized it was Bernie the third base coach, so he tried to kick the umpire again. Joey saw his grandmother out on the field with her cane going after the ump. Joey's mom was trying to control Grandma and Joey started back at the ump. Bernie tightened his grip while Abe helped him, and he could not move. Mom got Grandma off the field and as the ump gained control, he called Big Joe to home plate. He was pointing at Grandma as he said loud enough for all to hear, "If she is not in a car in one minute you forfeit." Big Joe looked at mom and said, "take her to the car NOW" and three boys immediately went and helped to get her there in less than a minute. The ump then looked at Joey and said, "HE IS OUT OF THE GAME...NOW and if he is not gone in 30 seconds you lose." Abe immediately dragged Joey, who was still crying with anger to the car. The ump said "PLAY BALL" as Joey and his grandma were put in separate cars. The Mantle's won in the bottom of the seventh. The ump headed for his car but on the way, he told Big Joe there will be a full report on this to the league. "That kid should be banned." The Mantle's left and Big Joe called his team together and the parents with them. He told them all what a great year they had, and he would call them about the team picnic. Then he turned to Joey and said, "That is not how we do it. That is not how we act." to which Joey replied, "But I was safe." Big Joe quickly responded, "YOU SAY ONE MORE WORD AND I WILL SLAP YOU RIGHT HERE." Even though his dad had never hit him he knew he would now, so he shut up. He also knew this was not the end of it. So, he went back to the car while dad said goodbye to the players and coaches.

Mom was in the kitchen waiting when they got home. Mom, Abe, and his wife had taken Grandma home. Dad told Joey to sit at the table. He proceeded to tell him all the things a good dad, as well as a good coach, would tell their son who had just done what Joey had done. Abe said similar things as well as did mom. Finally, dad said, "Do you have anything to say?" Joey thought for a couple of seconds and said "Did you guys see Grandma out there with her cane and all? HOLY MOLY" at which point mom said "GO TO YOUR ROOM" and he did.

An hour later dad and mom came to Joey's room. Joey immediately stood up and said "I AM SO SORRY. I know I was wrong." Dad responded by saying "Joey, at the team picnic you will stand up and apologize to the team and whatever parents are there. GOT IT?" Joey replied, "yes dad no problem." Also, son, there is one more lesson here. Your actions COST US THE GAME. We would never have played that poorly in the seventh inning. It is not the most important lesson but when you lose control of yourself you just cannot win at any game. ESPECIALLY a championship game. GOOD

NIGHT and I love you. Mom echoed the words and they both left Joey alone in his room.

As he lay in bed that night there were so many things going through his head: He was wondering if grandma was the only grandma to be thrown out of a little league game. He also was thinking that if he were ever in a brawl again, the two people he would want most on his side, were Muscles and Grandma K. He had already learned how good winning felt. The Golden Gloves and going undefeated in the regular season had taught him that winning made him feel really good. Conversely losing that playoff game was the worst feeling he ever had. He hated it. Not losing in any competition would motivate him for the rest of his life but as bad as losing felt, his being the reason why they lost their first championship game was almost unbearable. As he grew tired and started to nod off, he vowed that any team that he ever was associated with would NEVER be able to say again that Joey was the reason they lost. As his eyes grew heavy, he thought of Shirley winking at him as she walked by him during the kindergarten Halloween dress fiasco. Someday, he mumbled to himself, someday.

FIFTH GRADE – COMING OF AGE

It was the last week of July. He was excited that finally, he was out of quarantine for what happened in the Championship baseball game. Plus, this would be the year that he would be old enough to play football and basketball for St Charles. Also, mom had given birth to another baby, a boy, who would be named Lawrence. Joey now had two little brothers and the family had five children. One more was still a couple of years away.

Joey couldn't wait to teach his brothers all the things that dad had taught him. Both Douglas and Lawrence would be high school stars. He would coach them when they were young, and he would end up coaching Lawrence in high school. In a year Douglas would be traveling up to the Parma Show lot to play ball with Joey and his friends. Exciting times indeed.

Joey's buddies were showing up at the house to welcome him out of jail. "Let's play some ball" Joey hollered as they walked towards Ridge Road and the Parma Show parking lot. Roger was already there and ran down the street to meet them. As he approached, he said, "welcome back Amigo. You have a surprise waiting for you at the lot." Joey said, "I don't like surprises" to which Roger responded, "someday you will like this one my friend." By the left-field wall stood two twin girls named Sheryl and Carol. They lived by the reservoir where dad had taken the Lou Gehrigs to practice every day. They flirted constantly with the boys but especially

Joey. Joey smiled and started to put on his ball glove. Roger said, "Hey dope, go talk to them. They are on their way to the library and asked me if I knew you. I told them you were on your way up here and you talked about the two of them all the time." Joey glared at Roger and said, "I have never talked to these girls" to which Roger replied, "it is time that you start." Joey told his buddies to pick up sides and make sure he was included and walked over to the two girls. "Hello," he said. They both giggled. Carol said, "it is good to see you" and as Sheryl started to speak Joey said, "I gotta go play this game, I'll see you later." They both stood there for a moment and said "OK" and then started walking toward the library. As Joey got back to his buddies and asked, "whose team am I on?" Roger laughed and said "MAN, that was really smooth." Joey said, "let's play ball." And they did.

In the second week of August, Saint Charles would begin football practice. Joey had about a week to get ready to play a sport he had never played before. The boys had cut down their trips to the Parma Show lot and began playing football in the backyard. They played tackle football in cheap helmets and old retread football pants. After dinner, Big Joe would continue teaching his son basic football fundamentals. (Big Joe was a huge high school football star along with his brother George. They were a dynamic duo on the field. The two brothers garnered all sorts of attention. Simply put they were high school rock stars. World War II was in full swing when Big Joe graduated and there would be no chance of him playing college ball. He would be off to war to serve his country).

While the boys would play tackle football games in the backyard, mom could not help but watch. She also watched in the evenings when Big Joe coached her son. St. Charles football equipment pass out was on a Friday and practice would start on Monday. IN FULL PADS. In those days there were no non-contact days. There would be full contact on the first day of practice. Dad told Joey he would drive him to practice and stay and watch. At 5:00 Joey went down to the basement to put on his equipment. While dressing he could hear his parents talking. Mom was asking Big Joe if he really thought their son was ready to play football. She said she had been watching Joey play tackle in the back yard and she thought he played timidly and was afraid of contact. Dad just looked at her and said, "I guess we will find out."

The team was the Lightweight team which meant players could be in grades 5 through 8 with a maximum weight of 110 pounds. Joey would be one of the youngest and smallest players there. He weighed fifty-eight pounds. At least sixty kids were at practice and the Head Coach knew Big Joe from his high school days. He asked Big Joe if his kid was as tough as his daddy. Big Joe responded, "I guess we will find out." As stretching began he walked away to a spot where he could watch practice.

Stretching ended and the coach said, "we will start with the Nutcracker drill." (Nutcracker drill was a physical drill. Today coaches would never start practice with this drill on the first day of practice. It was actually a two-on-one drill in a 10-foot square made by the players. Everyone would be able to see the drill. There would be a ball carrier, a blocker, and ONE defensive player. On the coach's command, the ball carrier would run straight ahead, the blocker would block, and the defender would have to make the tackle. This was not a drill for the faint of heart.)

Coach called out a boy named Danny who was in eighth grade and a returning starter. He weighed one hundred pounds. The blocker was also a returning eighth-grader and was 110 pounds. The defender's name was called out. IT WAS JOEY. When Big Joe saw the matchups, he moved closer to the drill so he could watch. He was about to find out about his son's courage. The boys lined up, the older kids were smirking and yelling to Danny "SMASH HIM DANNY, SMASH HIM." The younger boys were completely quiet. The coach yelled, "SET....GO." Again, just like the Golden Glove fight, Joey would benefit from the practice time he had spent with Big Joe. As the big blocker was moving toward him, Joey gave him a head fake, grabbed the side of his jersey, pulled him sideways, and disengaged (just like Big Joe had shown him.) Then squared up and met Danny full force with a violent frontal shoulder tackle which knocked Danny on his ass. (Just like Big Joe showed him) The other kids were stunned. There was silence, Danny was getting up slowly and Big Joe was trying not to smile. The coach had just seen his star running back get flattened by a fifth-grader half his size. Joey started to head back to the groups as the coach called out two more eighth-grade returning starters for offense and much to everyone's surprise he called out Joey's name AGAIN for defense and said get lined up. Joey buckled his helmet and came out again. Big Joe who had relaxed and moved back, now moved forward again. The coach again said "SET...GO" this time Joey had moved up closer to the lead blocker who was only about ninety-five pounds, and he was expecting Joey to do the same thing, but this time Joey had timed the cadence and actually got a 'half a second' head start, he drove right into the blocker who was somewhat hesitant and hit him square on at full speed knocking him back into the running back who tripped over him. Again, there was a stunned silence. This time Big Joe did smile because this was something he had NOT shown his son. The practice moved on and was soon over. Joey headed to the car but heard the Head Coach say to his father "I guess we found out." Big Joe just smiled and walked to the car. He told his son 'nice going' and drove home for dinner to an anxious mom who was waiting at the door. Joey went down to the basement to change and shower. Mom closed the kitchen door and said to her husband "WELL?" Dad responded, "He is tougher than his dad....and smarter, much smarter." He then proceeded to tell his wife what he had seen at practice. Mom smiled with tears in her eyes and hollered downstairs to her son "COME ON LET'S EAT." Joey came up the stairs and they all sat down to eat, hardly talking about practice. Finally, she asked her son if he was going to football practice the next day. Joey looked at her like she had lost her mind. "OF COURSE."

After two weeks of practice and the first scrimmage, Joey found himself starting at cornerback on defense and third-team Quarterback on offense. His football career had begun.

That night he lay in bed thinking: being the first hitter is definitely the way to go, being a violent first hitter is even better.

The football season ended with a three and five record. Joey started every game at cornerback. He loved playing but was extremely miserable every time they lost. Meanwhile, school had started, and basketball would begin shortly. Joey's fifth-grade teacher was Miss Francis, and she was a knockout. Off the charts good looking. Joey was not sure how to act around her. This would be a totally different experience than having nuns for teachers.

There was a new kid in his class who had transferred into Saint Charles's. Joey wasn't sure where he came from but it wasn't Parma. His name was Gary. One day Gary came up to him as they stood in line to enter the classroom and asked Joey if he wanted to have some fun. Joey did not hesitate to say yes. Gary told him to watch him during class and especially watch closely when he would go up to Miss Francis's desk. During class, Joey kept his eyes on Gary. Finally, when it was individual worksheet time better known to teachers as 'busy work' Gary walked up to Miss Francis's desk, and laid his paper on her desk saying, "Can you help me with this?." She said "sure." As she was showing him how to do the math problem, Gary bent over a little closer. Joey was watching closely and after a few seconds, he was thinking what is the big deal? He kept his eyes glued to them both and finally he said almost aloud "Holy Moly he is looking down her shirt." Miss Francis always wore buttoned blouse's and Gary had the perfect angle to look down her blouse. Finally, the help session for Gary ended and as he walked back to his desk, he gave Joey a thumbs up. Joey just sat there. When the dismissal bell rang, Gary ran to catch his bus and Joey said, "see you tomorrow" and walked home. He walked home alone always vigilant for a Patrick sighting while he thought about the day. He could not get out of his mind what Gary had done. He was also wondering if it was a mortal sin. He got home, shot baskets for a bit, and then it was dinner time.

The next day he saw Gary before school. Gary said, "well, what did you think?" Before Joey could answer he said, "wait until you see what I do today." When they went into school Gary gave a quarter to a girl named Judy to change seats with him. He was now sitting three seats deep in the row directly in front of Miss Francis. When Miss Francis sat down Gary dropped his pen on the floor. He would do this two more times before she stood up and began to teach. At recess, Gary said to Joey "did you see me?" "What? drop your pen? what's so cool about that?" Joey asked. Gary responded, "Hey dope I was looking under her skirt." "Oh" said Joey. "Jeez, are you dumb?" The bell rang and they lined up to go back into class. Thoughts of the kindergarten episode with Louise the Chinese were still sticking in Joey's head. The next day Joey told Gary he was going to visit Miss Francis's desk. It seemed to Joey that would be a lot easier and less conspicuous than dropping your pen on the floor once every 5 minutes. In the afternoon while they had busy work Joey walked up to Miss Francis's desk and stood right next to her and asked for help. Miss Francis said "sure" and as Joey was placing his math paper on her desk while jockeying for the right position the horror of horrors struck. Joey tipped over the ink bottle that was open on her desk. Miss Francis screamed and immediately tried to keep the ink from running towards her and getting all over her clothes. The class watched in utter silence. They all knew how much she cared about her appearance. Joey tried lamely to help but only succeeded in causing the ink to spread wider on the teacher's desk. Finally, she said, at the top of her voice "Joey PLEASE GO SIT DOWN." She looked at him with near hatred in her eyes. The boys in the class were stifling their laughter and the girls were all staring at Joey. The bell rang as Miss Francis was still trying to clean up. She said to the class "GO HOME" and they did. While walking home Joey wondered if Miss Francis would ever smile at him again. The answer to that was no.

The months passed, and it was a warm day in late March. The schoolyard was filled with hundreds of kids playing. The fifth-grade bully was a boy named Robby. He wasn't all that big, but his older brother an eighth-grader was also the star Quarterback. Robby hung around with his older brother Lawrence and his friends which gave him a lot of protection. He took full advantage of it. Joey had played football with Robby in the fall. They got along but were far from friends. Robby would stay close to his brother and his buddies while on the playground. He would constantly torment younger kids and sometimes even his fellow fifth graders. His older buddies would always have his back. On this particular day, he started making fun of Joey. Calling him names and saying he was a pussy. All of course within the earshot of his big brother. Now Joey had not been in a real fight since Golden Gloves. His brawls with Patrick were so one-sided they could not be classified as fights. Joey fully understood that he could not let this kid push him around on the playground in front of his classmates, boys, and girls. As Robby was yelling Joey yelled "LET'S FIND OUT "and he started to walk at Robby. Someone yelled fight, fight, and immediately boys, as well as girls, started forming a circle. The older kids quickly got Lawrence and asked him if they should get involved. Lawrence said "No, I have seen this other kid at football, and this should be interesting. Let them fight." Robby started at Joey but he was puffing up like so many kids did in those days. Joey was on him quickly. He led with his right hand, and it landed square on his jaw. He followed up with jab, jab, right cross and Robby was on his back. Joey got on top of him and kept on hitting him till the bell rang. The older kids pulled him off, and they all ran to their lines to go into school. Joey knew he had won but he wasn't sure how badly, if at all, Robby was hurt. His class-mates were abuzz, but he said nothing. He took out his reader, kept his head down, and got ready for oral reading. Five minutes into the reading lesson the back door connecting two of the fifth grades opened and Sister Paulinus entered the class with a bloody-faced Robby by the hand. His nose was bleeding, his eyes were swelled, and blood came from his lip. UH-OH thought Joey, did I do that? As they walked to the front of the classroom the kids were dead silent. Sister Paulinus said, "Miss Francis may I interrupt your class for a few minutes?" Miss Francis, who had a very grim look on her face, said "Yes Sister of course." Sister turned to the class while still hold-ing Robby's hand and asked, "WHO DID THIS TO THIS BOY?" Joey knew his goose was cooked so he immediately stood up and said "I did Sister." The kids in Joey's class immediately started to murmur that Robby started it, but Miss Francis quickly yelled, "SILENCE." Sister Paulinus who knew who Joey was from having attended a number of football games this past fall, said "Joseph, Robby has something to say to you. Go ahead, Robby." Robby was truly battered but he looked at Joey and the rest of the class and said, "I am sorry I started that fight with you." Gary yelled out "I BET YOU ARE." Which drew giggles and laughter which ended as Miss Francis gave Gary a very dark look. Robby began again saying "I am sorry that I started that fight, I am also sorry that I have been a bully to so many of you. I promise I will not do that ever again." Sister Paulinus took Robby by the hand and said "Let's get you cleaned up, thank you Miss Francis." and they walked out the door. The rest of the day flew by. Joey caught both boys and girls staring at him the rest of the day but kept his mouth shut and when the bell rang got up and was the first one out the door. On the way home, he saw Patrick who was not close enough to catch him, so he yelled to Joey, "I saw you kick Lawrence's little brother's ass. Nice. Maybe I will leave you alone for a while." Joey just picked up his pace and headed home knowing that was not going to happen.

Fifth grade had two and a half weeks left before summer vacation when Miss Francis said to the class "I have an announcement. I will not be coming back next year." There were a number of fake moans which caused Joey to chuckle. He knew that most of the class hated her. Miss Francis continued "I am getting married in August and I think we should have a party on the last day of school. There will be refreshments, music, and dancing." There was an immediate buzz in the class. The girls were excited about dancing while the boys sat there in stone-cold silence. The next day at recess the girls had decided that they wanted to make this a date dance. The boys could ask a girl and they would be dance partners during the party. Miss Francis agreed and told the boys they had to ask someone before the party. She then asked, "Are there any questions?" Joey raised his hand. "Yes, Joey what is your question?" Joey stood up as that was proper protocol in fifth grade and said, "I was just wondering instead of dancing if I could fight Robby again?" The boys howled with laughter. Miss Francis's face got red with anger. She gathered herself and told Joey to go sit in the coatroom and so he did. He sat there for the rest of the afternoon. As he walked home, he realized he had two problems. One was who would he ask? Two, he had never danced with anyone but his younger sister at weddings. When he got home it was time to play baseball, so he did.

The next morning, he got to school early and began talking with Gary and some of the other boys. Gary told them all that he had already asked someone and that they should do the same. At recess that day a few more boys had dates and by the end of the week, many of the boys had asked girls to be their dates. Joey had asked no one yet, it was still about ten days away. At the end of the day, three boys came up to him and said that a lot of girls were not giving them an answer until they knew what he was going to do. Joey looked at them and said, "So." A boy named Eugene immediately replied saying "SO ASK ONE DICK HEAD." He decided he would ask a girl named Kathy, whose mom grew up with his mom. He also would travel down to the end of his street where Martin lived. Martin had told him about a new kid who had moved in a couple of months ago. He said the kid's name was Jackie, and he knew how to dance. He also told him that Jackie's mom let them dance in their basement with girls from the neighborhood.

The next morning, he walked to school and made arrangements with Martin to go down the street after dinner to meet Jackie. Martin said, "sure I will call you tonight after I talk to him." He called later that evening and told Joey that it was on for Wednesday and to come down at about 5:30. Joey thanked him and went to play ball.

The next day the kids in his class were talking about nothing but the party and who was going with who. Joey found Kathy just as the recess bell rang and he walked up to her and asked if she would be his partner at the party. Kathy quickly responded yes, and the other dominos fell into place. By the time Joey got home from school, mom was waiting at the door. Kathy had told her mom who she was going to the party with, and her mom called Joey's mom. Mom asked him as soon as he walked in the door "What's going on?" He proceeded to tell her what was happening. Mom started asking all kinds of questions like, "Does the teacher know? Do you know how to dance? We need to get her a corsage" and on and on. So many questions all at once had Joey reeling. "Mom," he said, "please slow down." Yes the teacher knows, it was her idea. I am going down the street after dinner to learn how to do the Stroll and the Hop and what are you talking about with the corsage thing?" Mom was all over it. "If you are going on a date you should be bringing your date a flower of some sort and what is the Stroll and the Hop? What happened to the jitterbug that you do at weddings with your sister?" "YIKES MOM" Joey responded. "The Stroll and the Hop are two dances that are popular today. I saw both on American Bandstand and tonight, I am going to learn how to do them. As far as the flowers there is no way I am giving her flowers, this isn't a date." Mom responded, "I am going to talk with your dad, and I am also going to call Kathy's mom tomorrow." They ate dinner and for the next six days, Joey went down the street and did the Hop and the Stroll.

The day of the party was finally here. Joey was the only boy who had a clue on how to do those dances. Some of the guys were flat-out hilarious trying to dance but Joey did so well that girls were asking Kathy if they could dance with him. She repeatedly said NO. The party ended at the bell and school was out for the summer. The kids said goodbye to one another and went home. Mom would ask about ten times how the dance was. Each time Joey would answer fine. Mom gave up on asking but later she called Kathy's mom. The two moms talked for a while and life went on.

That night as Joey lay in bed he thought about what he learned, besides the Stroll and the Hop in the last two weeks. If you can talk to girls like a human and you can make them laugh on top of being a good dancer and you're even a little cute you were going to have many girls interested in you. Joey would do all of those things for the rest of his life.

SUMMERTIME

It was summer again. Baseball, Ridgewood pool, and more adventures with girls. Joey loved the summertime. As school ended, he had asked his parents if he could take drum lessons. They said yes, but you must practice. The lessons would begin that summer and he'd have lessons twice a week. Along with the drum lessons he became a paper delivery boy. Patrick had given up his Cleveland Press route and Joey had gotten it. The truck driver for the paper felt like family seeing that he delivered the papers right in front of their house and had often stopped in to talk to mom and dad. For the first time in his young life, Joey had to deal with money. He was allowed to keep two dollars every week to do what he wanted. His parents put the rest into a savings account for him. He was becoming a grown-up. Another major event in Joey's life was taking place. Big Joe became the head football and basketball coach of the Saint Charles Lightweight teams. About 25 years later Big Joe would be enshrined in the St. Charles Hall of Fame as would his wife Phyllis, but that's a story for another day.

Many other things were going on that summer. The boys had discovered a new plastic ball called a whiffle ball. Now during the times when they could not play at the Parma Show lot, and they did not have baseball practice, they would be playing whiffle ball in his backyard. They would play until it got dark and the number of bikes that would be parked in his yard often reached double digits.

ENTER UNCLE EDDY

While summer was in full swing, mom's sister Aunt Florence decided to get married. Her husband-to-be would become known to the family as Uncle Eddy. A July wedding was set. Eddy would become part of family lore long after the adult family members would have passed on. Grandma K. couldn't stand him. You see Eddy had an aversion to holding full-time employment while Aunt Flo had a very, very good job. Another thing that drove Grandma crazy was Eddy showing up at all Joey's games and would not shut up. He always had suggestions on what Big Joe's teams should be doing as well as trying to coach Joey. Therefore, Big Joe also hated him. The truth of the matter was that Uncle Eddy was short about ten cards from his deck. Eddy's adventures began about two weeks after their July wedding. One late July day Aunt Flo arrived at Joey's house crying. Mom asked, "what's wrong Flo?" Flo replied sobbing that Eddy had gotten arrested, and she had to go bail him out. Flo didn't drive so she needed a ride and asked if Big Joe could take her to the Parma Police Station. Dad asked her what Eddy had done and Flo replied "shoplifting." Dad raised his eyebrows and he said "OK." He dropped Flo off, and she went inside to get Eddy. Together they walked back to where Eddy had left his car. About two days later Uncle Eddy showed up at Joey's house while he was outside shooting basketball. Eddy went over to Joey and started to show him how to shoot foul shots....underhand. After about five minutes of torture, Joey said to Eddy "Eddy what the heck did you get arrested for?" Eddy replied vigorously "MEENKYA JOEY I WUZ SHOPLIFTING." Joey said, "What did you steal?" Eddy answered, "a fishing pole." "A fishing pole?" Joey asked trying not to laugh. "Where did you hide it?" "In my pant leg" Eddy replied. "In your pant leg?" "Yea, Meenkya Joey I couldn't put it in my pocket. Meenkya I'm tellin' ya that chooch clerk wuzn't even looking at me. If I wouldn't have tripped walking out the door I would have had no problem, I'm tellin' ya that guy was a chooch." Joey looked at Eddy and said, "You are right Eddy I can't believe they caught you." Eddy said, "come on let me show you how to shoot foul shots." Joey threw him the ball, Eddy made ten in a row underhand foul shots, and walked to his car. Joey yelled "Where are you going?" Eddy yelled out the window, "to get a fishing rod. I am going fishing later." Joey hollered back "where are you going fishing?" To which Eddy responded "I don't know I have never been fishing, but someday I will teach you." and he drove away. Joey said aloud to himself "Oh my, and that guy just made ten foul shots in a row."

As Joey lay awake that night one thought kept running through his mind, and that was how sorry he felt for his Aunt Flo. He kept wondering how his favorite aunt could have married that CHOOCH.

Summer also meant it was time for the annual Saint Charles carnival. Joey had always attended in the company of his parents. This year he was begging to go with his friends. Mom and dad agreed figuring he could not get into trouble with them being so close. The carnival was a four-day event. For the first three days, Joey went to the carnival with his friends, Roger, Bobby, Henry, and Ducky. Joey had two dollars in his pocket of his newspaper route money. The carnival was packed. He noticed and remarked to Roger that this was the most girls he had ever seen in one place outside of being in school. Roger responded, "well let's get busy." They began to walk from booth to booth. They came upon a booth that gave you three balls and if you knocked the target off the rack, you would win a stuffed animal. Joey paid a dime for three shots. He hit them but not hard enough to win a prize. Roger said "let's move" but Joey said, "no, one more time." His first throw missed. On the next one, he knocked the target off the shelf and won a bear. He accepted the bear and said, "I have one more throw." Bang, he did it again and chose a stuffed monkey. His friends were loudly cheering, and Roger said loudly to the two guys running the booth "My friend here will wipe this booth out." To which the older of the two booth workers replied, "No he will not, two is the limit, MOVE ON." So, they did. As they moved deeper into the Carnival grounds Joey noticed that more and more girls were looking at him as he carried the stuffed animals. A couple of the girls had walked up to him and asked if they could have one to which Joey would respond "I have two sisters at home, and these are for them" and they kept on walking. Finally, they had reached the section of the grounds where there was legal gambling. The game, called Chuckle Up, is a spin-the-wheel game for real money. This would be Joey's first experience with gambling. He took a dollar from his paper route money that was in his pocket and put a dime down. By the time the night was done that dime turned into a dollar. Joey bought all his buddies a snow cone, and they walked home.

As Joey lay in bed that night staring at the ceiling, he thought, gambling is easy money. As he grew up, he would find out how not true that statement was when he and his friends would have a very close brush with death.

The next night was Sunday and the last night of the carnival. Joey's cousin, Bonnie asked him if he wanted to go to the carnival with her and her girlfriend Rhonda. (Big Joe's sister and her husband had bought the house next door to them the year after they had moved in. Aunt Millie and her husband Jack would end up having seven kids. Between the two families, there would be thirteen children.) Bonnie and Rhonda were both two full years older than Joey. Nevertheless, Joey had been flirting with Rhonda all summer long, every time she visited Bonnie. Rhonda was light years ahead of him when it came to knowing about the birds and the bees. Joey was always confident around girls because he didn't know what he didn't know. He asked his mom if he could go to the carnival and at the same time reminded her that THIS WAS NOT A DATE and that this was his cousin with whom he was going. To which mom quickly responded, "Rhonda is not your cousin" Joey replied, "she isn't?" Mom rolled her eyes and laughed saying, "yes be home by 10:00." Joey whined saying "how about 10:30?" to which mom fired back "OR DON'T GO," Joey said OK.

Later, Joey was waiting on the front porch for the two girls. They both said hello to his mom, and they headed up the street to the carnival. As they arrived Rhonda was already causing a stir with the older boys. Her tight jeans and halter top was doing the job they were meant to do. As they started to walk through the carnival grounds, she was gaining the attention of every teenage boy that saw her. Joey saw the stuffed animal tent and said, "You girls want a stuffed animal?" to which both squealed with delight saying "YES, YES!" so, they walked up to the booth. The guys working remembered Joey from the night before and while looking at the two girls they both just smiled, and one said "you are in much prettier company tonight." Joey gave them money for the first three throws and missed on all three. The worker whispered in his ear "relax kid." Joey laughed and bought three more throws. BANG, BANG, BANG, the bottles went flying and Joey turned to Rhonda and said "pick one out." She picked the biggest one she could. As she did Joey paid for three more balls and turned to his cousin and said, "your turn" Rhonda said to Bonnie "isn't he cute?" "He is if he wins me one of those too." BANG, BANG, BANG, all the bottles were down. Bonnie got a stuffed bear also and the workers told them to move on the kid made his quota for the evening. "Let's go play Chuckle Up." "What's Chuckle Up?" "You'll see." Joey put a dime on the numbers, and he quickly had two dimes. This really is easy he thought. He gave the girls each fifty cents and told them to play also. They did, and they all lost. Joey was almost broke, and it was 9:40. "We gotta go. Let's get some Cotton Candy and leave," he said.

By the time they crossed Ridge Road, the cotton candy was gone. Halfway down Dorothy Ave. about five minutes from home Rhonda grabbed Joey's hand and they walked hand in hand. About twenty steps later Rhonda stopped, turned, looked at Joey, and kissed him. Joey had now been kissed for the very first time. They would repeat the kiss about twenty more times. When they got home, they all said good night. "I hope I get to see you again, good night," Joey said, and Rhonda responded, "Good night, and I cannot wait to see you again either."

That night as Joey lay in bed, thinking of his first kiss, all he said was HOLY MOLY.

SIXTH GRADE, WHAT A BORE

Summer was over and that meant two things to Joey. Football was starting and so was school. It was a different grade and a different Head Football Coach. Joey was about to experience playing on a real football team. That was good. Big Joe being the new Coach was a totally different experience for his son. Dad was always determined that Joey would play because he earned it. He seemed to demand more from him than the others. Even though Joey had started at cornerback in fifth grade that meant nothing. He would have to earn it. He decided that the only way to do that was to be the most physical kid on the field, so once the whistle blew, he hit everything that came his way. Looking back years later when he was raising his only son who at the time was playing for Ohio University, Joey would give him the same advice. "Son, they are always going to be trying to recruit someone faster and bigger, and they may do that, therefore you have to hit anything that walks." He did and played in every game throughout his four college years.

School was starting and Joey was thinking that this would be a boring year, and he would be right, EXCEPT for one thing. When he walked into the classroom, his teacher Mrs. Grant greeted him and showed him his seat. As he was saying hello to the kids that he knew he saw a girl he had never seen before. He was stunned. She was the prettiest girl he had ever seen. He sat down and could not take his eyes off her. Every time he looked at her, she would smile at him. At recess, he started asking the boys he knew who she was. Billy told him her name was Karen, but Billy said "don't even think about it Joey, she is going with Monty." "Monty?" Joey asked "what kind of name is that and what do you mean she is going with him? Where are they going?" Billy said "you sure are funny Joey, they are boyfriend and girlfriend. They are going steady." Joey said, "seriously? well we will see, who is he?" "You know him," Billy said "he was in the classroom next to us last year and he was good friends with the kid you beat up. He is standing right there." "I know that kid," Joey said with surprise in his voice. His name is not Monty, it is Bryan. "Why do they call him Monty? They should be calling him Bucky Beaver. Are you serious, look at the teeth on that kid? Karen is going steady with him?" Billy said "yes but look at his hair. I wish I could do that with my hair, he looks like Fabian." Joey just laughed and they walked in line into their classroom.

In the first week of school, he became friends with Bryan. They hung out in school almost every day. They would be friends for the school year and then both would travel in different directions. Joey would soon realize that going steady in the sixth grade meant something entirely different than what the older kids talked about when they talked about going steady. Bryan would occasionally talk to Karen on the playground, but he never called her and when school let out, they went in separate directions. But it was generally accepted by the students of Mrs. Grant's 6th-grade class that Karen and Bryan were boyfriend and girlfriend. Joey would respect that because Bryan was his friend. However, every time Joey would look at Karen in class, she would be smiling at him. He would say hello to her but that was it. She was, after all, going steady with Bryan, and Bryan was Joey's friend.

Sixth grade was a bore. The year seemed to last forever. Football season had ended under Big Joe with a five-and-five record, a huge improvement over the previous year. The basketball season was a tremendous success. Big Joe's team was undefeated in league play but got beat in the first round of the playoffs. Joey did not start but he was the first guard to go in and played a lot. Needless to say, he had a tough time with their only loss.

In late March, Joey would put his basketball in his newspaper bag and when he had finished his route, he would go over to the St. Charles's school yard and play basketball with whoever was there. There were six baskets attached to the backboards. The backboards were nailed into the brick walls of the school and there were always games he could get in. One day the schoolyard was almost empty. Two boys were shooting around together and when they saw Joey shooting by himself, they asked him if he wanted to play HORSE with them. Joey said sure. As they played, they talked. The smaller of the two was named Chocko and the other boy was called Jebs. Joey introduced himself and Jebs said, "we know who you are." When they were done playing Joey asked if they would be there the next day and both said yes. He did not know it then, but both would become close friends of his and Chocko would become one of his best friends. Those adventures are yet to come.

As he lay in bed one night about a week before school let out, Joey was thinking about Karen and Bryan. He was wondering if Bryan and Karen were going steady why was Karen smiling at him every day, every single day. He began to realize he has a lot more to learn about girls. That too would be a story for another day.

THE HAUNTED BASEMENT

It was the summer of 1959. Joey was close to being a teenager. His body was starting to change. His hormones were running amok. He purchased a transistor radio with earphones so he could listen to Rock and Roll music. His dad gave him an old radio for his bedroom, and he would turn it down low at night and put himself to sleep. He developed a taste for both Rock and Roll as well as MOTOWN. He watched Dick Clark's *American Bandstand* and would practice the new dances that he saw down in the basement with the door shut so no one would see him. His mom and dad were having another child. The number of children would now be at six. He still loved baseball, football, and basketball but he would often find himself singing Rock and Roll songs. The year before the music teacher at St. Charles, Mr. Marvin, had started an eighth-grade chorus and a seventh-grade Glee Club. He visited all five sixth grade classes to evaluate and see if any of the younger kids would be able to sing with the seventh grade Glee Club. Joey was the only boy in sixth grade that was asked to join and join he did. His clothes started to matter. He still shopped with his parents for clothes but now he had an idea of what he wanted to wear. Pointed shoes replaced sneakers (unless of course, he was playing ball) and jeans replaced shorts. White t-shirts replaced striped t-shirts and on and on. He had always combed his hair but now it had to be a certain way. Elvis, Ricky Nelson, and Fabian all had the styles Joey would pattern himself after. Some of the kids in his sixth-grade class said he looked like Tommy Sands so he would always check the television to see if Tommy was on Band Stand.

At the same time, he was still a kid. He still liked to do kid stuff. He just tried to hide most of the toy soldiers etc. It was early July and he and his sisters, Grace and Tina, his brother Douglas and two of their younger cousins decided that they would have a haunted basement and charge five cents per every kid who would want to walk through. Boys as well as girls. The basement windows were completely covered, and the basement was pitch dark. Scary music was playing on the stereo record player and each kid took up a hiding place to jump out of as Joey guided the paying customers through the dark basement. No more than four kids at a time and they all had to hold the person's hand that was in front of them. Joey would hold the hand of the first person in line and guide them through the basement holding a flashlight that he would turn on just as Tina and Douglas and the cousins would pop out of their different hiding places dressed in their Halloween costumes.

Kids from the neighborhood started to show up. Soon there were lines waiting outside listening to the screams coming from the basement. The scariest part of the tour was the station manned by Grace. Grace was in a long black dress and had frizzed her hair and made it look as if it belonged to a wild woman. She was also able to contort her face in a very frightening way. She could spread her nostrils almost the full width of her face. Grace had the last stop on the tour. She hid in the downstairs full bathroom. On cue, she would be standing right by the door when Joey would open it with a lit flashlight under her chin. What made it more frightening was that Joey would lead the customers to the door, open it and nothing would happen. He would comment that the Wild Woman must not be home. He would take them to another part of the basement where Douglas in his devil costume would slither up from a large sink that only he could fit into. He would then start to lead the group outside. As they passed the wild woman's house Joey would say, "let's try again and see if she is home." As the door opened Grace would be standing there, flashlight lit below her chin, nostril-flaring, and cackling like a crazy lady, drawing screams from the customers as Joey hurried them up the stairs. Throughout the morning kids would come and go. The screams were always there. At about a half-hour before lunchtime, three girls showed up. Two were Grace's age and Joey had seen them before. The girl with them was older, and Joey had never seen her before. He greeted them all with a hello. The two younger girls giggled and said hi. The older girl introduced herself as Joan and explained that she had just moved in a couple of days ago and she lived right around the corner on Bertha Avenue. She also said she would be in seventh grade at St. Charles this coming Fall. He told her that they would be in the same grade, and she replied "I know." Joey was thinking as he told them about the haunted basement that Joan looked and acted much older than seventh grade. Nevertheless, they all paid their nickel and they started downstairs with Joey in the lead holding Joan's hand. The girls screamed every time they got scared and every time they got scared, Joan would get closer, much closer to Joey. By the time they got back up the stairs Joey's hormones were racing like it was the summer Olympics. The two younger girls said, "LET'S GO AGAIN". Joey looked at Joan who replied "SURE." As they started down again, Joey thought UH–OH. The first time that someone popped out they all screamed again but this time Joan grabbed Joey and kissed him. This happened every time the girls got scared and screamed. Again, when it was over, they headed upstairs and outside. Joey was sweating. The group went on the tour three more times. Each tour lasted longer than the previous one. Joan and Joey would take so long that the kids who were hiding were getting claustrophobic. Grace got tired of waiting on the last trip and jumped out screaming before the group had reached her. She stopped and watched her older brother in a lip lock with Joan. When Joey saw her standing there, he started screaming and they headed up the stairs. Mom came to the door and said it was time for lunch. Joan said "goodbye, I will see you later." and the girls left. Joey and his brothers and sisters went in to eat. They were having goose liver sandwiches on rye bread. They all were counting and dividing the money and talked about what they could do differently in the afternoon to make it scarier. While they were counting Grace raised her head and said, "Mom I saw Joey and Joan kissing" and went back to counting her nickels. Mom did not respond she just looked at Joey. Fifteen minutes later as the kids were getting up from their lunch she said, "kids I have a headache. Let's cancel the haunted basement for the day. Get a book and read under the tree." So, they did.

Later that night as Joey lay in bed he was thinking. Boy was that fun. Then he thought I wonder if mom is ok, she never has headaches. He fell asleep thinking about Shirley winking at him.

MAJOR DISAPPOINTMENTS

The summer ended with the Lou Gehrigs having an undefeated season but failing again in the city playoffs. Football was starting and after that was basketball. Joey would meet up with Chocko and Jebs after he finished his paper route, and they would play hoops at St. Charles. They would be buddies well into their sixties.

Late in August, Joey was given his first assignment of serving Mass. He and three other boys would serve the 6:00 a.m. Mass the last week of August from Monday through Friday. The 6:00 a.m. Mass was also known among the servers as the rookie Mass. Boys who had never served were often given that time slot because hardly anyone was there. The other boys were all older and if Joey forgot what to do, they would help him.

He was twenty minutes early, so early that the Church had not opened yet. Finally, the Priest came to the back door and opened it for him, and he went in and started getting dressed for Mass. The other boys showed up shortly and they set up the altar. At 6:00 a.m. on the dot, they would all walk out to the altar with the priest and the Mass would begin. About ten minutes into the Mass as the boys were kneeling facing the altar the server next to Joey poked him in the side and nodded to a door that was against the back wall. The door was behind the altar but off to the left. It led to the server's sacristy where those serving the next Mass would gather.

Joey looked at the boy and again he nodded toward the back door. The door had a round peep hole in it so the Priests that were saying the next mass could see out into the body of the Church. Joey looked at the door. He looked for about five seconds and just as he was looking away a finger came out of the hole. The finger did sort of a finger wave and then disappeared. Joey's mouth was opened wide in surprise. The other servers were laughing as if they were veterans. Joey was stunned. About 30 seconds later he got poked in the side again. This time he looked right at the peephole. A finger appeared again but this time a face had been drawn on it. Joey couldn't help but laugh this time especially when just seconds later another finger popped out. This one had a red face. The boys were all trying to hold in their laughter. Fooling around during Mass was punishable by death. Just as all four of the servers were getting themselves under control something else came through the peephole. Joey didn't recognize it but the boy next to him whispered, "it's a tongue." The tongue only lasted for a few seconds but all four of the servers were having a very difficult time keeping it together. Fortunately, it was time to dispense Communion and shortly after Communion the Mass was over and they walked off the altar as the next group of servers was going out for the next Mass. Joey took off his cassock and was beelining to the door when he noticed the other three boys weren't leaving. He stopped and went back in towards them saying "Is there something left for us to do?" Eugene the oldest boy said "Hell yes, we are going to torture those guys the way they did to us" and he showed the boys his fingers that had little faces inked on them. Joey turned and got out of there and headed home thinking he never would have guessed that serving mass could be so dangerous. Had the priest seen any of that....HOLY MOLY. He walked into the kitchen and his mom was waiting for him and asked, "how was your first Mass?" To which he answered "really fun mom, really fun" and poured a box of Tony the Tiger Sugar Frosted Flakes.

Football was starting and soon after, school would start. Like all seventh-grade boys, Joey's hormones were in full swing. Big Joe was now the Head Lightweight football coach. The boys were very excited. Big Joe's debut as basketball coach had led the lightweights to their first league championship. The guys were expecting more of the same in football. They would not be too far from wrong. School started in the first week of September. Joey had a bunch of new guys in his class. He knew most of them and thought this could be a fun year. Also, Shirley was in his class for the first time since she winked at him in kindergarten. Rumors had been spreading about Shirley for a while now. She was older and she looked older. She was one of the few girls who truly filled out her school uniform. A boy that Joey hardly knew, named Robert began talking about her on the first day of school. Robert was a boy that was two years older than the rest of the class and already well into maturing. He told Joey that Shirley hung out at Ridgewood Lake behind the swimming pool with the guys and girls that hung out there. Mostly older kids. Robert was always talking about her and the many different things she did with the older boys at the Lake. Joey did not completely understand all the stories but the ones he did he liked. When she would smile at him in school (and that occurred in about every class) his knees got wobbly and a bulge in his pants seemed to be there right along with his wobbly knees.

It was the third week of school when things got a little crazy in English class. The teacher's name was Mr. Fye. He was not a very good teacher and for a male teacher in grade school surprisingly he hardly had control of his class. In English class, Bob sat directly across from Joey. Shirley sat in front of him. Bob was always badgering her. She would turn to talk to him, but she was always looking at Joey when she did. Soon Joey was in the conversation, and they were having a good time. One day when they were diagramming sentences Bob took the eraser end of his pencil and started poking her in the back. She would half turn around all the while looking at Joey. Bob would stop poking and she would turn and sit straight in her seat. He would start again. Shirley turned but this time a little further around almost facing Bob. He now kept poking her and daring her to turn all the way around. She looked, smiled, and turned back to sitting straight ahead. Bob started again but this time telling her to turn all the way around. She started to turn again, then she would stop. When the poking started again, she would turn a little farther. Each time, the turn was almost a full turn, she was teasing Bob as well as Joey. Bob put his pencil down and started poking her with his finger. All at once Shirley full turned and faced him and Bob found himself poking her in places he shouldn't have been poking, right in class. Shirley quickly turned back straight ahead. Joey's knees were wobbling, and the bulge was bulgier. She turned and looked at him and winked just as the bell rang and they all got up to leave. At dinner time mom would ask Joey what his favorite class was, and he would answer English. She was very surprised but said nothing. Keep in mind mom was no dummy. This went on almost every day until one day Mr. Fye changed everybody's seats. And you guessed it, the three of them were separated far away from each other. English was not Joey's favorite subject anymore.

UNCLE EDDY AND THE ONE-LEGGED CHICKEN DANCE

Meanwhile, the Lightweight football team was undefeated. They were six & zero with two games to play. Their game coming up was against the only other undefeated team, Parmadale. The winner of that game would make the C.Y.O. playoffs. Joey started at cornerback as he had for the two previous seasons. On offense, he alternated with an eighth-grader named Billy at Quarterback. They would carry the plays in from the bench. Parmadale was an orphanage in Parma that had a school for grades one through eight. They were very well-coached and had very tough kids.

Going into the fourth quarter the game was tied at 0-0. Uncle Eddy was in full throttle. He was standing on the St. Charles sideline for the entire game. He was constantly yelling at the refs and twice the refs warned Coach Big Joe about the guy on the sidelines that was yelling at them. Big Joe responded both times that he didn't know the guy to which the refs would respond "he is on your sideline." Big Joe glared at Uncle Eddy numerous times but with the game, in the balance, his concentration was on the field not on the sideline. St. Charles had the ball on their own ten-yard line with about seven minutes left. Billy completed a ten-yard pass for a first down to their own twenty-one. It was Joey's turn to carry in the play. Big Joe turned to him and called fifty-one reverse. Joey stared at him for a second and took the play in. The play was an exotic trick play that they practiced every day for six weeks. It never seemed to be run correctly and now it was called in a game that would mean the championship. Joey called fifty-one reverse in the huddle. The players, to a man, raised their heads and looked at Joey with eyes wide open. Joey who was one of the only two seventh graders in the huddle looked right back at them and said "fuck it make it work" and they broke the huddle. They came up to the line of scrimmage and Joey placed his hands under the center. He called "SET" and the ball was snapped through his legs that were spread wide and right to the fullback. The fullback caught the ball and headed right into the middle of the line as Joey did a full turn and faced him. As the fullback hit the line, he handed the ball to Joey who had his back turned to the Parmadale defense. He took the ball as the fullback got smacked and started to run around the RIGHT offensive end. On his second step, a defender broke through and had him by the ankle. Joey pulled his leg out of the defender's grasp and looked to the offensive LEFT side and saw no one there. That's where he headed, turned the corner, and headed for the endzone. Now Joey wasn't big, but he was fast, and he started to pull away. He felt someone behind him and looked over his right shoulder and saw no one close. The only thing he was aware of was the St. Charles crowd screaming as he ran. He ran as fast as he could and suddenly, he was crossing the goal line and the ref was putting his hands up signaling TOUCH DOWN. His teammates hustled down the field, and he was mobbed. As they all turned and headed back up the sidelines there was a commotion going on out on the field. There was a flag on the ground right next to a ref who was also on the ground. Big Joe was in a strenuous discussion with another ref with a white hat. There were two auxiliary policemen who were escorting Uncle Eddy off the field and to his car. They told Eddy to GET OUT or he would be arrested. Eddy quickly got in the car and drove away while many of the St. Charles fans were screaming at him. As Joey got closer to where the play started the refs were marking off a 15-yard penalty against St. Charles that also nullified the touchdown. Big Joe was quickly getting the next play in to the team with Billy. Billy fumbled the snap and Parmadale recovered. They threw a touchdown pass with no time left on the clock and St. Charles lost. As Joey stood on the sidelines he kept asking what had happened. Of all people, it was Patrick who was there with other eighth-graders watching the game and ran up to Joey and said "GREAT GAME, GREAT RUN. YOUR CRAZY ASS UNCLE RAN OUT ON THE FIELD DOING SOME KIND OF ONE-LEGGED CHICKEN DANCE AND AS YOU WENT BY THE REF RAN INTO HIM AND FELL!" Joey was stunned. He just stood there while his dad yelled to him to "GET OUT AND SHAKE HANDS" and so he did. Parmadale won the championship and Joey would not PLAY in another football championship for about eleven years. Uncle Eddy would stay away from family gatherings for about two months. It took a lot of pleading by Joey's mom to get dad to forgive and forget. By Thanksgiving Day Big Joe had calmed, but, in his heart, he had not forgotten nor forgiven.

That night Joey lay in bed staring at the ceiling. He was thinking how glad he was that Patrick wasn't running up to him to throttle him again as well as wondering why losing a game was so absolutely painful. The pain of losing any game would never go away from him. Before he fell asleep there was one other event that had occurred that had him completely bewildered. What the hell was a one-legged chicken dance?

THERE WAS NOTHING THERE

Football season ended. Basketball practice had begun. It was Thanksgiving Day. Turkey, mom's rice, pumpkin pie, and football on T.V. It was his second favorite holiday. But also, there was a High School football game played every year between the East and West Senate champions. The game was called the Charity Game. This year the game was between a Catholic High School and a public High School. The Latin Lions were playing the John Marshal Lawyers. The game would begin at nine a.m. Thanksgiving morning. Every year St. Charles would charter a bus and take any 7th or 8th-grade cheerleaders and football players to the game which was played at Cleveland Stadium. The stadium held 86,000 people, but only about 12,000 people would attend so finding a seat was not hard to do. Joey and a few of his buddies, Ray and Billy would be going to the game. The bus would leave at 8:00 a.m. sharp and bring them all back to St. Charles later. The boys got there early and got seats in the back. As the bus was filling up Shirley and two of her girlfriends were getting on. They walked to the back of the bus and Shirley said to Billy who was sitting next to Joey "Get up I am sitting here." Billy looked at Joey who was already pushing him out of the seat and promptly got up. Shirley sat down and sat very, very close to Joey who was holding his breath. They talked on the way down to the game and Shirley being light years ahead of Joey made a number of suggestive comments to him, often whispering them in his ear. Joey started to think that this was the day. Today he would finally find out what the big deal was that caused such a ruckus eight years earlier with Louise the Chinese. The bus pulled up to the stadium and everyone got out and easily found their seats. About 74,000 were empty as the game began. They watched, they cheered, and they talked. At the end of the first quarter, Shirley got up and said she would be right back. She would not return until just before halftime. She sat down and whispered in Joey's ear "follow me." They both got up and as they reached the top of the stairs she took his hand. Usually, Joey was very at ease with the girls he had known BUT Shirley could very well be the Holy Grail and he was extremely nervous. She led him up another set of stairs and when they got to the top there was no one there. There were many seats but all empty. Shirley said, "come on over here." She took him around a corner and showed him a door. She pulled it open and turned on the light and quickly shut the door. The room was small and held some brooms and mops. But it was big enough for what Shirley had planned. She quickly turned to Joey and began kissing him which he more than readily returned. Somewhere in the middle of the third quarter, they took off their coats and his hands began to wander under her shirt. He fondled her for a while and then placed his hand inside her slacks and started to work his way down. Shirley quickly unbuttoned her jeans and Joey slid his hand inside her panties. He kept groping and fondling but he became nervous. Nervous turned to fear and soon fear turned to terror. THERE WAS NOTHING THERE. Shirley immediately took his hand and placed his finger inside her. She kept moving it back and forth while Joey stood completely puzzled. He thought to himself maybe she is looking for what is supposed to be here. All of a sudden, she was moaning. The moan kept getting louder and louder as the finger went around faster and faster and then all of a sudden Shirley gave his hand back and said "Let's get back to our seats." Joey was a lot of things. Puzzled, scared, puzzled again. The game was just ending as they met Billy and Ray on their way out. You missed a heck of a game, said Ray. To which Shirley quickly responded "he certainly did" to which Joey responded "OH". The drive home flew by and as they all got up Shirley whispered in his ear "That was fun. We must do that again BIG BOY" as she walked away. Joey just kept mumbling "there was nothing there. There was nothing there." Ray looked at him saying "where?" But he did not answer.

That night as he lay in bed, he had many thoughts. Why was there nothing there? With finding nothing why was it still so much fun? Why did my hand get so wet? As a matter of fact, why did my pants get so wet? I have to get to confession soon and lastly if there was nothing there why was there such a commotion in Kindergarten over Louise the Chinese's dress? I am going to have to talk to Shirley about this. But that would never happen.

Saturday was confession day. Joey went to church with his mom and dad. Confession was serious business and Joey had practiced for two days on what and how he would tell the Priest. As they walked into church there were lines at each confessional and mom chose the shortest one. When they got to the line of choice standing at the front of the line was Shirley. She looked and laughed, and Joey could not help but do the same. His confession to the priest went without a hitch. As Joey kneeled doing his penance he was thinking if impure thoughts were ten Hail Mary's and impure thoughts, as well as impure deeds, were ten Hail Mary's and ten Our Fathers, what's next? He would find out soon enough.

In school Joey and Shirley would talk in English class but they never could find time alone. Shirley sometimes stopped in the gym to watch Joey practice, but they certainly didn't talk there. Then the week before Christmas, she was gone. Joey would never see her again. She was gone. English class would never be the same ....EVER AGAIN. Still confused, Joey had decided he had to go to the library and get a book on human anatomy. He looked at pictures of both men and women. When he got done with both he simply said to himself....OH.

A FAMILY CHRISTMAS TRADITION

Thanksgiving was over and basketball was underway. November and December went by in a whirl, and suddenly it was Christmas. Joey's favorite holiday. Mom and dad had started a tradition with their family. One that would go on well into their grandchildren's lives. On Christmas Eve ALL their kids had to be in bed at 8:00 p.m. Santa would bring the tree as well as all their gifts. On Christmas Day they all woke up at almost the same time. Usually well before the sun rose. They would wait until told they could come down the stairs and then they would all come down together to see the gifts under the tree for the first time. They then would open their gifts together. Dad had an 8mm camera by the late '50s and every Christmas morning was on film. Three days after each child had his 7th Christmas, they would have a meeting with mom and dad and at that meeting, they were informed that there was no Santa Claus. Each of them reacted differently to the news when their time finally came. When Joey learned he at first didn't believe it. He thought and certainly hoped it was not true. He argued with his parents but finally, the truth dawned on him. When it finally did, he cried. Joey would later tell his friends and family that other than the deaths of his mom and dad it was the worst day of his life. Later that evening dad would say to his mom, this kid who boxed in the Golden Gloves at five years old and not only didn't flinch but flattened the kid in round one cried like a baby when he learned there was no Santa Claus. He waited for mom to respond and when she didn't, he flicked on the lamp and realized that she was crying too. Every year, mom and dad would have a meeting before New Year's with each child who had just been told there was no Santa. The meeting served the purpose of explaining their new role for NEXT CHRISTMAS. Mom and dad explained that they would be treated the same way as if they still believed in Santa. On Christmas Eve they would go to bed with the other children and wait for them to fall asleep. When they were sure that they were asleep they would sneak down the stairs and help decorate the tree and set the gifts. They were warned not to spoil Christmas for the younger kids. There was never a brother or a sister who had the secret of Santa Claus revealed to them before it was time. Joey as well as his brothers and sisters would do the same thing with their children on Christmas Eve. Their children would do the same for their kids.

Basketball season was underway and Big Joe's team would go undefeated in the regular season and win their second straight league title. Joey started at guard, but the rest of the team was made up of entirely eight graders. The pursuit of the elusive City Championship consisted of having to beat two other west side divisions winners. The Saint Charles undefeated lightweight basketball team beat them both and were now playing for the first basketball City Championship in the school's history. The entire school was on fire with excitement. Unfortunately, they lost by a large margin. Winning lots of baseball games and now basketball games, then losing in the City Championship title game was becoming frustrating for all involved. Despite winning almost every game in both sports the one loss a year was devasting. Only winning the whole thing would be acceptable. This would become the mantra for the entire family both boys and girls for many years to come.

The sadness over another City Championship loss was quickly dispelled with the announcement that mom was pregnant again and was expecting their sixth child. The family was ecstatic and looking forward to having another brother and/or sister.

Winter came and went. Basketball was over and summer baseball had not begun yet. Springtime became a time of playing outdoor hoops. Joey's cousins had moved to Parma Heights, and Big Joe's mom and sister moved into the house next door. Joey talked his aunt into putting a basket up on their garage and basketball would be played there for many, many years, well into Joey's adult life.

That night while he lay in bed, Joey's anger and tears of frustration turned to tears of another sort. He realized that his mom and dad, by creating and supporting the myth of Santa Claus had created some of his best Christmas memories. He was truly lucky to have parents who loved him so much that they fibbed a little just to bring joy into his life.

UNCLE EDDY

I t was a Saturday morning in mid-May. Joey, Jebs, and Chocko were playing a game of HORSE on the new hoop in Auntie Olie's driveway while they were waiting for some other guys to show up to play some three-on-three basketball. (HORSE was a shooting game that kids played when there weren't enough guys to play a regular game.) As they were playing a car pulled up, parked next to Joey's house and Uncle Eddy got out. He walked through Joey's backyard to where the boys were playing. "MEENKYA Joey what are you guys doing?" he asked. "Playing Horse" Jebs and Chocko answered simultaneously. Both boys knew Uncle Eddy and like most of Joey's friends who knew Eddy, they knew they were in for some laughs. Eddy had already become a family legend. He immediately responded by saying hello to the fellas and then asked, "Can I play?" Chocko said "SURE we are playing for a dollar a man. So, the winner would get three bucks." Eddy said, "Meenkya fellas I cannot play for money." "Why?" asked Jebs. "Because I am in Gambler's Anonymous. I cannot be betting." UH -OH Joey was thinking. Here we go. "Fine," said Chocko "how about we play for a beer?" (These guys were in seventh grade and had not even tasted a beer, so they were hardly being serious. This was ball-bust Uncle Eddy time.) To their surprise, Eddy answered, "MEENKYA fellas I cannot do that I am in Alcoholics Anonymous." Jebs immediately jumped into the conversation saying, "Eddy is the fishing rod story true?" "Fuck yeah it's true that Chooch wuz lucky to catch me" to which Joey responded by saying "EDDY you don't shoplift anymore right?" "Meenkya Joey no way. I am in Kleptomaniacs Anonymous. I can't do that." Chocko immediately got back involved in the conversation by asking "Eddy are you in any other anonymous groups?" "Just one other" Eddy replied. "Well, which one is it? "Meenkya youse guys are too much. I am in Peeping Tom's Anonymous. I got caught because that chooch of a dog would not stop barking." "So, are we going to play or what?" Joey said, "Eddy you don't mind if the three of us play for dollars do ya?" "No, it's ok." "One last question Eddy." Joey couldn't resist asking, "are you in Get A Job ANONYMOUS? Because I never see you going to work." "HEE, HEE, HEE, Meenkya Joey, I'm telling ya, you're a funny guy. Let's play, chooches."

They played a game of HORSE. The boys put their dollars in a hat, and they started to play. Eddy shot a barrage of underhand shots as well as hook shots and other trick shots that were in what seemed to be an endless repertoire of bizarre basketball shots. He eliminated the boys one by one and won the HORSE contest. He said, "IT WUZ NICE PLAYIN WITH YOU CHOOCHES" and he walked over to the hat holding the dollars and took his winnings. "Hey" yelled Joey "What are you doing?" As Eddy was walking to his car Chocko yelled "I THOUGHT YOU WERE IN GAMBLERS ANONYMOUS?" Eddy got in his car and started the engine. As he pulled away, he yelled out to the boys "I AM....WHEN I LOSE....SEE YOU CHOOCHES LATER."

That night, as Joey lay in bed staring at the ceiling, he was thinking. What exactly is a Chooch? Not finding the answer in his head, he then thought, maybe the family has Uncle Eddy wrong. Is it possible that he's smarter than we think?

RE-ENTER PATRICK

The school year was drawing near to a close. Joey was getting closer to being an eighth-grader. In a K through 8th school like St. Charles, eighth graders were the kings. Seventh graders were called Moldies, and they were harassed on Moldy day which happened throughout the school year. Joey had not been harassed much, largely because he played on the same teams as many of the eighth-graders and it was very difficult to harass a teammate. Also, they had huge respect for Big Joe, combined with a certain amount of fear.

At St. Charles, the eighth graders were let out of school earlier than the rest of the kids. Their last 4 days in school were designated Moldy week. This meant that tormenting the seventh graders became a full-time sport for those who were shortly going to graduate.

Much to Joey's surprise, Patrick somehow was actually going to graduate, and he dedicated his last 4 days of school to being the chief Moldy hunter. Joey became his #1 target. If any of the seventh graders got caught the older kids would and often did any number of things to them. Pink bellies. noogies, wedgies, and the worst fate of all was pantsing. Which meant removing the boys' pants in front of whoever was in the schoolyard. Years later when Joey was in college, he would watch his buddies streak completely naked. All of them thinking how cool it was to run down the street with no pants on. For seventh-grade boys, it was the ultimate humiliation.

On Monday of Moldy week, Joey was extremely alert. His goal was to not be on the playground for a lengthy period of time. During recess, a lot of the boys would stay in and work on extra credit and not go out. But the lunch hour was a different deal. Everyone had to go outside. Joey's plan was to go home for lunch Monday through Thursday. The eighth-graders had Friday off and were strictly forbidden to come back to school. Monday went perfectly for Joey. He walked home for lunch and did not show up back at school until the bell rang and the students formed their lines to go into the building. All the teachers would be outside standing by their homeroom's lines. That afternoon his buddies had told Joey that Patrick and a bunch of his guys had been searching all over for him and were pissed that they could not find him. After school, he took a longer way home and Monday ended safely. Three more days to go. Tuesday began the same way. Inside for recess and home for lunch was again the plan. When the lunch bell rang Joey headed out the back door of the school and would cross Ridge Road to go home a block away from school. He felt good as he crossed the busy street with no sign of any eighth-graders. He was feeling safe. He knew Patrick was way too slow to catch him and felt he was out of danger. As he crossed Ridge Road, he breathed a sigh of relief. All of a sudden about six eighth-graders popped out of nowhere. They came from the Parma Show parking lot, they came from inside the Parma Library, and from behind Vic's Deli. Patrick was screaming "GET HIM, GET HIM" as Joey took off. He quickly realized what Patrick had done. He had gotten some of the fastest eighth-graders to chase Joey and hold him. Joey ran like hell and barely escaped the ambush. The boys would never miss eating lunch so while Joey escaped into his house they quickly disappeared. Joey breathed a sigh of relief and timed his arrival back at school perfectly. Nobody would stick around after school, so the walk home was uneventful. Two days down and two to go.

Wednesday at lunch hour it was raining. If Joey's dad was not working on a day it rained he would always pick him up for lunch as well as take him back to school. As he sat in his dad's car and drove down Essen he saw the boys waiting in ambush and gave them the finger as his dad drove by them. Later that night he thought, one more day, and I survived Moldy week.

It was Thursday. Last day for eighth-graders at school. It was also sunny, so Joey was on his own. Lunch hour came and Joey followed the same plan. As he crossed Ridge Road nothing happened. There was no ambush. He felt good. Now all he had to do is get back to school when the teachers were outside waiting for the school lines, and he would escape Moldy Day. This time however his timing was a little off. He got back to school earlier than he should of, so he stayed behind the school by the Wilbur Avenue entrance, which of course was locked. Patrick and his buddies were everywhere. They had him cornered and six of them overpowered him easily. Patrick yelled, "TAKE HIM BY THE GIRLS PLAYGROUND AND LET'S PANTS HIM!" Hearing this Joey started kicking, punching, biting, and whatever else he could do to get loose. They were carrying him by his arms and legs. He was able to grab a boy named Ricky and just kept punching him, but they were getting closer to the girls' playground and Patrick was yelling "UNBUCKLE HIS PANTS." While in a kicking and punching frenzy he could see large numbers of girls watching and waiting to see what was going to happen. Joey caught a glimpse of the girls and it seemed like every girl at St. Charles was watching to see him get pantsed. Joey just kept flailing. Before he could get the belt unbuckled, Ricky lost his grip as did one of the kids holding his leg and Joey found himself on the ground. He was kicking and punching and making it very difficult for any of them to get his belt unbuckled. The group became a circle surrounding Joey. The eighth-graders were not punching him they were just trying to control him. He could feel that they were starting to lose interest. Ricky gave up first. He was tired of getting punched. Lying on the ground Joey landed a solid kick on a boy named Joe's testicles. He was lying on the ground screaming. The rest of the boys were now deserting Patrick as the bell rang. Everyone started heading to their lines leaving Joey and Patrick staring at each other. As Joey got off the ground Patrick said, "No hard feelings Joey." to which Joey who was now standing said "no problem, Patrick but you are still a freckle-faced baboon" and he bolted to his lines.

Joey's tie was a mess, his shirt pocket was torn, and his pants had holes in the knees. His mom was going to kill him, but it was much better than being pantsed in front of all those girls. Mom and dad both asked what had happened to which Joey said he got in a fight with someone. Dad said, "looks like you got your ass kicked." Joey just looked at him and smiled and said, "I'm ok."

That night as Joey lay in bed staring at the ceiling, he had a couple of thoughts. The first was how did Patrick find that many kids to help him? (He would find out the next day that Patrick was paying those guys that helped him catch Joey a quarter apiece for each day). The second thought was about how many girls were watching to see Joey get pantsed. He thought wow they are as curious as I am to find out what is under there. Really all they have to do is ask and we could work something out. He fell fast asleep shortly after that.

It was summer vacation time. The Baby Boomers were growing up. Along with Rock-n-Roll, gimmick songs were being made. Songs like PA, PA, OOO MOW, MOW; Purple People Eater; The Lion Sleeps Tonight among many others and all became lifetime classics. Hula hoops, skateboards, whiffle balls, and comic books became part of the BABY BOOMER experience. Sleeping outside in a tent at night became commonplace for boys of Joey's age. Sneaking out of that tent at two a.m. also became commonplace. Knowing where girls were having pajama parties was vital information. The boys would sneak out of the tent and pay them visits. It was a great time to be a kid.

THE FIREMAN'S KID

Baseball at the Parma Show lot began again. More kids were showing up to play and Joey's little brother Douglas was allowed to go with Joey and get into the games.

This year however a problem would emerge. One of the neighbors who lived across the street did not want the boys playing there. There was too much noise as well as the fact that hit balls would come into their yard. They constantly yelled at the boys and told them to leave, or they were going to call the police and have them thrown out. Joey and Roger as well as many of the guys who were playing would laugh and tell them to go ahead and call them. This went on until mid-June and the games continued. The neighbors escalated their displeasure by keeping the balls that were hit in their front yard. This coupled with the balls that would be hit on the roof caused a shortage of baseballs that were in the boy's possession. Finally, in late June the last ball that the kids had was hit over the right-field poles and went into the neighbor's yard for a home run. The joy of the home run quickly ended as the man of the house ran outside and took the ball back into his house. The boys had no more baseballs. "What do we do now?" asked Kenny a relatively new player at the parking lot. "WE GO STAND IN FRONT OF THEIR HOUSE AND CHANT WE WANT OUR BALLS BACK," said Roger. "Great idea," said Joey and about fourteen boys walked across the street and began chanting. The man who took their baseball came out on the porch and said, "my wife is calling the police right now!" Within a minute the boys heard sirens. They scattered but Joey knew that the police would be there well before they could get away, so he grabbed his little brother and hid him behind some bushes that grew at the back of the parking lot. He said, "Doug, stay here and do not move. "OK," said Douglas, and Joey took off running. Two police cars pulled up and started to round up a few of the boys. Joey was one of them. Roger and Joey got into the back seat of the police car and the officer said, "Fellas, I am going to take you both home. What are your names and where do you live?" Joey answered first saying "I am Joey DeTorre, and I live right on the corner up there." The police officer immediately looked in his mirror and said, "are you Joey the fireman's kid?" Joey thought UH-OH and said "yes." The officer got on the radio and spoke to the other patrol car saying, "fellas this is Big Joe's kid." The officer in the other car asked "The fireman?" "Yes sir" replied the officer "I am taking him home." "Ok" said the other car "from what these kids already told me we are going to let them all go anyway. Talk to you later."

The police car pulled up to the front of Joey's house. Joey, Roger, and the police officer were getting out of the car as Big Joe was coming out the door. He said "hello Frank. Good to see you ...I think. Is my son in trouble?" Frank said "morning Joey, but I don't think so." Big Joe turned to his son and said "Well?" Joey then proceeded to tell the story. When he was finished his dad said, "Is that all?" Both Joey and Roger nodded yes at the same time just as Joey's mom walked out the door. Big Joe and Frank were talking, and the policeman had told Roger he could go. Mom said, "Hello Frank," and she looked at Joey and said, "Where is Douglas?" The policeman looked surprised. Dad said "my #2 son". Joey went "Holy Moly" and got on his bike. He hollered "I got him" and pedaled off at full speed. He got to the parking lot in about 45 seconds and as he pulled in, he said to himself, please be there, please be there. He jumped off the bike and ran to the bushes. There was Douglas, standing in the exact same position Joey left him in. Joey breathed a sigh of relief, as Douglas looked at him and said, "can I move now?" Joey laughed hard, and Douglas said "What? You told me not to move." "Get on the bike we will ride doubles" and he pedaled home. Douglas explained to his parents when they got home what Joey had done and both parents just smiled. All was well. The next day the boys returned to play with a ball Big Joe had given them. Around home plate were a half-dozen balls returned to them from the neighbors. There were no more complaints and lots more games.

That night Joey was thinking as he lay in bed. It is a good thing I have never told Douglas to jump in a lake. As his eyes closed his last thought was how lucky he was to have his two parents.

Summer ended. It was the last year for the Lou Gehrigs, and they got beat in the playoffs again not even making the City Championship. Joey's days of playing baseball for his dad were over.

THE TIMES THEY WERE A-CHANGING

American baby boomers were the first generation of American kids who grew up with Television. Shows like I Love Lucy; The Range Rider; I Remember MA, MA; Make Room for Daddy; Rin, Tin, Tin along with many, many others became a baby boomer way of life. If the Friday Night Fights were on Joey watched carefully with his mom and dad while never forgetting Abe's boxing lessons, JAB, JAB, RIGHT CROSS.

Friday Night television was followed by Saturday morning cartoons. MIGHTY MOUSE, CLUTCH CARGO, Tarzan movies, Looney Tunes with Bugs and Porky and Daffy Duck, Yosemite Sam, Donald Duck and his three nephews, Huey, Dewey, and Louie, and who could ever forget Goofy. The television was packed with kids' shows from about 8:00 a.m. to Noon on all three of the stations that were available at that time.

As America rolled into the 1960's television was beginning to have a serious impact on the American people. The 1960 Presidential election would prove just how influential it had become. The Republican and Democratic Conventions were both televised. Joey thought they were boring, but mom and dad were glued to the T.V. The Republicans nominated Richard Nixon who had just finished serving eight years as Vice-President for the outgoing President, General Dwight D. Eisenhower, a hero of WORLD WAR II. Nixon was a familiar name in American households. He regularly appeared in newsreels and his picture was often in the newspapers.

The Democrats chose a relative unknown as their candidate by the name of John F. Kennedy. A handsome charismatic young man whom almost no one had ever heard of. Plus, he was a Roman Catholic. There had never been a Catholic president. Only one other Catholic had ever run for the office. In 1928 Al Smith a Roman Catholic lost by a landslide. Nixon was a huge favorite.

For the first time in the history of America, the candidates would debate on National T.V. There would be a total of three. Joey's parents along with millions of Americans were glued to the television. Nixon was far ahead in the polls leading up to the debates. He would not maintain that lead. There was no keeping score in the debates, but people who watched them on T. V. and who were polled afterward said Kennedy was a clear winner. However, those polled who listened to the debates on the radio said it was about even. Kennedy was at ease in front of the camera. Whereas Nixon was clearly not. He had a sense of humor and Nixon showed none. He was young and handsome, and Nixon was not. He was eloquent and charismatic and again Nixon fell short. All these attributes and or shortcomings were very obvious on T.V.

The debates enabled Kennedy to pull even in the polls and he went on to win the closest election in United States history. J.F.K became the youngest Candidate ever to win a Presidential election as well as the first Roman Catholic. Television would become a major factor in every following election in the United States.

EIGHTH GRADE

Joey was blessed. His life was fun. Not completely fun, but never boring. The nuns were tough and in Joey's family grades were very important. Mom and dad would go over all of their children's grades with a fine-tooth comb every report card day. Joey would study. His parents would make sure that he did every single night. He loved History and Social Studies classes. He also loved to read. He had moved on from reading books like *THE HARDY BOYS* and *MISS PICKERELL* books to Chip Hilton Adventures and sports stories, with those skills as well as the Math, English, and Science classes that the nuns drilled into his head he would be more than ready for High School. Monday through Thursday nights from six-thirty p.m. to seven-thirty p.m. was a strictly enforced study and homework time before bed at about 7:45. But Friday night the children that were old enough could stay up to about 10:30 and watch T.V. together.

Summer was ending and football began. Joey had turned 12 in July. He was an eighth-grader now. The top class in the school. He felt like he was growing up. Football started very badly, Joey's dad was in the hospital and was unable to coach. He would be in the hospital for almost four months. He had received The Purple Heart in WWII while he was loading an American cargo ship when a Japanese bomber attacked. He fell two stories down into the hull. He would suffer the rest of his life with a herniated disc. The only game he was able to attend would be the very last game of the year.

The team was coached by his two assistant coaches. They would win only two games. After winning their first game in week five the coaches packed the entire team in cars and drove to the hospital where they pulled up next to Big Joe's ground-level room and waited for him to be wheeled to the window. When he appeared, they cheered and clapped for five straight minutes. It was the first time Joey had ever seen his dad cry.

Big Joe attended the last game of the season, and he could hardly walk. He watched the entire game. Losing by one point his son would run fifty-five yards for the game-winning touchdown on the last play of the game. Joey ran directly to his dad and handed him the game ball while the entire team ran over behind him screaming and cheering. That was the second time that he would see his dad cry.

Meanwhile, school was well on its way. There were five-eighth grades. Two were all girls, two were all boys, and one was co-ed. Joey and three of his buddies were in the co-ed class, there were five eighth-grade teachers. Four were nuns and one lay teacher was a female. Two of the nuns were brutal. Sister Catherine and Sister Joan were notorious for slapping the devil right out of you. Sister Joan was the all-time worst. She was in her early sixties and had a hair-trigger temper. Sister Marie was not as physical, but she too had a temper. Mrs. Gerard was a nice lady but had very little control of the boys in her class and Sister Agnes was the Mother Superior. In her late fifties, she commanded respect from her students as well as the other nuns WITHOUT using her fists.

It was an age when Joey developed a number of friendships. Some were lifelong. Dwight, Moose, Billy, and Daryl were in Joey's class, the co-ed class that was Sister Agnes's homeroom. All these boys were not angels. Dwight would eventually become Joey's attorney and they would be friends for life. Moose was a borderline hoodlum who Joey was very close to in eighth grade. He would be shot and killed at the age of eighteen. Billy and Daryl made up the group of five. When basketball started Moans became another friend of Joey's, as well as BIG FAT LOU, WONDER BOY, INKY, and J.P.

The last group was in the all-boys-only classes and would carry on their friendship with Joey well after high school. For now, they had a couple of things in common. They loved sports, they loved girls, and they loved having a good time. Often at the expense of their teachers.

The class day began at eight a.m. and went until two-fifteen in the afternoon. The students would travel from class to class with their homeroom. There was a 30-minute lunch period crammed in between and when the weather was nice a 15-minute recess outside. Joey and his buddies learned about the teachers who taught them very quickly. The previous class of eighth-graders had filled them in on their teachers in great detail. The boys knew what to expect and with whom you could mess. And mess they did.

Sister Joan was a classic. She would scream and yell while she taught and did not hesitate to punch you if you were fooling around in her class. During a tirade, she would point a crooked finger right in your face and scream. "LISTEN, MISTER." As she screamed, her nostrils would flare, and spit would come out of her mouth. If you laughed, she would punch you as hard as she could (which really wasn't very hard). As they were being punched the boys would try as hard as they could not to laugh, BUT as soon as she would point her crooked finger in their face they were doomed. You just could not help but start laughing, which of course would send her into a worse frenzy, and she would try her best to punch you harder. If you were unlucky enough to take a peek at your buddies while getting smacked (you didn't want to look because you knew they were laughing hard, but you always did), you would begin to laugh even harder while getting pummeled. Moose was very good at making faces during the pummeling and you would be laughing so hard you would actually be crying. This would happen almost every single day to one or more of the boys. USUALLY, Joey and his buddies were the most common offenders and were all sitting at the front of the room. Each developed their own style of taking the blows. For example, Joey would cover up like a fighter with his hands and arms over his face. This helped him not look at his buddies laughing but nevertheless, he did anyway and of course, he would laugh, and the beat went on. Moose would be moving side to side bobbing and weaving trying to dodge her punches, Dwight would get down on his knees pleading "SISTER, SISTER please don't hit me PLEASE, PLEASE." Inky would bury himself on his desk and not look up again until he felt her go away while the rest of us roared. The best thing about all of this was that the boys mixed up their responses. Nobody ever knew what was coming next. It is quite possible that the boys didn't know what they were going to do until they did it.

Sister Catherine's class was similar except she used a yardstick. Her episodes were not as frequent but when they occurred you better not be laughing unless you were some sort of masochist. The boys were definitely not masochists but that did not stop them from playing with the fire that could be Sister Catherine. She would start every class with a collection for the missions. She had a tin world globe that was a piggy bank and would bang a pencil on the globe which was the sign that mission collection was underway. Row by row would approach the bank while Sister Catherine would stand watching with her yardstick in hand. The rows would stand and walk by her desk and put coins in the bank. After a week of being in her class, Inky said "Watch this." When he got up to the bank, he banged a coin on the side of the bank BUT kept it. The boys followed his lead. Soon the march up to the bank became a parade. The boys danced their way up to bang their coins on the globe. Sometimes they formed a Conga line. Sometimes they hopped on one leg. The best was when they marched as soldiers of the WICKED WITCH OF THE WEST from the Wizard of Oz singing "O WEE OH OH...OH, OH" (they had no idea what the real words were. In today's world it is rumored that the real words were "Oh we love the old one", but at that time nobody knew or cared.) The class was in stitches. Part of the enjoyment of school became waiting to see what these guys would do next. The class was never disappointed.

One day it was announced on the P.A. that there would be a contest for what room could bring in the most mission money in a three-day period. The prize would be extended time outside for a week. Obviously, the boys, led by Moose, told the rest of the class "DO NOT give money to the missions in Sister Catherine's class. Save it and give in homeroom." That afternoon in Sister Catherine's English class when the nun banged on the globe bank, Joey turned to the class and reminded them not to give. Unfortunately, Sister Catherine heard him, and the top of her head started to come off. She rushed at him and started walloping him with the yardstick. She was whacking him hard. He quickly sat down but she kept hitting him. Unlike Sister Joan, this was really hurting. He was getting hit everywhere. Finally, as she was slowing down he made a big mistake. He looked at Moose and Dwight who were laughing hard as they pretended to play invisible violins. Joey laughed, hard, but it was like ringing the bell for round two. Sister Catherine started to whack him again only harder. Moose and Dwight plus the rest of his friends were laughing hard now. He heard them and then saw them, and he laughed again as tears were filling his eyes. This went on for what seemed like an hour to Joey but really it was about five minutes. Joey could not stop laughing, and Sister Catherine finally got tired of hitting him. She turned to the class while tapping the globe with her pencil and said "ROW ONE." This time there was no-nonsense, and everyone put money in the bank. Even Joey and his buddies only this time without dancing or marching.

Basketball tryouts began right after Halloween. Big Joe was out of the hospital, but the pain was hardly remedied. Almost everyone from the championship team from last year had graduated. Joey was the only starter returning from the previous year. He had played street ball with Moose and Dwight, and both were pretty good players. What they lacked in skills they more than made up for in aggression. Joey tried hard to get them both to play. He was not sure they would, but they showed up at the first practice. There were at least forty kids trying out for the lightweight team. Joey knew most of them by sight, but they had never been in any of the same classes. A boy named Moans immediately jumped out during the tryouts. Joey had played baseball against him as well as his buddy Inky. Moans was a very quiet, very shy kid, but it soon became obvious that he and Joey would be the backbones of this year's team. Dwight would scrap his way into the lineup. Moose would also be a starter and play underneath the boards. Moans would be a shooting forward. Larry, a very good seventh grader would battle Dwight for playing time. Inky, Wonder-Boy, Big Fat Lou, and Billy rounded out the other guard spot. The biggest surprise was Martin. The same Martin that wore a brace in kindergarten and walked to school each day with Joey. His brace had been removed, his polio had been cured and he became a center who played behind Moose. As Thanksgiving approached and they had scrimmaged a couple of other teams, Joey thought *this team is really good*. How were we able to lose all the guys that we did and still be this good? We have a real chance to win the city title. It was then that Joey realized that Big Joe was the reason. Even though it was hard for Joey to play for him, he was very glad he did.

GRUNT TALK

By the third week in December shortly before Christmas, Big Joe's team had won its first four games. They had entered the Our Lady of Angels Christmas tournament and had won their first-round game. The daily routine became a fun one. Wake up, go to school, along with your buddies, mess with the teachers, hustle after school to get your paper route done, and then go practice. What more could a kid want. It was right after the first game of the O.L.A. tournament and Christmas vacation had started. Mom had some of his friends over the house on a Friday night for sloppy Joes, potato salad, and just plain fun. Dwight, Moose, Moans, Billy, and a few other boys came over. As they sat around the kitchen table playing cards, the phone rang, and mom answered it. (This was the time of rotary phones and party lines). Mom seemed to know the person on the other end, as she talked, she would occasionally glance and look at the boys. She talked for about 15 minutes, said goodbye, and hung up. She looked at Joey and said "that was Marge Kelly, you know, Duke's wife. (Duke grew up with his dad and was now a big-time lawyer. He would represent Joey when he got in some trouble later in life but that will be a story for another day). "She and I talked at the O.L.A tournament. You met Kathy, Duke's daughter. She is a cheerleader at O.L.A." All the boys looked at Joey and smiled. Joey's response was a simple "Oh." "Whose deal is it?" About ten minutes later the phone rang again and mom answered.

She said "hello" and 10 seconds later she said, "he's right here" she handed the phone to Joey who asked, "who is it?" to which mom answered, "it's a girl." All the chatter stopped as the boys' interest was concentrated on which girl was calling him. They could only hear his end of the conversation that went like this "Oh Hi ….UHHH ok sure. Yes, I know who you are I saw you at the last game" (actually Joey had not seen her at all). Dwight started making monkey faces which caused Joey to laugh. He talked for about 5 minutes and then he said "yes, he is here too. Sure, put her on." He handed the phone to Moans saying "it's for you." At first, Moans wouldn't take the phone mumbling something like "sure it is, no way." (It should be mentioned at this point that these boys were all good-looking boys, but Moans was about two notches higher in the looks department, however, he was painfully shy). Joey took the phone and forced Moans to take it. The boys were really starting to chuckle and that soon would turn to outright laughter. They were hearing only Moans side of the conversation which went like this "hello… this is him…yes…no…yes…no…silence….no….laughter….no….more silence …." (By now the boys were rolling with laughter) Finally he said "ok" and as he looked at Dwight he said, "it's for you." Dwight immediately took the phone. (Dwight was also a good-looking kid who was not shy at all.) His conversation lasted for about 15 minutes ending finally with him saying "Ok that's great. We will all be glad to see you, yes even Moans, but first we have to kick your guy's asses in the tournament. Ok great, see you there" and handed the phone to Joey who hung it up. Mom said with a smile on her face "who was it, Joey?" "It was Kathy Kelly, who said one of her girlfriends wanted to talk to me. Her name was Linda, so we talked, and then Linda said, Sharon wants to talk to Moans, and we all heard how that went." Dwight immediately jumped in and added "then Joyce wanted to talk to me, and I told her we would meet them after the tournament game next Tuesday and we could talk after the game. She asked if it would be ok for them to call us, and I said sure, go ahead." It was almost 10:00 and mom said, "boys, it's time for you guys to go home. You all have practice tomorrow morning at 8:30. My husband will take you home." Big Joe came from the living room where he had been sitting and said, "let's go fellas." They all said thank you and piled into his station wagon and he dropped them off at home.

There were no league games over Christmas break, but they practiced Saturday and Monday before their second round of the tournament. They each received a phone call every night from each of the girls. Joey and Dwight continued to roast Moans asking him if he used sign language on the phone since he could not talk. After practice, in the locker room, they would practice grunt language for Moans. Dwight said, "Moans, here is how it works when you are talking to Sharon on the phone. One grunt means yes, and two grunts mean no." Joey quickly chimed in "and a lot of grunts in a row means that you are really hot for her. Let's practice" and he and Dwight would just start grunting and continued to talk GRUNT TALK while the rest of the boys were doubled over in laughter. Even Moans.

It was Tuesday and round two of the Holiday Tournament. The boys were all business. They did not dare look at the cheerleaders. The last guy they wanted to get pissed was Big Joe. So, they did what Dwight had said they would do they kicked their ass and won by thirty. As they shook hands and headed to the lockers Kathy said to Joey "we will meet you guys out in the main hall." The boys showered and headed quickly to meet the girls. As they came out of the gym there was Kathy and her three friends. They came immediately over to meet them. The girls introduced themselves one by one and as they did Joey and Dwight looked at each other and both were thinking the same thing. WE GOTTA GET OUT OF HERE. Moans on the other hand was smiling and was actually talking to Sharon. The minutes dragged by and seemed like hours for Dwight and Joey. They labored through their conversation. Finally, Big Joe came around the corner with Joey's mom who had been talking with Kathy's mom. "Let's go fellas" and Joey and Dwight quickly said goodbye and headed to the car. They all got in but Moans. He was still inside talking to Sharon. Big Joe went to get him while

Joey and Dwight just kept shaking their head and saying "how could girls that sounded so good on the phone look so bad?" Joey whispered to Dwight so his mom couldn't hear "I don't even want to know what they have under there." Moans got into the car and as they started to pull away, he looked at Joey and Dwight and started grunting very, very fast. They all laughed....hard.

The girls called the next day and the next, but Joey and Dwight told whoever answered that they were not home. Moans meanwhile would tell them at practice how much fun it was talking to Sharon, and then he would grunt.

Friday was the semi-final game. The girls were there but not cheering. However, they sat right behind the St. Charles bench. As they walked out for the opening tip-off Dwight said, "Jeez did they have to sit right there?" to which Moans answered with a series of fast grunts. They all laughed....and then won by eighteen points.

After the game, the girls were waiting. Dwight and Joey walked right to them. Moans walked over to Sharon who was standing by herself. Dwight immediately told Linda and Joyce "we are not allowed to talk to you. We have to go." Both girls almost simultaneously said, "WHY?" Dwight answered, "Coach won't let us he doesn't want our legs to get weak, we play for the championship on Friday" Linda immediately said loudly "WHAT ABOUT MOANS? HE IS TALKING!" Joey responded as he and Dwight left "Moans does not understand English or speak it for that matter. Gotta go sorry." and they were out the door and in the car. Joey's mom said, "that was fast," to which Dwight said, "not fast enough." Moans and Big Joe got into the car and off they went.

The girls never called Joey or Dwight back. The only one who showed up at the Tourney championship game was Kathy and she sat right next to Joey's mom at the game. St Charles won the tournament by eight points. Joey and Moans both made all-tourney first team, and Dwight got an honorable mention.

TOUGH LOVE

Joey loved playing basketball, but it was very hard playing for his dad. He loved his dad and knew he was a very good coach. He also knew that the other players loved playing for Big Joe, but dad was much more demanding of his son than he was of anyone else.

Joey would hurry home to do his papers. Sometimes he had teammates who would help him, and he often would pay his little brother Douglas and some of Douglas's friends to help. On days where he had a full complement of help the route which had forty-eight houses was done in fifteen minutes. Some days his dad would help. They would put the papers in the car, and he would drive slowly as Joey and his minions would jog next to the car and hustle to the houses with the paper.

It was the second week of January, three weeks before the City Playoffs would begin. A huge snowstorm struck at about noon on a Wednesday. By the two-fifteen dismissal bell, it was almost a blizzard. No one would help Joey with his paper route on this day, he was on his own. He borrowed a bike from Big Fat Lou (who had ridden it to school that morning before the snow had started) and pedaled it home through the snow. He fell several times but got home, put his papers in a bag, threw the bag over his shoulder, had his basketball equipment bag in the front basket of his bike, and struggled through his route. After falling several more times

he finally finished and hurried into the gym for practice. He was twenty minutes late and Big Joe glared at him as he came in. He ran through the gym and headed upstairs to change. He put on his shorts, socks, and practice jersey and then realized he had forgotten his tennis shoes. He was horror-stricken and somewhat panicked. He looked frantically for an extra pair of tennis shoes hoping that maybe one of his teammates had that he could borrow. But there were none. Looking around again he noticed that someone had worn Hush Puppies to school that day, black Hush Puppies. Hush Puppies had RUBBER bottoms and soles, so he put them on. (Hush Puppies were a type of loafer that not-so-cool boys would wear.) Joey knew he looked ridiculous, but he had no other choice, so he put them on and went to practice. As soon as he stepped on the floor the other players broke out in massive laughter. Amidst the laughter, Joey inserted himself in a shooting drill. Big Joe was on the other end of the court and heard the boys laughing. He turned around and saw the cause. He blew his whistle and practice stopped. In a very loud voice, he said, "THE CLOWN BUS JUST LEFT. JOEY, WHERE ARE YOUR TENNIS SHOES?" To which Joey very meekly replied, "I was in a hurry, and I did not pack them." Big Joe said, "GO HOME AND GET THEM."

Everyone knew that there was a blizzard going on. Joey thought for a second and said OK, and ran back to the locker room, put on his street clothes, and ran through the gym and out of the door. He jumped on the bike again and tried to pedal. He fell six times and under normal circumstances, a ten-minute bike ride took almost 25 minutes. He got back to school ran through the gym went to the locker room to change all the while thinking practice is still going on. I am still going to be able to practice at least a little. He ran into the gym while practice was still going on. His hands were still frozen, so he grabbed a ball to warm up a little and Big Joe blew the whistle and said "Everybody up." The boys all gathered around their coach who said "Good job today fellas. See you tomorrow same time." Practice was over. The players didn't dare bust Joey's balls. There was just silence as Joey glared at whoever looked at him.

The boys filtered out and as they left Dwight, Moans, Billy, and Big Fat Lou stood by Joey's locker. Dwight said, "Hey man if you don't have frostbitten hands and you can still shoot your dad won't even remember you were late." Joey half-smiled. Billy patted him on the back and said "don't sweat it, man." Moans walked over and was silent for about five seconds, and then started grunting, which they all laughed hard at. As they walked outside the snow was really coming down hard. Big Fat Lou asked Joey where his bike was. Joey pointed to a pile of snow and said, "Thanks man, and good luck riding it" and he got into his dad's car.

The basketball team rolled on. They finished the regular season, and they won their first two playoff games. They were playing in the City Championship semi-final. The game went back and forth, and the score was tied at the end of regulation. In those days there was no overtime the game would be resolved in what was called "Sudden Death" which meant the first team to score would win the game. The ball would be put in play with a jump ball. Big Joe had worked with his team once a week from November till January on a special jump ball play. It was simple. Moans would win the tip-off and tip it to Lawrence the only seventh-grader on the team. Lawrence would turn and pass the ball to the opposite side of the court to a streaking Joey who had taken off deep on the tip. Joey would catch it, make the shot and the game would be over. That's exactly how it happened. Game over St. Charles was going back to the City Championship for the second straight year, UNDEFEATED and vowing that this year they would win it all.

Preparing for the City Championship again was very intense. Big Joe was a bit louder than usual, and it seemed at the first practice Joey was getting yelled at more than ever. It seemed in Big Joe's eyes that his son was doing nothing correctly. Finally, as he again was being scolded for taking bad shots Joey turned away from his dad and gave him the finger. Some of Joey's teammates saw it, but they surely were not going to say anything. The practice was not fun and finally, it was over, and everyone went home.

Dinnertime. The entire family sat down to eat. Mom had made

liver and onions which was not the kid's favorite meal. They were relatively quiet as they struggled to eat their food. Mom was asking dad about practice. "LOUSY, " he said and proceeded to talk about all the things that went wrong. Out of the blue, Douglas the middle son, who attended every practice serving as the ball boy and developing his own game said "Dad" "what Douglas?" his dad responded. Douglas raised his middle finger and stuck it right in front of his dad's face. Joey, as well as his mom, both stared wide-eyed with their mouths open. Grace was shocked. The others did not really know what Douglas had done meant but they knew by the reaction on their father's face that it wasn't good. There was about a ten-second pause as dad stared at Douglas. In that 10 seconds, Joey's life flashed before his eyes. Dad said to Douglas "where did you see that?" to which he responded immediately "I saw Joey do that to you at practice." Mom almost spits out her coffee and Joey thought 'oh my, I am a dead man.' Dad's face was rapidly changing as he asked his oldest son "DID YOU DO THAT?" Joey paused briefly and then said, "yes, I did." "DO YOU KNOW WHAT THAT MEANS?" hollered Dad. "Yes, I do" was his response. "WHAT DOES IT MEAN, TELL ME NOW" demanded dad. "Jackass" was Joey's response. This time Grace almost spits out her milk, but she dared not laugh. "JACKASS?" At that dad almost laughed. "IT DOESN'T MEAN JACKASS. I AM GOING TO TELL YOU WHAT IT MEANS" and he proceeded to describe very graphically what it meant as the other children sat there bewildered. When he finished his description, he said to Joey, let's go upstairs. Joey got up and followed him upstairs expecting to get paddled, but his dad didn't bring the paddle. They walked into Joey's bedroom and his father turned and looked at him and asked " Why would you call your father a jackass in front of all the players. They respect me more than my own son." Joey looked at his dad with tears in his eyes. "I do respect you, dad. I am lucky to have you and mom as my parents. But you are always on me at practice and sometimes even in games. This year has been worse than last year. Other than winning I am not having much fun." Dad's response was "OK, let's go finish dinner." They went downstairs and finished eating as the other children were clearing the dishes. No one spoke but all had a surprised look at the changed demeanor of their father and their brother. Mom said, "finish eating and let's get on the homework." The children scattered and did as they were told. Joey finished and went to his room saying nothing.

Later that night dad came up to Joey's room and said, "you know why I have been on you right?" "Yes, I do dad, but I am the leading scorer on the team and if they haven't been able to figure out that it doesn't matter who my father is, then we should both be giving THEM the finger." Dad started laughing along with his oldest son. He said, "Good night, I will see you at practice and as he was walking away, he turned and said, "by the way, don't think for even a second that I thought you actually did not know what giving someone the finger really meant."

The next three days of practice went very well. Dad still was as demanding as he always was, but it was different now. He was having fun playing again. Joey as well as his buddies were eager to win the City Title. They didn't. They lost the City Championship again. This time by six points, their only loss of the season. Needless to say, once again being unable to win a City Championship, Joey as well as his teammates were heartbroken.

SISTER, SISTER

Time moved on. Any veteran schoolteacher in those days would tell you, if you asked, that the most difficult time in the school year to teach was the middle of January until mid-March. The kids were cooped up day after day and if there were no snow days it was a long winter.

By the end of January, Joey and his teammates were over the disappointment that came with the championship loss and were busy having fun again. In late January there was a thaw in the weather. For five straight days, the temperature was over 40 degrees and dry. Joey had an idea. It was time to get even with Sister Joan for all the punches she had bombarded him with. The windows on the second floor were old-style windows with no screens on them. When opened they were wide enough to crawl or fall out of. Kids were always opening them. Joey gathered his buddies just before the lunch bell rang to get lined up and go back into the school. He told them his plan. "I will get in line with you guys and go back into school with you. While everyone is getting their stuff from their locker, I am going to sneak out the front door and lie down under Sister Joan's window. Sister Joan is always standing outside the door as the class comes in. When you guys get in go to the back windows and open them. Start yelling for Sister and call her to the windows telling her I fell out. When she looks and runs out of the classroom yell down to me and I will get up and come back in the front door. We will all be sitting in our seats by the time she gets back in the classroom. What do you guys think?" Dwight said "I am in. This will be really funny." Moose said, "you know what I think." "What?" said Joey. "That you are either stupid or nuts or have bigger balls than all of us put together." Dwight quickly added, "Or all of the above." They all laughed and started into school. The students headed to their lockers, then lined up and headed to their next classes. Joey headed down the stairs and snuck out the front door. He ran to his spot on the ground and waited. He looked up and saw his buddies gathering around the windows. Dwight was making his patented monkey faces and they were all laughing. All of a sudden Joey heard Moose yelling "SISTER, SISTER, COME HERE QUICK!" They all started yelling for Sister Joan. When she heard the yells and she saw the boys and some girls standing around the windows yelling for her, she came over and looked out and saw Joey lying on the ground. Moose was saying "He jumped out Sister, he jumped out." Sister let out a yell "aaaggghhh" and headed out the side door. Dwight yelled, "GO MAN GO NOW!" Joey got up and bolted back in the front door. He ran into the classroom and jumped in his seat. The class was buzzing and trying not to laugh out loud. Sister Joan got downstairs where Joey had been lying. She was a bit puzzled to see the spot empty. She looked around and then looked back up at the windows. They were closed. She immediately headed back to her classroom. She came in the door somewhat out of breath and looked and saw the entire class sitting at their desks with their hands folded waiting for class to start. She looked at Joey's desk and there he was. He too was sitting with his hands folded. She let out a yelp "aaaagggghhh" and ran over to Joey who was already saying "don't worry Sister, I'm ok, I'm ok" as the punches started to land. Immediately the entire class was roaring. She kept punching Joey and he kept saying "Don't worry Sister, I am OK, I'm alright" but he could not help but continue laughing along with everyone else. Suddenly there was silence. Sister Jane, the Principal, was standing at the door watching. She said, "SISTER, please come out here." As Sister Joan walked out the door Moose said, "your ass is grass buddy" and Dwight added, "and those two nuns are the lawn mowers."

The two nuns were in the hall for about five minutes talking to one another. Sister Joan came back inside only saying to Joey, "Sister Jane wants to see you outside." As he got out of his desk and headed to the hallway a number of the boys started to hum the funeral dirge. Joey was thinking that could easily become his theme song. Sister Jane looked at him as he came out to the hallway and before she could speak Joey started talking "Sister this was all my fault. It was my idea, and it was meant as a joke. I am to blame, and I am sorry." Much to Joey's surprise, she asked a question that caught him totally off guard. "Does Sister always punch you like that?" Joey was silent for a couple of seconds and then answered "Sometimes but not a lot. Those are playful punches. She never is trying to hurt me." There was an awkward silence as Joey finished talking and was waiting for whatever was coming next. Finally, Sister Jane said "Don't ever do this again or I will take you right to your father the Fireman. Now go back to class." The rest of the class time was somewhat subdued. With a minute left in the class Sister Joan said to Joey "your punishment for that little stunt will be to outline Chapter 8 in your Civics book and give it to me when you come to class tomorrow." Joey would spend the rest of the day answering his buddies' questions about what happened. After school, he headed home and did his paper route.

That night as Joey lay in bed he thought to himself: Maybe I am nuts. The next thought he had was a question to himself, why did Karen keep looking at him and smiling. She was not in his class but every time he passed her in the hallway her eyes would find him, and she would smile. Joey thought to himself you are really nuts if you make a mistake with her. She is going with Duane, the star football player who was the biggest, strongest, toughest, most man-like boy in the whole school. If you start fooling with his girlfriend you will certainly get hurt. He lay awake for a while longer and finally fell asleep. It had been a very stressful day.

About two weeks had gone by and school was school. The playground during lunch was organized chaos. About six hundred kids (probably more) jammed the playground. Recess was a bit less chaotic because the 7th and 8th-grade recess was held separate from the younger kids. However, there were still about four hundred kids on the playground. The girls would stand on one side while the boys would play several different games.

Last Man Up or in the winter when there was snow, they would play Last Tackle Up. These were simple games. They started with about a dozen boys being 'IT.' The 'IT' players stood in the middle of the schoolyard. The rest of the boys usually between 30 and 50 lined up in a straight line on one side of the schoolyard. Their goal was to make it to the other side without being 'tagged' by one of the 'IT' players. If they were tagged, they would also become 'IT.' If there was snow on the ground the game became Last Tackle Up. The rules were basically the same in both games EXCEPT the 'IT' players in Last Tackle Up had to tackle the runners not just tag them. These were physical games that resulted in torn pants, ripped shirts, and bloody noses.

The boys would also play games like keep-away or more often than not, football. On this particular day, it was football, eighth vs. seventh graders. They were playing with a rolled-up tin foil ball that was a little bigger than a baseball. Joey was playing quarterback and he had the tin foil ball in his hand just as the bell to line up was ringing. He let loose with a Hail Mary. As the boys watched Duane streak down the sidelines. The pass was intended for him. At the same time, Sister Joan and Sister Catherine walked around the corner. Time stood still. Joey was about thirty yards away when he launched the tin foil ball. He had a clear view of the disaster that was about to happen but was powerless to stop it. The ball was thrown high and for a few seconds, Joey thought maybe disaster would not strike. But it did. The ball came down and hit Sister Joan right below the eye. She didn't fall but she was hit hard, and she was dazed. Sister Catherine immediately grabbed her and as the students walked by the two nuns to get in their lines both boys and girls could not help but notice that Sister Joan's eye was puffed and swollen. The ball had also caused her cheek to bleed. Dwight and Moose who were jogging to their lines with Joey and Billy looked at Joey and said "you did it now man." Joey simply said "I DIDN'T DO IT ON PURPOSE." and they got into their lines. Normally they would almost immediately be signaled to begin walking into the school, but not this time. They stood and watched as Sister Agnes and Sister Marie walked past the lines to the two nuns. They were still watching as the nuns went into the building. As they were waiting to be called into the school, Joey said to his buddies "I am going in there and tell them I am sorry, and it was an accident." Moose responded quickly "ARE YOU NUTS?" the stunt you pulled a couple of weeks ago and now you give the same nun a black eye? "KEEP YOUR MOUTH SHUT!"

After what seemed like an hour the nuns came out to get their lines. As they walked in the door the students were told to line up against the lockers and make room for all the kids still coming in. There was no room for everyone to be standing in the hallway, so some actually had to stand along the steps. The principal of the school was standing in the middle of the hallway waiting next to Sister Joan who had an icepack on her eye. Dwight said "UH-OH." Joey started to get out of line to go say he was sorry but both Moose and Dwight stopped him with Dwight saying "Let's see what happens." Sister Jane walked over to Sister Joan and asked her to "Please show the students your eye." Sister Joan pulled down the ice bag and showed a puffed red bruise below her eye and the bruise was still growing. Sister Jane immediately asked "WHO DID THIS? I AM ONLY GOING TO ASK ONCE." She was greeted with silence. "Sister Jane waited about a minute and then said, "WE WILL STAND IN THIS HALLWAY UNTIL I FIND OUT WHO DID THIS." More silence...as the time moved on Joey said "I have got to tell them. There is no way that someone is not going to tell her who it was." This time it was Duane who whispered "Nobody will tell." Joey looked at him and his buddies and remained silent.

After fifteen minutes Sister Jane said, "I AM WAITING." Again, she was greeted by silence. A half-hour had gone by and still, no one responded. The nuns huddled and were talking to each other in whispers. They came out of their conference with Sister Jane saying "THIS IS YOUR LAST CHANCE." Dwight looked at Joey and whispered, "be cool fool". At that moment, a girl raised her hand saying "Sister, Sister." Moose, Billy, and Dwight all said almost in unison "OH SHIT" while Joey was thinking, I knew it, I am dead.

Sister Agnes knew the girl, so she said, "Yes, Carol what is it?" Carol quickly asked, "Can I go to the bathroom please?" You could hear some giggles while Joey looked at his buddies and they almost burst out laughing ....but didn't. As Carol went to the bathroom Sister Jane said, "TEACHERS GET YOUR STUDENTS INTO HOMEROOM when the bell rings in five minutes, we will have shortened afternoon classes." Sister Joan walked down the stairs with the school nurse and the day went on. The classes were very subdued and shortly the day ended, and school was over. Joey walked home alone to do his paper route thinking to himself "Thank you, God!"

That night he lay in bed thinking I can't believe that no one told on me. Nobody wanted to be a squealer or tattletale. Not even the girls. As his eyes closed, he knew that he would remember that for the rest of his life.

FIRST MAJOR DECISION

Joey's grade school years were rapidly growing to a close. It was late February. Eighth graders were making decisions on where they wanted to go to High School. Those going to Catholic High schools had to submit a letter of application to the school of their choice and then wait to see if they were accepted. Those going to public school did not have to apply they just had to inform the High School in their district that they would be attending.

For many, this was the era of Catholic Education. Of the two hundred and fifty boys and girls in eighth grade, two-thirds would be going to Catholic High school. Joey's class of boys would have the opportunity of attending the new all-boys high school in Parma. Padua Franciscan High School would be accepting graduating eighth-grade boys only. That meant that those boys choosing to attend Padua would be the school's first graduating class ever. The class of '65. They would also be starting their Athletic programs from the ground up. Freshman football would begin in August. Joey's parents had told him the choice of Catholic schools was his. Secretly they were hoping he would choose Padua. It was only ten minutes away and a little cheaper than the established schools. Big Joe felt his son would have a much better chance of playing sports there.

In the first week of February Joey came home from school to find his mom and dad waiting for him. Mom said "Sit down we need to talk to you. Tonight, after your younger brothers and sisters go to bed we will discuss where you are going to go to High School." Joey promptly responded, "I already know." Mom and dad looked at each other and dad said, "ok but we will talk later this evening." "Sure, " said Joey, "it's still my choice though, right?" "Yes, Joey it is still your choice but as you know it must be a Catholic high school," responded mom. Joey said "OK" and went to change clothes and get ready to do his paper route.

Later that evening after the younger children went to bed Joey and his parents sat again in the kitchen. Dad said "well, tell us your choice" "OK, Cathedral Latin" was Joey's response. Mom and dad were stunned. They turned and looked at each other and then turned back to Joey. (It should be noted at this part of the story that Cathedral Latin was an all-boys school located on East 107th and Euclid Avenue.) It was at least an hour away. The journey would consist of walking up the street to Ridge Road, getting on the 79-bus, riding it to West 25th & Lorain, then getting on the Rapid Transit and taking it to University Circle, getting off the transit, and then either walking a mile to school or catch another bus for the rest of the journey. It would take an hour at least).

Dad said, "why there? You have never been there and have no idea the time it is going to take you to get there...and back. You will make the trip twice a day. Also, the neighborhoods that you will travel through are not at all like Parma." Mom quickly jumped in saying "Have you thought about Padua?" To which Joey just as quickly answered "I AM NOT GOING THERE. It is not a real school." "All right, " said dad "Go finish your homework. Your mom and I have to talk. We can get together tomorrow again to finish the discussion."

And talk they did.

The next morning was Saturday. Dad and mom had talked for a long time. Dad did not have to work again until Monday. As they sat at the breakfast table mom was working in the kitchen. Joey knew that she was listening to the conversation that was just beginning between him and his father. Dad started by saying, "your mother and I talked for a long-time last night. So let's start with you telling us why you want to go to Latin." Joey thought for about thirty seconds. He responded with a question "I have to go to Catholic school, correct?" His father nodded yes. "And I will be using some of my paper money to help pay for it, correct?" His father's face changed as he spoke, but he said nothing as he nodded yes again. Joey continued by saying "Latin is a real school. Tough kids, great football, and lots of tradition. I want to be part of that." Dad got up kissed his wife on the cheek and said to his son "Let's go." "Where?" said Joey. "Cathedral Latin where else?" They got up and walked outside. They got into the station wagon and before they pulled away, he told his son "I am going to take you the exact route that you will travel. I cannot take you on the rapid transit, but we will travel all the way to Cathedral Latin and then come home. It is 10:05." He started the car and off they went. On the trip, there were very few words spoken. Joey kept his eyes open and watched out the window.

The first leg of the journey was down Pearl Road which became West 25th Street on the near West side of downtown Cleveland. As they traveled the view changed as well as the people. In the year 1960 Parma was 99.9% white. The route they were taking through the near West side was older buildings about 50% white 35% Puerto Rican and about 15% Black and those numbers were changing very rapidly. When they got to Lorain Road, they drove through downtown and then got on Chester Avenue. They proceeded east towards Latin. As they passed East 55th the people changed as did the homes. The farther east they went the fewer white people they saw. By the time they got to East 107th and turned right, there weren't any white people at all. They pulled into the parking lot of Cathedral Latin and parked. Dad looked at his watch and said, "It is 10:55. It took us 55 minutes by car with very little traffic. Add to that a minimal fifteen or more minutes by bus and rapid transit during the weekdays." He then pulled out and took him to the University Circle Transit station and said, "This is where you will be dropped off by the Rapid Transit. I am not sure if there is another bus to take you to the school from here or if you have to walk." He turned the car around and headed down Euclid Avenue towards home.

The trip home took almost a full hour. When they got there, mom was waiting in the kitchen. Dad said "son you sleep on the trip we took and tomorrow you will choose your school. But understand that where you choose to go and once you start you will certainly finish there. If you flunk out or get kicked out, I will beat your ass."

It was a nice day for hoops, so dad told him to go out and play. As Joey went outside to shoot hoops Chocko and Jebs showed up and they played some basketball. Meanwhile, dad turned to mom and said, "it is his choice, we should stand by his decision, whatever it is, but I meant what I said about finishing." Mom nodded in agreement. Inside, both hoped that Joey would choose closer to home. But mom had this feeling inside her that her oldest son was going to be different, and his life could go in a lot of different directions. She wasn't wrong.

The next day was Sunday. Mass day for the entire family followed by family breakfast. By eleven a.m., the family had returned home, changed out of their church clothes, and sat at the family table waiting for bacon, eggs, and hash browns. Mom cooked and then served the breakfast and just as the kids were about to get up dad said, "Sit back down for a minute, your oldest brother has something to tell us. Joey, go ahead." Joey wasted no time answering. "I am going to High School at Cathedral Latin." For the younger children Cathedral Latin could have meant the moon, they had never heard of it and really did not care much. But for mom and dad, it was big. Mom said, "finish the application and we will get it in the mail tomorrow." Dad said "Good choice son." Joey hugged both his parents as the rest of the kids went to whatever and began their day.

HEMO THE MAGNIFICENT

School was in the February muck and mire. Winter was getting old in Cleveland, Ohio and school was getting boring, for students as well as teachers. In a very rare event, it was announced to the students that there would be a movie in the auditorium/gym for sixth, seventh, and eighth-graders in the afternoon. That would be about six hundred kids sitting on two different levels and watching a movie screen that would sit on the stage. It was the only time in Joey's nine years of school that such an event was held. Eighth grade classes and one seventh grade class would sit in the balcony while the other grades would sit on folding chairs on the gym/auditorium floor. All afternoon classes would be canceled. The movie would be *HEMO THE MAGNIFICENT.*

At recess, Joey and his buddies were discussing the afternoon movie. Moose was asking "who the hell was Hemo the Magnificent?" Billy said, "I believe he is a Martian." They all laughed and continued the discussion. Dwight said, "I think the name is really Homo the Magnificent." More laughter. BIG FAT LOU said, "NO, NO, NO Hemo is a transexual." "What is a transexual?" asked Moose. "Half man and half woman" added Lou. "Which half is where?" asked Dwight. "Who's on First," laughed Joey. Billy said, "they are He/She's" to which Moose asked, "what is a He/She?" Billy asked Moose "have you been sleeping through all of this?" Joey said, "HE/SHE is the new first baseman for the

Yanks." They were all doubled over with laughter as the bell rang and they went to their lines each boy wondering who Hemo the Magnificent was. Lunch came and went, and it was time for the movie. Sister Agnes warned them about their behavior during the film. The balcony entrance where their class would sit was about five yards away from coming out of their homeroom door. Escape was unthinkable. Nevertheless, as they made the short walk to the balcony, Big Fat Lou asked in a whisper "I wonder if I could sneak over and sit with the girl's homeroom?" They all snickered as they took their seats. They sat down and five minutes later the movie began. It turned out that the movie was an educational film about blood and the circulatory system, and the boys were bored within about ten minutes. Fighting boredom Joey started to look around focusing on the girls' homerooms to see if he could see Karen without Duane noticing he was looking at her. In the process of his reconnaissance, Joey said to Moose, "where is Dwight?" Moose started to look and couldn't find him and as he was looking, he said to Billy who was sitting next to him "where is Dwight?" Billy looked, and he could not find Dwight either. Moose looked at Joey and shrugged his shoulders whispering, "he has disappeared. Martians got him." said Big Fat Lou and the whole row laughed. Joey quickly whispered "shut the fuck up" and he turned to look around. Sister Agnes had gotten up from her strategically placed seat by the door and had walked over and away from the boys to wake Eugene who had fallen asleep.

Joey saw that the back door was slowly opening, and Dwight popped his head in. As soon as he saw that Sister Agnes was busy with Eugene he stealthily hurried and sat down next to Joey. The boys were laughing as he sat down. Joey said, "Where you been man?" Dwight started to take Coca-Cola bottles out of his shirt and pass them out (this was before coke machines had cans) while saying to Joey "I snuck across the street to the gas stations and bought five bottles of coke a cola." I have been standing outside looking through the crack of the door when I saw Sister Agnes go over and roust Eugene and here I am." Joey laughed and said, "that took some balls." While Dwight finished passing the bottles out Moose turned to him and asked, "where are the chips?" The boys were laughing again, and Dwight pulled out five small bags of potato chips and passed them out. Joey said, "Hey you are one short" to which Dwight just raised his eyebrows. They drank their cokes and ate their chips without getting caught. The movie finally ended, they hid their trash as the bell rang for dismissal and Dwight's stunt would end up in the boy's stories forever.

DISASTER STRIKES

Joey's eighth-grade year was almost over when disaster struck. It happened in Sister Marie's literature class. Sister Marie was a pretty good teacher in a difficult subject matter for eighth-grade boys. She taught literature. She never used violence to discipline a student. She almost never had to and if you were out of line, it was a written assignment having to do with literature that would be your punishment. Joey and his buddies almost never fooled around in her class. This is why what happened next was so very unexpected.

The class was in the process of reading and discussing Mark Twain's book "Tom Sawyer." The class was quiet as Sister Marie was conducting the discussion. Joey and his friends were scattered in the seats that they were assigned. Sister was standing in the middle of row two and teaching from the aisle. The closest of Joey's friends to where she was standing was Moose. They both were out of Joey's viewpoint as they were back and to his left. The class was calm, and most were paying attention. All of a sudden, Sister Marie was screaming at Moose. As Joey looked over his shoulder to see what was going on Sister Marie walked closer to Moose who was sitting at his desk and slapped him very hard, and the slap caught him right in the face. Blood started pouring out of his nose. As she began to slap him again Moose realized he was bleeding and jumped out of his chair just as her slap hit him again. Now standing Moose tried to slap her back. As he did, he called her a fucking bitch. The class was stunned. Moose was yelling and calling her names. She responded with another slap that caught him on the shoulder. Joey jumped out of his seat as did Dwight. They both reached Moose at the same time. Joey got between him and the nun and said, "Moose, Moose, what are you doing?" Dwight was at Moose's side trying to calm him. Moose was in a rage that Joey and Dwight both had seen before in seventh grade when Moose had beaten up an eighth-grader who was trying to bully him. That fight did not turn out so well for the eighth-grader. Sister Marie backed away as the class sat in stunned silence. Moose had calmed just a little but took his books and threw them at Sister Marie and stormed out of the room but not before he called her a fucking bitch one more time. The quiet was deafening. Sister Agnes had heard the commotion and had seen Moose storming out and heading to his locker. Sister Marie was beginning to gather herself and start teaching again when Sister Agnes asked her to come outside in the hallway. Joey and Dwight, who both were at a loss for words, maybe for the first time in their lives, sat back down. The class was in shock. Sister Agnes popped her head in and told Donna to get the principal. When Sister Jane arrived the three nuns talked outside for the rest of the class period as a stunned and silent class sat there. The bell rang and once the kids hit the hallway the conversation was all about what they had just witnessed. It didn't take long for the other students to get wind of the story and by the end of the day, nobody was talking about anything else.

The most puzzling thing was nobody saw and heard what caused the eruption. The next day various kids, mostly girls, were called to the office to tell the principal what they knew. The girls were frightened by the fact that there was a policeman present also. In the end, everyone was able to say what they had seen after the battle started but no one knew what started it. The next day Billy who lived near Moose told the boys Moose was "Gone. He is out of school." The boys were not surprised. Moose had gone way over the edge. However, they were also sad. Joey especially. Moose was his friend, and he always had his back. Now he was gone.

Joey saw Moose only once after that. They said hi but didn't talk much. Years later he found out that Moose at the age of nineteen was shot and killed. Joey was saddened again.

REMARKABLE JOURNEY

The school year was about over. It was May 5th, 1961, and a remarkable event was going to happen. America was going to send the first American ever into outer space. The Russians had performed the feat less than a month earlier by sending Yuri Gagarin. Alan Shepard became America's first man in space. The newly elected President, John F. Kennedy, had boldly promised the world that an American would be the first man to walk on the moon. This was step one in that remarkable journey.

St. Charles had planned for the radio broadcast of the launch and retrieval of Astronaut Shepard. It would be heard over the P.A. system in every class. The flight itself would take only about 15 minutes and would be finished in time for the student's lunch hour. Joey's class sat in complete silence for about thirty minutes listening to the radio during the space mission. Dwight was the exception to the tranquility. From the very beginning of the final countdown until the moment they would pull Shepard out of the water Dwight would whisper, "he's not going to make it." He repeated this somewhat pessimistic warning about every five minutes. Eventually, Joey looked at him and whispered "Please shut the fuck up."

As the flight headed back to the atmosphere, the class, as well as the entire school, was listening both with anticipation as well as apprehension. Finally, the P.A. announced that the capsule had splashed down into the Atlantic Ocean. Every student knew that it wasn't over yet. They had to find the capsule and then fish the astronaut out of the water and get him on the Destroyer that was picking him up. Finally, after a prolonged silence the radio announcer said the capsule has been sited, found, and Alan Shepard has been brought on board. At that moment, every classroom in the school erupted with cheers. It made Joey proud that he was an American. The bell rang and it was lunchtime. Dwight hollered to Joey "See I told you he would make it" as he ran down to the cafeteria. Right then Joey should have known that he would eventually become a lawyer.

HAPPY ENDINGS

It was the last week for eighth-graders, May had come and gone. For the rest of the school, however, classes would go on for a week after the eighth graders were gone. The last week for eighth-graders was fun as well as eventful. Monday, Tuesday, and Wednesday they took tests for half a day and then went home. Thursday, they had off. Friday night was graduation. Saturday and Sunday there were all sorts of graduation parties. Monday was the entire school picnic at Euclid Beach.

But what many of the eighth graders looked forward to the most was Tasty's. Tasty's was a high school hang-out. It had a booth that sat as many as six with jukeboxes in each booth, a counter that served food and ice cream, and a check-out register that had cigarettes. The cigarettes were often sold to teenagers. St. Charles students were forbidden to go there under pain of expulsion. But once they were out of school the kids would flock there. Joey and his buddies would be no different. On Wednesday, the last half-day of school for eighth-graders he and his buddies headed right for Tasty's. On the way there Dwight was repeating to the guys a theory that he had told them many times. Dwight believed that if a girl smoked cigarettes then she probably put out. Billy and Big Fat Lou would always agree with Dwight repeating the theory that it was gospel. Joey would laugh and say no way. If Moose would have been there, he would have sided with Joey. But he wasn't.

As they walked in the front door, they immediately could see that the place was mobbed. Cigarette smoke was everywhere, and the place was filled with girls. Most of them also being graduating eighth-graders. Joey turned to Dwight and said "hey man look at all these girls, and most of them smoking. Don't let them see that bulge in your pants or they will think you are a weirdo." They all laughed as they looked for seats. There were none. Karen was there sitting with two other girls. She looked up at Joey and said "Hi, we have two seats here sit down." Dwight and Joey sat down, Big Fat Lou and Billy said they had to go, and Wonder Boy sat with his girlfriend who was in another booth.

The jukebox was playing songs and the waitress, who was at least sixteen, came over and said, "You boys have to order something or leave." Dwight promptly asked, "Do you smoke cigarettes." She looked at him like he had three eyes and said without smiling "what do you want to order?" Dwight looked at Joey with the deer in the headlights look and Joey said we will each have a large coke and asked Karen and her friends if they wanted anything to which they all responded, "no, we are good." Joey breathed an inward sigh of relief as he only had fifty cents. Karen began with small talk by saying to Joey "so how are you?" Joey answered "good" as the cokes were set on the table and the waitress left. Joey was taking a sip of coke as Dwight said to all the girls "do any of you girls smoke?" Joey almost choked and spit out his coke as he started laughing hard. Now all three of the girls were looking at him and Dwight like they both had three eyes. Joey was still laughing a bit when Karen said "I don't smoke but I love your smile. It was the first thing I noticed about you in sixth grade." Joey's face got a bit flushed and was about to respond when a girl named Laverne said to Dwight "I smoke is that OK?" to which Dwight grinned and said, "more than OK." Of course, he spent the rest of his time talking to Laverne. Joey said to Karen "thank you, I heard you broke up with Duane." She said "yes and I told Joan to tell you. Did she?"

Just at that time Moans came in and saw them sitting in the booth. He walked over and said, "hi do you have room?" Karen said "sure" and as she slid over, she grabbed Joey's arm nodding for him to slide closer. Which he did. Moans sat down next to Dianne and Dwight looked at him and grunted twice. Now the three boys were laughing pretty hard and Moans was included in the three-eyed looks that the girls were giving them. Karen looked at Joey saying "I don't know what you guys are laughing at, but I do know that the bunch of you are always having fun. So did Joan tell you or not?" As he was about to answer Karen, much to his astonishment, he heard Moans say to Dianne. "Do you smoke?" to which she replied "Yes I do" at that Dwight looked at Moans and grunted three times. The boys were now doubling up with laughter and the three girls could not help but laugh right along with them. Joey turned his attention back to Karen and said, "No I haven't talked to her recently." Karen responded, "Duane and I have been broken up for almost 4 weeks now" to which Joey replied "OH." They continued to talk and laugh for about an hour. Moans had money and bought everyone some cokes and bags of potato chips. The jukebox played songs like "BLUE MOON", MY GIRL," "SITTING IN LA, LA" and a bunch more as the boys made them laugh over and over again. Finally, Dianne said "sadly we have to go." Karen and Laverne both said, "yes we do it is getting late." As they were just about to leave Karen said to the entire table "how about we all come over my house tomorrow? My mom works all day." Dwight said immediately, "I am there." Joey said, "me too" and Moans said ditto. The girls got up and as they did Karen said, "be there at 12:30" and they walked out the door just as " BEND OVER, SHAKE A TAIL FEATHER" blared out of the jukebox. Moans said "let's go shoot baskets" so they did until Joey had to do his paper route.

That evening Joey had a difficult time sleeping in anticipation of the next day. He fell asleep while thinking about all the things that could possibly happen on Thursday.

Thursday morning arrived. He jumped in the shower and then had a bowl of Rice Krispies, the cereal that talked to you and as always, he would put his ear close to the bowl to hear the snap, crackle, and pop of the talking cereal. The conversation with the cereal never disappointed him. When he finished, he asked his mom if it would be ok to meet Dwight and Moans after lunch. They were going to hang around with a bunch of other eighth-graders. Mom said, "of course just be home by 4:00 to do your paper route." "Thanks, mom, can I use the phone in your bed-room I need to call those guys."

Joey's family had two phones. One hung on the kitchen wall and had absolutely no privacy. The other was in his mom and dad's bedroom and was very private. He would just have to be concerned that his sister Grace would not try to listen in on the kitchen extension. He made the call and they all agreed to meet at Vic's delicatessen at the corner of Ridge and Essen no later than 12:15. The three boys arrived at Vic's almost simultaneously and they began to walk to Karen's. Karen lived on the other side of Ridge Road which was at most a fifteen-minute walk. They talked about baseball and basketball and the school party that was on Monday at Euclid Beach. When they got to the corner of Karen's house Joey said "Stop. I need a favor from you both." "Just ask" replied Dwight. "O.K. you both need to promise me that you are not going to ask the girls if they want to have a smoke. That's a bull shit theory anyway." Dwight immediately went into his Uncle Eddy imitation saying "MEENKYA JOEY you think we are a couple of CHOOCHES OR WHAT?" They were all laughing as they walked up to Karen's front door where she was waiting with her two friends. "Come on in and sit down." They did. Each boy sat next to the girl he was there to see. Before anyone could say anything, Dwight looked at Laverne and said, "Hey you want to have a ciga-rette?" The three boys looked at each other and started laughing so hard they had tears in their eyes. Lavern said, "No thank you Dwight" and the three stooges laughed again. The girls looked at each other as if to say what is with these three? Joey quickly acted and said, "Ladies it is just a silly inside joke that has nothing to do with the three of you." Karen responded "that's cool. Let's turn the radio on." She turned on WHK the local radio station and they listened to rock-n-roll while they talked about all sorts of things. The girls continually giggled and laughed at most of the things that these guys would say, no matter how outrageous they were. As the afternoon went on there was less and less talking going on. Dwight started necking with Laverne (that is what the kids of the day called repeated passionate kissing.) while Karen said to Joey "let's go upstairs" and after that invitation, he had no idea where Moans was going to go, and he didn't really care.

For about the next hour or so the couples carried on just like other young teenagers would do in a house with no parents. Joey had taken giant steps forward in his knowledge of the female anatomy and learned quite a bit from when he was at the Charity football game with Shirley. Kissing was becoming an art for him. Whatever would happen after that depended on how far the girl would go. Joey would go as far as the girl he was with would let him. Pushing the envelope also became an art form. He knew exactly where to put his hands and exactly what to do with them when he put them there. With Karen, he proceeded until she said no. Neither one of them had ever gone "ALL THE WAY" and Joey had no idea how to get there. But on this day, they did just about everything else. When Karen began a low moan Joey knew from his time with Shirley that he was doing something right. They sat and talked upstairs for a while and just when they were beginning to start again the phone rang. Karen answered and conversed for about 2 minutes. When she got off, she yelled downstairs "MY MOM IS GETTING OUT OF WORK EARLY SHE WILL BE HERE IN ABOUT FIFTEEN MINUTES. YOU GUYS HAVE GOT TO GET OUT OF HERE." The three couples all were in different stages of undress. Immediately all six teenagers were scrambling for shoes, socks, and whatever other garment had been placed somewhere. They would have made better progress, but Dwight started chanting the Lone Ranger's theme song as Moans was pretending to be riding a horse and yelling "HI O SILVER AWAAAYY." They both started laughing hysterically. Veronica and Dianne were sitting on the couch literally rolling with laughter as

Joey ran down the stairs. He too started to laugh but he quickly realized he could not find his shoes. Karen came downstairs and yelled at the girls in a panic telling them to start straightening up the house. Moans pulled up his horse saying "WHOA HORSEY, WHOA BOY." Dwight stopped the Lone Ranger music and walked up to Joey who was desperately looking for his shoes and said in his best Tonto voice. "UMM KEMO SABE ME HELP FIND UM." The three boys were now laughing so hard they were crying. "UMM KEMO SABE I FIND THEM HERE UNDER COUCH. UMM I THINK WE SHOULD VAMOOSE KEMO SABE." Laughing non-stop they were out the door, Tonto, Joey, and Moans still riding his horsey saying GIDDYYUP, GIDDYYUP, and the boys crying and laughing at the same time. Meanwhile, Karen was yelling out the door "DON'T GO TOWARD RIDGE ROAD. SHE WILL SEE YOU. GO DOWN THE STREET AND GO AROUND THE BLOCK." The boys turned around and started to hustle the other way, to Karen's horror Dwight stopped, turned toward her standing at the door and folded his arms Indian style, and said "UMM PRINCESS SUMMER FALL WINTER SPRING YOU LOOKUM VERY PRETTY WHEN YOU ARE IN A STATE OF PANIC. WE SEE YOU IN ONE FULL MOON AT GRADUATION. WE GO NOW." They ran very hard down the street laughing the entire way. While on the way home they talked more about Dwight being Tonto and Moans riding his horsey than they talked about what went on with the girls. When they got to the corner of Essen Joey asked, "are you guy's helping me with my paper route?" to which in unison they said "NO". "I know," said Joey "see you tomorrow at graduation."

That night at about 7:30 the phone rang. Mom answered it and called upstairs to Joey. "Joey, you have a phone call, it's a girl." Joey asked his mother if he could use the bedroom phone to which she responded "yes but be off in 20 minutes". "OK, no problem." "Hello," he said "Hi," said the girl on the other end of the phone. "It's Karen." "Hi. Are you OK? Any problems with your mom?" Karen replied "No, she had no idea." They talked for about fifteen minutes finally ending with a goodbye and see you at graduation.

The next night was graduation. It was held in the church and almost every year it was packed. This year was no exception. The graduation ceremony went without a hitch and when it was finished the graduates would gather in the auditorium for cookies and punch.

As Joey grew older, he had very few memories of that evening. But one memory was captured in pictures and in later life, he would enjoy looking at it. Of all the nuns that you would expect to take a picture with Joey and his buddies, it wouldn't be Sister Joan. Nevertheless, he had at least four photos of Sister Joan arm in arm with Joey, Dwight, Billy, Wonder Boy, and Inky. The look on all their faces was that of old friends saying goodbye. Even Sister Joan had that look.

The night ended with Joey and his friend's saying goodbye and making plans for Euclid Beach on Monday. There was one more event connected with St. Charles and that was the school picnic.

On Monday, the boys met at Joey's house at 12:30. Big Joe would drive Joey, Dwight, Moans, and Billy to Euclid Beach and pick them up at 5:00. They would meet the rest of their buddies there. Big Joe dropped them off in the parking lot and told them exactly where he would pick them up. The boys got out of the car and as they were walking through the lot Billy and Moans were talking about all the rides they were planning on going on while Dwight and Joey said almost nothing. Finally, just before they entered Billy said to Joey "what about you two guys, you going to ride the Thriller and Racing coasters with us?" Joey said, "Sure I am going to do that, BUT what I really want to do is take as many girls on *OVER THE FALLS* as I possibly can." Dwight echoed "I AM IN MAN. I made a list of all the girls I knew that smoked. I'm going to try to take all of them on *OVER THE FALLS.*" Moans grunted three times and they all were laughing as they walked into the park. They rode as many roller coasters as they could in the first hour and a half. Finally, Joey said, "I am heading to *OVER THE FALLS*. I will be hanging out in that area. Make sure we meet up before my dad gets here." Dwight said, "let's go" and Moans said "I will catch up to you" and they went their separate ways.

OVER THE FALLS was two rides in one, the first part was a boat ride through a dark tunnel. The boat held four people and was pitch black inside. Occasionally there would be ghosts and other such creatures popping out, but it was not scary. When you got to the end of the tunnel the boat would become a ride. The pulley would take the boat up over one hundred yards and then send you almost straight down into the water. The tunnel took about seven or eight minutes to get through; the drop took about ten seconds.

Joey and Dwight stood around outside the entrance to OVER THE FALLS. It was probably the least crowded ride in the whole park, however, there was no shortage of girls walking by. It didn't take long. The first girl that went by was Donna, an eighth-grader at St. Charles. She was with her friend Kathy. Joey looked at Dwight and said, "Here goes nothing." He asked Donna if she wanted to go on the ride with him and she said yes. Dwight followed in the boat behind with Kathy, and as the Roller Derby announcers would say "THE JAM WAS ON." Joey and Dwight did not keep count of how many girls they would go on the ride with nor was it a contest. They both had agreed that spending time this way was better than riding roller coasters all day long. They just hoped the girls would say yes....and they did. Donna and Kathy came back twice more. But there were Carol's and Judy's, Jo Ann's and Lions, and Tigers, and Bears. Most came back at least one more time. Karen showed up with Laverne and when the ride was over the two girls asked Joey and Dwight if they wanted to go ride some roller coasters with them. They both said no, maybe later. The girls said, "OK we will see you in a bit" and walked away.

Joey and Dwight were perfect gentlemen. All of the girls knew that there would be necking. When the boys' hands would start to roam, they would either let them roam or say no or don't. If they said no the boys would always stop. If they let them roam then roam, they did. This went on for at least an hour and it was approaching 4:30 p.m. when disaster struck. Dwight recognized two cheerleaders from Our Lady of Good Council school who the boys had beaten in basketball. Dwight said to Joey "let's ask them if they want to go on the ride." So, they went up and Dwight said, "I know you don't know us but." Before he could finish one of the girls said "oh we know you. I am Barb and this is Monica. You guys played basketball against our school. By the way, where is your cute buddy?" "you mean Moans?" asked Dwight. Marie said, "Yea him, he was really cute." Joey jumped quickly into the conversation saying "when basketball ended his parents took him back to Czechoslovakia. He hasn't come back." Barb said, "Gee that's too bad." Dwight said, "you want to go on the ride with us?" "Sure," both girls said so they got in line to board the boats. What neither of the boys saw was Karen and Laverne walking over to the ride.

Fifteen minutes later as the boats splashed into the water and as they were exiting the ride Karen who was crying and Laverne who was trying to console her were waiting by the exit of the ride. Karen screamed at Barb "this is my boyfriend! What are you doing?" Joey and Dwight were speechless, but Barb responded immediately "Your boyfriend? Honey, you have to be kidding these two have ridden this ride with half the girls in this park." She turned to Joey and said "that was fun call me" and she walked away with Monica right by her side. Karen was sobbing and she too turned and walked away just as Moans was walking up with Billy.

Dwight and Joey were standing with their mouths still open and hadn't said a word. Billy said, "What the heck happened?" Joey, who was still a bit stunned pointed at Dwight and said, "He bit her." Billy just stared and Moans laughed. Dwight went immediately into his Uncle Eddy impersonation "Meenkya Joey, I ain't no Chooch. I didn't bite anyone. Meenkya I'm tellin ya." Now all four boys were laughing. Billy said, "we gotta go meet Big Joe" and off they went.

That night as Joey lay in bed with all sorts of thoughts running through his head, Karen puzzled him. Why was she crying? He felt bad about the fact that he had made her cry. What he didn't know was that he would see Karen only one more time in his life and that would be two years later. His thoughts gradually shifted to the fact his days at St. Charles were over. He was a Latin Lion now. As he started to doze off, he was replaying the OVER THE FALLS rides that he took today and thought, Jeez what a great life.

DO YOU REMEMBER THE 1960S?

- CHANGING TELEVISION STATIONS BY HAND
- AMERICAN BANDSTAND
- THE TWIST
- 45 RECORDS
- ROGER MARIS AND MICKEY MANTLE
- NIKITA KRUSHCHEV
- 33 ALBUMS
- COMIC BOOKS: SUPERMAN, BATMAN, ARCHIE, LITTLE LULU
- CIGARETTE COMMERCIALS
- EARMUFFS
- BEING PULLED BY CAR BUMPERS ON SNOW COVERED STREETS
- DICK CLARK
- ALAN SHEPARD
- WOOD PANELED STATION WAGONS
- THE MARLBORO MAN
- TV DINNERS
- JFK ASSASSINATION
- DRIVE-IN MOVIES
- SHINDIG
- BEATLES ON THE ED SULLIVAN SHOW
- RFK ASSASSINATION
- BONANZA
- TRANSISTOR RADIOS
- CUBAN MISSLE CRISIS
- THE HOWDY DOODY SHOW
- DANCING SOUTHSIDE
- MLK ASSASSINATION
- SLEEPING OUT
- VIETNAM WAR
- PITCHING PENNIES
- BELL BOTTOMS
- THE FLINTSTONES
- MINI-SKIRT AND GO-GO BOOTS
- TURTLENECK SWEATERS

PART 2

THE HIGH SCHOOL YEARS

t was the summer of 1961. The next ten years would prove to be a change in just about everything in America. Racial change, reaction to an unpopular war, political assassinations, music, dancing, morals, dress, technological advancements, television, automobiles, drive-in movies, The Cold War, the Space Race, as well as numerous other events would cause the Baby Boomers to evolve unlike any other of the previous American generations. The number of Baby Boomers would eventually peek at seventy-eight million. By the late 1960s, for the first time in American history, more than 50% of Americans were under the age of twenty-one. The economic power held by the Boomers at first went unrecognized but by the mid sixty's their influence was economically felt everywhere. It helped that television was growing right alongside the Boomer generation. Television shows, as well as commercials, started to gear their shows and advertisements toward teenagers and children. This population explosion did not move with the speed of a glacier it moved with the speed of a tornado. It was not a gradual change; it was a massive revolution and not always a peaceful one.

REVOLVING DOOR FRIENDSHIPS

Joey's life was undergoing major changes of its own. There would be a steady flow of friends moving in and out on a continual and simultaneous basis. The fact that he had chosen to attend a High School so far away from the neighborhood he grew up in would expand his life experience far beyond those who spent all of their time growing up in Parma would ever have. His exposure to so many different influences and cultures would make him different than his siblings as well as his parents.

Grade school was over, the Lou Gehrigs was dissolved, and it would be the first summer of playing baseball on a team that was not coached by Big Joe. Joey and many of his friends, however, would continue to play on the same team in the summertime. In the spring of 1961, St. Charles had started its own baseball team for the first time in the school's history. Joey started at second base and was also the backup catcher. Moans played third base, Big Jim was the Ace of the pitching staff, Inky and Wonder Boy played in the outfield, while Duane started at first. Joey had tried very hard to talk Dwight into playing but he had repeatedly said, no, thanks I am not a baseball player. The team had a record of fifteen & three and got beat in the semi-finals of the City Championship. At the end of the season Coach Haskins held a team meeting. He told the players he was having a summer team of thirteen- & fourteen-year old's that would travel and play other suburbs that had teams in the league. Tryouts would begin in a week and the team would be made up of players from all over Parma, not just St. Charles kids. When the meeting was over, he took Joey, Moans, and Big Jim aside. He told them that if they were going to play, they would not have to try out, but they had to let him know before tryouts began. On the way home the boys talked it over and agreed they would play on the team. They just had to talk to their parents. By the week's end, all three had called Coach Haskins and said they were in. Unknown to Joey, Coach Haskins had also contacted Jebs and Chocko (both were public school kids) and recruited them as well to play on his team. It would be a fun summer.

Neighborhood baseball continued at the Parma Show parking lot. Players continually showed up to play ball there. Joey's brother Douglas as well as some of the guys in his age group added to the player pool. The introduction of the Wiffle ball and bat brought backyard baseball back into play. Parma Show in the daytime and the backyard for night games. Mom, now not being plagued with hard balls hitting the house welcomed the boys playing in the backyard. It was going to be a summer of baseball as well as girls. What more could a thirteen-year-old boy ask for?

In between morning games in the show parking lot and evening games in the backyard, Joey would often spend his time in the afternoon at Ridgewood pool. The city of Parma recognizing the population boom that the city was experiencing built two public pools. One was on the eastern side of Parma on State Road and was called State Road pool. The other was built right across from Parma City Hall and the new shopping mall called Parma Town. That pool was called Ridgewood. It was also right next to Ridgewood Lake. Joey often went swimming right after lunch and would return home in time to do his paper route. The pool was always crowded both inside and out. On the outside of the pool was Ridgewood Lake. A large group of older teenagers hung out there. Parma teenagers at this time were starting to gravitate in certain areas and hang out there. They were not gangs per se, but they hung together, and often times there were fights. The Ridgewood Lake Boys were the largest of these groups and the fiercest. There were always a large number of girls who would hang out with them. Other groups existed throughout Parma. There were the Parma Circle boys, the State Road boys, the Forestwood boys, the York Town boys, and Joey and his buddies became known as the Vic's Boys. They often could be found sitting on the ledge of Vic's Deli which was right across from the Parma Show. There were older groups also. These guys were all old enough to drive. They hung out at Manner's drive-through and Bearden's drive-through which were right across the street from each other. During the 1960s on Friday and Saturday nights and in summertime almost any weeknight, there would be a parade of cars, as many as fifty at a time circling in and out of both the drive-through restaurants. There were car hops taking food orders and 'cherry' cars rolling through the parking lot with radios blasting. It was a carnival atmosphere. Summertime was becoming more fun every year that Joey got older.

One day that summer dad came home with a tent that slept four and had a ceiling tall enough for the boys to stand up in. Within days after putting the tent up it became somewhat of a hangout. If they weren't playing baseball somewhere then they were hanging out in the tent. Comic books of all types were all over the floor. Batman, Superman, Green Hornet, Archie, and many others. The kids would buy them and swap them, and they left them on the tent floor for everyone to read. Joey and his friends would begin to sleep outside in the tent. "SLEEPING OUT" became the rage. They would stay up half the night reading comic books then at about one in the morning they would leave and prowl the neighborhood.

One late June morning while the boys were choosing up sides in the Parma Show lot, a boy whom no one had ever seen before came walking over and asked if he could play. Roger asked him what his name was, and the boy answered "Keith." Roger looked at Joey who shrugged. Roger turned and said, "sure we are just starting to pick up sides." "Thanks," said Keith. He ended up being on Joey's team. He wasn't good but he wasn't terrible. They played all morning. While they played Joey noticed that Keith was using a glove made for a 7-year-old. The glove barely fit on his hand. The games ended and Joey asked Keith if he had a bigger glove. Keith said he had just moved in with his aunt and uncle and this was all he had. Joey said, "don't sweat it. We have plenty of gloves in my garage I will bring you one tomorrow." The next day Keith was there waiting as the boys arrived in bunches. He had his tiny glove with him and while sides were being chosen Joey walked over to him and gave him a glove from home. He said thanks a million times and Joey said don't worry about it a million times. Keith became a regular player and one day about three weeks later while he and Joey were talking between innings Joey asked him why he had moved to Parma. Keith's response left him speechless. He said, "my dad and mom were killed in a car crash. The only place I could go was to my uncle's home in Parma, so here I am." Joey had no idea how to respond to that. Finally, he said, "well, you are more than welcome here." Keith would become Joey's friend for about the next 3 years. In that time period, Joey made Keith welcome with any of the guys that would come and go in his life. Keith was always included with any group that he was hanging with at that particular time.

Joey's friendship group was constantly changing. He had his neighborhood friends who were the first kids he hung out with, kids like Roger, Wayne, Bobby, and many others who played ball at the Show parking lot. Eventually, they would disappear from his life as he grew older and would be replaced by guys who came from all over and some from entirely different backgrounds. With the improvement in technology and transportation, The Baby Boomer generation became much more mobile than any of the generations that preceded them. The next four years of his life would indeed prove to be an adventure.

It seemed as though summer ended before it got started. School was beginning and the journey to and from school would provide as many lessons and learning experiences as the time he spent in classrooms. This included grade school, high school, and college. He had chosen Cathedral Latin High School. He would travel through some of the toughest neighborhoods in Cleveland to get there. There were many boys who lived on the west side of Cleveland who would attend Latin. It was a football powerhouse. However, there were not many kids from Parma. Joey's friends Moans, Inky, and Big Jim would also attend. By the end of the school year, Joey would be the only one left. The boys rarely traveled to school together. Joey would travel solo until he was sixteen and got a car. Moans, Inky, and Big Jim lived far enough away from him that the first leg of the journey put them on a different bus. They would meet up during school and then travel part way back to Parma together and split up to take different busses home.

Joey's mom would wake him every day at 5:30 a.m. He would be out the door by 6:00. He would take a ten-minute walk up the street to Ridge Road and there board the number 79 bus to get to the Rapid Transit station which was located just outside of

Downtown Cleveland. A trip that would take at least 20 minutes through a neighborhood that was predominantly Puerto Rican. He would get off his bus and travel down a long set of stairs that was isolated from the main streets above it. From there he would wait and then board a rapid transit train that would take him to the east side. Usually, there were other kids on the rapid that were either traveling to Latin or Latin's rival school Benedictine. The 20-minute rapid transit would then take him to one of two destinations where he would catch one more bus. He could get off at East 105th and take a bus from there or go one exit further to the University Circle station. Both of those stations had drawbacks. The East 105th exit was in the heart of the ghetto. Joey had been warned by older kids that he knew that there were many incidents of Latin guys getting "jumped" by neighborhood kids. The next exit was the University Circle exit which was right next to the campus of Case Western Reserve College. From there he could walk about two miles on the last leg of his journey or catch another bus that would drop him off on Euclid Avenue a block away from school. On the surface choosing the last leg of the journey would seem to be an easy choice. But the University Circle rapid station had one major drawback. To get out of the station you would go down a long set of stairs to a long quarter-mile tunnel. In the years of making this journey, Joey would run into homeless people who were living there. On some days there were a number of sleeping bodies spread throughout the tunnel. He almost always opted to exit at University Circle, and he almost never chose to walk. The whole journey took over an hour if there were no transportation issues. However, there usually was. Especially if it snowed.

A YEAR OF LIFE LESSONS, MAJOR DISAPPOINTMENTS, AND AS USUAL GIRLS AND LAUGHS

Freshmen football practice started the week before Labor Day. Even though Joey weighed only 110 pounds, he made the long journey to practice alone. None of his buddies played football. He reported to the gymnasium for the first freshmen team meeting at 7:45 a.m. thinking he was 15 minutes early. When he walked in the door he was stunned. There were almost one hundred boys already there and more coming in the door. The coach started the meeting exactly at 8:00 a.m. He explained the rules and finished by saying we will all jog over to Ambler Field. Wear your tennis shoes and carry your spikes. "LET'S GO" and off they went. Ambler Field was a good two miles away. They practiced for almost two hours and then jogged back. They did the same thing in the afternoon. For three days the routine was the same. Joey practiced with the Quarterbacks, and he was the smallest guy in that group. On the fourth day at the team meeting, the Coach said, we will practice this morning and a cut list will be posted at noon. Tomorrow we will pass out equipment to those who have made the cut. At practice that day they ran the plays that they had been installing. There were twelve teams of offense. Joey was Q.B. 12. His team got three reps and practice was over. They walked back giving the coaches time to post the cut list. A huge crowd of boys was jammed around the bulletin board. Joey made his way to the front and there he saw his name. He was cut. He teared up but held the tears back. He wasn't going to let these guys see him cry. He walked out the door and started the long ride home. That night at dinner he said to his family "I got cut from football today." His comment was greeted by total silence. Mom and dad both said, "we will talk after dinner." As dinner ended, they sent the younger children to play. Both parents were sympathetic. Dad said, "son life is sometimes tough. When you get bigger try again." "Are you disappointed?" Joey asked. "OF COURSE NOT, " dad said. "Are you?" "Yes," he said….very." Mom said, "you will be alright, we love you and basketball is next." "Okay," he said and went to his room.

That night while Joey lay in bed staring at the ceiling he was thinking. They made their decision without even giving me a chance to hit anyone. It was completely based on my size. I was too small. I will always remember this. How could they know if a small kid could play or not without giving him a chance? He went to sleep still feeling awful.

DEAD BODY

O n a day in late October, Joey was running late for school. He had missed the number 79 bus he usually took and now he was behind schedule. When he got off the rapid transit at University Circle, he thought that he could still be on time if he ran and not waited for another bus to take him. So he took off running. He was cutting through the high school that was across from Latin. In the bushes that surrounded the school, he tripped over a pair of feet that were sticking out of the bushes. He looked down but did not stop. He got into the building just as the 2-minute bell was sounding. He quickly went to his locker and sprinted to his classroom. He made it just as the late bell was ringing. About an hour later while he was in second-period class an announcement was made over the P.A. system. ANYONE WHO CUT THROUGH THE PARKING LOT ACROSS THE STREET THIS MORNING BEFORE SCHOOL STARTED, PLEASE COME DOWN TO THE OFFICE IMMEDIATELY. Joey sat and thought for a bit. He was wondering if he should go. Upon thinking further, he decided that he had done nothing wrong, so he told Brother Larry the Latin teacher that he needed to go down to the office. Brother Larry looked at him and then said go ahead. Joey went down to the main office and told the secretary that he had cut through the parking lot across the street. She told him to please sit down and wait for a minute and she walked into the Principal's office. About thirty seconds later she came back out and said follow me. He followed her inside, and as she opened the door and nodded for him to go in, just as two older boys were walking out. When he walked in the door he immediately knew something was wrong. The principal was there as well as the assistant principal, a policeman in his uniform, and a guy in a suit. Joey was thinking *Holy Moly what is going on here*? The principal said "sit down please Nicholas. This is Detective Farmer and Officer Krupke. Detective Farmer would like to ask you some questions." Joey sat and waited as the detective asked, "did you cut through the parking lot across the street this morning?" "Yes, I did. I was running late and did not want a demerit." "Did you notice anything peculiar in the lot?" Thinking only for a few seconds he responded, "no I did not." Officer Krupke said, "take your time and think about it. You are not in trouble." Much more relaxed with the policeman's comment Joey sat and thought. After a few seconds, he remembered the feet in the bushes and said "actually I do. I tripped over a pair of feet that were sticking out of the bushes." Detective Farmer immediately asked, "why didn't you tell anyone?" Joey was a bit puzzled but answered by saying "I see people lying around almost every other day at the rapid station. I thought it was another homeless person. It happens all the time. Did I do something wrong?" The police officer said, "Son, that body was a dead person, and it wasn't an accident." Detective Farmer asked, "did you notice anything at all besides the feet sticking out?" "No, I did not, I just kept running so I would not be late." "Can I see the bottom of your shoes?" "Sure," said Joey and held up his feet. "Can you take them off?" Joey did and set them on the floor. Both policemen studied the shoes and said, "nothing here, you can put them back on." The principal said to Joey, "you can go now, thank you." He hurried out of the office and stopped in the washroom before going to his next class. As he stood looking in the mirror at himself, he muttered out loud, Jesus that guy was dead. A stall door popped open, and a freshman named Onie came out and looked at Joey and said "man, Jesus has been dead for a while now." Both boys laughed and walked out the door and headed to class.

At family dinner that evening Joey told his mom and dad the story. Neither said much but later that night he heard his mom telling his dad "I bet they do not have any dead bodies in Padua's parking lot." "I bet you are correct on that one Dar."

Later that night while Joey lay in bed staring at the ceiling, he could not stop thinking about the meeting with the policeman. He said to himself, geez oh man, those feet belonged to a dead person, and it wasn't accidental. I wonder why they looked at my shoes. I must be much more careful. One thing I know for sure, I will never let my parents transfer me to Padua. Sleep did not come easily that night.

CUT AGAIN

Joey spent the next month playing basketball with Chocko, Jebs, Moans, and Big Jim after school and on weekends. November came quickly as did Freshmen basketball tryouts. On the first Saturday of November, there were three tiers of tryouts with each session lasting an hour and 15 minutes. There were about seventy-five total boys trying out. Anyone not cut on the Saturday sessions would come back on the following Monday. A cut list would be posted in the athletic department on Monday morning. They were going to cut about fifty boys and eventually keep fifteen of the last twenty-five. On Monday Joey got up early to catch an earlier bus. He hustled to school and hurried to see the posted cut list. Anyone's name on the list would be cut, and anyone who was not cut was expected at further tryouts after school. Joey had brought his basketball stuff fully expecting to be in round two. As he went through the list, he saw his name. He was cut. Big Jim's name was also on the list, but Moans was not. Moans had made round two. This time Joey was not heartbroken, he was pissed. He caught up with his buddies in between classes and congratulated Moans on still being on the team. He finished the school day and before he did his paper route, he told his mom he had gotten cut. Mom hugged him and asked if he was ok. He said "yep, no problem" and went to do his papers. Big Joe was working at the firehouse, but he called Joey later and asked him the same question his mom had asked him, to which he responded, "I am fine." Moans went to tryouts and two days later he made the team. He called Joey after he got home from tryouts to tell him. Joey congratulated him and then Moans dropped the bombshell. He told him he was probably not going to play. He said he didn't feel like playing on a team where he probably would not start, and Joey wasn't on the team with him. Joey was almost speechless but immediately responded by saying, "Moans if you didn't make the team but I did I would be playing without you." "I know but you are different than me." They talked a bit about other things for a while and then hung up.

That night as Joey lay in bed, he was thinking about how unfair life was. He would give anything to have made the team and was still mad and somewhat shocked that he did not make it while his running mate on the eighth-grade team that went to the City Championship was choosing to not play. His bitterness would not go away for almost four years. He fell asleep a very unhappy kid.

The next day Moans quit the team.

Joey's buddies all transferred out of Latin at the end of the first quarter to public schools. All three went to a newly created public school in Parma. In school, Joey had met a number of other freshmen whom he hung around with during the school day, but they were all east siders who lived far away from him. His best friend in school was named Vic. He was an eastside kid living in a changing neighborhood. Vic was a two-sport starter both in freshman football and basketball. The two boys were almost inseparable during school but on weekends Joey still hung with his old friends.

I AM SPARTACUS

nky, Big Jim, Moans, and Joey hung out regularly. Joey's parents made him sit and do his homework just about every night during the week. But the other three guys were out and about almost every night. Joey would hook up with them on weekends however, weeknights were homework nights. One Tuesday night Big Jim called him and said to meet us at the Parma Library. Joey said, "seriously, the library?" Jim said, "7:00, be there." The library was on Ridge Road, right next to Vic's Deli. It was a 5-minute walk for him, so he told his mom he had to go to the library and do a report. Mom said fine but be home no later than 8:30. Joey headed up to the library at about 6:45. When he got there, he was amazed to see all of the kids his age everywhere. It would seem that everybody had reports to do for school because from the library to Vic's the sidewalk was jammed with boys and girls. His buddies saw him and said, "come on, let's sit on Vic's ledge in front of the store and watch the girls go by." So they did. This went on for the next few months until late November when it was too cold to sit outside. The library had hired a police officer to prohibit anyone from loitering in the library. From September until it got cold, Joey had a lot of books to read and a lot of reports to do.

One warm late October night as they sat on the ledge watching the girls walk by a very good-looking girl who was with two of her friends stopped and walked right up to Moans and said, "I see you guys here a lot, my name is Denise." As mentioned before Moans was a very good-looking boy but very shy nevertheless, he answered with a "Hello." Denise was trying to make small talk with Moans but was not having much success. As Joey watched their interaction mentally comparing it to the waiting room at the dentist's, he was also looking at one of her friends. As the conversation between Moans and Denise was dying out Joey decided to take some action. He walked up to Denise and said "Hi, I'm Joey. I'm his friend" pointing to Moans and winking at Denise's cutest girlfriend at the same time. Denise saw the wink and laughed hard as well as her girlfriend who immediately stepped up and said, "Hi I am Charlyn," as she reached out to Joey and shook hands. The third girl not to be left alone walked over to Big Jim and Inky and all of sudden everyone was in conversation. As always once they got warmed up the boys created lots of laughter. After about twenty minutes Charlyn said, "Denise we have to go, my dad is picking us up in 5 minutes." The girls said goodbye with Denise asking, "will you guys be here tomorrow?" While looking at Charlyn Joey said, "I only have so many reports I can use as an excuse so how about the night after?" The girls laughed and said, it's a deal, and hurried to meet Charlyn's dad. As the boys stood there Inky asked, "did any of you Chooches get their phone numbers." To everyone's surprise, Moans said, "I did." Joey laughed and said, "man you never cease to amaze me. They will be here no doubt"...then he said to Moans, "How about you just sit on my lap the next time we meet some girls. You can be my Charlie McCarthy dummy. Just sit on my lap and move your lips while I do the talking. Guaranteed we will get lots of chicks." Moans responded, we already get lots of chicks. They were all laughing as they headed home.

Two nights later Joey met Moans at the library. Again, there were tons of teenagers. As they were sitting on Vic's ledge Denise and Charlyn came up smiling and saying hello. They had talked for a bit when Joey asked Charlyn if she wanted to take a walk across the street behind the Parma Show. He said that there is a cool little alley next to the theater that I can show you. She smiled and said "ok." Then giggled and said, "I have never been in an alley." As they started to cross the street Moans yelled "hey where you going?" Joey said "Charlyn has never seen an alley, so I am going to show her. You both are welcome to come." "Sure," said Denise and pulled Moans off the ledge, and away they went. They necked for about a half-hour and Denise said we have to go. My dad is probably looking for us already. Joey said to Charlyn, "before you go can you give me your phone number?" "Sure" was her answer and off they ran.

Friday night the guys went to the Parma Show to see the movie, Spartacus. Moans, Inky, Big Jim, Keith, Fritz, and Joey all went together. For these guys, there was more to going to the show than just seeing the movie. First, they would sneak in one by one. Once in they would see if there were any girls. If there were they would sit right behind them and try talking to them. If they liked the girls, they would ask if they could sit next to them and if they said yes then anything could happen. On this night there were not any girls for them to try and meet so they watched the movie. The ushers in the show were usually hostile, largely because Joey and his buddies were always rather loud. This evening two ushers followed them to their seats and stood in the aisle behind where the boys were sitting. If any of the boys got loud, they would be thrown out. The two ushers were waiting to do just that if anyone got out of line.

The movie was good and held their interest. The ushers standing in the aisle irritated them, but nobody wanted to get thrown out of a good movie, even though they had not paid to get in. It was near the end of the movie, Spartacus (played by Kirk Douglas) had led a slave rebellion and now had been captured. The Roman General who had caught the slaves was now going to crucify them along the roadside to make an example of them. He wanted to make a special example of Spartacus BUT he did not know who he was, so as the slaves were sitting and waiting on a hillside for whatever fate was coming to them, the General, on his horse yelled to the slaves, "if you tell me who Spartacus is, I will spare the rest of you, and you will not be crucified." Kirk Douglas, being the hero of the movie jumps to his feet and yells "I AM SPARTACUS." Quickly realizing what their leader was doing one by one the captured slaves stood up and yelled "I AM SPARTACUS, I AM SPARTACUS, I AM SPARTACUS!" All of a sudden in the middle of this very dramatic scene, Big Jim jumps up and stands on his seat and yells "I AM SPARTACUS." The ushers immediately reacted and started to remove him. Accompanied by one of the ushers he goes peacefully. As he gets halfway up the aisle Keith jumps up on his seat and yells "I AM SPARTACUS" which immediately gets the attention of the second usher who quickly begins to remove him too. Inky then stands on his chair and yells "I AM SPARTACUS." The first usher runs back down the aisle and starts to remove Inky. One by one the boys do the same thing and one by one they are getting thrown out of the theater. As Joey stands to yell all of a sudden EVERYONE in the show was yelling, "I AM SPARTACUS. I AM SPARTACUS. I AM SPARTACUS!" Joey and Moans were laughing so hard they were crying. As they were escorted out the rest of the guys were outside listening to the uproar inside the show, and they too were laughing their asses off. As they stood outside Joey yelled, "we have to get out of here. Let's go to *BUDDY'S*" (Buddy's was a pizza place right down the street). The boys took off, but it was hard to run because they were all laughing so hard. The rest of the night they ate pizza, played pinball, and laughed. Most of the guys had to be home at 11:00 so they broke up and went their separate ways saying good night and then yelling "I AM SPARTACUS."

Later that night as Joey lay in bed he smiled and said to himself "I am Spartacus" and soon fell asleep.

THE FALL TURNS TO WINTER

Joey's friends had transferred leaving him to travel to and from school by himself. He was still unhappy that he had not made the freshmen football or basketball teams and that disappointment, coupled with the fact that there was no school baseball team led Joey to question his decision not to go to school closer to home. His grades were decent enough and he studied harder than he ever had before. Mainly because his parents made him stick with it. During his Freshman year, he was rarely in trouble at school but that would change in time.

Winter was in full swing. Christmas as always was Joey's favorite Holiday. In his younger days, he eagerly looked forward to the day when his parents would take him downtown to the May Company department store to see Santa Claus. Now that he was older and did not believe in Santa anymore, he envied his younger brothers and sisters who still were believers, and he enjoyed watching them on their visits downtown to see Santa. When Joey's mom and dad told him there was really no Santa Claus, he had been heartbroken.

He loved snow days. There was nothing better than waking up to find out school was canceled. He would roll over and go back to sleep. Later he would go outside. Sledding, snowball fights, snow forts, and playing keep-away with his brothers and sisters and their dog Muscles made the winter seem to just fly by. He would remember lots of things about winter in Cleveland, Ohio. When he was just starting to be 'cool' which was somewhere between sixth and eighth grades, he would constantly argue with his mom about wearing boots and winter hats. There was no way he could look cool in winter boots with buckles. There was also no way he would ever win these arguments. The battles with his mom about wearing a winter hat were epic quarrels. Joey wore his hair in the style of the day, like Elvis and Ricky Nelson, and Fabian. It wasn't possible to put Brylcream in your hair to get it to stand up and back while wearing a winter hat. It just could not be done. Mom saved the day by coming home from the store with a pair of earmuffs for Joey to wear. He did, and they kept his ears warm and did not mess up his hair.

At the same time, Joey grew farther and farther from Moans, Inky, and Big Jim. As would happen so many times in his life his friends were a revolving door. As older friends left, they were always replaced by newer ones. Sometimes he and his buddies would separate only to come together again a short while later. Moans had found a girlfriend named Annette. She was two years older than Moans and far more experienced in regard to sex. Actually, she lived only two streets from Joey, and he could look out his front door and see her house. Her mother was a barmaid in a very swanky bar-restaurant called The Thunderbird. She worked every night from about 7:00 p.m. until 3:00 a.m. Moans would go there just about every night and needless to say he was getting laid on a regular basis. Soon Big Jim, Inky and Fritz, and Inky's older brother all started to hang out there. Annette had girlfriends that would show up which made her house much more fun for the guys to hang out in and Inky's brother had a car. It was a constant party. Joey's mom would not let him go anywhere near the place.

Meanwhile, Joey had begun to call Charlyn. They talked on the phone almost every night and on Friday nights Joey would take her to the movies. Charlyn lived about three-quarters of a mile away from Joey, about five streets passed Annette's house. Joey would walk up the side streets to her house, say hello to her mom, and then walk her to the movies. When the movie was over, he would walk her back home, kiss her goodnight, and then walk back to his house. They would be an on-and-off couple for the next five years. They both flirted and would see other guys or girls, but both seemed to like one another considerably. They would "break up" numerous times but somehow they always would make up.

On Saturdays, Joey began hanging out with Chocko and Jebs as well as Roger, Keith, Yonko, Fuco, and others. They would play basketball whenever they could and sneak in the Parma Show on Saturday nights. They would head to Buddy's pizza afterward. Needless to say, girls were regularly on their minds, and it seemed that there was always plenty to meet.

Joey was just finishing a period of time where he did not play with an organized football or basketball team. It was a strange feeling for him. Joey and his pals were always looking for a place to play hoops. One day as they were sitting at the table eating the family dinner Big Joe looked at him and asked, "how would you like it if I put up lights on Auntie Olie's garage and you could play basketball games at night?" Joey's response was a resounding YEEESSS. The next day while he was at school Big Joe brought a fireman over the house who was a part-time electrician and they put lights up on the garage and around the driveway. It was now ready for nighttime hoops. After dinner was finished dad said "Put on some warm clothes and bring Douglas with you. I will be out in the back." Joey grabbed Douglas and said, "get dressed and let's go." As soon as he stepped out the side door he knew what was up. He could tell that there were spotlights on the garage next door. The boys ran around the corner and immediately saw the lights. "Douglas, go get the basketball!" Joey yelled. He turned to his dad and said "Dad, thank you very much." Douglas came out with the ball and the two boys played for an hour when Douglas was called in to get ready for bed. Joey stayed outside and shot baskets until 9:00 p.m. when mom called out, "time to come in." The next day he hurried home from school and paid Douglas, and a couple of his friends to help with the paper route. When he got done, he ran into the house and called Jebs and Chocko telling them to get three more guys and we will play hoops at about 6:00. They both had the same response;

it will be dark by then. Joey said, "just get 'em." At 6:00 sharp five boys were standing knocking on his door. He hustled outside, ran next door, and turned on the lights. "Pick up sides," he said. They did and then played to one hundred by ones. There would be basketball in that yard, on that court for the next fifteen years. He and his buddies would play basketball there well into their thirties.

That night as Joey lay in bed looking up at the ceiling he was thinking "I have a great dad." and fell asleep smiling.

It was early May; school had a month left. Joey had stayed late after school to play hoops in the open gym. He really enjoyed showing up the members of the freshmen basketball team. At about four o'clock he left school for home. He was going to walk to the University Circle rapid station. It was a beautiful sunny afternoon. As he walked down East 107th Street, just before Carnegie Avenue, Black kids suddenly surrounded him. His first reaction was where did all these kids come from. They seemed to appear out of nowhere. There were at least ten and they all surrounded him. The leader was a bit bigger than Joey and got right in his face. He was about two inches away. The look in his eyes was like none other than Joey had ever seen. He had been in his share of fights growing up but had never seen a look like it. The boy said, "give us your money." Joey looked over the group but there was no way he could run. He said, "I can't, I need it to get home." One of the boys who was standing right behind the leader of the group said "GIVE HIM YOUR MONEY SUCKER. WE DON'T CARE HOW OR IF YOU GET HOME." Joey turned and paused for about five seconds. One of the boys whistled and all of a sudden, they ran and scattered in all different directions. Joey was stunned and wondered, why did they run? Then he saw a police car turning the corner onto 107th Street and he knew why. He jogged quickly to the transit station, ran through the tunnel and up the stairs, jumped on the first car of the train that was just pulling up, and sat down in the seat.

That night as he lay in bed he was thinking about what he saw while looking into the leader's eyes. He was trying to understand what he had seen in those eyes. He thought for a long time, and it finally came to him. Hopelessness. Those kids didn't care what happened to them because their life seemed to be without any hope. They were not afraid. Very dangerous he thought. As he started to doze off, he was thinking WHAT NEXT? He would find out soon enough.

Joey began hanging with the guys from the other side of Ridge Road. Chocko and Jebs began to bring other guys with them to the hoops games under the lights. Roger was still around but he wasn't a basketball player so Joey would only see him on occasion. Keith was with Joey on a regular basis and guys who had names like Moga, Leech, Fuco, and others became regulars in the backyard basketball games. Yonko was friends with these guys, but he wasn't a basketball player either, so he came and went.

A boy from Pennsylvania had moved in with his uncle and aunt across the street from where the guys were playing nighttime hoops. He had a 1959 Chevrolet Impala, a white convertible with a red interior. One night he walked across the street to watch the basketball games that were going on under the lights. In between games, he introduced himself as Pete and that he was from Pennsylvania. He asked if he could play. Chocko said, "Pete? Like Pete Maravich?" They all laughed and Jebs said "sure you can play. If we know you are going to play regularly, we will make sure we get another guy, so we have an equal number, and nobody has to sit out. We can alternate for now." So, they did. Pete would show up regularly and became known to the group as Pennsylvania Pete. Joey was thinking that his convertible could come in handy this summer since none of these guys were old enough to drive yet.

The boys played basketball there on a regular basis and as the weather got warmer more guys would show up. One evening in early April at around 9:00 p.m., Roger came running into the yard very excited. He said, "you have to see this, JoAnn was undressing in front of her window. Come on now or you will miss it." Joey, along with Chocko, Leach, Keith, and a few others took off and followed Roger through the backyards. Pete, Jebs, and Moga stayed and kept shooting. JoAnn was a 20-year-old girl who lived up the street next to Patrick. She was a bit of a tease with the younger boys and was extremely good-looking. The boys ran and as they got to her backyard, they quietly snuck up to look in her window. All five of them started to jockey for position and when they saw that she was standing right in front of the window without any clothes on, they pushed and shoved to improve their view. As they were pushing and shoving each other no one noticed that JoAnn's friend who lived in the house right behind her was cutting through her backyard. As she came from around the garage she saw the boys and was startled. She stopped and yelled, "WHAT ARE YOU BOYS DOING!" Startled, Joey turned and looked, and as he took off he heard Keith yell, "SIGHTSEEING." The boys scattered in all directions with Joey and Chocko circling around the front of the house and ran like hell to where Jebs and Moga were still shooting hoops. They immediately got involved in the shoot-around and started playing a 2-on-2 game. The other boys headed towards Ridge Road. Joey assumed that they all had gotten away. When the game ended, he told the guys he was going inside, and that they should take a different way home. Joey went in, said goodnight to his mom, and went up to his room and waited. After an hour the phone hadn't rung, nor was there anyone ringing their doorbell, Joey got in bed and fell asleep. The next day he left school right at the dismissal bell, so he was able to get home before his papers were dropped off. He got off the number 79 bus and headed down his street. He was carrying his books like the cool guys did, and as he passed JoAnn's house he was thinking about what they had seen the night before. His thoughts were still lingering in his head as he walked by Patrick's house. Suddenly Patrick's front door burst open, and he was running toward him with a full head of steam. It all happened so unexpectedly and so fast that Joey did not react in time. Patrick tackled him at full tilt and as his books went flying Patrick slammed him to the ground, pinned him, and buried his face into the grass. Joey was having a difficult time breathing and could not budge the 220-pound oaf. Patrick's mother was screaming from the front door "PADDY, PADDY, GET OFF HIM, GET OFF HIM." Patrick had Joey pinned on his stomach and was yelling in his ear "WHAT WERE YOU DOING IN OUR BACKYARD LAST NIGHT? WHAT WERE YOU DOING?" Still trying to escape Joey answered saying "I wasn't. Get the fuck off me." Patrick punched him in the back of his head while his mother was still yelling for him to stop. Patrick slid Joey into a headlock and said, "Mrs. Murphy said a bunch of boys was looking in her daughters' window last night, I know that was you and your buddies." "No, it wasn't. I was playing basketball under the lights by my house all night, ask my mom and dad." Patrick hit him again and said "if I ever catch you back there I will beat your ass a hundred times and if I ever catch you looking in my sister's window I will kill you. Got it?" "Yea, I got it." Patrick got up using Joey's head to push himself off the ground while saying to his mother "I'm coming mom, what's for dinner?" Joey started for home. He picked up his books and then stopped. Patrick had his back to him. He let him get a few more feet away from him and then yelled "HEY PATRICK!" and Patrick stopped and turned to say "what?" Joey yelled, "ARE YOU SURE?" "AM I SURE OF WHAT?" Patrick yelled back. "Are you sure being a freckle-faced baboon that you can really count to 100?" And with that, he bolted. He walked into his kitchen and mom asked, "why are your clothes so dirty?" Joey said, "I was wrestling on the way home, sorry." He changed clothes and got ready to deliver his papers.

That night, as he lay awake staring at the ceiling, he thought that seeing a grown woman without any clothes on was worth the pummeling he had taken from Patrick. He also thought that the next time he would see Patrick, he would ask him how many times he had watched Joann naked in her window. Laughing to himself, he fell pleasantly asleep.

UNCLE EDDY REAPPEARS

It was one of those early warm spring days that were always welcome in a winter-ravaged Cleveland, Ohio. Nine boys had gathered in Auntie Olie's backyard to play hoops. Three-on-three games and the winner would keep playing. The first game had just finished. The winners were standing around drinking water while others were shooting around when a car pulled up to Joey's house. Chocko was first to see who it was, and he called out "IT'S UNCLE EDDY." Uncle Eddy's reputation for being off the wall had spread around and those guys who knew him couldn't wait to talk to him. Jebs looked at the guys who hadn't met him yet and said, "wait until you get a load of this."

Eddy got out of his car and was walking over to the court. He had a WWII fighter's helmet on with goggles. Joey said, "OH SHIT HERE WE GO." "Meenkya Joey how youz Chooches doing?" Chocko said, "great to see you, Eddy." Joey followed with "hey Eddy how you doing? Where ya been?" "Meenkya Joey, I just got back from a flea market." Pennsylvania Pete asked, "What is a flea market?" "Meenkya who is this Chooch?" Jebs said, "Eddy that is Pennsylvania Pete." "Meenkya I ain't never seen you before, where you from?" Guys started laughing. Chocko said, "Eddy he is from Pennsylvania. That's why we call him Pennsylvania Pete." "Oh, what's your real name?" Pete answered "Pete." "Meenkya, I grew up in Pennsylvania. The coal mines. That wuz sumthin, Meenkya that wuz hard money. My whole family mined coal. Did I tell you guys I played football for Pitt?" Joey said, "about a hundred-and twelve-times Eddy." "Meenkya Joey, you sure are funny." Pete asked, "Eddy, The University of Pittsburgh?" Eddy said, "Yea there too." Eddy was getting excited. "I got to share with you Chooches my new idea. Man, it's sumthin." Moga says "Let's hear it, Eddy." "O.K. I am going to Japan." "Japan?" asked Chocko, Jebs, and Moga all at once. "What are you going there for?" "Meenkya I am going to recruit some Sumos, what else?" "Sumos, what for?" "For hockey." "Hockey? Seriously what are you saying?" asked Jebs. "Meenkya you chooches don't know nuthin. I am going to be their agent." "Agent? Agent for what?" "Hockey?" "Ice hockey?" "Yea what other kind is there? I am going to bring them back to America to play pro hockey. "You think Japanese Sumo wrestlers can skate?" They are all over 300 pounds." Yonko chirped. The boys were laughing pretty hard now, but Eddy continued, "I am going to make them goalies. They can lay in front of the goal. No way they can hit the ball into the net with Sumos lying in front of it." Joey said, "puck Eddy, they try and hit the pucks, Eddy." "Yea that too."

There now were nine boys laughing their asses off. Out of the blue Eddy said, "I got time for one game of foul shots, best of ten, who wants to play?" Pete immediately said, "I will play you, ten foul shots twenty-five cents for every made foul shot." Eddie said, "I cannot do that I am in gamblers anonymous." Chocko said "I will take the bet, Pete. I have Uncle Eddy. Put your money in the hat, all singles if you have them. You go first, Pete." Pete took two warmups, made them both, and then Uncle Eddy took two warmups, shot them underhand, and missed them both. Pete looked at Chocko and laughed thinking he had a lock. Chocko said, "you want to make it 50 cents a shot?" Pete said "sure." Pete shot and made six. Uncle Eddy shot and made nine. He walked over to the hat that held the money and put $1.50 in his pocket. Chocko picked up his share and Pete just stood with his mouth open and stared. Eddy said, "I gotta go. You guys want to see what I have in my trunk from the Flea Market?" Joey said sure, and he and seven other boys walked with

Eddy to the trunk of his car. Pete was still in the driveway staring at the basket.

Eddy opened his trunk and said, "look at these babies." The boys who had been laughing hard for the last twenty minutes looked inside the trunk. Yonko said, "please tell me he doesn't have a Sumo in there." The boys laughed, still looking, but they couldn't see anything. Jebs said, "there is nothing in there." Eddy said, "Meenkya you guys are not only chooches but you're blind too" and he pulled out his flashlight and shined it on the floor of the trunk. The boys looked again and Moga yelled "HOLY SHIT THOSE ARE FLEAS." The boys backed away from the trunk and Joey yelled "close it, Eddy." Eddy closed it while saying "of course they are chooches, they are from the Flea Market. See you all later." "Wait," said Chocko "what the hell are you going to do with all those fleas?" "Man, youse guys are serious chooches. I am going to train them for the flea circus." "CIRCUS?" "Yea a flea circus. We are going to have all kinds of flea acts. I am going now to get some parakeet perches so we can teach the fleas how to trapeze. Maybe tomorrow I will be back, and you can watch them juggle." Joey quickly yelled, "Eddy keep those fleas away from here, my mom will shoot you." "Gotta go, see ya." The boys walked back to the hoops court where Pete was standing and mumbling "he made nine and shot them underhand, underhand." Joey said, "let's play some hoops."

That night while Joey lay in bed staring at the ceiling, he was laughing to himself. He thought, all my buddies think that Eddy is just putting them on. Man if they only knew.

EMBRACE THE MADNESS

School ended and it was summer again. Joey had just finished his first year of high school. Time it was a speeding by.

Summers meant baseball in the Parma Show parking lot along with whiffle ball in the backyard and also being on an organized baseball team. Big Jim, Moans, and Inky were again on the same team. It was good being around those guys again. By the end of the summer, he would once again be hanging out with them on a regular basis.

This summer, however, it was also Pennsylvania Pete, Keith, Chocko, Jebs, Yonko, Fuco, and sometimes his cousin, Jake. Whoever else was around was always welcome. Girls came and went. He was in a time where Charlyn and he were on the outs but that was a regular occurrence and Joey was fine with that. Like buses, it seemed that there was always another one coming along.

Pete was a critical player in the fun they had that summer. He had a car, and he had courage. Their summer escapades were always fun. They would regularly hop in Pete's convertible and go looking for girls. Often times they would head down to Lorain Avenue cruising for Cleveland girls. The convertible made the task somewhat easy. However, the area was a bit dangerous and soon they stopped making that trip and stayed right at home and cruised Parma. Top-down and the radio blasting while girls wearing short shorts were always walking somewhere. One night just as the summer sun was setting Joey and Pete were driving along Ridge Road, top-down with WHK playing all the new tunes as loud as they could be played. As they were nearing the new Parma Town Mall there were two girls walking on the street both wearing short shorts. Pete said, "Holy Moly, we have to take a shot at these two" and he pulled over on the next side street and waited for them to approach. They were on Joey's side of the car and were very good-looking. One, with her platinum hair, looked just like the actress Carol Baker. As they got close to the car Joey said, "HELP ME, I'M CRAZY." The girls started laughing and before Joey could say something else the Carol Baker lookalike started screaming "JOEY, where have you been all my life?" She ran up to the car and put her arms around Joey's neck and kissed him. At first, he did not recognize her but as they came up for air and she released his neck he said, "Renee?" She said, "yes, and kissed him again." Meanwhile, Pete was parked on the wrong side of the street and staring at the scene with his mouth wide open. The other girl was still standing on the sidewalk looking just as surprised as Pete. As Joey and Renee came up for air again, Pete said "Hey get in. We'll take a ride." Renee immediately jumped in the back seat. Joey opened the door and got in back with her. Renee hollered to her girlfriend to get in front. As she got in, she said to Pete "Hi, I'm Connie." Pete said "Hi, I'm Pennsylvania Pete" and they took off. Both girls were a year behind Joey in school. Renee looked much older than fourteen. She was also one of the girls Joey had taken on the ride OVER THE FALLS during the school picnic at Euclid Beach a year ago. Actually, they had ridden that ride together about five times. He had not seen her since, even though she lived about a block away on the other side of Ridge Road. Joey was thinking, 'my oh my has this girl grown up.' Pete asked, "where to?" "Make the tour man," he said. The tour was to drive through the Manner's Big Boy on Pearl Road then across the street over to Bearden's. "Make that circuit and then head up to Manner's on Broadview and then go park at Metropolitan Park. By then it will be dark so you could park there until it closed at 10:00 p.m." They did and had a great time. When it was time to go, they drove the girls a block away from Renee's house. The girl's parents had forbidden them to get in cars with boys, but girls don't always listen to their parents, do they? Renee got out of the car saying call me and Joey said "ABSOLUTELY" as they were driving away. Joey had to go home also, and as he got out of Pete's car, Pete said, "You Ohio boys sure know how to have fun." Joey smiled and said, "Later Amigo, EMBRACE THE MADNESS" and walked in his door.

That summer Joey's cousin Jake had moved into Parma a block away on Bertha Avenue. Jake had a pool table in his basement and he and Joey played pool there all the time. Like all basement pool tables, it had many quirks. Learning them was half the battle. On days when Joey wasn't playing baseball, he would go there and practice. His aunt would let him in to play even when Jake was not home. Big Jim, who Joey did not see very often at this time, fancied himself a pool player. He actually had been playing in a pool hall and bowling alley in Parma Hts. called Braden's. Those tables were made of slate. Jake's table was wood. Joey had never played on a slate table, but he got to know every curve and quirk on Jake's table. Jake lived a stone's throw from Annette's house where Moans and those guys often hung out. One day when Big Jim ran into Joey as he was walking up the same side street but both with different destinations they began to talk and catch up on old times. When Joey mentioned that he was going to play pool at Jake's, Big Jim said, "We should play sometime." Joey said, "sure bring your paper route money." The next day Big Jim called and asked Joey if he wanted to play pool that evening at Jake's. Big Jim said I can stop there before I go to Annette's. Joey called and asked Jake who said "sure." He called Big Jim back and said it's all good. See you at 7:30 and don't forget your money. "No problem" replied Big Jim. They started at 7:30. They played straight pool to fifty. Joey won the first game for two dollars by ten balls. Big Jim said double or nothing. Joey said, "sure that's only fair." He won the second game by twelve balls. They played a total of five games, all double or nothing. Joey won them all. He won a total of thirty-two dollars that night. Big Jim left saying, "don't spend it I will be back." "Ok," said Joey and when he left, he gave Jake half his winnings to which Jake responded, "no way do I want this." Joey said, "I will beat this fish all summer long it is your table you get half of what I win." Jake said "ok, sounds good. You going to play him tomorrow?" They both laughed as Joey said, "good night, see you tomorrow."

The next morning, before they played ball at the Show parking lot, he called Renee and asked what she was doing later. She said that she was going over to Connie's, and would he like to come over. Joey asked if he could bring a friend. She said, "yes bring two, Janice will be there also." "Okay we have no car, but we will walk over." "Fine," she said. "How about 7:30?" He called Chocko and Keith and both said yes, they would go. Jebs was going to his girl's house who lived right across the street from Connie and said he would walk over with them. The four boys walked together and had a great time with the girls. At 10:00 Connie told the boys they had to leave. Jebs was leaving his girl's house also. So, they walked down the side streets and then cut up Gerald Avenue towards Ridge Road. It was a very warm summer night and most of the houses had their front doors open. Out of the blue Joey said to Keith, "I will give you a dollar if you open that front screen door and go in their living room and sing two verses of PAPA HOO MOW, MOW." Keith asked, "how far do I have to go in? "Far enough for us to hear you." Joey said, "fine we have a deal." They both spit on their hand and shook. As Keith started towards the door Joey said "wait." Keith walked back to him, and Joey told him, "do not run to us. Run by us. Keep running when you get to Ridge Road. We will meet you inside Buddy's pizza...Got it?" "No problem," said Keith and started back to the door. Chocko said "let's start walking." They got about ten yards and still heard nothing. Jebs said, "what the fuck is he doing?" "Knowing this guy, he is probably sitting down with them eating popcorn and watching T.V." quipped Chocko. Joey said, "I am going to go back and check on him." "No way, Chocko said, "DON'T DO IT." "You guys keep walking I need to make sure he's ok," said Joey, AND AT THAT MOMENT THEY HEARD PAPA HOO MOW, MOW; PAPA HOO MOW, MOW; and Keith burst out through the door running at full speed. He ran right through the group of boys and without breaking stride said "Buddy's." The boys started to walk but heard the door burst open again. A man in his fifties carrying a Billy Club came bursting out the door. He stopped at the group and asked if they had seen someone run this way. Chocko replied "yes, he ran right through us. He turned right at Ridge Road." "Thanks," said the man and started to chase again. Jebs said, "What are the odds that if that guy keeps running, he will have a heart attack?" "JEEZ JEBS I HOPE NOT," said Joey. As they were approaching Ridge Road the man from the house was walking back, very much out of breath. He stopped and started asking the boys, "did you know that guy?" Choco replied, "Hell no what did he do?" "He was in our living room and was screaming." Joey said, "HOLY MOLY" "I AM GOING HOME AND CALLING THE COPS." "Good idea," said Jebs. The boys got to Buddy's in about ten minutes. Keith had already ordered two pizzas and sat with his hand out waiting for the dollar. Joey reached in his pocket and gave it to him. Chocko asked, "What the hell took you so long? Were you having dinner with them?" Keith said. "No, I got in the house and could not stop laughing. I was waiting but I kept laughing to myself. Finally, a woman walked out of the bathroom with cream covering her face and her hair in giant curlers. She looked like a Martian Albino and started screaming. I wasn't laughing anymore I was scared shitless. So I sang the song and ran and here we are." The boys could not stop laughing at the story. They ate their pizza and went home.

A couple of days later the fellas were bored. They were, after all, teenage boys. If they weren't playing ball or chasing girls then it was the mischief that came in all shapes and sizes. Joey, Roger, Pete, Yonko, and his cousin Jake were in Jake's basement playing eight ball for fun. Joey had a thought, "What are you guys doing tonight?" They all muttered and said, "nothing special." "Want to have some fun?" Roger said, "yes, for sure" Joey laughed and said, "Here is a thought. We cut a hole in a sheet. Place Pete's head in the hole. We put powder all over his face and I put my sister's Beatle wig on his head." The boys were already laughing. "We go in Pete's car down to Metropolitan Park where the kids park in their cars and neck and maybe more than that." Pete quickly said, "NO WAY ARE YOU DRIVING MY CAR." "Calm down chooch. You will drive your own car. We will park it on the west side of the park. Leave it unlocked. We will then walk through the woods to the east parking lot and hide in the woods. When a couple pulls up Pete waits about five minutes and then quietly walks down and silently stands next to the car watching them but saying nothing. The one streetlight in that lot will be shining on you somewhat. You will be looking pretty creepy. If in five minutes they haven't noticed you then make some type of creepy noises. We will be in the woods on the fringe if something starts to go wrong we will be right there. Raise your hand if you are in," said Joey. All the hands shot up except Pete's. "No way," said Pete. The boys all started talking at once. "Come on man this will be fun. We have your back, and nobody will chase you into the woods you look way too scary." "Okay, we gather later in my backyard. We head down there at 9:30. It will be dark when we get there. "Pete you in or not ?" "Okay," Pete sighed, "Let's do it."

At 9:15 they piled into Pete's car. His face was covered in powder. He would put the rest of his costume on in the park. They got to the park, and everything was in sync. Pete put the sheet on, and the wig went on last. They walked through the woods for a quarter of a mile and waited. In about ten minutes a car pulled up in perfect position. They turned off the engine and headlights. Pete waited about 5 minutes and then slowly walked out of the woods and just stood in front of the car leering. Nothing happened for a while. Finally, Pete started making a groaning and grunting sound which went on for about two minutes. Suddenly the girl started screaming. "OH MY GOD, OH MY GOD." Her boyfriend started the car. Backed up as fast as he could go and peeled rubber to get away. The guys were laughing almost non-stop. Roger said, "Let's do it again." "Okay" was the unanimous opinion of the group so they checked Pete's powder and took their position in the woods and waited. They didn't have to wait long. Another car pulled up to park. Pete waited until they got settled and then started toward the car to do his thing. After about five minutes the exact same thing happened. The girl started screaming and yelling. The driver slammed his car in reverse as if to pull away but then floored it and drove directly at Pete trying to hit him. Fortunately, Pete was anticipating something like this and scampered behind the nearest tree. The guys in the woods stood with their mouths ajar. The girl in the car was still screaming as the car sat and idled. As she started to calm down the driver's side door opened, and her boyfriend stepped out and went to the trunk. He came back with a tire iron, and she started yelling at him to get back in the car. He told her to shut up and he walked to the fringe of the parking area which butted up against the woods and stopped. He started screaming into the wooded area. "I will kick your ass. Come on down here you pussy." All of a sudden Yonko started screaming. No words just shrieking and screaming. The other guys quickly joined in. Yelling incoherent shrieks like wild banshees. It sounded like there were lots of them, not just five. The driver started to walk back to the car as the shrieking from the woods continued. When his girlfriend told him to get back inside this time he listened. As he backed out, he stopped again and got out of the car, and yelled "STAY HERE AND WAIT YOU PUSSIES I WILL BE BACK SHORTLY." He got back in the car and peeled out. The boys decided that they had time for one more car to torment before the park would close so they got Pete ready and hid. Ten minutes went by, and no cars appeared and Jebs said, "let's go home." They started to walk down the slope that led out of the woods. Suddenly three cars came speeding into the parking lot and slammed on their breaks. At least ten guys got out of the cars carrying baseball bats. They all started yelling and calling for the boys to come down to meet them. "Holy Moly!" said Jake. "They have way more guys than us and they are all carrying baseball bats." Jebs said, "don't sweat it. I know these woods. We can go up the slope and circle to our car and be gone before they know we left." "Good plan," said Roger and they started to follow Jebs. Unfortunately, Yonko started screaming and throwing rocks at the invaders. The rest of the guys followed suit. Roger said, "yea, that's it cover our retreat" and he started throwing whatever he could get his hands on. All of a sudden loud bangs were going off in the woods. Joey turned back and looked down at the cars and said "Those Chooches aren't throwing rocks they are throwing cherry bombs. Let's get the hell out of here." Jebs led them to the top of the slope and said, "follow me our car is about half a mile on the other side of the park. Let's run." And run they did. As they got back to the car, they could still hear loud bangs coming from where they had just left. "Open the car, Pete and get your costume off and leave it here." "the sheet too?" "Yes, Chooch and let's move it." He took off his costume, got in the car, and got behind the wheel. As the bangs were still going off, they went out the back way of the park to Stumph Road, crossed Pearl Road, and took the backroads back to Joey's house. They got out, sat down, and laughed. Joey turned to his cousin and asked, "Well Jake how did you enjoy your first adventure in Parma?" Jake looked at his cousin and said, "you guys are really nuts." They all laughed but, in his mind, Joey was completely agreeing with him. He looked at his cousin and said, "CUZ, EMBRACE THE MADNESS."

About a week later Chocko, Joey, Keith, and Roger were shooting pool down in Jake's basement again. There was no money being played for, so things were getting pretty boring, pretty fast. After Roger had missed the eight ball for about the twentieth time, he put the stick down and said to Joey, "Why don't we take Jake on a PA, PA, HOO MOW, MOW hike?" Keith immediately said, "a dollar." Chocko says "I am in." But Jake who had almost had his wiener blown off on his first adventure with his cousin and his buddies said, "What the heck is that?" Chocko said "it's easy man, no sweat. We walk down the street and Keith sings PA, PA, HOO MOW, MOW!" Jake responded by saying "I call bull shit. It cannot be that simple." Joey said "don't worry cuz, I would never let anything happen to you. I have a match coming up with Big Jim and I need your pool table." They all laughed and walked out the door heading towards Dorothy Avenue less than a block away. They walked down Dorothy going away from Ridge Road. They talked and laughed as they walked. Halfway down the street Chocko said, "stop" and looked at a house that had its screen door open, and said to Joey "how about it?" Joey nodded at Keith and Keith headed toward the door. Jake just stood there wondering what was going on. As Keith was walking up the porch Joey turned to Jake and said "when you hear the song, we run our ass off. Follow me." Jake was in the process of saying "hey I am not"....PA, PA, HOO MOW, MOW!" interrupted the question. Keith was bursting out the door and Joey said "JEEZ HE CHANGED HIS STRATEGY! LET'S GO." and they took off. Seconds later the door burst open again and there were two older men running out the door. The chase was on. As they got to the crossroads Joey said, "follow me and then split up at the next corner." He glanced to see if his cousin was with them, and he was right behind Joey. When they got to the crossroads they split up and went in different directions. The two older men had already stopped and were heading home. Probably to get their cars. Fifteen minutes later the guys were sitting on Joey's front porch laughing. Joey was giving Keith a dollar while Chocko was complaining about Keith saying "HEY MAN YOU LEFT WAY EARLIER THAN THE LAST TIME YOU DID THIS. We need more head start time." Keith responded with "I ain't no Chooch, the last time I almost got caught, be ready to go when the band plays." They all were laughing hard. They settled down and were sitting around talking when Jake asked, "Hey cuz is there anything you guys do that doesn't include running and being chased by someone?" They all laughed hard and headed home.

Summer vacation was nearing an end. All the summer vacations would seem to end so fast. School would start in about three weeks. Girls had always played a big part in summer. Charlyn would pop in and out of Joey's life and while they would see each other and go out it seemed like it always ended in an argument, and both would stay away from each other for weeks at a time. As the summer was ending it was still Renee' who held Joey's interest. The problem was that Joey would almost always lose interest after no more than a week. He liked girls a lot. He just could not stay for long.

In the summer of 1962, Rock-n-Roll was rollin. The Twist was the new dance craze. The Four Seasons had their first hit *"Sherry."* Joey's favorite song was Dion's *"The Wanderer."* It just seemed to fit how he was with girls. He embraced the madness. He had seen Renee several times and fun with her was really fun. It was early afternoon, and he was playing H.O.R.S.E with Jebs, Chocko, and Yonko for a quarter a game. Chocko and Joey could shoot the lights out with a basketball. Jebs was an excellent player in every game he played in, but he couldn't shoot like those two. Yonko was awful but a ton of laughs to be around. In between games Jebs said to Joey "I am going over to Sandy's house tonight at 7:00 and Renee is going to be there as well as Suzie, you want to come with me?" "Yep, I am in I will call her when we get done here." Yonko quickly asked, "can I go too?" Jebs asked, "do you have interest in Suzie?" "I want to see if she will let me put my hands under her shirt." (For a 14-year-old, Suzie was very well put together). Joey quickly responded with "GOOD LUCK WITH THAT. I tried at Euclid Beach two years ago and she slapped me." They all laughed. Yonko asked Chocko "what are you doing tonight?" "Nothing" was his response. "I may go to bed early." Again they all laughed hard. Yonko said, "bologna, you are going to find Katrina and take her to Forestwood." Now they were all howling. Chocko responded with, "I will take the fifth," and the laughter only got louder. The group broke up. Jebs said to Joey, "I will meet you two at Sandy's. I forgot I told her I would be there at 5:00. Yonko don't embarrass me, or I'll beat your ass." Again, all laughed and knew it was quite possible that Yonko would indeed embarrass him, and it was doubtful that Jebs would go after him, but you never knew what could happen at any time with Yonko. As they walked away Joey told Yonko to meet him at Vic's by 7:00 and they would walk over together.

That night Joey left his house at 6:55 and headed up the street towards Vic's. He saw Yonko heading towards him and said, "Man you must be revved up to get under that shirt, you are never early." They walked up the street, cut through the Show parking lot, and continued to walk up Snow Road. As they walked up Snow and were getting close to Ridge Road, Yonko said, "take a look at this guy. What's his deal?" Coming towards them was a six-foot, 3-inch white kid who was strutting the strut down the street. It was a very different walk that had his arms swinging and a certain bounce to it.

Yonko said, "I think this kid is a fag." "So what?" said Joey "he ain't bothering anyone" and they continued to walk towards him. About two feet before they were ready to pass one another Yonko jumps up next to the kid and starts his patented shriek laugh while pointing at the kid who on a closer look was definitely not a kid. He was more of a young man who was about seventeen or eighteen years old. Joey had seen this act of Yonko's before. Normally it was quite funny but not this day. The kid stopped walking and reacted immediately. He raised his hands in a boxer's position and started bouncing around like Muhammed Ali while saying loudly "I'M FROM NEW YORK, I'M FROM NEW YORK, I'M FROM NEW YORK AND I WILL KICK YOUR ASS." Yonko kept up his screeching laugh as the kid kept bouncing. Just as he turned, ready to punch, Yonko backed off and shut up. Yonko was definitely not a fighter. The KID was now yelling RIGHT IN Yonko's face. "YOU CLEVELAND BOYS ARE PUSSY'S." Before he could throw on Yonko, Joey yelled "HEY." The boy turned and stopped bouncing. "Why don't you and I go right over there behind those buildings, and we can take care of business." The kid was bouncing again and shouting "NO FUCKING WAY MAN, YOU AND HE WILL JUMP ME. NO WAY MAN." "You want to fight it's just you and me over there. You cannot fight in the middle of this intersection; the cops will be here in less than a minute." The kid started bobbing and weaving again and continued his I'm from New York patter. Joey said, "let's do it or we are out of here." The kid stopped bouncing and looked at the strip mall parking lot across the street and after about 15 seconds he said, "let's go." They walked to the intersection and crossed all the while Joey was thinking, I have a bad feeling about this kid. He is much older than us and there is no fear in his eyes. They got into the parking lot and squared off. There was no more Ali shuffle or bouncing around. He was in a solid boxing stance and was a good seven inches taller. Joey as always tried to get the first punch in, but the New Yorker blocked it easily and countered with a powerful right that hit him on the forehead. Joey got into a boxer's pedal and tried jab, jab, right cross. His reward was a jab to his cheek and a right hook to the side of his face. The

New Yorker was landing, and Joey was not. He continued his pedal trying to assess how he could land a punch against this kid. He went to the body and tried to punish him with inside body blows and this had some success. When they got out of the clinch the New Yorkers' jab was landing again. Joey was losing. Time to change tactics. To himself he said, screw this and made a running football tackle on the kid. The New Yorker was surprised and went down on his back with Joey on top. Joey struck him hard twice in the face, but the New Yorker was a street fighter also and landed a knee right to Joey's abdomen. Joey got two more punches into his head and his nose started to bleed but at the same time he lost leverage and the boy got on the top of him and started to pummel him. He covered up with his arms, but the hits kept coming. The only punches Joey could land were to the side of his head and if he left his face uncovered he usually took a hit. He tried to knee him and caught him in the groin but not his nuts. At that moment Yonko yelled "CAR! I THINK IT'S A COP." The New Yorker jumped up and Joey was shortly behind him. The police officer pulled up next to them and said, "You boys alright?" Both kids answered, "yes, we are just messing around." The officer looked at the bloody nose of the New Yorker and then back at Joey. After looking at Joey for about twenty seconds he asked, "Aren't you Joey the fireman's kid?" "Yes, I am officer." "Are you sure you are ok? This boy is a bit bigger than you " "I am fine officer, thank you." "Well then let's see you all leave this lot. I will check back in about five minutes." "Ok thanks officer" and the policeman pulled away. When he pulled around the corner out of sight the New Yorker said, "ok let's finish." Joey's response was "FUCK OFF I am done." The New Yorker laughed and said, "I knew Ohio boys were pussies." just as the officer was pulling back around the corner. Joey looked at the New Yorker and said, "tell that to your nose" and he and Yonko continued on towards Sandy's house. The New Yorker walked the other way. The officer drove by Joey and Yonko and nodded. As they walked, they talked. Yonko kept going on about how Joey had kicked the New Yorker's ass. Finally, Joey looked at him and said "Are you fucked up? That guy was beating me badly.

If we keep fighting he finishes me with a very thorough ass-kicking. Now shut up." They walked for a while in silence. They got to the end of Sandy's street and Yonko said "stop." Joey looked at him and he had a wallet in his hand and a number of bills. He counted out forty dollars and started to hand Joey half. "What's this for?" "I picked up his wallet that fell out of his pocket. Half of this is yours." Joey said, "no, we have to find him, give it to him." Yonko said, "NO WAY. We will never find him. Besides, he started the fight, now take the money." "I DON'T WANT IT; you started that fight. Get the hell away from me." They walked in complete silence. Just before they walked into Sandy's driveway Yonko said "ok, I will give it to the church." Joey looked at him and said, "if you say one more word just one I will smack the shit out of you right here in her driveway." At that moment Renee came running out of the house yelling "Joey, where you been all my life" and put her arms around his neck and laid a kiss on his lips. The others came out and they all sat down on the porch. After an hour they left, and Joey and Renee left to go to Buddy's Pizza. Moans, Annette, Fritz, Big Jim, and Inky were all there. They all talked for a while and then Joey walked Renee home and they sat on her back porch until 11:00 when Renee's mom came out and it was time for Renee to go in the house. She did and Joey walked home. On his way home he was thinking about how much fun Renee' was and how good-looking she was. He thought to himself I really like this girl. He wouldn't see her again for two years.

That night as Joey lay in bed staring at the ceiling a number of thoughts crossed his mind. First of all, Yonko is an idiot, a funny idiot but an idiot, nonetheless. I should have known better than to mess with a kid that size and at least two years older than me. I am very lucky that that police officer showed up. I hope he doesn't tell my dad. That money will never see the inside of a church. He fell asleep thinking how much fun Renee was.

UNCLE EDDY STRIKES AGAIN

About a week later Joey, Jebs, and Chocko were finishing up Joey's paper route after playing basketball all afternoon. They got to the corner of the street and ran into Moans, Big Jim, Inky, and Fritz who were sitting on the corner of Vic's. They all sat down on the ledge and just hung out. It was rare that the two separate groups that Joey hung out with were together. They all knew each other but seldom hung out. As they sat and talked, and watched girls walk by a car went by and blew it's horn. The driver slowed down, made a left, and came back and parked in Vic's parking lot. The guys watched him get out of the car and walk over to them. Eddy was dressed in Bermuda shorts and black knee socks. He had a fishing hat on, and from it dangled eight hooks and a dozen lures. "Meenkya Joey, how are you? I see all the Chooches are here with you." The fellas all said, "Hey Eddy how you doing?" Each of them knew they were going to have some laughs. They all listened as Eddy was telling some fishing story when Chocko said "Eddy, no offense but you stink" "You sure do Eddy where you been." added Joey. "Meenkya Joey I wuz just about to tell youse guys. I just came from a skunk festival." "A what?" asked Jebs, "What the fuck is that?" chimed Big Jim and the revelry began. "I am tryin to tell youse chooches. All the skunk owners enter their skunks in a contest. They walk them around on a leash and give them orders to do things like sit or jump, you know stuff like that." "You walk skunks on a leash?" asked Fritz. "Yea lots of entrants. Nice prize money also." The fellas all looked at each other and were trying hard not to laugh. Inky asked, "How did your skunk do?" "Not so good the prick wouldn't listen to me. Man, I'm tellin ya that wuz sumthin. Whenever I gave him an order, he just did what he wanted." "What kind of orders did you give him?" "I told him to bark three times and he just looked at me." Laughter now was in full tilt as the boys kept asking questions. "What place did you finish in?" "We didn't, the chooches threw us out." "Threw you out? Why?" "My skunk stunk." "Your skunk stunk?" "Yea that's what I have been tryin to tell ya. My skunk stunk." Laughter was king now. "Eddy, didn't they all stink?" Fritz chipped in immediately with "pet skunks all get deodorized." Big Jim turned to Fritz and asked, "How the fuck do you know that?" "My Grandma had one." "Jesus," said Chocko, "this just keeps getting better and better. Was your skunk deodorized Eddy?" "Meenkya no I read the rules but I didn't know what that meant." The boys were now laughing so hard that they were crying. "Eddy where is your skunk now?" "I took him off his leash and left him there. When I left, they wuz running around trying to catch him and he kept spraying them. The other skunks were going nuts. Meenkya I'm tellin ya it wuz a skunk riot. I had to get out of there." The boys were absolutely roaring. "Eddy go home and shower please because you smell just like your skunk." "Meenkya okay why didn't youse say sumthin?" As he walked back to his car he stopped and went inside Vic's to get a pop. "Watch this," said Chocko. Within two minutes Vic's wife who was working the register was chasing Eddy out the door with a broom yelling for him to go home and bathe. Eddy was trying to give her money for his pop, but she was locking the door while she was still screaming at him. He got into the car and as he left, he pulled up next to where the boys were sitting and rolling with laughter. "See ya fellas I got to look for a new pet." As he pulled out of the drive, he yelled back to them "I GOT A FREE POP HEEHEEHEEE." The boys laughed for another five minutes and then the group broke up and they went their separate ways.

That night as Joey lay in bed, he was thinking about the Skunk Festival, and he smiled, skunks on leashes and he chuckled, Skunk riots, and he was giggling louder now. Bark three times, and he laughed harder. So hard, that Grace in the other room yelled...what are ya doing? All a tired Joey said was "me and the fellas ran into Uncle Eddy today." Grace responded saying, "Oh, that explains it... goodnight."

About three days later Joey was going swimming at Ridgewood pool. He was looking forward to seeing a girl named Myra whom he had just met at the Parma Show on Saturday night. Myra was another of those girls that Joey seemed to attract that never looked their age. She too was fourteen looking like seventeen. As he was approaching the pool, he would be walking right past Ridgewood Lake and probably the Ridgewood Lake boys. He knew a lot of those guys from playing sports either with or against them. He wasn't worried about it. As he walked past the lake there were a ton of guys and girls having loud fun in a large group. Suddenly the attention of the group turned towards a boy who was walking from the group right at Joey. Joey kept walking but the kid yelled "HEY YOU, WAIT." The kid jumped over the fence and continued towards him. A herd of guys and girls followed close behind. Guys jumped over the fence and the girls stayed behind it jostling to see what was going to happen. As the kid got closer Joey recognized him as the younger of two brothers both of whom were somewhat scary. He went by his initials J.B. His older brother was named Ralph. J.B. said in a loud voice "I HEAR YOU ARE LOOKING FOR ME." Joey looked around the group who had surrounded the confrontation and knew almost all of them. He saw no animosity in any of their eyes so he thought he wasn't going to get jumped; it must be something else. He looked back at J.B. who was exactly the same height as he was but was at least two years older. "Why would I be looking for you. I don't even know you." "Well, you are going to know me now" and started to take off his T-shirt. Rule number one immediately kicked in, always be a first hitter. As J.B. got closer to him and was starting to yap some more Joey hit him square in the face and another fight was on. This was a kid his own size so his boxing skills would prove useful. J.B. was stunned but still came at him. JAB, JAB, RIGHT CROSS followed by a right-hand hook, and J.B. was bleeding from his nose and mouth. He still kept fighting but like all these wannabe fighters they always kept their hands far below their face as they tried to dance. Joey just waited till he got close again and then it was JAB, JAB, RIGHT CROSS with the right landing flush below his eye. J.B. was very angry, bleeding, and frustrated. He then made a big mistake. He led with a kick that Joey caught in midair. He fell backward and landed flat on his back. Joey dragged him along and every time he raised his head, he caught Joey's right fist with his face. This continued for a while then Joey jumped on top of him. He began to pound him again as he was being pulled off. He fought to break loose and when he did, he was face to face with the older brother who was carrying a handheld blackjack. Joey had not been in this situation before and wasn't sure quite what to do when all of a sudden about 5 guys from the crowd got in between the two. Their leader was a guy named The Sabre who Joey had played ball with. He knew the other four also. The Sabre said loudly "this was a fair fight and your brother lost. Let it go it is over." The older brother who went by Bo looked at The Sabre and then at Joey and said, "he is right you won, nice fight." Joey said thanks and looked at The Sabre and said, "Can I go now?" "Yeah, no problem, nice fight. You are welcome to hang out with us down at the lake if you want. "No thanks I have a girl to meet. See you when I see you" and walked away. As he walked, he heard someone running up from behind him and he wheeled around with his fists clenched. "Wait, wait, nice fight." It was Zac one of the boys who stood behind The Sabre. He was older than Joey and lived only a block away. They played baseball and basketball together. He said, "listen if the older brother comes after you let us know, those two are bad, bad news. That kid you fought needed to get his ass kicked. You made us St. Charles boys proud. Now go meet your girl and see you around." "She is not my girl and thanks again."

The rest of the day was spent swimming with Myra. He walked her over to Parma Town where they had a coke and a burger. They poured dimes into the jukebox that sat on the table in the booth. Songs like "Run Away" by Del Shannon, "Crying" by Ray Orbison, "Blue Moon," "Lovers Who Wander," "She Cried" and at least a dozen others. Most of his paper route tip money found its way into that jukebox. He waited with her until her ride picked her up. He left to walk home only this time he stayed on Ridge Road all the way to Essen. On his way home his thoughts were of Myra. As he walked in his side door, he thought I really like this girl. He would see her twice more and then never again.

SCHOOL STARTS – 10TH GRADE

It was back to school. While the school year would be almost uneventful, he would finish the year with eighteen demerits. Twenty-one would get you tossed. There would be many new friends. Murray Hill was just around the corner and guys like Rocky, Carmen, and Dominic would for a brief time enter his life. He also became friends with Black kids. There weren't any African American families living in Parma at that time. He would always feel that even though the school was a very good one he learned much more about life on his way to and from the school. Both good and bad. He would draw on both as he got older. There were some ethnic students as well and just some plain old tough kids that were from the eastside of Cleveland. Vic was one of the latter. He and Joey had become very good friends in school. A friendship that would last until college. Eventually, Vic would flunk out of college and be killed in the Vietnam war. But at this time like most kids of this era, nobody had even heard of Vietnam. Sports, girls, and fun were what made their world go around and Joey was completely bought in on all three.

As his demerits piled up in his sophomore year, he came dangerously close to being tossed out. His demerits were not of a serious nature, but there were many. If his tie was untied and the wrong teacher saw him, he would get one. If he was fooling around in the wrong class, he would get one. Tardy for class and so on and so on. He was actually living two lives. One that revolved around his scholastic world. Both in-class and to and from school. The other was in his own neighborhood. Again, there were almost three different groups that he could find himself hanging out with at any given time. One thing he was finding out about his life, it was never boring.

It was Friday afternoon. Joey finished his paper route and had an hour to be home before dinner. He walked over to Vic's to see if anyone was there. He found Moans, Inky, Big Jim, and Fritz. They were talking very loudly and laughing. Joey walked around the corner and said, "what's up?" Big Jim responded quickly by saying, "we are just reminiscing about Moans fight with Pretty Boy Ray on his last day at Latin." Pretty Boy Ray was Ray Lawson an upperclassman at Latin who the guys had nicknamed Pretty Boy. It seemed that his girlfriend could not stop talking about how good-looking Moans was. It was driving Pretty Boy nuts. He started harassing Moans in school pretending it was just about him being a freshman and Pretty Boy being an upperclassman. It was supposed to be just fun, but it wasn't. Each incident got worse as Pretty Boy was getting more and more pissed because his girl would not stop. The banter continued as Joey pulled himself up on the ledge to sit. "How bout it man, you going to give that girl a twirl?" laughed Fritz. "When you going out with her?" added Inky. Moans responded by saying "man I have never talked to that girl in my life." "She does think you are a cutey though," laughed Big Jim. "Fuck off Jolly Green Giant." "Ok, but it was fun to watch you kick the shit out of that Pretty Boy on our last day at school. He wasn't so pretty when you were done with him." Joey said, "Man I am so sorry I missed that. Everyone has told me you absolutely destroyed his ass." Fritz jumped in, "does this mean you are a lover and a fighter now?" Moans shot back, "Hey why don't you get laid for the first time? I heard there is a bus load of blind girls going to be at St. Charles for church later. Maybe you could sneak up on one and tell her you are Elvis Presley." The boys were laughing. "By the way, Keith is coming up here with his new girlfriend," said Joey. "Actually, I see them crossing the street right now. "What's her name?" "I think it's OO(h)." "OO(h)"? Is she Oriental?" "Not sure I have never seen her." "Why is he coming here?" "He is taking her to Parma Town and said he would stop if we were here." Keith was arm and arm with his girl about fifteen yards away. The boys were all looking to see who Keith was seeing. Slowly their jaws dropped to their chest and Big Jim said "OOOOO(h), that is a very ugly girl" as Keith was just coming into earshot. "Hey," said Keith. "How you all doing?" "Great" "This is Madeline." When Keith said her name all the guys immediately looked at Joey who had a huge grin on his face. They all talked for a while and then Keith said, "We gotta go. Going to do some shopping at the Mall." Fritz said, "So nice meeting you, don't do anything that I wouldn't do." To which Moans responded under his breath, "Well I wouldn't do that," pointing at Madeline. Just as the guys were breaking up Moans asked Joey what he was doing later. "I'm taking Charlyn to the show this evening." "Man, you, and that girl on, off, on, off. We ought to start making book on how long it will last each time." "Hey," Joey said changing the subject. "We are playin hoops in the backyard tomorrow you are all welcome. About one o'clock. Later fellas." "Yeah see ya later, nice one on the OOOO(h) thing" and they all laughed as they moved on.

His mom was becoming worried a bit. Joey was not allowed out after dinner on school nights and his sudden interest in the Parma Library made her have some apprehension that he wasn't really going there to study. Couple that with, on his progress report he was getting demerits. Not big deals by themselves but they were starting to add up. As she thought about it, she realized that this would be another year that Joey didn't play sports for the school. That night she talked about the situation with his dad. Big Joe thought for a minute then told her, "I have an idea. Let me work on it" and the conversation ended. Two days later he said to his wife "let's talk about Joey. My idea is I am going to put together a team to play in the rec leagues made up of kids who got cut from their high schools" and he did. The team he put together could have beaten a lot of high schools. He had a big front line and shooters in all positions. He had the same results with the older kids that he had with the younger ones at St. Charles. They didn't lose a game in the Parma Rec leagues in four straight years. Their only competition would come in the Cleveland city-wide tourney and for the next four years, their chief rivals were the Central Y Jokers and the Central Y Hawks. These games were always for the championship of those tourneys. They won two and were runners-up in two. Most importantly Joey improved in school.

School was largely unremarkable for him. It was filled with laughter, there were no more dead bodies and he managed to only get jumped once on his way to and from. During his freshman year, he had seen a kid in the hallways that walked kind of funny. He never met him but sophomore year the same kid was in a few of his classes. His last name was O'TOOLE, but his nickname was Onie. It turned out that Onie had a disease that would get worse every year. His different walk would eventually lead to him being a cripple and from there it would kill him. But for now, his funny walk was not very noticeable, and he and Joey would begin a friendship until he died. Onie was hilarious and proved to be every bit the cut-up that Joey was. They spent day after day getting in minor mischief and laughing their ass off. Onie also had some immunities from getting in trouble at school. He had an older brother who was in the same order as the priests and brothers that staffed Cathedral Latin and his parents were huge donors. They had a biology class as well as a Spanish class together. Onie was smart. He nicknamed the Spanish teacher Pico which in Spanish meant beak. Obviously, the teacher had a big nose. Soon the entire sophomore class was calling him Pico.

A PENNY FOR YOUR THOUGHTS

They also shared a biology class. Once every other week the class lab was held after school for about an hour. Attendance was mandatory. One of the labs was dissecting a frog. You and a partner would cut the frog up systematically and when the hour was up, they would wrap the frog, put their names on the wrapping and put it into a tank, and finish the lesson the next time they had class. Onie was Joey's partner and frog dissecting lasted for three weeks. There were many laughs. On the third and final week of frog dissecting class Onie chose to look up some answers in his text while Joey continued to dissect their frog. As the dissection was nearing completion Joey noticed something shiny inside his frog. He hollered to the teacher "THERE IS SOMETHING in here." The teacher just rolled his eyes. Joey now was dissecting intensely because he knew something was inside. He looked over at Onie and waved for him to come over and see. Onie said no, gesturing that he had to find the answers he was looking up. Joey kept digging and there it was. He again yelled out "Hey Brother Larry look, it's a penny. There is a penny in my frog." Brother Larry again rolled his eyes and said, "Sure Joey." Joey said, "but there is please come here and take a look." Brother Larry said, "finish up your work there are only 15 minutes left." Joey was getting pissed, this guy wasn't believing him. He looked up again and over at Onie who was literally rolling with laughter. Joey then looked around and noticed that almost everyone in the class was laughing. They could not hold it back any longer.

He sat there frustrated while thinking, why are they all laughing. He yelled out again "Hey I am not kidding there is a penny in my frog." This caused outright hilarity and now hooting at Joey. His buddies yelled out things like keep digging man maybe you will find a dollar, another yelled, maybe a treasure map, and another yelled; maybe it is a pirate's frog. Even Brother Larry was laughing. Joey was really pissed now and then suddenly it dawned on him. Someone put the penny in the frog while it was wrapped up. That's why Onie was sitting somewhere else pretending to be a studious student. Joey yelled across the room of still hooting boys "YOU PUT IT IN THERE, YOU DICK" and now he was laughing. But to Brother Larry, it wasn't funny anymore. He looked at Joey and said, "Joseph stick around after class." The laughter ended suddenly. Everyone knew that Joey had just stepped over the line. Onie however was frightened. He knew that Joey was going to be in trouble and didn't want to see that. The bell rang and as the students filed out of class Onie went up to Brother Larry and confessed to putting the penny in the frog. Brother Larry curtly said, "I figured, now get out I have to take care of your buddy." Onie left and Brother Larry looked at Joey. He said, "you know you cannot use that kind of language in this school, right?" "Yes, Brother." "So here is what I am going to do. You will have ten demerits." "TEN?" questioned Joey. Brother Larry's quick response was "let me finish OR we can go upstairs and meet with the Assistant Principal which I would bet that the best you could hope for is a two-week suspension. Your worst-case scenario could very well be expulsion. So, do you want to let me finish?" "Yes," replied a some-what subdued Joey. Getting tossed out of school would be met with severe consequences by his parents, especially his dad. Brother Larry continued. Like I said "Ten demerits. Five of which I will turn in tonight and you will begin serving immediately. Five of which will disappear if you finish this semester causing no problems in this class ever again. Do we have a deal, you have ten seconds to answer?" Joey quickly said "Deal." "Now get out." In the hall Onie was waiting. Joey looked at him and said, "STAY THE FUCK AWAY FROM ME" and went to his locker and headed home.

LIKE A TURTLE

At Latin, every boy had to take a typing class. The class was taught by a 5ft. 8-inch Brother who was about two-hundred and sixty pounds named Brother Oscar. Almost all that weight was carried in his mid-section. He had a short fuse and hands that seemed to be the size of hams. He was nasty. He would walk behind the boys while they were typing and if he even thought they were looking at the typewriter he would hit them extremely hard in the back of the head. To Brother O it was cute, but the boys hated him. Every class began with the students praying out loud together before sitting down for class. Brother Oscar would stand almost sideways during the prayer so he could see the class as well as the crucifix in the front of the room. One of the things that would send Brother O into a frenzied rage is the typewriter bells ringing while prayer was being recited or a lesson being taught. To get even with this guy who would hit them in their head with great regularity, the boys at great personal risk to themselves would ring the typewriter bell whenever they could. Whenever they thought O wasn't looking. Often times during prayer and any lesson that he was explaining. You could see the anger in his face, and some claimed there was often smoke coming out from his head. Onie was a regular bell ringer and never got caught. He also never got clipped in the back of the head. Joey often took shots to the back of his head, and he hated O with a passion. One day after school Joey had just finished serving his final demerit and he was making his way through an almost deserted building. Practice was going on in the gym which was on the other side of the building from the door Joey would be exiting through and almost nobody was there an hour after school. Joey was walking down the hall and would be leaving around the hallway corner to his right. The hallway he was currently walking in intersected with a main hall in the lowest level of the school. As he walked around the corner to the exit, which was about ten yards away, he heard a noise coming from the intersecting hallway. He stopped and looked. The noise was coming from someone who was lying in the hallway on their back about 50 ft. away. They had fallen and could not get up. Joey immediately started to walk over to help whomever it was that had fallen. It seemed like he could not turn himself over. It was like a turtle who was on his shell. Short little arms waving about and trying desperately to right himself. However, he was just too heavy in his mid-section to get himself up. As he walked closer Joey realized who it was. It was Brother O. Joey stopped. He turned and walked back to where the halls intersected and turned the corner. He stood and watched. No way was O going to get up without help. His mind was racing. He wondered if he was hurt. He looked around behind him to make sure that there was no one there and then peeked around the corner to watch Brother O. He then yelled in a gruff deep voice. "HEY, ARE YOU OK?" O answered immediately "yes I am not hurt I just cannot get up. I fell and have been lying here for a while, thank God you can help me." Joey looked around again, he knew he was about to play with fire, but he just could not resist. He poked his head around the corner and in a high falsetto voice he said, "Brother O, this is your guardian angel, God is trying to make up his mind if he is going to let me help you." "WHAT?" screamed Brother O and his turtlelike arms started going a mile a minute. In a falsetto voice again, Joey said "I am waiting on his answer, "I am sorry just try to be patient." O yelled, "WHO ARE YOU?" The response came back again in a high voice. "I already told you Oscar who I am." Brother O asked in a pleading voice "For the love of God please quit fooling around and help me." Joey switched voices to the deepest baritone voice he could muster and yelled "OSCAR THIS IS GOD. DO YOU PROMISE TO STOP HITTING THE STUDENTS IN YOUR CLASSES?" Brother O responded somewhat meekly "yes, yes, I do." "GOOD I AM GLAD THAT MAKES ME VERY HAPPY. NOW GET YOUR FAT FUCKING SELF OFF THE GROUND YOU FAT ASS BULLY." with that Joey was out the door and on his way to the Rapid Transit. The next day O was standing outside each of his classes staring at every guy as they went in the room trying to figure out who was God. Joey tried to be as normal as possible. He looked right at him as he walked in and said, "afternoon Brother." O never found out. Joey's only regret was he could not tell any of his friends until after he graduated. O never punched another kid that year and the next year he was transferred somewhere else. Years later as he sat in Onie's apartment who by this time was unable to walk at all, he told him the story and they both laughed and laughed until they cried.

That night as Joey lay in bed staring at the ceiling he again found himself laughing, but he also was thinking, what if I got caught, got demerits, and got thrown out of school? What kind of kid does that knowing how much it would hurt my parents? Is there something wrong with me? He stared at the ceiling for a good five minutes. Finally, he heard a deep voice coming from somewhere....Joey, THIS IS GOD, don't worry about it, that prick deserved everything he got. Joey breathed a sigh of relief thinking, the Lord works in mysterious ways, and went to sleep smiling.

A new phenomenon was beginning to sweep through high school. Isometric is a strength-building exercise, as well as weight-lifting. The belief that weightlifting led guys to be muscle-bound, slow, and unathletic was quickly being debunked. Joey chose to participate in both forms of conditioning as well as a stretching routine all of which he did alone in his basement. He would begin his sophomore year at five feet, six and one hundred-twenty pounds. He would enter the summer vacation of 1963 at five-eight and one hundred-sixty pound. To say he was feeling good about himself would be an understatement.

His thoughts went back to his earlier time in the Parma Show parking lot while playing baseball when Rhino and his buddies bullied him. It was early June and the last week of school. Joey was at home preparing for summer vacation and trying on bathing suits. They wouldn't fit. He left his room to go to the full-length mirror that was upstairs and take a look at himself. He was only in his underwear and had never seen himself in a full-body mirror. He was stunned. He stared at himself for at least five minutes. He decided he needed a new bathing suit and he also had to pay a visit to Rhino.

The summer vacation of 1963 would be the most eventful summer of his teenage life. For the next three years, his out-of-school friends would be Moans and Company. Big Jim, Joey, and Moans were all invited to try out for a very good traveling baseball team. They did and all three made it. Keith, Fritz, and Inky were not invited but tried out anyway. Those three did not make it. The three who made it talked about not playing if those guys were not on the team, but that was a short-lived conversation. They all wanted to play.

Some of the guys had already turned sixteen. Joey would be sixteen in July. Sixteen was the magic number for getting a driver's license. First passing a written test would give you your temporary license. The temporary license enabled you to drive if accompanied by a licensed driver. The second requirement was you had to pass an actual driving test which included parallel parking. By summertime, both Moans and Fritz had passed both tests and had their regular driver's licenses. Joey and Inky turned sixteen in July and Big Jim in August. None of them had cars yet so the summer was still a time of walking to where you were going. They started to hang out at Annette's more and more at nighttime. Annette's mom still worked at a bar and did not get home until 3:00 a.m., so it was the ideal place, especially knowing that on any night girls would also show up. The Shimmy, Shake, and South Side were the dances of the day. Joey would play records in his basement and/or listen to WHK on his radio while practicing those three dances religiously. He had learned much earlier in life that girls loved guys who could dance and so he worked at it. Baseball at the Parma Show was over. It just died out and it seemed the younger kids did not want to play there. The travel teams' games were always at night. Baseball practice was in the morning three times a week and summer basketball was played in the backyard regularly. At night "sleeping out" would take place. To Joey's mom and dad, it meant Joey and his friends would be sleeping outside in tents at one or another of the boy's houses. Occasionally it would be Joey's turn to host the sleep out and they would sleep in Aunty Olie's screened-in porch next to Joey's house. The truth was most of the time there was no sleep out anyplace. They would hang around at Annette's and then prowl around from 2:00 in the morning until about 7:00 in the morning when they headed home and went to bed.

Often, they would leave Annette's and head to Knollwood apartments where they would enter an apartment building and go downstairs to the laundry room where they would talk and smoke cigarettes the rest of the night. They would tell stories and talk about girls. It was on such a night that Keith made a revelation. They were all laughing and sitting in an almost all-dark basement enjoying just hanging out when Keith said "Fellas I have to tell you something. I lied to you all." Deathly quiet followed as everyone became interested as to what the lie was. "I told you guys that my parents both died in a car crash. That is not true. The truth is my father shot my mother and then shot himself. I found them both." His confession was followed by complete and utter silence. The only sounds were the breathing of one another. Nobody had any idea what to say. After a five-minute silence Fuco, who hung out with Joey but not very often with this group, spoke out. He said, "Ya know when I grow up and have children I think I am going to name my first daughter Machu Pichu." Following a ten-second silence, Moans and Joey both started laughing and the rest of the group followed suit. "Why would you do that?" laughed Inky. "Why not name her the Grand Canyon or Forest Rain?" While the laughter was starting to spread Big Jim said, "I don't get it. What's a Machu Pichu?" The laughter increased and Fuco said, "it's Pecan Pie." Rolling now, Big Jim asked "why would you name your daughter after a pie? Don't get me wrong I like Pecan Pie but as a name for my daughter I don't know." Very loud laughter now. "Listen Numb Nuts," said Moans as he addressed Big Jim. "Machu Pichu is a place in South America." "Why would he name her after a place in South America?" "Yea Fuco why didn't you pick a place in America? Like Grand Canyon." "That would be a great name for a girl" blurted Inky. "Or Princess, Summer, Fall, Winter, Spring," said Moans. "Or Honolulu Lulu." Fuco quickly responded, "My second choice was Butch." Now the laughter was becoming a roar. The suggestions continued for the rest of the morning. Finally, as the sun began to rise the boys ended the conversation, said goodbye to each other, and started home. On his way-out Joey said to Moans and Big Jim "Remember, we have practice in about three hours." Both groaned as they walked away.

That night as Joey lay in bed staring at the ceiling thinking...his father shot his mother and then killed himself. I can't imagine anything worse. I'm gonna have to make myself be kinder to Keith. He had a hard time sleeping that night.

REVANCHE....AS PEPE LE PEW WOULD SAY

It was St. Charles carnival time. The carnival was five days long. Joey loved the carnival and it always brought back memories of his first kiss with Rhonda. He wondered briefly what had happened to her, but the thoughts quickly disappeared. The gang would meet at Vic's and attend at least for two nights. Charlyn was again out of the picture for Joey and there would be many girls at the carnival. They arrived and immediately headed for the throwing booth. Within thirty minutes Joey and Moans had two stuffed animals each. Big Jim had one. They started to head to the Chuckle Luck wheel when Joey stopped. He handed his animals to guys who hadn't won any and said, "hold these for me please." To the group he said, "Cover me," and he walked over to three guys who were standing together talking. His buddies had seen the look in his eyes, and they had seen that look before. Trouble lie ahead. Joey walked up to the three and tapped one on the shoulder. It was Rhino. Rhino looked puzzled. Joey said, "why don't you and I go across the street behind the barber shop, and we can have a talk." "I don't know you" responded Rhino "I think you do." Rhino studied his face and then it dawned on him, "I remember now." "Good let's go." "Why?" "Because I told you I would remember, and I do, let's go." Rhino was now fat. He must have gained 40 pounds. Joey didn't care, he had no intention of wrestling with him. Rhino had no choice it was either go and fight or lose face. They got behind the barber shop and Rhino dropped his hands and started to dance around. Joey could not believe he was this stupid. He waited and then it was JAB, JAB, RIGHT CROSS, and Rhino was bleeding. He advanced again, and it was a lead right hook that got him on the chin. Rhino was having a hard time breathing. He came at Joey again and it was more of the same. Rhino looked at his buddies who were surrounded by Joey's friends. He turned back to Joey and said, "That's it, I cannot breathe." "Fine but understand every time I see you, I am going to kick your ass. Got it?" "Yes, I got it" and the group dispersed. As they headed back to the carnival Joey said, "Can I have my animals back?" They all laughed and headed to Chuckle Luck.

Joey's summer routine was a teenage boy's delight. Baseball, basketball, and girls. Annette's house had become a regular hang-out in the evenings. Moans was there constantly. Annette would be the first girl he ever slept with, and he did so as often as possible. It was like a party every evening. There was a steady stream of girls who hung out there as well. They played albums and danced. On weekends they would go to dances that were held at the different V.F.W. Halls throughout Parma. These dances were packed. Lots of girls and many groups of guys that were prevalent throughout the Parma neighborhoods. Fights erupted regularly but the dancing went on.

Joey had become attracted to a neighborhood girl who had just started to hang out at Annette's. Her name was Violet and Joey thought she was very sexy. The first time that they were necking at Annette's she took his hand and put it under her shirt. She had nothing on. He said to himself, this girl is a keeper. She was. For about three weeks....and then again, he would move on. Not quite knowing why but he just did.

In late July, Joey and Inky went to take the written part of the driver's test that would enable them to have earned their temporary driver's license. The kids called it their temps. Both boys passed missing one question apiece. Now it would be time for each of them to find someone who would teach them how to drive so that they could take their driving test and earn their regular driver's license. It would take Inky about three weeks, and it would take Joey about 6 months. Moans had already earned his regular driver's license but didn't have his own car yet.

TWO TYPES OF JAIL

Trouble came their way near the end of summer. As usual, they were at Annette's. At about 11:30 at night, a boy they called The Hut showed up in his car. He was with Roger who Joey had not seen for a long time. They walked down the stairs to a basement filled with loud music and dancing. They greeted one another, and The Hut immediately started leering at the girls, Violet in particular. Joey went over and sat next to Violet who got up and sat on his lap. After about thirty minutes Roger said "The Hut and I are going to the reservoir and drive on the grass in his Old's. Does anyone want to go?" Six of the ten guys there said "OK". They kissed the girls they were with goodbye and piled in the car. The reservoir was about two square miles of flat grass. In the daytime, kids were always playing there. Cars were strictly prohibited from entering. The Hut told the guys to get out while he eased his car over the curb. Roger got back inside. The rest of the guys got on top of the car and held on to the roof or wherever they could get a grip. The Hut left his lights off so not to attract attention and began driving in a pitch-black night, on a field of grass that had six guys hanging from the roof. He started driving pretty slow but after about ten yards he started to pick up speed. When Joey heard Roger yell out the window "YEEEHAAA" he knew it was time to get off. As The Hut accelerated Joey yelled "SCREW THIS" and let go. He hit the ground and rolled and continued laying there and he watched the silhouettes of his friends, one by one, letting go of their grip. As all six were laying on the ground, The Hut was going at least 30 miles an hour. Suddenly there were red flashing lights pulling up on the grass. Moans yelled "Cops," but they all had seen the lights and were up and running. As they ran Joey yelled "split up" and immediately Moans yelled, "meet at Annette's." There were many different exits from the reservoir leading to side streets that they could use to get to Annette's house, so they split up and ran. Joey found himself paired with Fritz. They chose the longest route which was even made longer since every time a car came down the street the two would hide in shrubbery or behind a tree. They headed toward Ridge Road and then cut up the side streets. As they came around the corner which was about fifty feet from Annette's they saw a somewhat crowded front yard. All the guys had made it back except The Hut and Roger. His buddies were with their girls and Violet ran to Joey, jumped, and hugged him. They kissed for a while and then Annette said in a loud voice "YOU GUYS HAVE TO GET THE HELL OUT OF HERE my mother gets off work in 20 minutes." The boys looked at each other and Moans said "where can we go?" Annette said, "you can stay here Moans, but the rest have to go." Moans quickly responded, "NO WAY I go where they go." There was silence while all were thinking of what they could do. Fritz said "My cousin Hank lives right around the corner; he has a car. I am going to get him. Two minutes later, Hank's white Oldsmobile convertible came flying around the corner with Fritz in the front seat. Hank sometimes hung out with these guys but wasn't exactly a regular and not very well-liked. He said, "my parents belong to a country club in Ravenna, we can spend the rest of the night there." "Great," said Big Jim "Maybe we can play croquet or something" and headed towards the car with the rest of the group following. "WHOA!" said Hank in a loud voice. "I can only take four of you, my cousin and three others. I do not want six guys tearing up my upholstery." SILENCE.... Both the guys and girls stood somewhat dumbfounded. Annette ended the silence with "YOU GUYS GOT TO BE OUT OF HERE IN ABOUT 5 MINUTES." With this, Joey walked up to the driver's side of the car and said, "How about this Hank? I drag you out of the car, we all beat the shit out of you, tear up your upholstery and take your car anyway." Hank looked at Fritz who said, "LET THEM IN AND LET'S GET OUT OF HERE." They kissed their girls goodbye and headed to Ravenna.

The last hour had been a non-stop adrenaline rush so when Big Jim started to lead the song "Ninety-nine Bottles of Beer On The Wall" five other voices yelled immediately "SHUT UP" and he did. They reached the country club in about 45 minutes. There was a gate, and it was half-open. Fritz jumped out of the car and opened it all the way. There were no streetlights in the driveway, so Hank drove with his dim lights on. He drove to the back end of the country club by the pool area and pulled his car up next to the locker room. As they headed inside, he said, "We shouldn't turn the lights on, so use your lighters to see." The lighters flickered, and they all sat down on the floor in silence. In a few seconds, the silence was broken by laughter that became contagious. Hank kept schussing them and each time he did the laughter got louder. Big Jim said, "Hey guys this is better than sleeping out." Again, his comment was met with a massive "SHUT UP." They sat in the dark and talked about all sorts of things that fifteen- and sixteen-year-old boys would talk about. Lots of questions were directed at Moans regarding getting laid. Being the only one of them who had ever done so he was considered an expert on the subject. Once that conversation began the questions started and went on for a while. Fritz asked, "Moans do you wear a rubber?" Keith followed with "How does it feel to wear a rubber?" Big Jim asked, "do you keep your eyes open while you are on top of her?" That one drew one big almost in unison "SHUT UP" Joey asked, "do you only do it lying down?" This was one of the few that Moans would answer with "No." Joey quickly followed up with "what other ways have you done it?" Moans replied, "standing up from behind and sitting on a chair." Big Jim asked, "The next time you do it can I watch?" Joey said, "Guys 1, 2, 3" and this time in complete unison came "SHUT UP." Unbeknownst to them all while this revelry was going on, back in Parma the police had begun questioning Roger and The Hut. They were questioning Roger as they wrote a ticket for The Hut. Roger had been a friend of Joey's since he was six years old but tonight that friendship was about to end. It seems that one of the questions they had asked Roger was who was with him. Roger had answered them by saying "Joey DeTorre" to which the policeman responded with the ever-famous question "The fireman's kid?" "Yea," said Roger. When the police were done writing the ticket one of the officers drove over to Big Joe's house at about three in the morning. Both mom and Big Joe came to the door fearing the worst. The officer told them what had happened and said to Big Joe "you might want to get your son home if you can before he gets in more trouble." Big Joe said thanks to the officer and started getting dressed. Mom asked, "where are you going?" "I am going over to Annette's to see if Joey is there and then I will bring him home." When he got to Annette's the girls were all sitting on the porch. Big Joe asked them where his son was. Violet said they all had been there, but they had left. "Where did he go?" Annette quickly said, "we don't know they didn't say." He then asked was anyone hurt. "No, they were all alright." "Any idea where they might have gone?" Annette's answer again was "no they didn't tell us anything." "OK thanks," he said and left. Big Joe returned home to a worried wife. He told her that the girls said that no one was hurt but they didn't know where they had gone. Mom quickly said "They were lying, " His dad said "I know" we will see in the morning. He will be fine." Mom followed him to bed while saying "I hope so."

Meanwhile, as the fellas were grilling Moans about the birds and the bees car lights appeared to be pulling into the country club. Hank quickly said, "shut up and put out your cigarettes." The boys sat very still in the pitch-black locker room. They were perfectly quiet as the car went by them. They sat that way for over ten minutes, and they started to think any danger must have passed. Suddenly the light switch was turned on and there stood two policemen. "Holy Shit" said one of the officers and they both pulled their pistols out and pointed them at the group. All the hands immediately were raised high in the air. "What the hell do you guys think you are doing here. Stand up and put your hands against the lockers. Don't even think about turning around." Joey was thinking, is this really happening. I am standing with my hands against a locker room wall while two cops have their guns pointed at me. The officer said to his partner officer "call for two more cars to come here." He then asked again "what are you doing here?" Hank started to turn towards him, and the officer said very loudly "DO NOT TURN AROUND. KEEP YOUR HANDS ON THE LOCKERS AND TELL ME FROM THERE." Hank did as he was told and then explained to the police that his parents were members and they had nothing else to do so they came here to wait for the pool to open. They were just sitting around talking. That's all. As he finished two more police cars pulled in this time with their flashers on. Four more officers came in and they all barely fit in the room. They started to pull out their weapons but the officer in charge said, "don't" and then said to the boys, "Keep your hands up, turn towards us, and sit straight down." The boys did exactly as they were told. He then said, "you can put your hands down." The police decided they would bring them to the station. They put the boys in the police cruisers and had someone call the club manager to see if they wanted to press charges. As the police cars started to pull out of the club the procession of the three police cars with two boys in each car stopped. A car was pulling into the club lot as the police cars were pulling out. They stopped to talk. Their conversation lasted for some time. Hank who was in the back seat with Joey said "I bet we are going to be let go. That is the manager talking to the police." The officer driving said to Hank and Joey. "You might be allowed to leave. That's what that conversation is about." The conversation went on for about twenty minutes when the officer in the front car got out of his vehicle and walked back to the car Joey was in. He said to the driver "we are taking them in and booking them. The manager was trying to get ahold of the owner but there was no answer. So, in we go." The officer said, "Sorry fellas, but you heard the man."

They were not put in cuffs, but they were searched, and each had to put their belongings in a large envelope with their name on it. They were then taken to three rather large holding cells and in each was a picnic table. Two boys in each cell. The last two to be brought to their cells were Keith and Fritz. The officer who accompanied them said, "We are still trying to get in touch with the owners. We will let you know." It was now six in the morning. The boys could see each other as the cells were lined up three in a row. Keith was standing in the middle of his cell just staring at the picnic table while the others were talking in low voices to each other. All at once Keith jumped up on top of the table in his cell and started singing "JAILHOUSE ROCK" at the top of his lungs. Big Jim immediately started clapping in time and soon THE WHOLE PURPLE GANG was participating. The revelry took up right where it had left off before the police had shown up. They were all laughing, singing, and having a good time. At 9:30, an officer came downstairs to their cells and said, "I am glad you all are enjoying yourselves." We still haven't been able to contact the owners so because you all are minors, we are going to release you in the custody of your parents or guardians. They are being called now, and when each of your parents arrives you will be released. Try and keep the noise down." And he walked back up the stairs. By ten-thirty, Joey, Keith, and Fritz were the only three guys left in their cells. When the officer came down again, he called Joey's name saying his dad was here to pick him up. The fun was over. He picked up his envelope that had all his belongings and then walked to the car with his dad who was noticeably angry. They got in the car but before his dad put the key in the ignition he turned to Joey and said "I have been looking for you all night. Your mom was worried sick. A Parma police officer that I know came by the house and told me about your escapades at the reservoir and that I should try and find you and bring you home. I went to Annette's then to Manners as well as Bearden's. Both were already closed so I went home and told your mom you were ok and probably would be home in the morning. Then we got the call from Ravenna police and here I am." Joey said "Dad I am so.... His dad immediately said, "DO NOT SAY ANOTHER WORD OR I WILL BEAT YOUR ASS RIGHT HERE IN THE POLICE PARKING LOT." Joey wisely chose silence. The drive home was about forty minutes, and he knew the worst was yet to come. His mind was filled with all sorts of thoughts. But there was one that he just could not get out of his mind. His dad was looking for him and even went to Annette's. How did the police know he was involved in the reservoir fiasco? By the time he got home, he thought he knew. He would take care of it later but for now, he had to make things right with his parents. They got home and mom was waiting at the door. Her eyes were puffy, and you could tell she had been crying but you could also tell she was very angry. Before Joey could say a word, she said, "get out of those clothes and get in the shower. You have been in jail all night. We will sit and talk after you clean yourself up." Joey considered telling her how clean the jail cells were but the look in his father's eyes said keep your mouth shut. Up until now, this had been an exciting adventure but after seeing his parents, he felt awful. He also knew there was more to come. He showered and got dressed and headed to the kitchen where both his parents were waiting. The rest of his siblings were conveniently playing outside but he knew Grace was hiding somewhere so she could hear what was going on. Both mom and dad talked to him for about forty-five minutes. Asking him all kinds of questions and telling him how disappointed they were. Dad talked about how embarrassed he was that the Parma police had come to their house to tell him about his son, AGAIN. In the lecture dad mentioned that your buddy Roger told them who else was involved. The officers knew me so one of them came over to tell your mother and I. Joey had already figured that out and sat there in silence. As the conversation was ending his mom said "your punishment is that you are grounded for the rest of the summer. You can go to baseball practice as well as your games. You will do your paper route and come home immediately after. I have talked to Moans, Inky, and Big Jim's mothers and they are all doing the same thing. We are finished here." Joey asked if he could go to his room and both parents said to go ahead. As he went up the stairs, he realized that the punishment they were talking about was at least 6 weeks and then some. YIKES! He lay down and quickly fell asleep. He slept until midafternoon. When he got up and went downstairs the atmosphere was different. His brothers and sisters were playing, and his mom had sandwiches for him. She had become much more relaxed. Dad was on his lunch hour and was sitting at the kitchen table. He too seemed much more relaxed. Joey instantly decided to take a chance. He looked at both parents and asked, "Am I allowed to have phone calls?" Dad answered immediately "yes." Joey thought one down two to go. "Am I allowed to play Wiffle ball and or basketball in the backyard?" This time it was his mom who answered immediately "Yes." Joey thought two down and one to go. He also was realizing that his mom and dad had anticipated these questions and already knew what was acceptable to them. Okay, he said to himself here we go, the big one, and asked, "Am I allowed visitors?" This time his mother and father looked at each other before answering. Joey thought they may have disagreed with the answer to his question. Mom answered "Yes." Holy Moly, Joey thought three for three. He said "Thank you and I am very sorry. I have to go get ready to deliver my papers."

The papers were dropped on the corner. The truck driver waved to Joey and moved on. Joey put half his papers in the bag and delivered them to the lower half of the street first. He worked his way back up to his house and reloaded his bag with the rest of his papers and then did the top half of the street. There would be no help for him, so the route would take longer than normal. As he got to the corner, he looked at Vic's and decided to take a walk to the front of the building, not expecting that any of the guys would be there as they were all being punished too. As he turned the corner at the end of the building the whole gang was there including Keith's girl, OOO(h). All of them. Laughing and carrying on as normal. Joey was stunned. He immediately said, "HEY I THOUGHT YOU ALL WERE BEING PUNISHED." They all laughed. Fritz said, "no way my dad just laughed." Keith said, "my aunt and uncle didn't care. My uncle was just pissed that he had to drive all the way down to

Ravenna." Joey looked at Moans, Inky, and Big Jim "what about you three Jamokes?" They laughed. "Our mom's reconsidered and let us out." Big Jim said "Jamokes? That's an Uncle Eddy word." And they all laughed. Moans asked Joey "you are in for the rest of the summer? That is more than 6 weeks. A bit much don't ya think?" "FUCK YES but that's the way it is." On that note, Keith said "We have to go. We are going to the show later to see the Elvis movie where he sings "*JAILHOUSE ROCK*" see you guys later." As they walked away Big Jim said "OOOOOO(h)" and the gang started to laugh again. Joey said, "gotta go, see you all when I see you." Big Jim said, "WAIT." Joey stopped and turned. "Can I have Violet while you are in jail?" Moans saw it coming and quickly got in the way saying, "Let it go man let it go." Joey stopped and laughed saying "you're right Moans" and then turned to Big Jim and said "if you can get her, you can have her. Gotta go."

The next day he spent playing fast pitch whiffle ball with his brother Douglas. He then worked on his basketball skills and did his isometrics and lifting. He called Violet and they talked for a while. He told her he would not be around for six weeks. She responded by saying "Annette's isn't the same without you being there." "I will call you tomorrow and they said good night." Joey spent the night watching TV in Auntie Olie's patio. After one night he already was losing his mind. The next day was more of the same. Whiffle ball, basketball, and paper route. Two events broke the routine. While Joey was playing whiffle ball with Douglas, Roger stopped over. He said, "I heard you are grounded." Joey said, "you heard right. Why did you squeal?" "I didn't squeal I just told them who I was there with." "You don't think that's squealing?" "Joey, the cops put a gun to my head. I had to tell them." Joey stared at him to see if he was joking. Seeing that Roger was seriously lying Joey led with his right and caught him under his eye. Roger was not totally stupid. He was about twenty-five pounds heavier and three inches taller than Joey. He went right at Joey and took him to the ground. Douglas ran into the house yelling "Joey is fighting in our backyard." His dad was off work that day and came running out. Roger had Joey in a headlock while Joey was punching him as hard as he could in the stomach. Big Joe yelled, "That's ENOUGH." Both boys stopped immediately. Big Joe said, "Roger go home." As Roger walked away Big Joe looked at his son and said, "Don't think for one minute I don't know what that was about" and he went back inside and told his wife everything was OK. That evening Joey was in Auntie Olie's patio watching TV when he heard his mother's voice saying, "Joey you have a visitor." Joey got up and went outside the patio. Mom was with Violet. She turned to Violet and said "Nice meeting you. Joey, Violet goes home at 11:00." Both Joey and Violet said OK as his mom walked away. "Hey, great seeing you. Come on in." They both sat on the chaise lounge and soon they were lying next to one another and soon after they were intertwined. Shortly before 11:00 Violet said "I have to go; I don't want your mom getting upset. Can I come back tomorrow?" "Of course," he answered. They kissed goodbye and she headed home. Shortly his mom came out to check and said, "nice girl." Her oldest son replied "Yep, thanks for letting her visit" and he laid back down to watch the late show. The next night Joey was sitting on the patio and feeling sorry for himself. He couldn't help but think that this was just like being in jail and how horrible it would be to spend your life in prison. He was having a real problem dealing with the fact that after being grounded for only three days he still had almost six weeks left. While thinking of these unpleasant thoughts a voice from the darkness outside of the patio said "Hi." It was Violet. "Can I come in?" she asked. "OF COURSE, GET IN HERE." They hugged, kissed, and laid down together on the chaise lounge. About five minutes later the patio door opened and Joey and Violet immediately broke from their clinch. The Hut walked in, said hello, and sat down to watch television. Joey and Violet said nothing while they both looked at each other and lay back down to watch the television show that had caught the attention of Clevelanders of all ages, GHOULARDI. The Hut pretended to watch the TV, but he couldn't stop leering at Violet. Finally, Joey stood up and said to The Hut "let's go outside I want to talk to you." Joey started to walk towards the side street where The Hut's car was parked, and The Hut followed him. Joey turned to him and said, "MAN YOU HAVE TO LEAVE." The Hut quickly asked, "Why, I didn't tell on you Roger did." Joey said "I know and now you have just told on Roger. That problem has already been addressed. However, if you do not leave and my parents see you here when I am supposed to be grounded, I will never be let out again." The Hut said "jeez Joey I am sorry. I will go. Is Violet going to leave also? Does she need a ride?" "No Hut. Violet and I are going to get married, and my mom said she can visit any time she wants." "Oh, ok. Congratulations I wish you both luck" and he turned and got in his car and left. When Joey got back in the patio Violet was standing and waiting for him and asked him "How did you get him to leave?" I told him that if my parents see him, I might be grounded forever. He asked if you needed a ride home and I said yea she does. "WHAT" she screamed. Joey laughed and said, "HEY, I am only kidding." "You better be. What did you really tell him?" I told him that you were allowed to stay because we are going to get married." Violet was startled again and looked at Joey and said, "we are only 16, I cannot do that." "I know that. I can't either. But you see The Hut has an I.Q. of about sixteen so he completely bought in and said congratulations to us both." By now they were both laughing hard, and Joey walked her to the front of his house and kissed her goodbye. As she left, she told Joey that she had to go away for the weekend with her parents, but she will see him on Sunday, Monday at the latest. On Sunday morning after the family went to Mass, they all sat down for a breakfast of bacon and eggs. While they were eating dad said we have something to say. He looked at his wife, and said, go ahead. Mom looked at her oldest son and said, "we are ending your grounding starting tomorrow." Dad quickly added "you handled the punishment without complaining and you apologized at least five times. We think you learned your lesson." Joey was ecstatic. He got up and hugged his mom, grabbed his dad's hand, and shook it saying to both "THANK YOU THANK YOU THANK YOU" and for no reason at all started doing a new dance called Southside in the kitchen. Grace immediately stood up and danced with him. The family laughed and clapped, and Joey was a free man again. What a great life.

That night as Joey lay in bed staring at the ceiling, he was thinking, did Roger really think that I would buy into his lame-ass story that they put a gun to his head. My oh my, if one week of being kept in my house is that bad, I certainly never want to go to prison. I need to start making better choices.

A SUMMER OF WINNING AND LOSING

The next day before he went to baseball practice for the Parma ALL STAR Travel team Joey sat down to a bowl of Sugar Frosted Flakes with Tony the Tiger on the front of the box. He said to his mom and dad "I FEEL GRRRRRREAT." They both were laughing when Joey said, "I have something to tell you." Both mom and dad looked up from their breakfast expecting the worst. "I am going to try out for the varsity football team at Latin. I weigh almost 165 pounds now. I have been doing isometrics as well as lifting weights. I know I am as good as a lot of those guys and the coaches haven't seen me hit anyone. I think I can make the team." Both mom and Big Joe expressed their happiness, and both told him how proud they were of him. Dad immediately asked if he had been doing any running in his conditioning program to which Joey responded that he has been running at baseball. His dad said, "you still have about 10 days before August 1st and tryouts begin, I would use that time to build up your legs." "I will, thanks, dad. I have to go to practice now." He hugged his dad and kissed his mom saying "See ya later Alligator" to which his mom said, "after a while crocodile." He laughed as Moans was beeping his horn outside to pick him up for baseball. When his mom was sure he had left she said to Big Joe "well what do you think?" Big Joe hesitated for a minute while he thought about her question. Mom grew impatient and finally said "WELL?" Big Joe said "Phyllis, you are not going to like what I think but here goes. I am positively sure he is good enough. There is also no doubt in my mind that he is tough enough. He has gained at least 30 pounds since the last time they cut him. You can see that in the way he is hitting the ball in baseball. Those bloopers and weak singles that he was hitting two years ago are now line drives and some have reached the fence. He made that ALL-STAR Team not only on his fielding but now the kid can hit as well. But honestly Phyllis, he's in the wrong school. I knew this when he chose Latin, but it was his choice. If he had gone to Padua or the new public school Valley Forge, he would be a three-sport starter. Latin gets their kids from the entire city of Cleveland plus Joey hasn't played Freshman or J.V. also add the fact that he is not the kind of kid that those coaches like. He wears his hair like Elvis Presley, he has gotten lots of demerits, and on top of all that he beat up their starting J.V. tailback in a fight last spring. I am pretty sure that he is not what those coaches are looking for. His only chance is they have contact drills before they cut him. If not, he won't make the team again. Sorry, but you asked."

Joey got home from practice and got ready to do his paper route. He paid Douglas and two of his friends a dime each and the route was done in less than 30 minutes. When they were done, he headed to Vic's to see if anyone was hanging out there. As he walked around the corner all his buddies were there waiting for him and started cheering and clapping. "Welcome back," said Moans, and the revelry began. Big Jim said, " I heard you had some words with that squealer Roger." Keith quickly added. "I heard it was way more than words. He said he kicked your ass, but I will tell you his face looked pretty bad and yours doesn't." Joey changed the subject by asking, "What's going on tonight?" "Welcome home party tonight at Annette's." "GREAT, I AM THERE." "Violet is chomping at the bit," said Moans and they all laughed, and the group started to break up and head home. "See you all at about 7:30" and off they went. That night they had lots of fun as usual. Joey told them all that he was going to try and play football at Latin AGAIN. All of his buddies nodded in agreement. The only one who seemed to be unhappy was Violet. But Joey didn't seem to notice. The group broke up and headed home at about one a.m. with Joey reminding Big Jim and Moans that they had their first tournament ALL-STAR game tomorrow night in Euclid. Moans said "can't wait" while Big Jim just grumbled. "What's wrong?" asked Moans. "I am not the starting pitcher in the opening game," whined Big Jim. "Don't sweat it man you will pitch game two. It is a one-and-out tourney, so we need to win them both to play in the winner's bracket. "Don't be a baby." The next day they won the first game and Big Jim pitched a shutout in the second game. Moans hit a grand slam and they were in the winner's bracket.

FIGHT NIGHT

That Saturday a girl named Charise that they had gone to school with at St. Charles and occasionally hung around Annette's invited Joey and the boys to a party at her house. No dates were allowed. Joey, Fritz, Moans, Keith, Big Jim, Hank, Fuco and Inky all went to the party together and there were more girls than boys. Charise had a crush on Joey and her girlfriend Rita felt the same towards Moans. There was dancing and laughing as the boys found themselves pairing up with the different girls who were there. Just as Charise was talking to Joey about going upstairs a boy named Ralph came down the stairs and said, "turn the music off and listen up." Everyone there knew him from school. They turned the record player off and listened. He looked right at Joey and then looked around the whole room. He said in a very loud voice. "MY BUDDIES AND I ARE WAITING FOR YOU AT THE CEMETERY DOWN THE STREET. IF YOU ALL AREN'T A BUNCH OF PUSSIES THEN MEET US THERE IN FIFTEEN MINUTES." He turned again to look at Joey and left. There was silence. The guys as well as girls knew exactly who his friends were. Charise broke the silence by saying, "please no fighting especially here." The boys knew that they had been called out and they would be heading to the cemetery, but the surprise was that they didn't have a beef with these kids. Actually, they had played ball with them at St. Charles and the one kid's father was an assistant coach in football with Big Joe. Moans looked at Joey and said, "LET'S GET THESE GUYS." Joey would use that phrase the rest of his life and every time he did, he thought of Moans. It was a quick ten-minute walk to the cemetery. Inky immediately headed upstairs to use the phone and called his older brother. When the guys got to the cemetery they were stunned. There were all kinds of kids standing against the cemetery fence. The boys who had issued the challenge were already inside the fence which was about twelve yards high and had barbed wire on the top. As he walked toward the fence Joey heard someone call his name. He looked and saw Dwight standing alongside the fence waving and he walked over to him. Dwight and Joey shook hands and Dwight asked "do you guys need any help? It seems that you are outnumbered." Joey said "no it is supposed to be a fair fight. Stick around and we will talk afterward." As he headed to the fence he stopped and turned around and said to Dwight can you hold my white-on-white shirt for me? Dwight responded, "no problem but how about those nice tailor-made pants and those Stetson shoes?" Joey laughed and said, "you want me to fight in my underwear?" They both laughed and Joey walked up to the fence and climbed over along with the rest of his buddies. Dwight was right, they did have two guys more than he and his buddies had brought along with them. Joey was surprised that when he saw the extra two guys, they were twin brothers he had hung around with at St. Charles. They started to pair off and Big Jim yelled, "I knew you pussies would not fight us fairly. You knew you needed those extra two guys." The crowd was bigger now that the girls from the party had arrived. Hank, who was outside the fence yelled "WAIT I will help you even it up" and started to climb the fence. The problem was Hank's arm was BROKEN and in a cast. As the boys started to square off a '57 Chevy came screaming down the street next to the cemetery. The driver slammed on his breaks right next to the fence. The doors opened and Inky and his older brother Dale jumped out of the car. Inky saw Dwight and walked over to him while Dale ran up to the fence, climbed over, and started screaming, "OK, OK, WHO WANTS TO FIGHT? WHO WANTS TO FIGHT?" He looked at the twins who had not paired up with anyone and screamed. "YOU TWO WANT TO FIGHT, LET'S GO. LET'S GO MAN." The twins said, "NO, NO, we are just watching." "GOOD" Dale yelled, "WATCH FROM THE OTHER SIDE." The twins climbed back over the fence and now the fight was even. Joey yelled to Hank, "you sit out it's a fair fight and we don't need any help with these punks." As the fight began Dale climbed over the fence and watched. The battle was on. Joey squared off with Frank, the son of Big Joe's assistant football coach, and immediately started with jab, jab, right cross landing all three punches. Suddenly someone jumped on his back and the two boys took Joey to the ground. Joey yelled, "I got two on me, I got two on me." Someone yelled, "who is the pussy now?" Almost immediately he felt the extra body being pulled from his back. He went right back to work on Frank and nailed him two more times. Frank tackled him but Joey landed on top and ripped his t-shirt, he had his knees on Frank's shoulders and was getting ready to punch him again when Frank said, "kind of like football used to be ain't it?" Joey looked at him and the anger left him. He liked this kid and had no beef with him. He had him pinned and had him bleeding. He had no desire to keep beating on him. Joey said, "yea and you weren't any good at that either." In the next moment, someone outside the fence yelled "COPS" and two squad cars with their lights flashing and sirens blaring were racing down the street. Someone yelled "FENCE IN THE BACK" and they all took off towards the back fence. Joey had no time to get his shirt and was running full speed in his Stetson shoes and his tailor-made pants. He reached the fence on the run and jumped halfway up and started to climb. As he neared the top, he felt someone climbing right behind him. He turned to look, and it was Hank trying to climb with his broken arm in a cast. Joey looked at him and said, "what the hell are you doing here?" Hank answered somewhat out of breath "Playing tiddly-winks what else would I be doing here?" Joey laughed and said, "be careful this is tricky up here" as he climbed over the barb wire top. He was very careful to not rip his tailor-made pants or cut his chest open on the barbed wire. Hank said "don't worry" as Joey jumped from the top and landed safely in bushes that surrounded the cemetery. Hank followed him as Joey watched with a nervous eye. He got to the top. Joey said in a loud voice "STAY AWAY FROM THE BOARD THAT IS PROPPED NEXT TO THE FENCE IT ISN'T STABLE." Hank said, "don't worry I have climbed a lot of fences" and he stepped on the board to balance his jump. The board moved and Hank fell, face first. Joey tried to break his fall and they both tumbled into the bushes. Joey asked, "you OK?" Hank quickly answered, "NO. I think I broke my ribs, and my nose is bleeding." Joey helped him as he struggled to get up and Hank said "listen I parked my car on this street. I have to go get x-rays." Joey said, "OK I will help you." Hank said "NO I will do it by myself. You stay in the backyards and head up the street. I will be alright. If you stay in the backyards, you can make it back to the party without getting caught. We will meet up later." With that, he walked out of the backyard and headed up the street to his car. Joey was thinking, what next. He too headed up the street but traveled through backyards while hiding in the bushes. He had traveled through one backyard when he heard some rustling in the bushes that he was in. He thought just what I need, a dog. He became dead silent and didn't move. He crouched in the bushes for a minute that seemed like an hour. He didn't hear anything, so he carefully proceeded forward. Suddenly a hand shot out of the bushes. Joey jumped and a voice said, "here, take this." It was his shirt, and it was Dwight who was in the bushes. Joey said "thanks" and started to talk but Dwight interrupted saying, "I live right around the corner. Stay in the back yards until you get to 54th street. Cross the street and you will be back at the party." Joey was saying thanks and starting to make conversation. When he got no answers to his questions, he realized that Dwight had taken off. It was like he vanished. As Joey made his way through the backyards, he was thinking that when we get older that sneaky fucking kid is going to definitely become my lawyer. He would never know, although he had asked him many times, how Dwight knew about the fight, or where to find him in the bushes, but just like later in life, Dwight was always there for him.

Joey returned to the party and walked in the open side door. As he walked downstairs, he could hear the music playing loudly but when he got down there no one was dancing. The basement was packed. The guys they had just fought were all there. They were sitting on one side of the room opposite Moans and company. Frank was standing in the middle of the room and Joey found himself standing right next to him. He quickly assessed the room and saw no hostility in anyone's eyes. He glanced at Moans who just shrugged. Rita was sitting on his lap. His focus then went to Frank who was trying to make light of an awkward situation. His shirt was ripped and dirty. It had grass stains all over it. His right eye was swelling, and his face was bruising. His nose had dried blood under it. As Joey continued to look around the room, he noticed that none of his buddies had any bumps or bruises showing. Charise walked over and stood between Frank and Joey. As she took Joey's arm in hers, she said "PLEASE NO FIGHTING." As Joey was about to say something the side doorbell rang, and it was the police. Two cruisers had pulled in the drive. Two officers were coming down the stairs while two stood outside by the front door. Joey thought here we go again. I am about to get a life sentence of never being allowed out of my house again. The officers entered the basement and the first one asked, "whose house is this?" Charise answered "Mine, I am having a party. There is no booze just some dancing and some laughs." "We heard you guys had a fight here." "No sir," said Charise "there has been no fighting here." "Yea I know," said the officer "but there was across the street in the cemetery." He looked at Joey and asked, "were you fighting?" "No sir," said Joey. As he spoke, he held his arms out to show how clean his clothes were and said, "does it look like I was fighting?" The officer then looked Frank up and down and said, "tell me you weren't fighting." Frank said, "no I was not. We were having a scavenger hunt and that's how I got looking like this." The girls giggled, the boys chuckled, and the two officers grinned and then said in a loud voice "HERE IS THE DEAL. THIS PARTY IS OVER. I WANT THE BOYS TO LEAVE TWO BY TWO. IF YOU DROVE THEN GET IN YOUR CAR WHEN YOU GET OUTSIDE. He looked at Frank and said "LET'S START WITH SCAVENGER BOY. GET OUT AND IF YOU COME BACK, YOU WILL BE ARRESTED." The boys all left two by two. When they got outside, they piled in Moans '57 Chevy and drove to the Red Barn, got some burgers, and stood outside talking about the night's escapades. Joey said, "man I thought they were going to say it is the Fireman's kid again and I would be in my house for the rest of my life." They talked for a while and finally Big Jim said, "please take me home we have a game tomorrow, and I am pitching." Fritz, who had heard what happened to his cousin said, "I need to check on Hank. I will let you know how he is in the morning." They all left. Joey walked the block to his house, got home, and went to bed.

The next day Joey was up early. He was helping his dad scrape their house. He had a game at two o'clock so he wanted to get as much done as he could before he left. He was up on the scaffold making good progress when a car pulled up to the side of his house. He took a quick glance and saw that it was not a police car, so he kept on scraping. As he was working, suddenly he had an urge to turn around, so he did and there stood Frank's dad staring at him. Joey stared back and said, "Hi Coach" and kept on scraping the house.

"I heard you had some fun last night," said Frank's dad. Joey turned and looked at him and said "I guess so." "I heard you kicked the crap out of my son." Joey turned again and said "I never kicked him" and kept on scraping. "Is your dad home?" "Yes, he is, go on in." Joey kept on scraping saying to himself, this shit never ends. A half-hour later Frank's dad came around the back of the house and said to Joey, "good luck in your game today." Joey responded with "Thanks Coach" and watched him walk away and get in his car. Shortly afterward, Big Joe came out and said, "that's enough son, you have a game to play. Your mom fixed a sandwich for you. Go eat." An hour later Moans was beeping his horn and Joey ran out, got in the car, and turned the radio up to full blast as The Kingsmen were singing "LOUIE, LOUIE." Joey looked at Moans and said, "LET'S GET THESE GUYS" and off they went. Joey's buddies, Inky, Fritz,

Keith, and even Hank showed up for the game. Violet and Annette also showed up. Joey's mom made sandwiches for the team while his dad bought a case of Pepsi for after the game. His brothers, Douglas, and Lawrence were also there playing catch and Wiffle ball in the outfield. Big Jim pitched another shut-out and the boys continued their advance in the winner's bracket. This wild summer still had four weeks left.

The next night as Joey lay in bed staring at the ceiling, and he was replaying the events of the last two days, his first thought was how could the only guy who didn't fight come out hurt much worse than all the guys that fought put together? Barely awake, Dwight popped into his head handing him his shirt. He sighed and said, how did that guy do that, he never ceases to amaze me.

SOME GUYS NEVER LEARN

ootball practice started on the first Wednesday in August. Joey's mom had talked him into getting his hair cut. He listened and then decided to let his dad give him a buzz cut. Wednesday morning some guys who lived near State Road and also went to Latin picked him up to go to practice. They got there about 7:00 that morning and got dressed for the seven-thirty meeting in the gym. There were over one hundred kids there from grades ten through twelve. Coach explained the schedule for the week. Two-a-days were Wednesday, Thursday, and Friday. They would have only one practice on Saturday with the first cut list to be posted after it was over. Those that made the cut would start again with two practices on Monday. When the coach finished, they all jogged the two miles to Ambler Field. The morning practice was physically demanding. They were not yet in pads so there were no contact drills, but the conditioning drills dominated the first session. They finished two-and-one-half-hour practice with sprints up Ambler Hill. They were not allowed to drink water until they returned to school. They had to again jog the two miles back to Latin where they had about forty-five minutes to eat the lunch they had with them. Joey was trying out for defensive back and running back. On his jog back to school he knew he had made a couple of mistakes. He said to himself, you are an idiot. This is the Cathedral Latin varsity football team. They had played in the city championship game at Cleveland stadium thirteen times and had won twelve. Did he really think that the strength training he did this summer would be enough? Did he really think that the amount of running he was doing in baseball would be enough? He quickly became a lot less optimistic that he was going to make the team. He was also thinking that he made a mistake going out for running back. He was a Quarterback, that's what he had been his whole life and while he knew that Q.B. 1 was pretty good, he felt that he was way better than the kids that played behind him. If only I can make it to Monday. Contact would start then, and he felt that his stock would go up when they started to have contact drills.

The afternoon practice was more of the same. It seemed to him that Ambler Hill had gotten higher. He got home that night and ate dinner and his mom made him drink lots of water. He walked over to Annette's and stayed for about thirty minutes and left. Violet seemed hurt, but Joey said, "I am tired and sore, I am going home." After he left Violet said to Moans and Annette "I have never seen him like this. Do you think that something is wrong?" Moans said "Listen, what he is going through right now is extremely difficult both physically and mentally. He is a pretty tough kid, but this is different. He is trying to play football for a real school. It's not easy." Violet responded with tears in her eyes "I HOPE HE GETS CUT." "WHOA," said Moans "I wouldn't say that around Joey if I were you or he won't be the only one who gets cut." Violet again started to cry. Annette and some of the other girls started to console her and eventually, she stopped. They sat and talked for a bit and finally Big Jim said to her "Hey Vi, I am here for ya, and Joey had already told me that if I can get you to like me then he would let me have you." Immediately Violet burst into tears again. Much louder ones this time. Moans looked at Big Jim and said, "are you the biggest dumb ass I know or what?" Big Jim looked at him and said, "I guess so, how many dumb asses do you know that are taller than 6-feet 6-inches?" Moans looked at him and they both laughed, while Violet cried even harder.

For Joey, Thursday and Friday were exactly the same. He would get home, eat, lie down, and fall asleep. Violet would stop by and talk to his mom, but Joey was in his room and there would be no waking him. Saturday was here. One single practice and then the first cut list. If Joey could make the first cut, he knew he had a chance. There was an atmosphere of apprehension during Saturday's practice and when it was over the players hustled back to school to see the posted list. They were all somewhat surprised that it was already posted. They crowded together to see if their names were on it. There was both joy and sadness. When Joey saw his name on the list he turned and walked outside to wait by the car for the other guys to check and see if their names were there too. They came out and piled in the car. Of the six guys who were sharing the ride to practice together, Joey was the only one who had not played Freshman or J.V. The other five had played for 3 years. They were all cut except Todd who had started varsity as a sophomore. The 50-minute ride home was dead silent. When he walked in the door at home his mom and dad were waiting for him. All he said to them was "I GOT CUT....AGAIN" and went up to his room. Mom called the family when dinner was ready. The atmosphere which was usually boisterous and filled with laughter was somewhat subdued. Mom broke the silence saying to Joey "I almost forgot to tell you. Your baseball coach called and said to tell you that tomorrow you will have to catch both games of the double header. Cliff broke his hand during baseball practice this morning and he is out for the remainder of the season. He wanted to know if you would be up to it. Those are two huge games. Win them both and you guys will go to the Nationals. He wants you to call him." For the first time that evening, his eyes came up from his plate. His whole family was looking at him. His dad said, "Son if you can't, you can't. You have had a grueling four days." Joey got up and mom asked, "where are you going?" "To call my coach." came the response. About fifteen minutes later he returned to the dinner table and was very surprised to see the whole family still sitting there. He sat down and started to finish his Royal chocolate pudding. After his second spoonful, his mom said "Well?" Joey gave her a puzzled look and said, "well what?" Dad quickly interjected, "Your mom wants to know what you said to the coach and so do I." Joey was looking at his parents like they had three eyes. "Exactly?" he asked. "Yes," said his mom. "OK," I said "LET'S GET THESE GUYS, and then I said goodbye. I am still very sore. Do you mind if take a hot bath right now? I am really sore." "Sure, go ahead." After his bath, he told his parents he was going to lie down for a while. He did and he slept until seven-thirty the next morning.

The double header would start at 1 p.m. They needed to win both. Joey had breakfast and was about to take another hot bath when Moans called. "What's up, man? Are you OK?" "I am fine. Just a little bit sore." "WHEW, Big Jim is telling everyone that you were not going to play today." "You know better than that. Big Jim is a DILL ROD. What time are you guys picking me up?" "11:30, you sure you are OK?" "Hey" "What," said Moans" "LET'S GET THESE GUYS! See you at 11:30." Joey went and took another hot bath.

The next day Moans and Big Jim picked him up and headed for Brookside Park where the final games of the National qualifying tourney would be played. There would be four games played that day and the surviving team would travel to Florida to play for the national title. Joey was sore all over, but he knew it would get better as his body got loosened up. Big Jim was going on and on about how he should be pitching in the first game. His logic being if we lose, he doesn't get to pitch. He was actually making sense but finally, Moans yelled at him saying "WE AREN'T GOING TO LOSE. SO PLEASE SHUT UP." Big Jim did and two hours later the boys had won and advanced to the final game. Moans again was the hero with a four-for-four-game and three R.B.I.'s. Joey threw out two guys trying to steal but went hitless. J.W. the number two pitcher gave up three hits and one run. It was now Big Jim's turn. As they started to warm up for game two Joey was shocked to see Jebs on the other team playing third base. He walked over to him as they were getting done with infield practice and said "HEY MAN what are you doing. I thought you were playing for Parma Heights." "I was," said

Jebs, "but we lost and this team from Mentor who beat us picked me up so here I am." They both said, "good luck" and the game began. Mentor would be batting last. In the first inning, Parma scored three times and going into the bottom of the 7th led three to one. Big Jim was pitching well although Jebs had hit a home run for Mentor's only run so far. They were three outs away from going to play for a National Championship. Big Jim struck out the first batter but walked the second guy up. All of their family and friends were at the game yelling and cheering. Violet and her friends were all there also and were screaming on every pitch. The people rooting for Mentor were just as loud. Everyone was standing. Even Joey's two little brothers weren't running around anymore and were watching the game with interest. Big Jim walked the next batter and men were on first and second. He called time, and Joey went out to the mound. Jim was whining that he was tired. Very tired. Joey said, "look man we are 16 years old. 16-year-old boys don't get tired right? And besides, no one else can pitch. You are the man." Jim looked at him and then said, "I will be ok." and Joey returned to home plate. The next batter scorched a line drive down the third baseline. Moans dove to his right and made a spectacular diving catch, he jumped up and threw the ball to double the man off second, but the second baseman muffed the ball and it rolled into right field. Two outs and men on second and third. Joey yelled out to his teammates "ONE OUT AND WE ARE THERE. LET'S GET THESE GUYS." As he was heading back to home plate Coach Haskins called time out and headed to the mound. Joey saw him and sprinted towards him yelling "WAIT." When he got there, he said to him in a low voice so Big Jim could not hear them, "Coach I know what you want to do. Intentionally walk him, right?" "Yes" came his answer and Joey immediately followed up with "you are right BUT the batter after the guy we walk will be Jebs. Between you and me I don't think Big Jim can get him out." Haskins thought for a minute and finally said "no we walk this guy and pitch to Jebs." Joey said, "Ok coach, let's do it." They got to the mound and Coach Haskins explained what they were going to do. Big Jim looked at the on-deck circle and quickly said "Jebs is the next guy up." Joey looked at Haskins but didn't wait for him to speak. He looked at Big Jim and said "you struck him out twice already today. Do it one more time and I will have Violet put her tongue in your mouth." Both Big Jim and Coach Haskins burst out laughing. Big Jim said, "let's do it." They intentionally walked the next batter and Jebs came to the plate with the bases loaded. Joey looked at him and said, "you get all curve balls man" and Jebs laughed. The first pitch was a screaming fastball right by Jebs for STRIKE ONE. Same pitch on the next one and Jebs had no chance. STRIKE TWO. Joey watched as Jebs moved to the front of the plate, so he signaled for the fastball. This time, however, Big Jim was shaking him off. He signaled fastball again and he was shaken off again. "TIME OUT" screamed Joey and he went out to the mound. "Whatcha doing numb nuts. He has no chance at hitting your fast-ball. Throw it and let's go home." "Ok," said Jim, and Joey went back to the plate where he again signaled for the fastball. Again, Big Jim shook him off for the third time. Again, Joey yelled "time." By now the umpire was yelling and Haskins came out. He stood silently as Joey lit into Big Jim. "ARE YOU BRAIN DEAD. He is praying you throw a curve; he is waiting for it. He has moved all the way up in front of the plate. He has no chance of hitting the fastball." The umpire yelled, "OK COACH BREAK IT UP." Haskins looked at the two boys and said to Joey "I believe he should throw the pitch he wants. Joey stared at him incredulously for a second and headed back to home plate. The ump yelled "play ball" and Joey flashed the sign for the fastball. Big Jim shook his head yes and then fired his fastball right at Jebs. Jebs went to the ground and the pitch just missed him. Joey had a sick feeling in his stomach. He had seen Big Jim use this tactic before to set up his curve ball. The problem was that Jebs had seen it too and he started to move up even farther in the box. Joey sighed, hoped, then gave the signal for the fastball. Big Jim shook it off and Joey reluctantly gave the curve ball signal. Big Jim wound up and let it go. The ball had lots of spin and looked the size of the moon. It was heading right down the center of the plate. The idea of the pitch was to make it look like it was going to be a strike, but the ball would curve outside, and the batter would be swinging at a bad pitch. Joey knew that by standing further up in the box Jebs would be hitting the pitch before it broke away from him. As the ball got to the plate it seemed to hang there forever. Jebs swung and hit it off the fence in left field scoring both runs. Game over. Season over. Just like that.

The pain of losing would last a while, however, Joey and his buddies didn't speak much about the game. Summer was fading fast. Joey had ended it with Violet and when she had asked why he was unable to give her an answer. She was a tough girl so there were no tears, when she asked him if there was someone else Joey answered, "not that I know of." A frustrated Violet said "OK" and walked away wondering why? The strange thing was that Joey walked away wondering the same thing.

Later that night as Joey lay in bed staring at the ceiling he thought, almost out loud, I know Big Jim will never learn but I am stunned that a coach would not know better. He fell asleep but woke up numerous times that night and each time he would be thinking the same thoughts.

A WALK IN THE PARK

It was Labor Day. The last day of summer vacation. The boys had decided to go to Chippewa Lake Park. Chippewa Lake was an aging amusement park along the same lines as Euclid Beach and Geauga Lake Park. All three parks would find themselves closed within the next five years as a new major amusement park called Cedar Point would put them out of business. Inky had his parents' car and would drive, which made Moans very happy. Inky would also drive Joey and Moans along with Big Jim and Fritz. They all met at Joey's house and piled in the car. As they drove south down Pearl Road in Parma Heights police radar targeted Inky and asked him to pull over. Twenty minutes later they were on their way again with Inky the proud owner of his first speeding ticket. When they got to the park, they headed toward the roller coaster where they went for a couple of rides and then explored the rest of the park. Much to their surprise, there was a serious shortage of unattached girls, and they became bored. They decided to go home much earlier than they were anticipating. As they were finding their way toward the exit, they noticed a walk-through Fun House/Haunted House. Joey said, "Man we have got to go in there." They all agreed, bought their tickets, and went inside. It was the most crowded place in the park. As they were coming out of the House of Mirrors that led through to the dark and haunted part of the Fun House Joey said "look" as he was looking at the ceiling that led into the darkness, "I bet we can crawl up there." They waited till a group of people went by and then Joey said, "give me a boost." Fritz boosted him up and Joey found himself on a wire mesh ceiling that was actually a crawl space that extended over the dark, haunted rooms of the Fun House. He hollered down to his buddies "YOU AREN'T GOING TO BELIEVE THIS, COME ON UP." Moans and Inky quickly got lifted up while Fritz and Big Jim flipped a coin to see who would stay down below. Fritz won the flip and got the boost from Big Jim who then was going to stand guard. They spent the next hour traveling atop the actual fun house. They could see people walking below going from room to room. In the rooms that were dark, they started making scary noises. The people below believed that the noises were part of the fun house. Eventually, they got carried away with themselves. They started directing their yells right to the patrons. Fritz started it by yelling "I am the God of HELL FIRE AND I AM GOING TO FIND ALL OF YOU WHO HAVE LARGE NOSES." They all quickly got involved. Inky yelled, "WE SEE EVERYTHING YOU DO, GET YOUR HAND OUT OF THAT GIRLS PANTS." By now they were all firing away barely able to get the words out because they were laughing so hard. FRITZ YELLED AGAIN "THE GOD OF HELL FIRE COMMANDS YOU TO LEAVE YOUR GIRLFRIENDS BEHIND AND GO." Joey hollered in his best witch's voice "I SEE YOU MY PRETTY" and on and on for almost an hour. It was time to leave when Fritz stepped over the line. One of the girls walking in the dark witch's room had on cutoff shorts and a string bikini top. He reached down while she was staring at automated ghouls and ghosts and untied her bikini top which immediately fell to the floor, and she was topless. She started screaming at the boy she was with accusing him of untying her bikini. He laughed and said, "I didn't, I thought you did it yourself." She screamed "OH SURE" and the fight was on. The boys watched for a bit as the argument escalated. Moans said, "This has been a really good time, but I think we should get outta here NOW." They immediately started to crawl to the spot that they entered from. It took them a while to find it but when they did, they wasted no time dropping to the floor and heading toward the exit. Leaving, they passed the fighting couple who were accompanied with two park employees and were heading to the dark rooms of the fun house. The boys made it to the exit and were doubled up with laughter. Big Jim was having an ice cream cone and said, "Man that took a while tell me about it." Moans said "not now we gotta keep moving." They were just about out when they saw a hut like building with a sign saying JUNGLE LARRY'S WILD ANIMAL SHOW – ONE DOLLAR. Fritz said, "a dollar, are they kidding; besides, we just left a wild animal show in the fun house." They all laughed and started to walk again but Joey said "wait." There was an open window. No screens, no glass, just open at the top of the wall. The wall went up about eight feet and the open window just above it. He said to Big Jim "let's go over there and put me on your shoulders I want to see what's inside." "No" yelled Moans "we need to leave." "Relax man" said Joey "it will only take a minute." And he walked over to the wall where Big Jim put him on his shoulders. Joey looked in and almost immediately yelled "HOLY SHIT THIS IS THE ALLIGATOR PIT." The boys all laughed. Joey again said directly to Big Jim "get me the hell down Dufus this really is the alligator pit!" Big Jim let him go and he jumped from his shoulders. As they took a few steps and were walking towards their waiting buddies a guy in a safari jungle outfit with a bullwhip on one side of his pants and a holster on the other came out of the building screaming, "WHAT ARE YOU JERKS DOING? GET AWAY FROM THE BUILDING. THOSE ARE LIVE ALLIGATORS IN THERE." The boys started walking with Inky saying "Oh boy here comes another day in a jail cell. I hope it is as nice as Ravenna's was." It was funny but nobody laughed they just kept walking towards the parking lot while Jungle man kept following and screaming. When they heard Joey say "WHOA," they all stopped and looked back. Big Jim had stopped, and he was beginning to talk to Jungle man who actually turned out to be Jungle Larry. The boys stopped and now slowly walked towards Jim and Larry. "Larry calm down man. It is cool. Nobody meant no harm. Larry, I love watching you on TV, I never miss your show. The lions, tigers, and bears are so cool, and you are really brave to do what you do." Jungle Larry calmed down. He said, "your friend was in the alligator hut while we have a show going on, just didn't want him to go any further." Big Jim continued in his best Eddy Haskell voice. "Gee Larry thanks so much. We are so sorry. We just don't have the money to pay for your show. You are our favorite African Safari Man. Nobody else compares to you." Jungle Larry got on his walkie-talkie and was talking to someone. Moans and Joey looked at each other thinking, here we go again. Jungle Larry got off the walkie-talkie and said, "I left you guys some passes at the exit gate for my show this Saturday." He turned and was hurrying back to the building that he came from when Big Jim yelled to him, "THANKS AGAIN LARRY. CAN YOU GET US SOME TICKETS FOR THE Mr. JINGELING SHOW, THAT WOULD BE GREAT TOO?" Larry stopped and looked back giving a big farewell wave. When the boys got to the car they were doubled over with laughter. Moans said to Big Jim "I didn't know you and Jungle Larry were on a first-name basis. Joey quickly echoed. "Big Jim, that may have been your finest performance ever." They were howling with laughter as they neared the exit gate and Inky said, "should I stop and pick up our tickets?" Moans quickly yelled, "HELL NO YOU CHOOCH, LET'S GET OUT OF HERE." The 45-minute drive home was filled with laughter. As they were driving on Pearl Road still laughing about so many things that had happened a police car turned on his flasher and pulled Inky over again. The officer walked up to the driver's side and said, "can I see your license son?" Inky was seriously rattled. As he fumbled through his wallet to get out his license the officer said, "I see you have one of our tickets already." Inky said, "Yes sir. I got it this morning." The policeman took his license and returned to his car. Ten minutes later he came back to the car and handed Inky his license and a pink ticket. The officer said "I have some advice. You have had your license for less than a month and have gotten two tickets. Both on the same day almost in the exact same place. Continue at this rate and in two more months, you will not have any license at all. So, I gave you a pink warning slip. It is not a ticket but please drive slower" and he walked away. Inky gave a sigh of relief and they continued home. They dropped

Joey off first then he mentally started to prepare for the long bus and rapid transit trips and a full day of school. Summer was over.

That night as Joey lay in bed his mind was filled with questions. Is it possible that Big Jim is really friends with Jungle Larry? Did Inky set a new record for the number of speeding tickets gotten on the same journey? I wonder if that girl ever found her top? I hope nobody ever tells Uncle Eddy about the alligator hut. He fell asleep trying to decide what was the funniest escapade that happened that day.

FOOTBALL, YOU BET

The end of summer brought fall, and fall brought football. Having been cut again, Joey couldn't wait for neighborhood football to begin. The Vic's boys had started playing other neighborhoods about two years ago. The rumor had circulated that these guys were pretty good. They actually practiced two times a week, and sometimes three. By mid-September, they had played three different neighborhoods and had beaten all three soundly. While they took their neighborhood football seriously, they took their dancing equally as serious. Joey, Moans, and a few others kept up to date with the latest dance styles. As a group, they would attend dances every weekend in the local VFW Halls. Live bands, girls, and sometimes fights became a regular way of life. Joey had learned years earlier, that if you could dance well, the girls would always be around. He had become a very good dancer and it was fun. Friday night and Sunday nights would be dance nights. On the third Sunday of September, the boys had won their third straight neighborhood football game. That same evening, they would spend dancing in the VFW Hall. The Ridgewood Lake Boys usually occupied about a quarter of the space in the Hall. Joey kept a wide distance from them. He was careful not to dance with their girls, even when they came up to him and asked him to. He had learned to be cautious about three months earlier. On that particular night, Annette had invited some of her friends to hang out with Moans, Joey, and Big Jim. They went to Manner's, all packed together in Moans' car. Joey was sitting in the back seat, next to a girl named Carol, and Kathy was sitting on Big Jim's lap. Joey and Carol weren't doing anything, both were hardly interested in the other. However, from where Carol's boyfriend stood, it didn't look that way. Moans had pulled into the parking place, and the driver's side door was right against the speaker that was used for ordering food. When Carol's boyfriend, Terry, saw her in the car, he immediately thought she was with Joey. He sprinted up to the back window behind the driver's seat, started screaming, grabbed Joey by the neck, and began to pull him out of the window. Joey couldn't move and Moans couldn't open his front door because the speaker blocked it. For the first time since Patrick, Joey was taking some hits and was unable to respond. Carol jumped out the other door yelling, "I am not with him, I'm your girl, he is just a guy!" Joey was seething when he finally got loose. He quickly climbed over Kathy, who was still sitting on Big Jim's lap and got out of the back door. Terry had calmed down. He and Carol were arm-in-arm. As Joey started towards him, Terry said, "I am so sorry. I know you are a good kid, and I well remember our football days. Carol explained everything. I am sorry I just lost control." Joey had already made up his mind that this kid was going to get hit regardless of what came out of his mouth. As he approached him a police officer who was hired by Manner's to keep fights to a minimum and keep kids in their car, walked into the parking lot. He saw Terry, Carol, and Joey all outside their cars. The officer quickly walked over and asked, "is there a problem here?" They answered that there wasn't. The officer then said, "you all need to be inside your vehicles." "No problem," said Terry, and he and Carol headed towards his auto. The officer turned and looked at Joey and said, "Are you Joey DeTorre? The fireman's kid?" "Yes," Joey answered, and he put punching Terry off for another time. Joey went back to Moans car, not feeling very good about the fact that he had been hit repeatedly and had not been able to respond. He said to Moans, "take me home." Moans' said, "don't worry about it." Joey responded with, "this isn't over."

On Monday night Joey and his buddies were playing three-on-three hoops under the lights when a car pulled up and parked next to Joey's house. The Saber, and two of his buddies, got out of his car. Jeb said, "uh-oh," and looked at Joey. They stopped at Joey's side door to say hello to Big Joe and Joey's mom. Twenty minutes later, they came out and walked over and watched the end of the hoops game. When the game was finished, The Saber asked Joey if he could talk to him. He said, "sure." The Saber, in an exaggerated announcer's voice, said, "THIS IS A PUBLIC CHALLENGE TO PLAY A NEIGHBORHOOD FOOTBALL GAME THIS SUNDAY!" We hear you guys are pretty good, and we want to play you this Sunday at 2:00 p.m. at Parma High School. Not all the guys were present, so Joey said he would let him know on Wednesday. One of Saber's friends, Denny, asked: "you aren't afraid, are ya?" Joey and Jebs both glared at him. The Saber said, "call me and let me know by Wednesday." As he walked away, Joey yelled, "I need your phone number." The Saber responded saying, "I just gave it to your mom when we were inside." He got in his car and peeled off as they left. By Wednesday night, after contacting all of his guys, Joey called The Saber and told him the game was on. The Saber said, "great, the first team to score twenty-one TDs was the winner, and you must win by two. Half-time would be the first to score eleven TDs." The Vic's boys practiced on Thursday and Saturday afternoons. They would play the game with their usual fourteen players and all fourteen showed up for both practices. After practice, they had discussed that the scoring rules were much different for them in this game. They had played the other neighborhood games in two halves of 40 minutes each. The guys really wanted to play the Ridgewood Lake Boys, so they didn't think much about the rules. They felt that they were really good and so it didn't matter. Big Jim and Chocko played wide receiver. Both were very good and had great hands. Big Jim was 6'5" and Chocko was 5'6", Mutt and Jeff, but both could catch. Jebs and Moans were excellent running backs and very, very tough kids. Nobody was in pads, so the offensive line got in each other's way and held. All fourteen players would play both ways. One thing all these neighborhood games had in common was they were physical. This one would be no different.

Sunday came. Joey and his buddies were warming up in the pregame at 1:30 in the afternoon at Parma Senior High School. Their entire team was throwing, running, and catching in warmups. At 1:40, the Ridgewood Lake Boys had about ten guys. Big Jim walked over to Joey and said, "do you think these punks will have 11?" Joey answered saying, "how should I know, why don't you go over and ask The Saber?" "Noooooo, thank you," said Big Jim. "that kid is a lunatic." Joey responded, "they're all lunatics." About five minutes later, cars started to pull into the Parma High School driveway, and they headed to where the football game was going to be played. The cars kept coming. More and more and more carloads. Carloads of girls, as well as many, many, carloads of boys, all of who would be playing in the game. The girls spread out blankets on the sidelines, popped open some beer cans, and got ready to watch the game. The end-zone side of the field where The Saber stood was packed. They had at least forty guys. It seemed they were everywhere. The parking lot was filled with cars. Fritz, Moans, and Inky walked over to Joey. Fritz said, "I feel like Custer." Inky immediately said, "you guys know what Custer said at his land stand, right?" "What," said Fritz. "No" "Where'd all these fucking Indians come from?" Moans laughed and said, "don't worry, they're not going to scalp you." To which Joey quickly responded, "don't be so sure of that." Moans said, "Fuck 'em," while Joey said, "Let's Get These Guys," and the game began. Joey knew that Terry was going to play in the game, and when he came to the line of scrimmage, he located him playing right corner, and formulated his own private game plan. After the Vic's Boys scored on the first drive, Joey knew where he was going to line up every play. The next time they had the ball, he put three receivers to the side of the field, away from Terry. Then Moans, and, or Jebs, would lead Joey on a quarterback sweep around the corner, to the side away from the three receivers. As Joey came around the corner, Moans or Jebs would block the outside linebacker and Joey would run straight at Terry. He didn't try to run around him, he ran right at him. Each time he ran into him, he delivered a forearm to his head or chest, or whatever part of his body was available. He ran this play eleven times in the entire game. When Joey wasn't running into him, they were throwing the ball at him. Big Jim and Chocko alternated catching passes in his area and sometimes over his head. About the fifth time, they ran the quarterback sweep, Terry tried to go low on Joey. Joey saw it coming and made a quick juke move and Terry whiffed completely. He was on the ground and Joey went twenty yards before being tackled. Joey's teammates were all chuckling, and what was worst for Terry was the girls at the game were giggling at him. On Joey's way back to the huddle, he looked at Terry, smiling he said "I'm gonna fuck you up all day." That lit Terry's fire, he came right at Joey and the only fight of the day began. This time, however, Joey wasn't trapped in the back seat of an automobile. He led with his right hand and stunned Terry with a blow to the face. Quickly, The Saber and four of his guys came out to break up the fight. The Saber was yelling "WE WANT TO PLAY FOOTBALL; WE CAN FIGHT ANYTIME." and the game continued on. As each team went back to their huddles, Joey winked at The Saber and then smiled at Terry.

It was halftime. The Vic's Boys had completely dominated the first half. Their passing attack was brutal. Big Jim and Chocko were unstoppable, scoring three touchdowns apiece. Jebs and Moans had two touchdowns each. Fritz picked up a fumble on defense and also ran it in for a score. The Vic's boys led 11 to 1. The game was very physical but so far there was only one fight. Unfortunately, the first half lasted about 90 minutes and they were completely exhausted. The Lake Boys, however, had two full teams of offense and two full teams of defense. Some of those guys were not very good, but all of them were physical. The Lake Boys continually scored in the second half. They tied the score at 12-to-12, and they had now played almost three full hours. They upped the lead to 17-to-12 while the Vic's Boys were moving slower and slower. With the game getting shorter, Joey made a personal decision to continue on Terry. He called QB sweep, seven times in a row. Each time, he ran smack into Terry and fore-armed him hard. When he was about to call the play for the eighth time in a row, Moans said, "no way, Jose,' it's

Jebs and my turn." They took out a wide receiver and put Jebs and Moans in the backfield together. They finished the series with Jebs and Moans running behind one another's blocks, right at Terry. Jebs eventually scored and it was 17-13. However, the Lake Boys continued to score at will. When they were on offense, Joey, Moans, and Jebs continued to take turns running the ball right at Terry. After about four hours of playing, the game ended. Ridgewood Lake Boys 21, Vic's Boys, 17. The Lake Boys were whooping it up, but they also knew why they had won. Joey, Jebs, and Moans shirts were almost completely shredded and were barely hanging on their bodies. The Vic's boys gathered for a few minutes after the game. Joey looked at them and said, "you guys are tough-ass fuckers." Chocko, who was on the ground, got up, pointed at Joey, and said "we ain't the only ones."

After the game, almost all of the team headed to Joey's house. Big Joe was grilling out. More importantly, Joey's mom was making her famous potato salad. Mom had always cooked for the teams that Big Joe coached. Her potato salad, as well as her Sloppy Joe's, were off the chart. This was a cookout, so there were no Sloppy Joe's, but there was plenty of potato salad. When the boys pulled up to Joey's house all of the family was out in the yard. As Joey, Moans, and Jebs got out of the car, everything stopped. Mom's eyes were wide with shock and fear. She looked at her husband, then back at the boys, and exclaimed "My goodness, are you boys alright?" All three answered, "yep." With Jebs saying, "can't wait for your potato salad." Mom quickly asked, "where have you been?" To which Moans answered, "the game lasted almost four hours!" "Oh my God," said mom, "do you want to change out of those ripped-up shreds you are calling shirts?" Jebs said, "No, we are fine, besides Joey thinks it makes him look like Marlon Brando." Mom then asked, "who won?" "They did," Joey answered somewhat curtly. Big Joe looked up from his grill, he looked at the boys, and asked, "who won the fight?" Moans and Jebs both laughed and pointed to Joey. Joey quickly responded saying, "there was no fight." Big Joe started to call the other children for dinner and the guys helped pass out the paper plates, and dinner was served. During dinner, Annette stopped by with a carload of her friends. They got out of the car and said hi to Big Joe and his wife. They turned down all offers to eat, but Violet said, "I'll take some potato salad if that's ok." Big Jim shot out of his seat and got her a plate. The girls sat down on blankets while the boys were having some conversation. Mom and dad both tried hard not to listen. Annette was loudly saying, "It's Sunday night, VFW Hall night! Looking at Moans she said, "tonight we dance!" Big Jim jumped into the conversation saying "no way, I'm sore as hell. I can barely walk." To which Annette quickly responded, "you can't dance anyway." Joey, speaking with a low voice, entered into the discussion saying, "there is no way that I am not going to VFW Hall tonight! I'm going to dance and I'm going to flirt with Terry's girl." "No way," said Moans while looking at Annette, "I am going, he quickly added, and I am dancing, he added again. I'm with Joey on this one, we have to go." Turning to Joey he then said, "except, please Joey, don't flirt with Terry's girl. I am not sure a fight is what I need tonight." Violet jumped in saying "there is no chance that Joey will not be flirting with Terry's girl, along with every other girl there." "Maybe so," said Annette, "but that boy can dance." Fritz, put in his two-sense saying, "I am going with ya'll" and looking at Big Jim he said, "are you going to be a pussy your entire life?" And the back and forth between those two went on for ten minutes. Finally Moans said, "shut up, you two are like old ladies!" Mom jokingly yelled, "watch it." to which Moans quickly apologized. Keith said, "I am in, I have your back Joey." Moans said, "ditto for me unless a fight starts." On that note, they all laughed and headed home to shower and change, with Moans saying, "let's meet at Annette's at 7:30." Right on time, they all met at Annette's. Annette's friends said they would meet them at the VFW Hall. Joey got in Moans car to ride with him and Annette. Keith got in the back seat. As he sat down next to Joey, Joey turned to him and said, "don't get any ideas big boy" and the car filled with laughter. Inky drove the second car with Fritz and Big Jim. They pulled into the lot and got out of the car, then Moans and Joey walked in first with Annette in between the two. The second group was right behind them. As they paid the admissions and walked through the door to a packed dance hall, Fritz said, "here we go."

The Saber and his boys seemed to be waiting for them. When he saw them come in, he immediately headed toward them, followed by a number of his guys. Again, Fritz said in a low voice, "here we go." The Saber went right to Joey, and hugged him, saying, "you are every bit as tough as I remember you were in grade school when we played football together." He then shook hands with Moans, saying almost the same thing. All of a sudden they were surrounded by Ridgewood Lake Boys and were being congratulated on how well they had played. As the group made their way to the chairs that were being saved by Annette's friends, they were constantly being congratulated, as the Ridgewood Lake Boys kept seeking them out. The girls sat down, and Joey looked around the room. He saw Terry and his girl talking to The Saber. Joey looked at Terry and Terry averted his eyes, while The Saber whispered something in his ear. By now, Joey's group were all watching. It was Big Jim's turn now to say, "here we go for sure boys" as The Saber came over with Terry by his side, Carol stayed back, but she was staring. Terry came up to Joey and said, "I believe we are even now" and shook his hand and immediately headed back to the other side of the Hall. The Saber, who had been standing and talking to Moans, while watching what was going on, walked up to Joey, and said, "congrats again, man, now you are even, and you did it right. Let it go man, so the rest of us don't have to get involved." "Absolutely no problem," said Joey, they shook hands and went to find someone to dance with. The rest of the night was filled with laughter and dancing. One of Annette's friends, said to the girls while looking at Violet and Annette, "you both were correct, that boy can dance, and he is flirting with every girl in the place." As she got out of her seat, she said, "I'm going to ask him to dance," and she did, and he did.

That night as Joey lay in bed staring at the ceiling, many things were running through his head, Joey was thinking that Big Jim was correct, I am sore all over, and quickly fell asleep.

SHOCKING TIMES

Joey was beginning his Junior year in High School with one major change. His Auntie Olie had volunteered to take him to the rapid station at West 65th Street, near where she worked. This meant no more number 79 bus on the way to Latin. The rest of the trip, however, stayed exactly the same. He became very committed to getting his driver's license. He wanted to be able to drive all the way to school. As the summer had finished, Auntie Olie had volunteered to teach him how to drive. Her car was a bit smaller and would be easier for him to maneuver. They went driving as often as they could. By mid-September, Big Joe took him to take his driving test. He got a 95% on the driving part of the test, but he failed parallel parking. The officer who administered the test was somewhat surprised. He had aced the driving part of the test but just couldn't parallel park. His dad let him drive the family car home and while at dinner that evening, had told his mom "he actually drives very well. He just needs to learn how to park. From now on, he is allowed to drive with anyone who has a license."

Joey was somewhat bothered. Moans and Inky both had passed their driver's test, and both now had their own cars. He became determined to start driving to school. Meanwhile, his school days had become much calmer than they had been. He was studying and doing very well. His circle of friends had expanded. The boys he had traveled to football tryouts with lived in the State Road area and were being driven to school by a kid named Clark. These guys traveled in a group of three and paid him a dollar a week each. At school one day, Joey asked if he could get in their carpool. Clark said, "yes, for a dollar a week." By mid-October, he was no longer taking the bus and the rapid. He kept on practicing his parking, but unbelievably, he failed parallel parking for a second time. If he were to fail a third time, he would be waiting a year to try again. Just before Halloween, his dad said at dinner "there is someone stopping by later. I want you and your mother to come outside when he gets here." The side doorbell rang before they had finished eating. Big Joe went to the door and asked the boy who was there if he could wait for five minutes. "Sure," he said and waited outside while the family finished eating. When they were done, they all put on jackets and headed out. There actually were two boys outside waiting in two different cars. Big Joe said to the one, "let's see what you got." He turned to his oldest son and said, "check it out, I'm thinking of buying it for you." Joey's eyes got wide as he went closer to check out the car. This was definitely a kid's car! A '58 Ford Galaxy, with dual Hollywood mufflers, stereo system, and blue cherry lights. Without ever even driving it, Joey knew he wanted it. Father and son then took it for a spin. When they came back, Big Joe made an offer to the owner who said, "I have to think about this, I will let you know tomorrow." His dad said, "fine." The next day the two boys came back with the owner of the car saying, "if you are paying cash, the car is yours." His dad did, and now it was his. His dad let him drive it whenever he wanted as long as he had a licensed driver in the car with him.

School was school. Same old same old. His grades were good, and in his American History class, they were outstanding. The teacher of the class, who was also the athletic director, named Brother Mitchell, had remembered Joey from the eighth-grade city basketball championships. After the first quarter ended, Brother Mitchell asked Joey if he wanted to be in an accelerated American History class. Joey went home and talked to his mom and dad. He was very happy when his mom said how proud she was of him. He agreed to take the accelerated class and did very, very well in it. He made the Honor Roll in both first and second quarters. At school, he and Vic were still very close friends. Onie also became a regular member of the group and the guys from the State Road neighborhood were guys he was hanging around with more and more.

In early November, Joey had an idea. "Why couldn't he drive to school?' he asked his dad who surprisingly answered, "yes, as long as you have a licensed driver in the car," Joey called Clark, and they agreed that Joey would drive every other week. During the week's Joey drove, Clark would leave his car at Joey's, and he would serve as his licensed driver. Soon after, a kid named Flip joined the carpool. He said he would pay for gas if he could get picked up and dropped off every day. He lived on W. 25th and Denison, and Flip became part of the crew. Joey drove every other week, he learned how to drive on the interstate, in bad weather, and he learned how to maneuver in traffic jams. He was a good driver but still didn't have his license. But now he figured, he really didn't need one. School was going very well. His homeroom had won the intermural competition for flag football and basketball for three years in a row. A year ago, as a Sophomore, they played for the school champion-ship in basketball vs. Seniors in front of the entire student body. Joey had scored twenty-six points of his team's forty. They lost, he hated losing, but he felt sure the basketball coach would seek him out to try out again for the school's basketball team. He didn't.

One day, about a week before Thanksgiving, as Joey sat in Spanish class, an announcement came over the PA system say-ing, "The President of the United States has been shot." A stunned class sat with their mouths open. About forty-five minutes later, in Biology class, another announcement was made that President John F. Kennedy was dead. Shock filled the school. At the end of the day, Joey had a flag football championship game. His home-room played and won, but everyone's thoughts were elsewhere. The game ended about 5:00 p.m., but Joey didn't get home until about 7:00. As he went into the house he saw his mom crying and hugged her. His brother Douglas came into the kitchen and said, "I didn't do the paper route yet." "What?" exclaimed Joey, "why?" Douglas answered that they haven't been dropped off yet. "What, they are not here yet, it's almost 7:30 p.m." "That is correct" answered Douglas. Almost on cue, the paper truck pulled up to the drop-off spot. The driver blew his horn and waived and pulled away as Joey was coming out of the house. It was Friday night, and he was scheduled to go to Annette's. The gang was having their normal Friday night get-together. He started his paper route at about 7:45 p.m., and every house had someone standing at the door waiting for the evening paper. As he finished his route and was walking back to his house it began to sink in that this was an extraordinary time. By the end of the week, it would be even more so. When he got to Annette's, everyone was there. However, there was no loud music or party atmosphere. The opposite was true, it was very somber and almost every girl there was sobbing. This went on for the entire night. He had no special interest in any of these girls who were hanging around Annette's, so he just kind of sat and listened to the idiotic comments that were being bantered about. The idiocy would keep on coming. Saturday night, he took Charlyn to the show. She wasn't allowed in boys' cars, so for Joey, not having his driver's license yet, walking was still no big deal to him. She cried most of the night, and Joey was glad to take her home.

The next two days were trance-like. The conversation was always about the assassination. All types of rumors were widely circulated. Russians killed Kennedy, Johnson had a heart attack, Umbrella-Man, Babushka Lady, and so on and so on. The rumors would go on for years. There were all sorts of rumors about the accused killer, Lee Harvey Oswald. There was so much confusion, that the country seemed to come to a stand-still. Throughout the entire country, shock, grief, and rumors ruled. On Sunday morning, Joey called Chocko and Jebs to get some other guys and to play hoops at Auntie Olie's. They decided they would play at about 1:00 p.m.. As he was waiting for his friends, he was sitting around the TV with his family, watching the transfer of the prisoner Lee Harvey Oswald on live TV. As the transfer was happening in front of millions of viewers, a guy in a hat jumped out of the crowd and shot Oswald in the stomach. Joey stood and watched in complete disbelief. This can't be happening he said to no one who was listening. As his buddies arrived for basketball, most had not seen the shooting. They all went into the patio to watch the aftermath on TV. They were visibly bothered. The abundance of rumors and wild stories contributed to the unrest, not only for the boys but for the entire country. They blocked it out of their minds by playing hoops. The next day, schools were canceled. Because TV was in the process of capturing America, they got to watch the horror and sadness all over the next day. Joey, later in life, like most adults, would have to deal with difficult times, but nothing would bother him quite as the Kennedy assassination did. When he grew up into adulthood and had become a responsible adult with kids of his own, he would study the Kennedy assassination over, and over, and over again. He would form his own opinion on the event, but that opinion would continually change as more and more information became available. He would never stop reading about it.

That night, as Joey lay in bed staring at the ceiling, sleep was not coming easy. He said to himself, "the President of the United States was shot and killed, and I have watched the reruns almost one hundred times. The guy who killed him was shot and killed right in front of my eyes, live, on national TV. He didn't fall asleep until early that morning.

HAVING FUN AND A POOL HALL LIFE

Christmas time, Joey's favorite time of the year. It was a Friday night, about ten days before Christmas, and Annette's basement was full of kids, enjoying the music and dancing. Ever since summer, and the Ravenna jail incident, about every month or so, Keith would commemorate the event by singing "Jailhouse Rock." Tonight, he was standing on the steps going down to the basement, with the overhead lights off, and a number of flashlights pointed at him as he sang. The guys and girls sat on couches and chairs while clapping their hands in time with the music. Keith was in the middle of the song, and the side doorbell rang. Without waiting for someone to let them in, four Ridgewood Lake boys entered and came down the stairs. Keith was unfazed and kept right on singing despite the commotion and the fact that Annette had turned all the lights on. The Lake Boys had obviously been drinking and completely ignored Keith. They sat down while someone named Mack asked, "where is your beer?" Keith had stopped singing and the music was turned off. Moans quickly responded, "there is no beer." The Lake Boys were silent for a few seconds then started to size up the girls that were present. Nobody was coupled yet, so it wasn't that big a deal. However, making conversation had become difficult, to say the least. There was an atmosphere in the room that had not existed before. Joey was mentally preparing for whatever trouble was about to happen. Suddenly, the doorbell rang again, and in came Renee and three of her girlfriends. Renee was dressed in a black leather skin-tight slacks and a very tight black sweater. With her Carol Baker hair, she was drawing immediate attention. The Lake boys were practically drooling. The regulars at Annette's, including Joey, were very surprised to see her since she had not been around for quite some time. As her two friends sat down, Renee looked around the room, saw Joey, and yelled, "Joey, where have you been all my life?" She walked over, grabbed him by the hand, and took him upstairs to the living room while the Lake Boys sat somewhat stunned. Joey and Renee laid together for about an hour when one of Renee's girlfriends yelled upstairs, "hello up there, we gotta go!" Renee' hollered back, "in a minute," then said to Joey "I gotta go. I know you hang out here so that's why I came. If you want to see me again, then call me." She kissed him on the cheek and walked out the door. As Joey headed down the stairs, he saw the Lake Boys following the girls out the door. In his head he was thinking, this girl looked great, and promised himself he would call her and see her again. He never did....ever.

Christmas and New Year's came and went. Outside hoops were almost unplayable in Cleveland in the wintertime. Because Joey went to an all-boys Catholic High School and had parents that kept a tight rein on him during school nights, there was currently a severe shortage of girls in his life. Boredom had set in. He had finally taken and passed his driver's tests. He had Inky drive him to watch the parallel parking tests that were taking place at the test center. He quickly realized that when he had been practicing parking, with Auntie Olie, they had the sticks set up wrong. Joey fixed the alignment, practiced one day, took the test two days later, and parked the car on his first try. He now could drive his '58 Ford Galaxy all by himself. Hide the women and children.

One day, in late January, while sitting at Annette's, Moans said, "let's find a pool hall that doesn't check I.D.'s." Big Jim quickly named two local pool halls. However, he also said, "it's hit and miss as to whether they will card you or not." They sat and thought for a while, and decided that the following day they would go to

Braden's Pool Hall and see if they could get in. So they went, and as luck would have it, all of them got carded. None were eighteen years old yet, so the proprietor said, "bowl or leave." They walked out, got in their car, and drove over to Manners. As they were sitting eating Manners Big Boy's, Fritz said, "Cloverleaf Bowling Alley has a 24-table pool room and I have heard they never check I.D.'s." Joey responded, "that's a bit of a drive, but let's try it on Sunday."

Sunday evening Joey was waiting at home before getting picked up to shoot pool at Cloverleaf. It so happened that on this night, his sister had at least six girlfriends over the house. They were gathered in the living room to watch the Ed Sullivan show. It seemed a new band, called The Beatles, was going to be introduced to America on the show. The girls were all a buzz. Normally, Joey would flirt with some of Grace's friends, mainly just to aggravate her, but not on this night. The girls were locked into the TV. They eagerly were waiting for the Beatles to be introduced. The doorbell rang and in came Moans, Big Jim, Fritz, and Inky. The girls loved flirting with Moans, but not tonight. Inky immediately said, "let's get out of here, but Big Jim said, "nope, let's watch these guys." They all had a memory of Elvis Presley's first appearance on the Sullivan Show, where half the screen blocked out his lower body. They wanted to see what the Beatles would be like. The moment of their introduction quickly came, and four guys, with long hair, walked on stage and began singing, *"All My Loving"* There was immediate screaming in Sullivan's audience, as well as from the girls in the living room. They were absolutely going wild. Non-stop screaming through the whole performance. As the Beatles started their second song, Moans said, "let's get out of here" and they all made it towards the door. On the drive to the "Leaf", Joey said, "What was that? How about those haircuts?" Big Jim said, "yikes man, they will never last." They all agreed, and the talk quickly turned to nine-ball.

It was the beginning of a pool hall life. They were not carded, and the six boys got three tables. The many adventures that come with a pool hall, would dominate the next three years. They went almost three times a week and spent entire Sundays there also. In that time period, there arose a hierarchy based on a pool player's ability. Moans emerged as the top guy in the group, Inky was second, Big Jim was third, and Joey was a distant fourth. The other guys, like Fritz and Keith, dropped out of the picture. They still played sports, but their free time now was devoted to getting better at pool. The fellas became regulars at Cloverleaf pool hall. They got to know the guys that hung out there, and a whole new circle of friends, as well as adventures, would come into play. There were names like Hetz, Fats, Mouse, The Doctor, Larry, Da Door, and a host of others. There were about 25-30 regular players plus the occasional strays that came in looking for a game. Joey was surprised at how quickly they made friends, and how quickly they learned each other's skill levels. Low-level gambling was constantly going on. Joey continued to get better, but he became more skilled at getting "spots" from the people he played. He made money, not because of how good he was, but because he always got in the right game. It had been three months now, and they had not seen a fight in the pool hall. The bothersome thing was, that half of the regulars carried. Joey and his buddies were never strapped, but he often wondered what would happen if a fight would ever break out. By the next September, he would find out. The art of surviving in a pool hall was not how good you were but playing and obtaining a spot from your opponent. Straight pool was the game of choice, and sometimes 9-ball. More money could be made playing 9-ball but whether it was straight pool or 9-ball, it was always for money. For most of January and all of February, Cloverleaf became a home away from home. Moans got really good at the game, while Joey got a lot better every time he played. However, he always asked for a spot, usually got it, and with the right spot came winning money.

That night as Joey lay in bed staring at the ceiling, he had two thoughts. The Beatles, I should never have quit taking drums and saxophone lessons, and I know I am way better looking than Ringo.

BASEBALL AND A BOYS FIRST TIME

At the same time, school was going well. Joey made second honors and got three straight quarters of A's in Advanced American History. In the first week of March, baseball tryouts began. Again, a huge number of boys were trying out for the first baseball team in Cathedral Latin's history. Joey was a little apprehensive as he started to prepare for the tryouts being that he was cut from the two other sports he had tried out for, but baseball was his game. He was an outstanding second baseman and if he could hit, he thought he had more than a chance to someday get a minor league offer. School, pool, and baseball were the dominant forces in his life again. He went through a period of about three months without being involved with a girl. Tryouts started the first week of March, and when that week was over, there were thirty-five boys left. About twenty guys got cut without even being able to take batting practice. Joey had made all the cuts so far. He was an excellent fielder and Big Joe had taught him how to turn a double play way back when he was nine years old. He knew he was the best fielding infielder that was left on the team. It would come down to hitting. Easter vacation was later that year, and the weather turned warm earlier than usual. With just two weeks before the first game, they finally got to practice outside. It was now time to hit. Each day after practice a cut list was posted on the wall. By the end of Easter break after a full six days of outside practice, the roster was down to thirty-one. Twenty-four were expected to be kept, and so far, Joey was one of them. With about twelve tryout days left before their first game the Coach announced that seven more guys would be cut. The weather stayed nice, and for the next five days, practice was outside. Four more kids got cut, and five days before game one, there were only three more kids that had to be let go. With the strength Joey had developed in the off-season, he was pounding the ball. In the practice games, he was hitting 357 and had hit two home runs. He felt that he was the best infielder on the team, and nobody turned the double play even close to how fast he was pivoting and getting rid of the ball. He fully expected to make the team. After these scrimmage games, the team was down to twenty-four. Finally, Joey had made a varsity team at Cathedral Latin High School, and he would now be going head-to-head with a senior football player for the starting position at second base. The first game of the season was held at Woodland Park and Latin beat Collinwood 3-2. Joey did not start the game, but he pinched hit and got an RBI single to tie it. In typical Cleveland weather, the game was played in 33-degree temperatures as snow flurries took place the entire time. In this the first year that Latin would field a baseball team, the team was 12-6 and lost in the third round of the State Tournament. Joey would alternate at second base and hit 320. He enjoyed the season, but it bothered him that he shared time with a kid that was hitting 240 and wasn't close to Joey in fielding ability. He was venting his frustration one Sunday afternoon in the Leaf to Moans. Moans in his ever-present wisdom, put things in perspective by saying, "it's better than getting cut, right?" Joey thought a while and then said, "you are right, no more bitching."

His junior year in high school was ending quickly. He had not gotten in any trouble and his grades were good. He had developed new friendships not only with the guys he drove with to school but also kids from both the east side and west side of Cleveland. He became close with Vic and closer with the unforgettable Onie. Onie had become one of the fellas. His physical health had gotten worse, but he still walked well enough and hadn't started to deteriorate to the degree he would reach at the end of his young life. Onie was a first-class teacher ball-buster. Sometimes he made Joey laugh so hard they both would cry. He lived in a wealthy development located in Independence. His house was something that Joey had never seen the likes of. Occasionally, Onie would be taken home from school in the carpool with Joey and his buddies. It was out of the way, but Onie paid extra. One day, in the middle of a rowdy accounting class, Onie said "Joey, I need to talk to you." "Sure, how about lunchtime?" "It's a deal." At lunchtime Joey found Onie and sat down next to him, saying "what's up?" Onie said, "we have become good friends, so I'll share this with you, there's a girl in my development who does it, are you interested?" Joey said, "sure." Onie said, "ok, I will call her and see if I can set something up." The next day at lunch Onie told Joey, "She is babysitting for two little kids on Saturday night, they will be in bed by 8:00 p.m. and she said we could come over about 8:30. Are you in?" "Sure," said Joey, "by the way, what's her name?" "Kathy," said Onie. "Tell me what she looks like again" Onie described her, and Joey again said, "OK. I will pick you up Saturday at 8:15 p.m. and we will go over there." Onie said, "it's a deal."

That night, Joey drove his car to pick up Onie. Kathy was babysitting in Onie's development about a two-minute walk from his house. Joey beeped the horn; Onie came out and they drove to Kathy's. Kathy was not great looking, but not terrible either. Onie introduced them and in twenty minutes Joey and Kathy headed to the guest bedroom. They spent the next two hours there. Joey had intercourse for the first time. Along with that, it seemed that Kathy enjoyed oral sex, doing things with her mouth that Joey had never experienced before. After two hours, he was completely spent. They came out and sat down on the couch, Onie slowly walked over, took Kathy's hand in his hand, and said, "my turn." Kathy looked at Joey and said, "it's up to him," pointing at Joey. Joey decided to mess with Onie, he stopped, and thought for a while, seemingly to give Onie the impression that it was hard for him to make up his mind. Meanwhile, Onie was looking at him with a pleading look in his eyes. Joey messed with him for another minute, then he finally said, "sure go ahead," and so they did. About forty minutes later Onie and Kathy came out of the bedroom. Joey got up, said good-bye to Kathy, and he and Onie headed for the door. He looked at her and said, "I'll see you again." Kathy looked at him and said, "next time come alone." He said "OK" and took Onie home. On his way back to Parma he was thinking, "I will definitely see this girl again, and this time he did."

That night as Joey lay in bed staring at the ceiling, he thought... wow, my first time. Actually, it was not that big a deal...but the mouth stuff was off the charts.

UNCLE EDDY THE EASY RIDER

It was a beautiful Saturday spring day. Joey called a bunch of guys to play outdoor hoops at Auntie Olie's and about nine guys showed up. There were cars everywhere. While they were playing, Uncle Eddy pulled up and parked in his usual spot. Jebs saw him first and said, "it doesn't get much better than backyard hoops and a visit from Uncle Eddy. You guys who haven't met him are in for a real treat." The games continued while those guys that were not playing, kept glancing over at Eddy who was struggling with something he had taken out of his trunk. After 30 minutes, and the completion of two games, Eddy headed towards the fellas. Moga was the first to see him and said, "holy shit, look at this guy." Eddy was heading toward the driveway, he had on a Nazi helmet, a sleeveless Levi jacket, and fake tattoos on his uncovered arms that said, "Born to ?" He was also sporting Bermuda shorts, black socks, engineer boots, and sunglasses. The game stopped and the guys stood with their mouths wide open. Moans said, "Double holy shit." Fuco asked, "is it Halloween?" Chocko added, "this is going to make my day." Eddy said, "Meenkya Joey, how are youz guys?" "Hey Eddy," was the response that came from those guys who already knew him. The guys that didn't know him were still standing with their mouths agape. "Meenkya Joey, I need some help" to which Fuco responded, "you surely do, what's with the costume?" Chocko couldn't resist asking, "Eddy, the tattoo on your shoulder, Born to ? what does that mean? Eddy responded "Meenkya, Chocko, I thought you were one of the smart guys. I got this tattoo at a discount, and the guy ran out of ink. He only had enough for a question mark." "Oh," said Chocko. "Meenkya," said Eddy, "what a Chooch. I am a biker now; this is how bikers dress." Again, Chocko said, "OH," amidst mass hilarity, Joey asked, "How can we help you, Eddy?" "I can't get my bike fixed; I need some help from youse Chooches." Joey said, "ah, ok, Moga is somewhat mechanically inclined, let's take a look." The game stopped, and all nine guys walked towards Eddy's car, where all over the sidewalk were spread out bike handles, pedals, and one tire connected to the pedals. That was it. Eddy said, "I cannot get this bike to work. Meenkya, help me out." Moga looked down at the parts scattered over the ground and said to Eddy, "this isn't a motorcycle," to which Eddy responded, "No shit Sherlock, Meenkya Joey, I thought you said this kid was a mechanic. Why would I have a motorcycle, I don't want to kill myself. Meenkya, Moga are you silly?" "No Eddy, sorry, my fault." Moga looked at Eddy, then at Joey, then at the other guys who were standing around laughing, then back at Uncle Eddy and said, "Eddy, this is a unicycle." "A what?" "Unicycle, it has only one wheel, no handlebars, and two pedals. Clowns ride them in the circus and sometimes they juggle while they ride. However, I can put this together for you in about fifteen minutes." "Meenkya, thank you. While I wait, I will challenge youse guys in foul shots." He turned to the group and said, "the best of ten foul shots, for a dollar a shot." Eddy went over, grabbed a ball, started shooting underhand foul shots, and missed almost all of them. Two of the guys who had never played in the backyard before said, "OK, you're on. Start with Tommy, and I have the game after." Eddy said, "OK, put the money first in a hat." Both boys put 10 singles in the hat. Tommy shot first and made six. It was Eddy's turn, and he went ten for ten. Chocko was rolling on the grass laughing. The second guy, Richie, grabbed a ball just as Moga was returning. Moga said to Eddy, "your unicycle is ready." Eddy said, "thank you, let me beat this chooch first." Richie shot and made only three. Eddy made nine and said, "I'm going to go ride my unicorn." Moga said, "ah, unicycle Eddy." Eddy took the money out of the hat and said thank you to Moga as well as to Tommy and Richie. The boys went back to playing basketball. In the middle of the game, they heard horns blowing and guys yelling. The ruckus was coming from right around the corner on Snow Road. Wondering what was going on, the game stopped, and they walked around the corner to see what was happening. Cars were backed up from Ridge Road to West 79th street. At the front of the gridlock, in the middle of Snow Road was Uncle Eddy, still in his biker costume riding in circles on his unicycle and juggling two baseballs. Fuco said, "holy shit the three," Joey said, "Uncle Eddy's earned three Holy Shits today" as police cars were heading towards the traffic jam. Joey told the guys, "go home, I am heading inside and hiding." They laughed and quickly split. Joey watched from his bedroom as the police pulled up to Eddy and told him to get off the road. Eddy pedaled down West 79th Street, up to his car, put the unicycle in his trunk, and drove away.

SENIOR YEAR

The school year ended, and it was time for summer baseball. Joey, Moans, and Big Jim played together once again on what amounted to a Parma All-Star team. Joey would turn seventeen in July and be a Senior in the fall. Time, it was a flying by. Unlike previous summers, this summer was somewhat tame. The pool hall in the summertime was not crowded, but the Leaf and Annette's were now nightly hangouts. Drive-in movies were all the rage, and they were the best place to go with your girlfriend. Joey and the boys still went to VFW dances and Charlyn was still an on-again-off-again happening. There were new girls and acquaintances, but baseball, the pool hall, dances, and Annette's occupied most of his time.

Summer passed quickly, it was September, and it was Joey's Senior year, and an eventful one it would be. No matter what he did, this would be a year when trouble would find him. It started at school with the first day of the new principal's PA announcements. His name was Brother Cecil. Brother Cecil spoke in a somewhat effeminate voice, and he would start every announcement with the same words "Well Students." It didn't take long for massive mimicry to begin throughout the school. He started the first school assembly in the exact same way, and each time he said "Well Students" twelve hundred boys would begin laughing. It seemed every boy in the school had developed an imitation. However, Onie had one of the best. He thought about entering the talent show and doing a Brother Cecil imitation, but he didn't get past the audition. His impersonation always got huge laughs.

The second problem on the docket was a big one. In 1964, schools had no such thing as an early dismissal. Joey was scheduled into the eighth period (the last period of the day) study hall. Every educator knows that the toughest time slot to teach is the very last period of the day. Make that period a study hall, and fill it full of senior boys, and you have a recipe for disaster. It took only the first week of school for trouble to emerge. The Brother who was put in charge of eighth-period study hall went by Brother Steve. The study hall was filled with lots of Joey's buddies including Onie, Vic, and Flip as well as a number of guys who also had their shares of being in jams. It certainly didn't help that Brother Steve played at being a hard ass. All these guys had experiences with hard asses before, both young and old. They quickly recognized that this guy was a fraud. In the first week, he had given a demerit to every single guy in study hall. It seems he could not get the fellas to stop talking, as well as, to stop yelling his name out when he wasn't looking. DWEEEEEEEBBBBB, became the study hall war yell that actually spread throughout the school. Soon the guy couldn't walk down the hall without someone yelling DWEEEEEEEEEBBBBB. By early October Brother Steve was losing it. He had almost no control over the study hall. He tried to be a tough guy, but the boys just ignored him and laughed. One day, near the end of the semester after almost 90 days of Brother Steve presiding over chaos, he walked into the room and drew a large box on the chalkboard. On the top of the box, he wrote in quotation marks "The Crew." He then filled the box with students' names. There were twelve names written inside the box. He announced that they would officially be known as "The Crew." He went on saying, that from now on, any misbehaving, no matter who did it, the Crew would be punished. For the first time since the beginning of school, there was silence. The boys sat and processed the information. Suddenly, realizing he was immune to being punished a boy named Jeff, who was a non-crew member stood up and started doing monkey imitations which of course caused loud laughter from the entire room. A wide-eyed Brother Steve placed a checkmark on the board next to the Crew members' names, giving them all one demerit. Monkey boy sat down and then another non-crew member stood up and started singing "Mary Had a Little Lamb." More laughter and another demerit for the Crew. Another two non-crew members again got up, and they pretended they were Paul & Paula. They started to sing "Hey, Hey Paula." The class was now howling. Finally, Joey stood up and there was silence as everyone was waiting for whatever was going to come next. Joey clasped his hands together and said, "being that I have studied law since kindergarten, I have been chosen to represent the Crew, as they are clearly being discriminated against." A huge round of applause came from the Crew. Brother Steve shrieked "sit down!" Joey responded, "I'm sorry, I cannot. I would like to call my first witness, Onie from Onieville to testify. Onie, can you please come up here, put your hand on my history book while I swear you in." Onie immediately got up and drew a major round of applause from the entire class. The class was now in fall-on-the-floor laughing mode, as Onie raised both his arms in a muscle-man stance. With that, Vic fell out of his desk to the floor and lay there laughing. The classroom laughter was so loud they almost missed hearing the dismissal bell ring. When they did they all got up and bolted. It was Friday. It was Joey's turn to drive, so they ran to the parking lot, met the other guys, and pulled out of Dodge. They figured that all would be forgotten by Monday. They were very wrong. Monday came, and as they walked into the eighth-period study hall, the Crew had eight demerits on the board next to each of their names. Eighteen was get kicked out of school time, so most of these guys would now be at least over ten. The ruckus started immediately, but this time it was not joking or laughter, it was anger. Protests were launched involving everyone in the class. With ten minutes left in class, Brother Steve made the announcement that the Crew would remain in their seats after the bell rings. The mumbling got louder when Steve said, "you are here for 45-minutes. If you leave before that, you will get five more demerits each. I have work to do in the bookstore, you wait in this classroom, and I don't care how much noise you make." The end of the day bell rang, and the Crew didn't move. The other students got up and walked out the door with Brother Steve following them. Before he shut the door Steve turned to the Crew and said, "try me." He shut the door and went to the bookstore. The twelve boys sat there in silence looking at each other. Danny Z was the first to speak. He said, "we need to settle down, this is getting serious." They discussed the situation for about ten minutes, when Joey, who had said nothing, interrupted the conversation. He looked at the guys and asked, "Did Steve the Dweeb say we could make all the noise we want?" Onie quickly, and enthusiastically said, "yeah bro!" Joey looked at the other guys and there was total silence for about thirty seconds. He stood up and immediately started screaming at the top of his lungs. The seriousness was being pushed aside and one-by-one each of the boys joined in the screaming. The yelling, screaming, and banging on the desks could be heard in three-quarters of the now-empty school. They kept on screaming, yelling, and banging for about the next five minutes. It sounded like a classic Latin pep rally. The door started to open, the screaming stopped, and the boys were ready for Brother Steve to come in the door. A big surprise awaited them. It was the assistant principal who came in the door. This guy was a guy that no one messed with. He immediately asked, "what is going on in here?" There was a palatable fear in the room which led to dead silence. The AP said again "what is going on here?" Finally, Joey again (who was silently saying to himself, why did I say I was studying to be a lawyer) answered by telling the truth. "Brother Steve told us we had to stay here until he came back, and that we could make all the noise we want. So that's what we were doing." The AP, after surveying the room said, "get out of here." You didn't have to tell the boys twice; in a manner of seconds, they were out the door. The exception being Onie who said, "but brother..." The assistant principal looked at him and said with a maniacal look in his eye, "get out of here!" There were three days left in the semester, and Friday there was no school. The AP monitored the study hall for the next three days and there were no issues. They never saw Brother Steve in that room again. The second semester began with teachers who had free periods alternating days to monitor the Crew. They would do this until they found a full-time replacement. There was peace for the next three weeks. No demerits, just peace.

School went well for a while. Baseball practice would begin in a month and Joey was on the depth chart for second base number one. Needless to say, he was very excited. Problems were just around the corner, however, arising again in late January. A new full-time study hall mentor was assigned to eighth period. He was another guy who did not teach regular classes. His name was Brother Fred. Brother Fred made the same mistake as his predecessor. Taking the same approach that didn't work before. He played at being a hard ass and that rarely works as an educator. The assistant principal introduced him personally and warned the boys that any nonsense at all would be immediately punished. When he left the room, Brother Fred started by laying down the law. Such things like, there will never be any talking, unless given permission, you will raise your hand if you want to speak. If you do not have work to do, I will give you some. These were almost the exact same things that Steve had said. He then put twelve names in the corner of the blackboard. Every Crew member was again listed on the board. The guys all looked at one another, all thinking the same thing. Here we go again. Aside from the fact that Brother Fred had no clue about handling kids he also had a physical disadvantage. He was 5'6", heavy and round with a blond buzz cut. He looked just like Porky Pig. The boys wanted no trouble and each of them certainly wanted no more demerits. They were quiet and took out their textbooks, opened them up, and pretended to read. The first day almost ended without incident. With fifteen minutes left in the day, Flip put his head down to go to sleep. Brother Fred, who was sitting at his desk staring at the class, which he would do every day, immediately jumped up and literally ran over to Flip's desk and loudly screamed "THERE WILL BE NO SLEEPING, GET YOUR HEAD UP AND

A BOOK OUT!" Flip, who probably had more demerits than anyone in the room, said nothing and did exactly as he was told, period. He couldn't get any more demerits. It looked as if the incident was going to go away when someone suddenly coughed out the words "PORKY!" The guys who had all been pretty much thinking the same thing could not help but laugh out loud. Brother Fred's face turned beet red as did the top of his head, and you could almost see the smoke coming out of his ears. Fortunately, the bell rang, and the boys were up and out of there. In the car on the way home, the guys were laughing hard at Brother Fred. However, Joey, as well as both Flip and Clark, looked at Onie, and Joey said "we know that it was you that coughed Porky and it was hilarious, but man you've got to stop. This guy is as bad as Steve and demerits will be his next weapon." Flip quickly added, "man I have very little room for any more demerits, and I want to graduate." Onie responded by saying "OK, OK, no more Porky coughs." Everyone in the car laughed and no one believed him. The next day passed without incident and the weekend had arrived. When they returned to study hall on Monday, on the blackboard was written in large capital letters "REMEMBER – SILENCE." The guys all looked at each other and while keeping their mouths shut were hoping that chaos would not return. They constantly would remind each other by tapping their fists on their chests meaning, they all wanted to graduate. Things were looking up; another week went by without an incident. But in mid-February disaster struck. Brother Fred had not let up. He would stare at the class from the moment they walked in the door. It was as if he was daring them to challenge him. On a Wednesday in February, Danny Z asked Ronnie, who was sitting next to him, if he could borrow a pencil. Brother Fred with his eyes ever peeled, saw the exchange, and immediately stood up screaming "NO TALKING, you have one demerit!" and put a checkmark next to his name on the blackboard. Danny Z said, "Brother, I was only asking for a pencil." Fred's response was, "you want another one?" "No Brother" came Danny Z's answer, "I get it, no talking." The class ended with Danny Z now at eleven demerits for the year. The next day, Danny had snuck in the room ahead of time and had written on the board, REMEMBER – SILENCE, and signed it Porky. As the boys filed in, there was immediate and loud laughter. Joey quickly ran to the board and erased it. He looked at Danny Z, laughed, and said, "man, I am saving your ass." As the words came out, Brother Fred was walking in the door. Joey had erased the board just in time. Thirty minutes went by in relative silence. Suddenly, Danny Z, who was sitting in the back of the room in the corner, started swaying sideways in his desk. Side to side, side to side. Porky saw him and pretended not to pay attention. Other guys, Crew and not Crew, were starting to notice Danny Z swaying. Onie couldn't let this pass, and he started to sway in his seat. The jam was on. It didn't take long, soon the entire class, row by row, were swaying in their seats, in perfect silence. Back and forth...back and forth. Brother Fred seemed perplexed. He was not exactly sure how he should deal with this situation, so he got up and gave the entire class, Crew, and non-Crew, demerits. Immediately, the grumbling started. Joey quickly jumped out of his seat, "may I be given permission to speak your Honor?" Fred looked puzzled, but said, "yes, you may." Joey said, "thank you your Honor, and preceded to say, everyone in the room knows that I have been studying law since kindergarten, and I ask you, your Honor, what law have these gentlemen broken? They are making no sounds, and completely following the no-talking rule. Can you please explain before we take this grievance to the assistant principal? WHAT LAWS HAVE BEEN BROKEN?" Brother Fred was getting red-faced again, but he seemed at a loss for words. Joey pounced on his silence while saying "it is my humble legal opinion that all the demerits you gave out today be erased, and we, the students, will go on with the rest of the class in silence. Or I go down and see the assistant principal." Brother Fred was fully flushed and looking more like Porky Pig every second, but he went over and erased all the checks he had put on the board that day. The class vigorously applauded, and Brother Fred began smoking again. Joey quickly said, "whoa Brother, whoa, the boys are just applauding your generosity and wisdom." Fred stopped for a second then said "alright, then sit down in silence."

A few days passed and it would seem that Brother Fred was still not happy with what he had achieved in bringing order to this rowdy study hall. It seemed there were little pockets of whispering whenever he would let his guard down. So he took to moving around the room whenever and wherever the whispering was coming from. He would stand right over the boy he thought was guilty and stare at him. It was the one and only Onie again who lit the fire. You see, when Brother Fred had taken over the study hall, he had seated the Crew members all about the room, with the thought being, if they are not all together, we will have order. The real truth was, there was order. These guys all wanted to graduate, so they had stayed relatively silent in the study hall for over four weeks. Onie was sitting in the right front corner of the room. Fred was standing and staring over Danny Z's shoulder, who was seated in the rear left corner. Onie put his head down in a book, and in a falsetto, somewhat raised voice, he said "Over here Porky." Fred looked up, chose the wrong corner, and went and stood over Clark, who had done nothing. You could hear snickering, but no one wanted it to turn into raucous laughter. Flip was next to see Onie's wisdom in what he had started. From the corner where Flip had sat, he too put his head down and in a book and called out "Over here Porky." Brother Fred knew where that one came from and beelined over and stood and stared at Flip. It quickly was followed by Danny Z saying, "Over here Porky." And now it was rolling. Every time that one of the class said "Over here Porky" Fred would beeline to that corner. To the guys, it was like playing with a pinball machine. They could make it go wherever they wanted it to. They could barely contain themselves. This went on for twenty minutes, and at the bell, they all were gone. The study hall did this for three straight days. They would wait in silence until the middle of the class, then someone, Crew, or non-Crew, would start it all again. "Over here Porky." Friday ended; the guys headed to their cars. On the way home Onie asked everyone in the car, "how long do you think this clown will go on before the top of his head flies off?" "Forever!" Flip said, "he's an idiot!" Joey said, "not for me man, as much fun as I'm having, this is waiting to become another disaster. Baseball has started and on Monday Coach has written for me to be excused from last period study hall." "What about the rest of us?" asked Clark. "In my humble legal opinion Clark, I would get a library pass and get the fuck out of there." The entire Crew got library passes and graduation became a reality. Unfortunately for Joey, however, his biggest problem was right around the corner.

That night as Joey lay in bed staring at the ceiling, he asked himself...how is it possible that we landed two Chooches in a row as our study hall monitor? However, it actually felt good pretending to be a lawyer, maybe that's what I will be when I grow up and "Over here Porky" will be funny for the rest of my life. He fell asleep with a smile on his face.

A RUMBLE IN THE JUNGLE

It was mid-May and baseball was turning out to be very good for Joey. He hadn't received any more demerits which meant he hadn't gotten into anymore more trouble. He was playing every day, and he was hitting 320. There were about ten days left in school for Seniors and Joey was breathing much easier about making it to graduation when disaster struck. Those team members old enough to drive could drive over to Ambler Field for practice and go home from there. They often time carpooled with guys that they lived close to so they could leave practice together to go home. On this particular day, Joey went down to Marshalls Drug Store for a snack and missed his ride. He was dressed for practice and started to jog to Ambler Field to make it on time. On his way, he was suddenly surrounded for the second time in his four years by eight to ten Black kids. They wanted his wallet and slapped him in the face. He responded by saying, "I don't carry my wallet with me when I'm in my practice gear." The boy closest to him grabbed him by the jersey, and another boy stood and started to try to go through his pants pockets. Joey ripped his hands from his jersey and pushed the other kid away. As the other boys started to get involved, a car came flying up to the curb where they had Joey surrounded. The driver slammed on his brakes, threw the passenger side open, and yelled "get in!" Before anyone else could react, Joey dove into the car, slammed the door shut, and Coach McGuire sped away. He pulled up to the practice field and dropped Joey off saying "you know better than to walk this far alone in this neighborhood, please don't do it again." "Don't worry Coach and thank you very much" said Joey. "No problem. Keep hitting the ball son."

The incident was forgotten.....almost. There were four more days of school left for seniors as well as four more baseball games left. Joey was heading to Marshalls Drug Store again, but this time he was with four or five teammates. While they were buying snacks, Joey looked over at the counter and recognized the leader of the gang. It was the guy who slapped him in the face. He was sitting at the snack bar, drinking a Coke with a girl from John Hayes. Joey turned to his friends and said, "that's the guy who jumped me and slapped me. I'm going over there." One of his friends, Ricky, grabbed him by the arm but saw the look in Joey's eye and quickly let it go. Joey said "just have my back. Keep me from getting jumped from behind." Ricky said, "you got it, amigo," and off Joey went. He walked over to the counter and tapped the boy on the shoulder. As he turned around, Joey said "remember me?" The boys' eyes got wide with recognition, and he jumped up. Joey quickly punched him in the face and landed right under his nose, and the battle was on. The girl started screaming, and suddenly his buddies were coming in the door to help him. They were the same guys that had tried to help him steal Joey's wallet. Ricky and company reacted immediately, and a full-fledge battle was underway. The fight went on for what seemed like an hour but was probably no more than a minute. Police sirens could be heard in the distance, and with that sound, everyone split. The Latin boys headed quickly to where their car was parked, jumped in, and drove to practice just as the police were pulling into the drug store about a hundred yards away. A boy named Phil said, "whew, that was close." Joey said, "that's not over fellas, the store employees know we're from Latin, they don't know who the other guys were but there's sure to be a follow-up." The next day at school, during first period, there was a PA announcement asking the varsity baseball team to report to the gym. In the gym, there was the principal, the assistant principal, the head coach, and two policemen. The principal introduced the policemen and gave them the floor. They explained that the manager at Marshalls Drug Store said that a bunch of white kids in baseball gear was involved in a fight. We are following up on the incident, so we started with you guys and turned the floor over to the coach.

"Fella's," he said, "we are in danger of not playing our final four games. We need to know who was involved and why." There were about 20-seconds of dead silence. Joey stood up and said, "it was my fault Coach" and then he explained to everybody exactly what had happened, going back to being almost robbed, and slapped around about ten days earlier. Again, there was silence. The assistant principal asked, "who was with you?" Joey answered, "I don't know, I don't remember, there might have been guys that were there, I just don't know who it was." More silence. Ricky stood up "I was there, I was with him, I wasn't going to sit around and watch him get beat up." The assistant principal asked, "you all beat up one guy?" Joey quickly responded again saying, "I went after one guy, I don't know where the other guys came from, but I was surrounded again." Four other guys stood up and said the same thing as Ricky. "Those six guys came in the door, and we weren't going to let Joey fight them all." Joey again spoke up, saying "This is all my fault. If those other guys don't jump me ten days ago, this doesn't happen. I started this at Marshall's, these guys were just standing up for their teammate." The two policemen walked over and conferred with the principal and assistant principal. The baseball team sat in complete silence as the conference took place for about five minutes. When finished, the police turned to the team and said, "your school officials will handle this" and left. Joey and his five friends were told to just stay in the gym and the other players were sent back to class. The three administrators conferred for almost thirty minutes. Finally, as the five boys sat in the gym stands, the principal said, "well students." There wasn't even a snicker this time. And he said, "let's go to my office." So the five boys, the coach, and the assistant principal headed to the main office. The players sat in the outer office while the administrators conferred again. Finally, after

45-minutes of waiting, the door opened, and the boys went into the principal's office. The principal again, said, "well students, do you have anything else to add?" Joey again said, "I do! This was only my fault. If I'd have walked away then nothing would have happened, but honestly, I couldn't walk away." "OK," said the assistant principal, "this is what's going to happen from an administrative point of view, then Coach will tell you what's going to happen from an athletic point of view." The AP said, "it was off-campus, so technically we can do nothing. We do not approve mind you, but there will be no punishment coming from the school. Keep in mind, if Marshall's wants to press charges, or ask for reimbursement for the damage that was done, this will be the responsibility of you and your parents. If that would be the case, my advice to you all would be to get a lawyer. If there are charges pressed I'm sure you will be notified, and all of your parents will be summoned to school to meet with us. I suggest you let them know what happened. Coach, it's your floor." Coach told all the players to leave except Joey and that he would deal with them later. Joey was left alone with the three adults. Coach said, "Joey, we have four games left. You will be suspended for three. The tournament is over, that would leave one game left for you in a Latin uniform. I would certainly play you in that game. You have certainly earned it. I also respect you for how you handled your teammates." Joey thought for a minute as the coach watched him intently. He said "thank you coach for the respect, but I'm done. I'm going to graduate here in four days, I don't want to play here anymore." The coach stared in surprise, saying "Joey, you've had a great year, you need to reconsider, you have a full three days to think about it. Maybe your parents can help you rethink your decision." "Thanks again coach, but I am done." Of course, I will play summer ball, and I would appreciate it if you didn't share this incident with any college scouts." Coach again said, "think it over, you can go to class." That night Joey asked to talk with his mom and dad away from the ears of his brothers and sisters. They went outside on the front porch and Joey told them the complete story, starting with being jumped. His dad asked, "that's it, that's just the way it happened?" His dad said, "I think you should reconsider the last game," to which Joey said, "nope, I am not playing there ever again." Dad said, "alright, I'm fine with everything you did." Mom asked, "you are sure you are not suspended from school?" "I'm sure" replied Joey." "You are sure you are going to graduate?" Joey laughed, "I'm sure." Mom said, "I love you and I'm with your father."

About five days later mom and dad were called down to meet with the principal. It would be the first time ever his dad would visit his high school. When they came home they said nothing. Joey never found out what happened in that meeting. In the remaining three days that seniors were in school, it spread like wildfire. The baseball players met with Joey to ask him to play his last game. He thanked them but said he was done. The rest of the school looked at him with respect in their eyes. Numerous seniors sought him out after graduation to say a special goodbye. Danny Z said, "you made the Crew proud," and they laughed.

They all went on with their lives.

That night as he lay in bed staring at the ceiling Joey was reflecting on the last week. I should have left well enough alone. Why couldn't I do that, I am really surprised that my parents did not punish me, I wonder if they had to pay damages? As he yawned he had other thoughts, I am really glad that I have friends. I will never forget how my buddies stood by me, those policemen didn't want anything to do with this, my coach is a Chooch, and I would never play for him again. Sleep was very long in arriving that night.

BRUSHES WITH DEATH

A week following graduation Joey received a call from one of his east side friends at Latin. Rocky DiNardo had promised Joey that they would play a game of straight pool, and in the chaos of Joey's last week at Latin, they hardly saw each other so the promise had gone unfulfilled. Rocky was an Italian kid from Murray Hill, an Italian neighborhood about two miles from Latin. In the previous decades it was widely rumored that Murray Hill was the home base for the Italian mafia of Cleveland.

Rocky was calling to see if Joey could meet him at Severance Center the next day at about noon. The following day they met in the parking lot. The two were happy to see each other and made their way to the pool room. The pool room, like Cloverleaf, was alongside a fifty-lane bowling alley. It had twenty-four tables and there were always some big money games going on there. The room was sunken below the main floor. You had to walk down about eight steps to get to the tables. Rocky and Joey chose a table right by the entrance. They rolled the balls out on the green, but before they could establish what they would be playing for, Rocky saw someone upstairs at the snack bar which overlooked the pool hall. Rocky said, "I gotta go talk to somebody upstairs, you warm up and get used to the tables." "Fine" said Joey, as he scattered the balls. He started practicing certain types of shots with which he was still struggling. Fifteen minutes later, Joey was still practicing alone. Rocky was still upstairs talking when a very large somewhat ugly Italian guy came down the steps and into the pool hall. He stood in the doorway and seemed to block out the sun. Fortunately for Joey, he had developed the skill of eyeballing someone without them knowing he was watching. After about forty-five seconds of trying to practice, as well as keep an eye on the new guy, he said to himself, I am staying away from this guy. I've been very lucky to be able to recognize true bad assess and giving them a wide berth. He felt in his bones that this guy was dangerous, and he admitted to himself he was frightened. After surveying the room, Monster Boy walked up to Joey's table and said, "you want to play?" Joey thought to himself, oh shit. I've been staying away from guys like this my whole life, but this one seeks me out. Joey answered with all the politeness he could muster, without sounding like Eddie Haskell, "No thank you. I'm sorry, but I need to work on my bank shots." His new friend responded rather loudly saying "you mean you don't want to shoot pool with me? Why? You don't like Italians or what? What's your problem?" He answered again, "No man, it's nothing like that, I just need to practice." "Then practice with me," Monster Boy said in a voice much louder than he had been using. Fortunately Rocky chose that moment to look down into the pool room to see how Joey was doing. Seeing who Joey was talking to, he mumbled loud enough for the snack bar patrons to hear him, "Momma Mia, Madre' De Dios." He immediately bolted for the stairs and when he got there took them two at a time. Upon arriving, felt the tension in the room and said to Joey's new friend, "Meenkya, Patsy, how ya doin?" Patsy said, "OK, I'm good Rock. Is this guy with you?" "Yeah man, he is good people." "Well, he's being very rude." Rocky looked at Joey with eyes that said, are you nuts and said, "No, no, Meenkya Patsy, he is a great guy and a friend of mine." "Then why won't he play me?" "No, no, Patsy, Meenkya, he was just waiting for me. Go ahead, you two play, I will rack for you guys" and as he walked by Joey to get the balls, he whispered to Joey, "play him." Joey immediately understood and said, "No problem." Patsy quickly followed up by saying, "nine-ball man, two dollars on the five, and five dollars on the nine, we re-spot the nine-ball." Joey said to himself, oh fuck, and looked directly at Rocky. This was a very expensive game, and he didn't have the money to cover large losses. He was thinking very fast now. He usually carried the bottom half of a cheap pool stick that Onie had put liquid cement in the bottom of. It made a great weapon. He had a special pocket sewed into his leather jacket where he kept the club, however, it was summer. He wasn't wearing his leather jacket, so the pool stick was in the back seat of his car taking a nap. He knew if he lost to Gorilla Boy, he couldn't pay up and would probably get his ass thoroughly kicked. He also knew that if he won any money from this guy, he wouldn't get paid. His brain was moving as fast as it could. His street smarts were taking a major exam. Finally, he said, "Patsy, I cannot beat you in nine-ball, but I believe I can beat your ass in straight pool. How about one game to fifty for five dollars and time?" He looked over at Rocky, whose eyes were saying, man, you have a death wish. Surprisingly, Patsy said to Rocky, "Meenkya Rocky, I like your friend. Rack 'em, Rocky." Rocky grabbed the rack and again whispered to Joey, "lose, I will pay half." Patsy told Joey, "break 'em" and the game was on. After the first rack was in the hole, he thought to himself, I'm going to have to try really hard to lose to this Chooch. But lose he did. As Patsy was taking the five dollars, he started making fun of Joey's pool-playing ability. Joey was firmly biting his lip through the host of insults. He figured sore lips were better than black eyes, a broken nose, or worse. After two minutes of verbal abuse, Patsy moved to another table. Joey and Rocky paid the tab and quickly headed to the parking lot.

As they walked to their car, Rocky said, "Let me tell you, man, that is the craziest, baddest fucker on Murray Hill, and maybe in the whole universe. We are so lucky to be standing here right now without hearing police and ambulance sirens. Meenkya man, I am so sorry you had to go through that." Joey said, "No problem, pool halls are dangerous places, and I don't carry, so I work very hard at avoiding trouble." They talked a while longer, shook hands, hugged, and said goodbye. Like so many other people in his life, he would never see Rocky again.

About three weeks later, one of the guys he worked with brought a Cleveland Plain Dealer and had left it on the front seat of Joey's car. He usually only read the sports page, but the paper was face up, and Joey couldn't help but notice the headlines. "FATAL SHOOTING ON E. 107TH AND EUCLID." That was right in front of the Marshalls Drug Store where he, just three weeks earlier got into his infamous brawl. It seems three African American males were shot gunned right in the face in broad daylight. Two of the three had died, and one was in serious condition. The story was continued on page seven, so Joey turned, and there on the page, were pictures of the three guys being held by the police for the shooting. He looked, then looked again, then looked again one more time. Finally, he said to himself, I am lucky to be alive. It just so happened that one of the shooters was his newfound friend, Patsy Isabella, aka, Gorilla Boy. The same Patsy that Joey had played pool with three weeks earlier.

That night as he lay in bed staring at the ceiling, and just could not get to sleep, he repeatedly thought, I am so lucky to be alive. The next day he turned eighteen years of age.

LIFE GOES ON

Two weeks before high school ended, his mom and dad had told Joey that in spite of the fact he had a partial baseball scholarship to Bowling Green, college would still be very expensive. He would have to find a summer job to pay for what the scholarship would not cover. Joey had said, no problem, and he would. He turned his paper route over to his brother Douglas and the route would stay in the family for another five years. Meanwhile, he got a job at the May Company department store that would start the day after his graduation. His dad's friend, Abe, was also working to try to find him a job that would pay more. Inwardly, Joey had a lot of personal doubts about going away to college, but he wanted to play college baseball. Plus his buddy, Onie, had already started summer school at BG. Onie's health was now significantly deteriorating, nevertheless, his parents got him an apartment, packed him up, and sent him away. Before Onie left for BG, Joey visited with him and knew immediately that his health was declining so quickly that he soon would be back home. He would only last three months.

The day after he graduated Joey reported to work at May Company. They were having a tent sale, and so they had hired a number of college kids. As this was his first real job he was a bit anxious. The job was somewhat boring. He carried stuff to and from the tent and did very little of anything else. At two-thirty in the afternoon, a huge thunderstorm hit the Cleveland area. They tried very hard to secure the tent, but they had no luck. By three-thirty, the extra hired help were sent home. By seven o'clock, the storm had completely knocked down the tent and ruined thousands of dollars in merchandise. That night, he received a call from someone at May Company telling him they were laying off most of the summer help. His first job lasted less than twenty-four hours.

After three days of being out of work, his dad asked him to hang around the house that night. Abe and his wife, Gretchen, were coming over and he had some good news. When Gretchen and Abe arrived they sat on the front porch with Joey and his parents. Abe said, "Joey, I've got you a job at the Cuyahoga County Engineers. You start on Monday. You will be getting a call tonight or tomorrow explaining where you have to go." Joey said, "Thank you very much Abe, but I have never been good at math, and I know nothing about engineering." The adults laughed and Abe said, "Joey, you will be counting cars, you can count can't you? You will work six hours and get paid for eight. You must drive your own car to different places every day. The extra two paid hours will cover your gas. You have the six-a.m. shift to noon. Joey was silent. He look at Abe, then looked at Gretchen, then looked back at Abe, then Gretchen again, then finally he looked at his parents. He said to Abe, "ARE YOU KIDDING ME? I'M GONNA BE ONE OF THOSE GUYS SITTING ON THE CORNER WITH A CLIPBOARD IN THEIR HANDS?" "Yep," said Abe. "And I am actually going to get paid to do that?" "Yep," said Abe again. Joey kept on saying, "And I'm done, every day at noon?" "Yep. They will call you with the details." Joey got up, and said "Thank you, Abe," hugged Gretchen, hugged his mom, hugged his dad, then he finally hugged Abe and said, "Jab, jab, right cross." To which Abe responded, "you will flatten them, Joey." That night in the pool hall, when Joey told the guys what his summer job was they were incredulous and asked if they could get one also.

Monday came and he reported to Van Aiken Boulevard somewhere in Shaker Heights where he met his supervisor who explained the rules of the job and how to put the tallies on the board. He thought to himself, a chimp could do this job. He would never have a job that was even close to having this much fun until years later when he started teaching and coaching. Where else could you sit on the corner, flirt with girls, or sit in your car with the music blasting and harmonize to some Doo-Wop? Eventually, he ended up working with two kids who sang in a band. Kids would visit their car on their breaks to listen to the three of them harmonize. One day the kid he was paired with offered him a bet. Jason said, "I will bet you that you cannot sit in that tree for an hour and count your cars." Joey said, "what's the bet for?" "Two dollars," the kids said. Joey responded, "You're on" and climbed up the tree. After sitting in the tree for forty-five minutes something that Joey hadn't counted on occurred. Two supervisors showed up to check on his station. This is bad thought Joey, but I'm not going to lose this bet. So he didn't move and kept on counting. Eventually, after waiting for about twenty minutes, the supervisors left. He immediately jumped down from the tree knowing he had won the bet. He jumped in the car and said, "I won, but tell me what you told them." Jason said, "I told them that you had to go to the bathroom, and I had your count." Joey looked at him and said, "thanks" as the kid pulled out two dollars Joey said, "keep one." The kid looked at him quizzically. Joey said, "you could have won this bet just by telling them I was in the tree, so you keep half."

It was a summer of work if you could call it that, and baseball, beaches, girls, and the pool hall. Life couldn't get any better. On Friday of his second work week, Joey came home and found his parents waiting for him. Mom had a tear in her eye and dad handed him a letter that was in his hand. Joey's first thought was, oh man, I got drafted. However, the letter was from Bowling Green University, and they were withdrawing his scholarship. He looked at his parents and said, "No big deal. I was expecting something like this. Jake is going downtown to Tri-C Metro. I will register next week, and he and I will go together. It looks like I will still be living with you. My goal is to do that until I am a hundred years old." Everyone laughed.

Saturday morning was meant for backyard basketball. Chocko, Jebs, Moga, Yonko, Keith, and the whole gang was there and warming up. Big Joe came out of the house, hollered over to his son, and said, "come on over I want to talk to you." Joey thought, Uh-Oh. His dad said, "Son, are you OK with the BG thing?" He responded, "more than OK dad. I love my family and all the friends I have. It's a good life." His dad smiled and said, "go play." As they were walking away from each other, Joey stopped and turned. He walked closer to his father and in a low voice said, "you know why this is happening, don't you dad?" Big Joe looked at his son and said, "I think I do." Joey continued, "It was my high school baseball coach telling them what happened." Big Joe said, "I believe you're right, but son, know this, you did the right thing." "I know dad, thanks for everything" and jogged over to play hoops.

That night as Joey lay in bed staring at the ceiling he thought, "Fuck 'em."

Summer ended with Joey and Charlyn fighting for about the hundredth time. Joey made up his mind that this was their last fight. He'd had enough. It was time that they both moved on, and they did. School started in September. He and Jake drove together but rarely saw each other during the day. The Tri-C downtown campus actually had no campus. A large cafeteria filled up daily with kids waiting for their next class. Black kids would sit on one side, and white kids on the other. Two of his friends from Latin, Ron, and Vic were also enrolled at Tri-C and Joey met with them every day in the cafeteria. Ron's cousin, Jamie, was also enrolled and he was in a fraternity with a bunch of upperclassmen who were in their last semesters. He was twenty years old, soon to be twenty-one. Most of the guys sitting at the table with Jamie were also older. At eighteen, Joey found himself with nineteen-, twenty-, and twenty-one-year-old guys. Added to the fact that there was a severe shortage of good-looking girls, school became an instant bore.

In the early days of school, the older guys' discussions usually centered around a place called Viet Nam. Joey had read an article about Viet Nam in Scholastic Magazine during his senior year in high school but thought very little about it. But now, with the older guys constantly talking about that far-away country, he was paying closer attention. He had registered for the draft this past summer, but he was thinking very little about Viet Nam. It seemed the upperclassmen were very concerned about being drafted. The anti-war demonstrations had not captured much attention yet. What Joey did not know was that eventually that war, in that faraway place, would escalate beyond anyone's imagination. He did know about draft deferments, and his draft status was 2-S. He had paid little attention to this and the other deferments that these older guys were constantly talking about. He mentally made a note to ask around at the pool hall. One thing he did understand was that all these upperclassmen would be done with classes in December and if they were not still in school they would be eligible for the draft immediately.

In late October, the talk shifted to intramural basketball. It seemed that Jamie's fraternity had won two years in a row, but was unable to beat the Stingrays, an all-black team that was extremely talented. At the same time, Joey had talked Vic into playing on his dad's travel basketball teams. Big Joe now had two teams in different age brackets. Both were in the process of annihilating the Parma Muni leagues. Their toughest games actually came in practice when the two teams scrimmaged each other.

One day, as Joey and Vic sat in the cafeteria with other members of Jamie's fraternity, Steve, the President, mentioned that the fraternity basketball team would begin practice. He then invited Vic to play on the team. Their first practice was being held that night in the downtown armory. There were two premier teams in the league. The fraternity and their archrivals, the Stingrays. The Phi-Zi's, had never beaten them and had lost four times in the last two years. Most of the fraternity was sitting at the table and were anxiously waiting for Vic's response. Vic said nothing, but just pointed at Joey. The President, Steve, who was a Latin grad three years ahead of Joey, said, "sorry buddy. But we already have two guards." Joey responded, saying, "we aren't buddies." As Steve's ears got red, Vic quickly interjected, "Not like him" as he pointed again at Joey. Steve, whose ears were now bright red said, "he didn't even play at Latin." To which Vic quickly responded saying "Latin didn't have two guards like him either. He shoots way better than I do." Jamie, Ron's cousin, had been listening intently. He had already checked out Joey's basketball ability with Ron. Ron had told him that if Joey had been at any other high school he would have been a star. Jamie said, "let him come to practice. If he is better than me or Dale, then I will sit." Steve looked at Joey and reluctantly said, "you are invited to practice with us tonight." Vic smiled and Joey winked at Steve saying, "OK buddy, I will be there." That evening both Joey and Vic showed up for practice and within two minutes of playing, it was obvious that Joey and Vic should be in the starting line-up. By the end of practice, there was absolutely no doubt that if they were going to beat the Stingrays, these two guys would help them. Practice ended and as they walked to their cars, the two friends talked. Vic said, "this is a no-brainer, what do you think?" Joey responded, "my friend, I appreciate you and your effort, and we are clearly the best two guys on this team. But I have been used to being called a greaser, and a hood, or whatever so if they don't want me, then screw 'em and they will continue to get their asses beat by the Stingrays."

The next day, by the time Joey got to the fraternity tables they were all filled. As he was looking around for somewhere to sit, Steve told one of their pledges to get up and let him sit down. Joey said, "no, keep your chair, I can stand here for a while." The pledge was in near panic, and Steve eased his mind by telling him it was alright. He turned to Joey and said, "we want you to play." About ten sets of eyes were all focused on him, waiting for his answer. It came with a question, "am I going to start?" Before Steve could answer, Jamie said, "yes you will. You are quicker, faster, and a way better shooter. I will come off the bench when needed." "Ok," said Joey, "I'm in." A seat opened up and he sat down next to Vic who looked at him and said, "We just won the championship."

Meanwhile, the pool hall had become a much more significant part of his life. Entire weekends would be spent there. Time at Annette's had been reduced but they would still gather there on Friday or Saturday night. Joey's mom and dad still made him stay home and study on weeknights, but that got less and less. He was eighteen years old and halfway to being nineteen. One night in November, pool hall regular nicknamed De Door who Joey and Moans had gotten to know well sat down while Inky and Joey were playing. He was a Garfield guy that most of the players in the hall knew. He said somewhat quietly "I have a new gun, who wants to go outside around back and see it?" Joey and Moans both went while Inky stayed inside and shot by himself. The Doctor and Mouse came along also. They went around back. De Door took out his gun, and they all looked at it. It looked like a gun. When they all had seen it, he pointed it in the air and shot it. "Jesus," said the Doctor, "I am headed inside." De Door laughed and he shot again only this time it wasn't in the air. As he fired, he hit the half wall surrounding the parking lot. You could hear the bullet ricocheting, and both Joey and Moans got to the ground. As the echo ended, Joey quickly got up and said, "fuck this. I am going inside." Moans said, "dude, I am with you." Mouse and De Door were laughing and continued shooting as Joey and Moans reached the door. Moans looked at him and Joey said, "what the fuck are we doing?"

BIRTH OF TONUS 0

Friday nights in January were Leaf time. Joey, Moans, and the rest of the gang headed to Cloverleaf. On arrival Moans immediately found himself in a big-money pool game with a guy from the Garfield area named Frankie Scarfolo. Scar, as he was known was a good pool player and a wanna-be gangster as well as a pretty boy. His clothes were all very expensive. Tailor-made pants, white on white shirts, and very expensive Stetson shoes. He seemed to always have cash. He was also the type of guy that thought all the girls were looking at him. Joey knew they weren't because he thought they were looking at him. On this Friday night, the pool hall was packed. It was one of those very rare nights that found many of Joey's different friends showing up in one place at the same time. Guys that were not even pool players just happened to be there. All the tables were filled with players. Yonko, Chocko, Moga, Onie, Flip, and even a couple of Latin guys he went to school with. As Scar and Moans began to play straight pool for fifty dollars a game, a crowd gathered to watch. Joey was standing on the side, along the wall, just four feet away from the table. Moans led from the start, and as the game got into the fifties, you could tell Scar was becoming flustered. After an hour, Moans was leading seventy-five to sixty-two, when he made a tremendous bank shot. Joey said, "NICE SHOT." Scar, who was standing cue in hand, roughly six feet away, set the cue stick next to the table and slapped Joey very hard in the face while immediately bouncing into a fighter's position in the expectation that Joey would be responding. Joey took the slap and did nothing. He didn't move. The entire room went silent. Moans stood open-mouthed as Joey stood against the wall staring at Scar. After about thirty seconds Scar picked up his cue stick saying, "that's what I thought" and took his next shot. The pool hall was stunned. Joey's friends could not believe what they were seeing. Joey DeTorre got slapped in the face and had done nothing? Onie and Flip were incredulous, but Chocko whispered to Yonko "this isn't over yet, you watch." Thirty minutes later Moans went on a fifteen-ball run and won fifty dollars. Scar threw the money on the table and sat down. As the crowd started to break up, Scar looked at Joey and loudly said, "Apologize." Joey said, "What? Apologize? Seriously?" As Scar got out of his seat and once again said, "Apologize" the crowd was regathering. Before Joey could answer, Moans yelled, "He is not apologizing" to which Scar responded saying, "then I will have to kick his ass, he's a pussy anyway." Joey was standing perfectly still staring at Scar as he got out of his chair. He said, "How about this Scar? You take the gun out of the back of your pants, give it to someone, then you and I can have a go?" Scar looked around, then took his gun out of his pocket and handed it to Mouse saying, "hold it and keep it out of sight." He turned and said, "OK pussy" and started moving towards Joey. Silence settled over the pool hall. The crowd gave them room. Chocko said to Yonko, "I told you this wasn't over. Joey is going to tear this guy up." Before Scar could take three steps, he was hit three times in the face with very quick punches. It was now Scar who was stunned. He then made a serious mistake. He tried to take Joey down by grabbing his sweater. As he pulled Joey slipped out of the sweater and Scar found it wrapped around his own two hands. Before he could untangle himself, Joey was pummeling him with numerous blows to the face. Scar continued trying to disentangle his hands and arms from the sweater. When he did, he decided to try a wrestling move and as he went for the takedown, Joey kicked him square in the balls, and down he went. Joey was on top of him in seconds and just kept punching. Scar was pinned on the ground as he was being hit with blow after blow. By the time he had fought his way to his feet, the manager of the Leaf with two of his very big employees was breaking up the fight. Jack, the manager, knew them both and said to them "any more of this you and you both will be banned from here." Scar said, "OK." Joey just glared. Scar found Mouse and got his gun back and headed to the bathroom to clean up. Other than red marks from the original slap, Joey had no blood or bruises. His friends started to walk up and congratulate him. The Garfield guys were saying, you just kicked the ass of a guy who has a very large reputation. Again, Joey said nothing and moved back away from the tables. As he moved farther from the door he kept his eyes on the bathroom that Scar had entered. Moans immediately understood why Joey was wary. Scar had his gun back. Moans too became very wary. Eventually, Scar came out of the bathroom, he had dried blood on his lips and nose, and one eye was swollen and headed directly towards the front exit and left. Finally, Joey as well as Moans let their breath out and relaxed. His buddies started gathering around him again with Yonko taking center stage, saying, "That was too cool, just like Frank Sinatra in *Tony Rome*. You are Tony Rome!" Guys were laughing as Yonko continued with his bullshit patter. "Seriously man, that's Tony Rome stuff man. Put your gun down then I will kick your ass. That's genuine Tony Rome cool man." Joey finally answered by saying "I don't like the name, Tony." The laughter was coming easier now, and Fuco sensing a thaw in Joey's demeanor got into the ball busting saying, "OK, how about just Tonus?" Yonko picked right up, saying, "yes, yes, yes, from now on you are Tonus!" Chocko jumped in saying, "Let me be the first person to call you "Tonus." Fuco quickly added, "Sir Tonus." And everyone roared. From then on, his buddies regularly called him "Tonus." It was the first time Joey had a nickname, so he embraced the madness.

Three weeks later, Tonus, Chocko, and Yonko were drinking beer in the Thunderbird Lounge, having their normal conversation which always caused loud laughter. One of the two barmaids was constantly flirting with Tonus. He flirted back, but she was about eighteen years older than him. She was divorced and had teen-age kids. When last call came she said, wait for me and we will go somewhere. Tonus looked at Chocko and said, "I have nowhere to take this woman." Chocko said, "bring her to my place, my family is out of town, see if the other barmaid wants to come too." They waited in the parking lot as the two barmaids came out together. Their names were Janie and Beth, and Tonus asked if they wanted to go over to Chocko's? Yonko who had met a girl his own age in the bar asked if he could come along and bring her. Chocko responded, "sure man, the more the merrier. Just behave yourself." They all headed to Chocko's, and it took less than five minutes for Tonus to disappear into the back bedroom with Janie. He was somewhat nervous as she was almost twice his age. They spent an hour in the bedroom, and when they came out, the other women were gone but Yonko and Chocko were still there. Janie looked around and said, "I better get going home, I will see you at the bar" and she kissed him on the cheek. No sooner had she walked out the door when both Chocko and Yonko both started with "Oh, Oh, Oh" in a falsetto voice. "Oh Tonus, Oh Tonus," and went on and on. Tonus quickly realized they had been listening to Janie when they were in the bedroom. She was not a quiet lovemaker. Yonko changed the chant to, "Oh Tonus, Oh Tonus, Oh baby, Oh Tonus." They were all doubled over with laughter. Chocko wouldn't let up saying, "from now on, you are O Tonus." Yonko retorted, "no man, that doesn't sound right. How about Tonus 0?" And it stuck.

Finally, when he was home in bed at about six-thirty in the morning, Joey lay staring at the ceiling. Joey thought to himself, Tonus 0....hmmm, I like it......and quickly fell asleep with a smile on his face.

UNCLE EDDY - AMERICA'S NUMBER ONE
– *BOINGGGG* - PRIVATE EYE

The pool hall life continued. Sometimes Tonus and his friends, on weekends, would arrive late in the afternoon and stay until it closed at one a.m. It was Saturday, and Tonus, Moans, and Inky arrived at the Leaf at about 6:30 that evening. They were talking as they walked in the door and hardly noticed the guy sitting at one of the round tables that were positioned around the bowling lanes. More than half the pool tables were empty so Inky and Moans decided to play straight pool for five dollars. Tonus was left to wait for someone more suited to his ability level, so he spent his time practicing. As Tonus worked on his rail shots, he could not stop himself from checking out the guy sitting outside the pool room. He looked very strange, but also very familiar. His strangeness was causing Tonus to examine him even more. He was dressed in a long raincoat and wearing a Fedora. As Joey studied him, he was thinking this guy must shop at Goodwill. He decided to get a closer look, so he went out of the room and walked right by him as he was heading to the bathroom. As he was passing him he mumbled to himself, geez, this guy's not different, he's weird. I think he's wearing a fake nose and glasses, as well as an eye patch. He decided he needed to get an even better look as he returned from the bathroom. As Tonus came out he immediately noticed that the guy had left. As he got closer to the pool room however he saw the guy walking around the empty tables which were more than half the room. As Tonus walked in, Inky, who was just about to shoot a bank shot, stood up and said, "Have you seen that guy?" Moans quickly added, "there's something wrong there. He's walking around the room looking at tables, but it doesn't look like he has any intention of playing." Tonus eyeballed him closely and quickly said "hey. I don't mean to interrupt you guys but, have you looked closely at this guy?" Moans responded quickly "of course, he has a fake nose and glasses, as well as an eye patch. That's how all the cool guys dress nowadays. He seems like a normal guy to me." Inky and Tonus both laughed as The Doctor came into the room with his girlfriend, got a table, and started to give her lessons. The stranger immediately took interest and sat down in a chair that was next to their table. Tonus said out loud, "Man, this might get bad." Both Inky and Moans stopped shooting, looked over at The Doctor and his girl, with Moans saying, "You are Correct-a-Mundo. This could get interesting." Tonus said, "I am going over to talk to The Doctor and check this guy out closer." As he headed over Inky said, "Hey, don't flirt with The Doctor's girl." Tonus responded, "Don't worry, I've already scoped her out, I think she has three eyes and a cauliflower ear." And he headed for their table. When he got there he said to The Doctor, "You guys mind if I watch?" "No problem" and The Doctor introduced him to his girlfriend. As he did, he whispered to Tonus, "Have you checked out this goof sitting next to us?" Tonus responded saying, "Of course, that's why I came over." The Doctor said, "Thanks, but I'm carrying, I'm OK." Tonus said, "Is it my imagination, but is he wearing a fake nose and glasses, as well as an eye patch?" Jackie responded before The Doctor could speak saying, "Yes, and look at the weirdo's shoes." A surprised Tonus hadn't noticed, but this guy was wearing black Keds tennis shoes and they had lots of holes in them. At that very moment, the weirdo got up and moved across the room. He sat down again in an area where nobody was playing. The Doctor said, "Tonus, maybe you should say something to Jack, the manager of the bowling alley." Tonus said, "maybe I will" and walked back over to where Inky and Moans were playing. "Hey, I'm going over to talk to that weird guy, keep your eyes open." He grabbed some balls that were already made, picked up a cue, and walked over to an empty table next to where the strange man was sitting. He spread the balls out and started to practice. After shooting a few bank shots, the stranger turned to him and said, "Meenkya, Joey, you Chooch, you are blowing my cover." Tonus turned and stared at the guy as his mouth dropped to his chest. "Geez Eddy, is that you?" "Meenkya, you Chooch, you are blowing my cover." "My goodness Eddy, what are you doing?" "I am working, now leave me alone." "Working here? Doing what?" "Meenkya, seriously you are blowing my cover." "Cover, what the hell are you talking about?" "Listen Chooch, I am a private detective, I am here to see who has been pocketing chalk, and I have that couple over there under surveillance." Tonus was dumbfounded and was staring at Eddy while thinking, this guy has completely gone around the bend. He gathered himself and said, "Eddy, why are you wearing a fake nose, glasses, and an eye patch?" "Meenkya, Joey you are really a Chooch. I'm a private eye. I have to keep an eye patch on to keep my eye private." Tonus's head was spinning as the pool hall was starting to fill up. "What are you actually trying to find out?" "I told you I am looking for people who have been stealing chalk." "Chalk, yelped Tonus, Has the Leaf hired you to do this?" "Meenkya, no, I figured if I could prove my worth, I could show them what I have done, and that would help me get hired." "Geez Eddy, have you done this anywhere else?" " I have, but I've been thrown out of Yorktown and well as Biafore's." Tonus said, "I can't imagine why Eddy" and left to go back to Moans and Inky's table. Moans said, "who's your new buddy?" Tonus responded by saying, "you ain't going to believe this" and then told them the story. As more people were filling up the pool hall, more people were also starting to notice the strange guy sitting in the chair. Finally, The Doctor came over to Tonus and asked, "Do you know that guy? If not, I'm going to get Jack and have him tossed." Tonus responded saying "Don't. I will take care of this" and again walked back towards Eddy. He started to talk, but before he could finish Eddy said, "Meenkya Joey, I gotta go, I just heard that at Braden's bowling alley someone is starting to steal their chalk and I have to get there as fast as possible while the trail is warm" and he sprinted out the door. Again, Tonus found himself standing with his mouth wide open. He really didn't want to know how Eddy knew this; he was just glad he left. As he went back to sit down by Moans and Inky, The Doctor said, "My oh my, you made that work. He flew out of here, what did you tell him?" I told him there was a pistachio sale going on at Parma Town and those are his favorite nuts. Now the group was staring at Tonus, but before they could say anything, he said "Please don't ask."

ADVENTURES IN PARADISE

Semester exams were in a week. The basketball championship game was being held the first week of the new semester. The Phi Zi's were undefeated. They had beaten the Stingrays three straight times as Joey and Vic had both lit them up. They were now being called, Joey and Vic, the Dynamic Duo. Between the two of them in the three games against the brothers, they had combined for a total of one hundred and eighty points. After their last game, a Physical Ed teacher had come up to them and said, "I am Coach Starns. I will be the head basketball coach next fall on the new campus in Tri-C West in Parma. I would like it very much if you guys would try out. I am quite sure you both would make it. What do you think?" Joey responded immediately, "It's about five minutes from my house, I was already planning to go to school there. I am in as long as I am allowed to play baseball also." Vic said, "man, I am an east side guy, but I would like to play for the school, let me see if I can make it work." Coach Starns took both their phone numbers and said, "I'll be in touch. I'm looking forward to coaching you both. Good luck in the championship game."

Bad news struck at the semester, four days before the intramural championship Vic became ineligible. He had failed three classes and he was not allowed to play. As Vic sat in the stands watching, they would lose in the championship game by fifteen points. Afterward, he came into the locker room to talk with Joey.

His mom had told him to enlist in the army before he got drafted. Viet Nam was starting to heat up so if he enlisted he might be stationed somewhere other than Nam. Suddenly the sadness of losing the title was replaced with a grave sadness. The two friends hugged and said goodbye. Joey would never see him again.

In spite of the fact that school was very boring, Tonus's life at the pool hall was filled with a myriad of adventures. They were not always good adventures, but nevertheless, they were not boring. Christmas vacation had come and gone, as did basketball season. It was February in Cleveland Ohio, which is usually an especially dead time. One night at the Leaf, while his friends were playing, Tonus had no one who would give him the spot that he required so he found himself sitting once again with nothing to do. As he was looking out the glass he noticed that there were five girls bowling by themselves, so he walked out and sat at a table behind the alley where they were bowling. Four of the girls were about twelve years old, but the fifth girl looked to be his age or older. She was definitely in charge of the other four and Tonus automatically assumed she was their babysitter. As fate would have it, she was also a knockout and was flagrantly flirting with Tonus. As the girls finished another of their games, she told her friends that she was going to sit the next one out and came and sat down next to him. As their conversation developed, it turned out she was indeed babysitting her younger sister and her friends, and she found it very, very boring. Her name was Gail, and they all lived in Maple Heights. The younger girls were starting game five and she told them to go ahead without her. She was going to continue talking to her newfound friend. They did a quick huddle and giggled, then began bowling again. Gail's conversation with Tonus was becoming much more suggestive. Almost all of the suggestive comments were coming from her. There were blatant hints and after about twenty minutes of this, Tonus finally said to her, "do you want to go out in my car?" She immediately answered, "yes, let me go tell the girls." The girls giggled again and kept right on bowling. Tonus said, "wait here for a minute," and he walked over to Moans who was playing nine-ball and told him where he was going. Moans looked over at the girl and said, "Holy Moly, she's really nice looking. You lucked out man." Tonus winked, gathered Gail, and they walked out into the parking lot, found Tonus's car, and got into the back seat. They immediately started kissing and within about five minutes it became very passionate. As Tonus was thinking what his next move should be, the passenger door was ripped open, and an adult male grabbed Gail by the arm. Tonus was reaching for a blackjack that he kept under his seat, as Gail yelled, "Oh my God, it's my dad" and was quickly and somewhat violently pulled from the car. Her dad took a swipe at her and missed completely largely because his attention was now focused solely on Tonus. Tonus left the black-jack under the seat but quickly jumped out of his car and locked it. As Gail ran inside, her dad came at Tonus. He came around the front of the car, as Tonus headed towards the rear of the car. Tonus gathered himself and thought, this guy is in his forties, and he had no intention of fighting him. What transpired next was like a scene from Abbot and Costello or a Three Stooges movie. The older man was chasing Tonus round and round the car. After two trips around her father stopped to catch his breath. While they were looking at each other across the car he yelled, "she is fourteen years old!" For the first time in the evening, Tonus became afraid. He yelled back, "I didn't know, she said she way my age, and she certainly looks it." The last part of the comment lit dad's fuse again, and the chase was on, round and round, and round, circling around the car. After what seemed like a dozen circles, the father stopped again to catch his breath. Again, they found themselves staring at one another, but this time the father was reaching for something in-side his jacket. Tonus thought, Jesus, he has a gun! Fortunately, his hand came out of the pocket empty, and around the car, they went again. Every time the guy would stop, Tonus would stop. Every time he ran, Tonus would run. If cell phones were around with cameras, this would have been all over the internet. Finally, he rested again. Tonus gave it one more shot and yelled, "I told you, I had no idea she was that young!" and he broke for the back door of the bowling alley. As he ran, he turned and looked back at the dad that was still standing there and yelled "but if you really want to catch me, just follow me in here dick head" and he ran inside. As he came running through the doors he immediately saw a flurry of activity in the pool room. It seemed that Gail had run into the room and had told all the guys what was going on outside, she had told them her dad was trying to kill the guy she went out to the parking lot with. The hall quickly mobilized. Each guy was in position, and everyone had a pool cue in their hands. Some had handheld blackjacks, but so far, no one had drawn a weapon. If Gail's dad were going to come in here, he certainly wouldn't last long. As Tonus entered the pool hall, Moans tossed him a stick, and they watched through the coatroom to see what was happening in the front lobby. Gail and the young girls who had been bowling met her father as he came in the main doorway. The four younger girls were standing crying. Her dad came inside very out of breath, he slapped her, and now all the girls were crying louder, with Gail yelling "he didn't know, he didn't know! I didn't tell him" as Jack came around the corner with his two goons. Gail was yelling, "nothing happened, nothing happened!" Jack looked at her father who was still trying to catch his breath and said, "I think you should listen to your daughter and take the girls home. This will only get worse for everyone if you go in that pool hall." Gail was still saying, "Daddy, daddy, we didn't do anything wrong." Her dad hesitated and then said, "Get in the car girls" and they all left. The Abbot and Costello routine had ended. Jack and his goons came around the corner in the pool hall and said to Tonus laughingly, "you again?" Tonus quickly asked, "did that girl look fourteen to you?" Jack paused, looked at the two goons who were vigorously shaking their heads no, and Jack said, "no way, she could pass for twenty." Tonus said, "now you are seeing the problem." Jack responded, "I understand completely, but I'm thinking he might take them home and choose to come back with a gun. You should leave. You are not banned but get out of here for the night." "Got it," said Tonus, and he turned to Moans and said, "I will meet you at Kenny Kings." He hurried to his car and quickly drove away.

That night as he lay in bed, a number of thoughts were racing through his mind. He could have had a gun, he could have shot me as we ran around the car, I wonder if anybody was watching us run around the car like the Keystone Cops, how was I to know she was only fourteen, am I supposed to ask every girl I'm with how old they are now? I might as well be a eunuch. As he thought about the last part, he thought, that's not gonna happen and fell asleep.

ANOTHER RUMBLE IN A DIFFERENT JUNGLE

It was a week later; Gail's dad had not come back. The pool hall regulars were still talking about the fourteen-year-old girl who looked like she was twenty. Tonus was playing nine-ball with a kid called the Wiz. It was a Friday night; Tonus had gotten there at about 4:30 and had been playing nine-ball for almost two hours. Fifty cents on the Five, and a dollar on the nine, re-spot. He was playing out of his mind and was up about thirty-five dollars. He made the nine on his break and it paid double, with that Wiz said, "Enough is enough." He gave Tonus about forty dollars, and they walked over to the desk to pay the time. As they finished paying, Moans and Fritz arrived. Tonus headed back into the room and sat down next to the table where Fritz and Moans were playing. They weren't playing for anything, so the atmosphere was very loose. As more guys started to trickle in, Moans said "Tonus, Fritz has been telling me that we can make some money if we go down to La Q tomorrow. It's on West 25th Street and on Saturday afternoons the competition is quite weak. The guys that hang out there get paid on Friday afternoons and they like to shoot pool for money. He says the good players don't show up until the evening. What do you think?" Tonus answered immediately saying, "Man, I don't know how I can pass this up. It was only six months ago I almost got killed shooting pool at Severance Center. A month later we are out in the back parking lot while two total nitwits are shooting their new gun, and we had to hit the deck, so we wouldn't get shot. Ten days ago, I have to tell Scar to give his gun to someone so that he and I can fight, and last week, some forty-year-old man is chasing me around my car because I took his fourteen-year-old daughter into my back seat. Now you want me to go to a pool hall on West 25th Street, where hardly anyone speaks English and almost everyone is carrying a gun or a knife, or both to watch you play one of their guys for money. Geez, I can't think of a better way to have fun. So your question was, what do I think, so here is exactly what I think, I think that you are out of your fucking head. Not only that, I think that Fritz has his head so far up his own ass that you would not be able to hear him if he even said something that made some sense. Moans my man, I'm really getting tired of pool halls and the people that frequent them." "So, OK, we will meet you then tomorrow at noon, here? We should get back about four o'clock." Tonus just shook his head and said, "OK, fine, I'm in, but I do not have a good feeling about this." The next morning Tonus met Fritz and Moans in the Leaf parking lot. He had his leather coat on which had a sewed-in pocket that contained the bottom half of a cue stick with liquid cement in the very bottom. He said hello to both Fritz and Moans and got into the car. The drive took about twenty-five minutes. When they pulled up to La Q, Fritz started to parallel park on 25th Street. Tonus said, "Chooch, stop. Don't box yourself in. Pull down to the open spot a way up, nobody will be able to park in front of you there. It will be easier to leave." Fritz said, "Man, you worry way too much." Moans said nothing, simply because he had learned a long time ago that Tonus was right way more than he was wrong. They walked in the door to a room that had twenty-two tables but only two were occupied. Two guys were playing near the back, and a single player was practicing at the table just as you came in the door. Moans sat down right in front of him. Fritz sat down right by the door, while Tonus sat about a half a table away. The room had old-school scoring of classic wooden beads strung on wires over each table. The man playing by himself looked around and asked in somewhat broken English, "You play?" "Sure," said Moans.

Moans and Manuel decided to play straight pool for fifty dollars. The game was to seventy-five. They each put their fifty dollars in a hat, as two older guys came over to the table. One of the older guys introduced himself as the manager Carlos. The other guy was his nephew Ramone. They sat down to watch. Moans and Manuel lagged for the break. Moans won, Manuel broke safely, left enough of a shot for Moans to manufacture a six-ball run. The jam was on.

After about forty-five minutes Moans led by a score of 58-45. The pool hall was filling up and now there were about twelve tables in use while four more guys were now watching Moans and Manuel. During the game, Ramone had gotten up and moved his chair closer to the table. He was positioned almost directly in front of Tonus. Tonus had not realized how big this guy was until he had moved much closer to him. He got up and moved his seat, so he had a better view of the table. There were now about five more guys watching the match. Tonus looked around the room and discretely signaled Fritz to follow him into the bathroom. Once they were both inside, Tonus said, "When Moans gets into the sixties, whether he is winning or not, go start the car and wait inside for us." Fritz said, "why" and started to complain saying, "What if he wants to play another game?" Tonus said, "he won't, now do what I say." Fritz had seen Tonus's eyes like this before, so he knew not to continue arguing and said, "OK." Tonus said, "leave the washroom now, I will be right out. We cannot walk out together." Before Fritz could get whatever he was going to say out of his mouth Tonus said, "go now dimwit." and Fritz quickly walked out. About a minute later, Tonus retook his seat. Ramone had moved again, and he was now located off to Tonus' left, but still in front of him. There was a crowd watching the game, Moans had just finished another six-ball run, and the score was now 64-48. Tonus looked directly at Fritz and glared. As Manuel was getting ready to shoot, Fritz got up and walked out. On Moans next turn, he ran eight more balls, and his total was now seventy-two. He was three away from winning. Suddenly, Manuel started yelling in both Spanish and English. Tonus did not completely understand, but Manuel was pointing to the score beads on the wire that hung over the table. He was yelling mostly in Spanish, but Tonus and Moans both recognized the word cheating. Manuel was pointing at Moans and speaking much louder. Moans looked at Tonus who deliberately stared at the money hat and then slowly moved his eyes to the door. Six years of growing up together paid off. Moans knew exactly what Tonus was saying even though he was saying nothing. He got out of his chair and said to Manuel, "Are you saying I'm cheating?" Again, Manuel's response was a mixture of both languages. Tonus and Moans only understood a few words, like Si, Si. From that moment on everything happened at lightning speed. Manuel moved the markers to show he was winning by ten balls and started to walk towards Moans. At the same time, Ramone was reaching in his pocket. Tonus reacted quickly and reached for the pool cue that was hidden in his coat and hit Ramone in the side of his head while yelling, "Let's go!" Moans was way ahead of him. He knew what was coming, had already grabbed the money, and was on his way out the door. The crowd was stunned as Ramone crumpled to the floor. Tonus immediately bolted and he too was out the door. All the while, hoping not to get shot in the back. Moans had gotten to the car about five seconds ahead of Tonus. He opened the back door and jumped in with Tonus quickly piling on top of him. As he slammed the door shut, he screamed, "Go, Fritz, Go!" as the guys from the pool hall came running out the door. Moans was yelling "keep your heads down in case they start shooting." Tonus yelled to Fritz, "Go down 25th, hurry, make a right on the bridge to downtown, go across it, and get on 77 North." Fritz yelled "North? You mean South" "Listen dill rod, go north. Take it to the freeway, go west, if somehow they are following us we don't want to lead them to the Leaf, and move it!" As they got to the freeway heading west, both Tonus and Moans were peeking out the back window watching to see if they were being followed. Tonus said, "the first opportunity to get on the Turnpike, follow the directions and do it. Head east on the Turnpike, take it to Rt. 8, and get off. We will go to the Leaf from there." Fortunately, Fritz did exactly what he was told and about an hour later they pulled into the Leaf's parking lot. During the escape, a number of thoughts were running through Tonus's mind. The strangest being was the time Tony S rescued him in the Parma Show parking lot years earlier. He remembered how Tony S had brought clubs with him on that day. As that thought was traveling out of his head, Tonus realized he would be haunted forever by his next thought. He had been in a number of scrapes, but none like this one. He had punched a number of guys in brawls, but he had never hit a guy with a weapon. Especially a weapon like what he had in his coat. He would always remember the sound the club had made when he hit Ramone for the rest of his life.

As they pulled into the Leaf's parking lot, Tonus said, "pull in the back" Fritz responded saying, "why? We weren't followed." Moans suddenly screamed, yelling, "Just do what he says." Tonus said, "park over by the back wall." As they pulled up to the back wall he then said, "Park here and wait." He got out of the car, looked around the parking lot, and headed up the steep hill that surrounded the lot. He was glad he had worn work pants and old Stetsons. He found some bushes near the top of the hill, started digging with his hands, buried the pool stick beneath them, and headed back to the car. As he got in, he told Fritz to drive around to the front lot "BUT DON'T GET OUT, WE NEED TO TALK." Fritz did as he was told, while Moans was staring at Tonus and was seeing him, unlike any other time he had ever seen his friend. Fritz parked the car and they stared out the window. Finally, Tonus said, "Listen, we tell no one about this, ever. If anyone asks where we were, we were at Biafore's shooting pool. He took a long pause and said, "guys I have no idea what happened to the big guy I hit with my stick, but I know it was solid and the noise it made on his head was loud. I am not sure what kind of shape he is in." The three young men sat there in silence for about fifteen minutes. Finally, Moans said, "I'm good, we get it, right Fritz?" Fritz nodded yes, and Moans said "let's go inside." Tonus said, "I cannot right now, my hands are covered with dirt, and I am heading home to shower. I will catch up with you later on. Remember, say nothing!" and he walked towards his car. When he got home, he cleaned his shoes in the garage, went down to the basement, and took a shower. He had dinner with his family and then headed back to the Leaf.

That night sleep for Joey did not come easily. After tossing and turning for several hours, he decided maybe some fresh air would do him some good. As he stood in his backyard, staring at the sky, his thoughts were racing...

How badly did he hurt Ramone? It was self-defense, wasn't it? He was reaching for a weapon, wasn't he? Did I hide the cue stick good enough? Would it have been better to throw it in the lake? Why did I still go when I knew that this trip was going to go badly? In the morning I need to check the newspapers to see if anything has been reported. I have punched, and been punched many times, but nothing like this.

For the first time ever, Joey thought about where his life was going. In the last four months, he had a number of encounters that could have ended up much, much worse than they did. He finally fell asleep as he was thinking, my mom and dad do not deserve a son like this.

CPSIA information can be obtained
at www.ICGtesting.com
Printed in the USA
BVHW050929251122
652759BV00005B/105

9 781977 257116